ARCADE

A Novel

HUGO N. GERSTL

ARCADE

A NOVEL

HUGO N. GERSTL

 SAMUEL WACHTMAN'S SONS ⬛ DEKEL PUBLISHING HOUSE

ARCADE

Copyright © 2015 Hugo N. Gerstl.

All rights reserved under International and Pan-American Copyright Conventions. No part of this book may be reproduced or transmitted in any form or by any means, electronic or mechanical, including photocopying, recording or by any information storage and retrieval system without permission in writing from the publisher. For information regarding international rights please contact Dekel Publishing House, Israel; for North American rights please contact Samuel Wachtman's Sons, Inc., U.S.A.

Dekel Publishing House
www.dekelpublishing.com
North American rights by
Samuel Wachtman's Sons, Inc.
ISBN 978-1-888820-94-2

This book is a work of fiction. With the exception of certain anchors of fact, all the characters in this book are the author's creation. As in all novels, much of what occurs in this book originated in the author's imagination. Any similarity to persons living or dead or to events claimed to have occurred are purely coincidental.

Editor: Pnina Ophir

Cover images:

"*Creative Commons Tenement House at Próżna Street in Warsaw*"
© *Adrian Grycuk, licensed under CC BY-SA 3.0 PL*

Vienna Opera interior © Chaoss / Couple © Wavebreakmedia Ltd / Gloriette Vienna at dusk © Digitalpress / Ferris wheel against the evening sky © Milkovasa / Town hall in Vienna © Sborisov / Greenhouse In Vienna © Slavasav / Marian columns known as plague columns © Shchipkova Elena / Dreamstime.com

Open chapter fleuron images from @Truemitra - FreeVector.com

Cover design and typesetting by

For information contact:

Dekel Publishing House	**Samuel Wachtman's Sons, Inc.**
P.O. Box 45094	2460 Garden Road, Suite C
Tel Aviv 6145002, Israel	Monterey, CA 93940, U.S.A.
Tel: +972 3506-3235	Tel: 831 649-0669
Fax: +972 3506-7332	Fax: 831 649-8007
Email: info@dekelpublishing.com	Email: samuelwachtman@gmail.com

TO

Colleen Miller, Lisa Peaks, Laurie Harper, Pnina Ophir,

Jacob S. Lo, M.D., Anya Chernova, Herb Chelner, Barry Dolowich,

the late Gary Jennings – my literary mentor and

the greatest American novelist

And, as always

FOR MY LORRAINE

Novels by Hugo N. Gerstl
Published by Dekel Publishing Group

Arcade

Assassin

Legacy

Against All Odds

Billy Jenkins

Amazing Grace

Scribe

Misfire

Standoff

Nonfiction Titles by Hugo N. Gerstl
Published by Dekel Publishing Group

The Politics of Hate

How to Cut Your Legal Bills in Half

Birth is a beginning
And death a destination
And life is a journey
From childhood to maturity
And youth to age
From innocence to awareness
And ignorance to knowing
From foolishness to discretion
And then, perhaps, to wisdom
From weakness to strength
Or strength to weakness
And often back again
From health to sickness
And back, we pray, to health again
From offense to forgiveness
From loneliness to love
From joy to gratitude
From pain to compassion
And grief to understanding
From fear to faith
From defeat to defeat to defeat
Until, looking backward or ahead
We see that victory lies
Not at some high place along the way
But in having made the journey stage by stage
A sacred pilgrimage
Birth is a beginning
And death a destination
And life is a journey
A sacred pilgrimage
To life everlasting

- **Rabbi Alvin Fine**

BOOK I

LEV

1

No one heard Lev's screams. No one saw him vomit until his insides and his throat felt as jagged as a knife wound. He remained in the cabin for two days. During that time, he somehow managed to gather his wits together long enough to drag the remains of his parents and baby sister into the cellar. He found the ground beneath the snow packed so hard it was impossible for him to dig even a shallow pit to bury them. He cleansed the cabin of the slime. He ate almost nothing during that time. He felt weak with hunger and emptiness. With his last strength, he dragged three logs inside, placed them in the fireplace, and lit a fire. He watched as the tinder, then the logs, caught and a large fire roared.

Another day passed. Lev gathered the pitifully small collection of his family's heritage – the Bible, his father's prayer shawl, the handgun, the large kitchen knife, two candles, a box of matches, and loaf of bread. These he packed in a large pillowcase. Going to his parents' closet, Lev pulled out his father's heavy coat, which was much too large for him, but he put it on anyway. He donned his own worn shoes and rubber galoshes. Despite the holes in the soles, they'd be the only protection his feet would have. As an afterthought, he stuffed the blanket from his own bed into the pillowcase.

By that time, Lev was weeping uncontrollably once again. Soon, he realized that if he didn't eat something substantial soon he would perish. He returned to the kitchen, grabbed two small eggs which were sitting on a counter near the stove, cracked them open, and put them into a large ceramic bowl. Reaching into a cabinet higher up, he found some stale breadcrumbs and dried cherries, which he dumped on top of the eggs. Lifting a nearby pitcher of water, he poured its contents into the bowl and stirred the whole thing with a wooden spoon until it was the consistency of mush. He ate greedily and voraciously. While it did little to lift his spirits, Lev knew he would somehow have to go on living.

When the weak winter sun was at its highest, Lev emerged into the pale January day. Without so much as a glance backward to the place he'd called home for the past half-year, he trudged slowly through the snow in the direction of the large mountain to the north. He had no idea where he was going, and in his misery he did not much care, but he knew the last thing he wanted was to go into the village and tell the peasants what had happened.

That night, fortune spat in his face once again. An unexpectedly bitter storm raged through the valley. Snow blizzards made it impossible to see more than a few meters in any direction. Sudden loud noises, whether from the crack of falling trees or from gunfire, terrified Lev, so that he was paralyzed with fear. As darkness descended, he could see no farther than his arm's length. He was so busy thinking life could not be more miserable that he did not see the fallen tree before he tripped and felt himself reeling. By that time, it didn't matter. As he was falling, his head struck an overhanging rock, and everything went black.

"Almost froze to death."

"Would've if we hadn't happened by."

"Tough break for the kid. I remember the family from last September."

Voices swam above his head as he drifted into and out of sleep. Vague memories of being hungrier and thirstier than he'd ever been in his life. Of being too tired to move another step. Of tripping. Of how good it felt to just lie down in the snow bank awaiting death. Slowly he felt himself come awake.

"Where am I?"

"North of Zakopane. Safe." A bass voice, gentle and patient.

"How long have I been here?"

"Since last night."

"You know?"

"Yes."

"It's warm. Aren't you afraid of …?"

"The men who shot your family? They'll never kill anyone again."

"I'm very tired."

"Sleep then. We'll watch out for you."

❦

Lev awoke late that afternoon. He smelled before he saw the rich, hot soup, filled with meat, celery root, carrots, onions, and potatoes, with a film of bubbling fat on top. Thick chunks of black bread with small pats of real butter. As he drifted into consciousness, he glanced around at his surroundings – a small, half-timbered room lit by four candles. A robust fire burned in a fireplace in the far corner of the room.

A dark-haired man, taller than his father, kept steady watch. Lev felt his body covered by a heavy blanket. "Where am I?" he asked.

"Alive," the tall man answered.
"In Poland?"
"Yes."
"You saved my life."
"God saved your life. I'm Gabriel Ostrowski."
"Lev Arkady."
"You're what, ten?"
"Almost eleven." The man's eyes were dark brown, as gentle as his voice. "Are you a partisan, *Pan* Ostrowski?"
"Gabriel. Uh-huh."
"Jewish?"
"Of course."
"How many are there in this camp?"
"Fifty. Men and women. Ten children, three of 'em about your age."
"I brought a gun and a knife," Lev said. "You can have them."
"Thank you, Lev," Gabriel said sincerely. "We've set up a school for the youngsters. Ilan, who's sixteen, is our teacher. I think you'll like him."
"We had a Bible in our cabin."
"Hebrew?"
"Yiddish. My Papa is …was … a teacher in Bratislava."
The large man picked Lev up and carried him over to the bentwood rocking chair in which he'd been sitting. He held the boy tightly and rocked quietly for several moments. Gabriel knew better than to say anything. Sometimes silence speaks more eloquently than words. After awhile, he asked, "More soup?"
"Please."
"You're not the only one in camp who lost your family, Lev. We all help one another to survive."
"If the Nazis …?"

"They won't. A bully keeps his distance when he meets someone who's not afraid."

"My Papa said there were lots of them. I remember when they marched through Bratislava. There must have been more than a thousand."

"We know the forest better than they do. We have many armed camps in the area. Guns and bullets, too. Oh, Hi, Maya."

A slender, dark-haired woman of thirty entered the room. "So the boy is up?" She reached out her hand to Lev and shook his hand, as though he were an adult. "I'm Maya Abramovitz. Welcome to *Selah Sholom*, the Rock of Peace."

"I'm Lev Arkady," the boy answered.

"I'm so sorry to hear about your father, mother, and sister," she said, reaching out and hugging the boy. "I lost my husband and my son a year ago. He would have been your age. The sadness never goes away, but you survive." She changed the subject. "We're expecting more freezing temperatures tonight, Lev. Come outside with me and make yourself useful by moving some logs from our woodpile to the houses."

"Uh … "

"Good," she said, winking at Gabriel. "You can't expect an old woman to do all the work.

Outside, Lev saw a dozen solid, neat log cabins, encircling a central quadrangle. Armed sentries stood guard next to a stone building with a single small slit window, the powder magazine, on one side of the quad. A small *shul*, the community house of worship, commanded the center of the field. A sturdy wooden fence surrounded the armed settlement. Close by stood a bakery from which emanated the steamy, sweet aroma of fresh-baked bread, a remarkably well-stocked dry goods store, even a doctor's office and an apothecary. Chickens strutted in the public square.

"Who owns all this?" Lev asked, holding Maya's hand.

"The community. Anyone takes what he or she needs. Some would call us communists or socialists I suppose."

"Communists? Socialists?" Lev didn't comprehend these large words, but the idea of a community, rather than one person, owning everything and sharing it with others in the compound sounded fair to him.

Maya continued, "Everyone has what he needs, but no more than that. No one has to go without. Nobody's rich, nobody's poor, everyone's pretty much equal, so no one has to pretend they have more or that they're better than anyone else."

"Who's the leader of the camp? Gabriel?"

"We don't have a leader. Whenever something important comes up, everyone meets on the public square and we talk things out. So far it's worked for us."

At that moment a rubber ball bounced against Lev's leg. Without thinking, he picked it up and hurled it in the direction from which it had come. He heard a remarkable sound, children laughing.

"Good throw!" a chubby boy his own age shouted. "Wanna' play?"

Lev looked guiltily at Maya.

"Go ahead," she said. "But make sure you only play for an hour. Remember, you promised to help an old woman."

◈

"So now we have eight in our class," Ilan said. "Tell us about yourself, Lev. You don't have to be shy. We've all survived many of the same experiences."

Lev looked around the room. A girl and a boy his own age. The other five, three boys and two girls, including Dovid, his newly-found friend from yesterday, ranged in age from nine to twelve.

"My family came from Bratislava …" Lev began.

"I remember Bratislava," one of the girls, blonde-haired and quite fair, said. "We went through there on our way from Budapest. They shot my father just outside Devin Castle." She said this with hardly a hint of emotion.

"We lived in a cabin in the High Tatras," Lev continued.

"Zakopane?" an older boy asked.

"Farther east."

"My older brother blasted three Nazis," the boy said proudly. "But on the way here, we were ambushed. My mama and I made it through."

As the stories unfolded, Lev surmised that the other children had all heard them before. An orphan with nobody left, a motherless sister and brother; arm shot off, a shattered knee, running and hiding through obscure corners of Eastern Europe. A *goy* who had hidden them in a barn for three nights. A *sheygetz* who tried to turn them in to the Gestapo. Unmitigated tales of loss and of woe and, Lev noticed, indomitable pride at having survived. Unmitigated joy that the *Boches* – the feared Germans – were on the run, beset with the same terror the Jews had felt for all these years.

After school that day, Lev questioned Gabriel. "How long do you think we'll be able to stay in *Selah Sholom*?"

"Hard to say. Poland won't allow an all-Jewish settlement to survive."

"But we could fight," Lev said stubbornly.

"We could," Gabriel said, lighting up a pipe and drawing on the tobacco. Lev found the cherrywood aroma as soothing as the man himself. "But why bother? Most survivors want to go to Palestine if they can make it. Less than a dozen want to stay here. Some would just as soon go home."

"Home to where?"

"Do you have any relatives anywhere, Lev? An aunt, an uncle …?"

"I don't know."

"They say the Americans are trying to patch pieces of families together. Someone came through here last week and said the allies were setting up DP camps."

"DP Camps?"

"Displaced Persons' Camps," Maya said, coming through door with a couple of birch logs. She hadn't bothered to knock.

The man puffed contentedly on his pipe. "Don't expect everyone to welcome us back to the new Europe with open arms. You say your father was a teacher?"

"Yes."

"Did he teach you anything about the Jewish experience in Europe?"

"Some."

"One in every six Jews who lived in Eastern Europe before the War has survived."

"But at least we're safe here," the boy said.

"For the moment."

❦

The moment lasted another month.

As February turned to March and the snows started to melt, what roads there were became mushy and impassable with the accumulated mud and detritus of a dying winter. At the beginning of March, during a gray, rainy day, Gabriel and Lev spent a few hours gambling at *sixty-six*. "Jews all over central Europe have played this game for years. Since it doesn't take a full deck of cards — only the aces, kings, queens, jacks, tens and nines – almost anyone can afford the twenty-four cards necessary for the game."

At eleven that morning, Gabriel asked Lev if he'd mind riding over to the nearest camp to deliver a message about troop movements he'd observed during the past week. Without hesitation, Lev agreed. Within the hour he was astride one of the camp's strong mules. Five kilometers into the ride, he noticed a large group of ragtag soldiers headed west. That would give him more news to deliver. He was not concerned, since they seemed not to have noticed him.

Although he did not know it, Lev had seen a remnant of an elite corps – seventy-eight German troops fleeing toward the frontier of the rapidly shrinking Reich. Gone were their coal-black winter greatcoats and their iron-toed boots. Gone was their swagger. Had one looked at the faces of these once indomitable princes of the *Reichswehr*, one would have seen gaunt, sunken eyes, stubble which had gone unshaved for days, a hunger so desperate they'd risk annihilation for a decent meal. Yet each trooper still carried a rifle and what little ammunition he had left, to ensure he'd make it home to whatever awaited him.

What Lev could not have observed was that as they came within sight of the camp where he lived, those Reich stalwarts smelled, saw, and heard everything they didn't have: fresh bread baking in a communal oven, the laughter of children, chimneys belching smoke, the wondrous sound of women's voices and the soft, inviting womanly curves they hadn't experienced for more than a year. It was too much for them to bear. In their desperation, they turned in the direction of the place, ready to raid, unaware that it was well-armed, and equally unaware of something else.

Coming from the southeast, the platoon commander of a well-fed, well-armed Soviet contingent had learned from his scout that a physically and emotionally bankrupt number of *Boche* troops were in the area. *Easy pickings, perhaps even another medal*, he thought as he ordered his soldiers to turn toward *Selah Sholom*.

※

It took Gabriel and several other men in the camp less than two minutes to move the women and children into an underground bunker. It was always the women the soldiers were after, he thought. It didn't matter whether they were young and attractive, like Maya, or old crones in their dotage. Prepubescent girls were special targets. "Just another piece of luck," he groused sourly to a comrade.

"The Jewish curse. If we didn't have bad luck, we'd have no luck at all," the man replied. "Looks like close to a hundred of them. Twenty of us. Where's your young friend?"

"Sent him to Keshan to deliver a message."

"Bright kid. If he saw them on his way there …"

"God knows. Probably best we take cover at the other end of the camp," Gabriel said.

"I doubt if either side would fall for that ruse."

"It's the only one we've got."

※

"More than fifty of them," Lev reported to the man whose name Gabriel had given him. Within ten minutes, the commander had explained the situation to his men and thirty of them were riding hell-bent toward *Selah Sholom*.

※

They might have survived had not that last shot been fired – a shot that by sheer coincidence penetrated the tiny window of the camp's powder magazine. The explosions that rocked the entire camp buried the twenty Jewish defenders alive when their dugout collapsed. The Russian forces systematically demolished the Germans and occupied the camp within half an hour.

By that time, the partisans from Keshan, who were within two kilometers of the camp, saw pillars of smoke rising eerily from the tiny settlement. More terrifying, they heard the screams and moans of women and children being not-so-systematically raped and slaughtered by the marauding Soviets. As Lev rode into what was left of the village, he saw a gross, fat soldier tossing an infant into the air as if it were a ball. The man cocked his rifle and shot the baby before it hit the ground.

Screaming obscenities he wasn't even aware he knew, Lev rode to within five meters of the brutish soldier, raised his handgun, and shot him in the face at point blank range. Insane with fury and grief, he neither saw nor felt it as another soldier, swinging his rifle like a bat, cracked Lev's right leg. Lev fell from his mule, shattering that leg. Just as the attacker was raising his rifle to end the boy's life, one of the Keshan partisans shot Lev's would-be killer.

By one that afternoon, the carnage was over. The camp was a smoldering memory. Its only survivor, a ten-year-old boy, lay writhing and moaning on the ground, half dead, ignored by all but the vultures who circled closer and closer.

2

Several hours – or was it days? – later, Lev awoke. He lay on a bed of straw in the back of a covered wagon. From time to time, the wagon hit a bump and the resulting spasm caused him to moan. He saw that his shattered leg was elevated and tied to a wooden slat. After one particularly horrendous bump, the man who was driving the cart, turned back to look at him. The fellow was in late middle age, with a full white beard. He wore a slouch hat and a scarf around his neck.

"Hello there," the man called down to Lev. "Miserable day," he continued, mopping his brow with his shirt sleeve. "Of course, it could be worse. You could be dead like the rest of 'em."

"H-how did you …?" Lev stammered. His pain worsened and lessened periodically.

"Looking for anything of value that might be left," the whitebeard answered. "Sorta' like the vultures," he continued. "When I saw 'em circlin' you, I looked closer and … that's how you come to be here." When he saw Lev's horrified look, the old man continued, "I'm sure in their present condition, none of the people in *Selah Sholom* would've cared. If I hadn't have been there, it would've been someone else. At least I'm more honest than most about it. I don't kill anyone to get what I need. If it happens to drop into my hands, well …"

Lev lay back. "I killed a man…"

"I'm not surprised. He probably deserved it. First thing we've got to do is get that leg fixed up," the older man continued.

"Is there a doctor nearby?"

"Might be," the man replied. "Not gonna' go there, though."

"Why not?" the boy asked. "If it's a question of money …"

"Money?" the man cackled. "Don't believe you got much of that."

"I could pay you back … somehow," Lev said.

"Don't need to be paid. I could afford a doctor if I needed one," the whitebeard replied. "Nope. A doctor's the last thing you need. They'd just keep you in the hospital forever and maybe saw your leg off if it didn't get better." The man lit a cheroot and started puffing happily. The stench wafted back and Lev felt himself choking. The whitebeard seemed not to notice. "I imagine you don't have anyone left, 'cept me, and I don't have time to sit around a hospital for weeks and weeks."

"So you're just going to leave me in the next village?"

"I didn't say that either. Someone I know in one of the other partisan camps might help."

By nightfall, Lev and the older man reached the outskirts of another partisan settlement, which didn't look much different from the one that had been destroyed.

"Hey, open up!" the man called. "Got someone here who needs some help."

A tall, rawboned woman approached. "Old Amos?"

"No, Methuselah. Of course it's me, Chaya. Who'd you expect, Father Christmas?"

"Sure, twice in a year," the woman answered. It was obvious from the offhand tenor of their greeting that the two of them knew and genuinely liked one another. "We heard about *Selah Sholom*. Is he …?"

"The only survivor so far's I can tell. His leg's broke in three places. It could be a problem. He's young, the bones are still soft…"

"And you know exactly what to do?"

Lev sat silently in the back of the wagon, listening to the exchange.

"Of course."

"An old coot like you *would* know a little bit about everything."

"Hell, woman, it worked on my old horse five years ago when the vet told me to just shoot him."

"*Christ!*" Chaya exploded. "The boy's a human being, not a horse!"

"My, my," Amos replied laconically. "A nice Jewish lady taking the name of Our Lord in vain."

"*Our* Lord?" Chaya said, raising her eyebrows. "When did you become religious, you old fraud?"

"Whenever it suits my purpose. Have I ever told you about the Lord's eggs?"

"Only four hundred times." As exhausted and in as much pain as he was, Lev couldn't help but enjoy their banter. "You really think you can help him?"

"Yep. I'll need your husband to help."

"He's a carpenter, for God's sake!"

"So was Our Lord Jesus, Madame," Amos said, bowing.

"Amos, you are absolutely incorrigible."

"At your service. Will you help me then?"

"I'll help the lad, provided it doesn't kill him. What's his name, anyway?"

"Umm … I really don't know. What's your name, boy?" he asked, turning his face toward the back of the wagon.

"Lev. Lev Arkady."

"His name is Lev Arkady, Chaya."

"Thank you so very much for that information, Amos," she said sourly. "I'll go get Shmuel."

※

When the four of them were inside the carpenter's home, Amos became serious. "There's no way to sugarcoat this, lad. You've got a choice – live with only one leg or die with both of them." Already chalk white, Lev turned slightly green. Amos continued, "A doctor might want to amputate, and you'd be lopsided but alive. Or I can give you the same treatment that once saved a good horse all intact. Say which."

Lev did not hesitate. He gave a tortured grin and said, "If I am not as good as a horse, I deserve to die."

"You're a brave young fellow. Try to bear that in mind, so you'll whinny and not screech when it hurts. Now Shmuel," Amos said, turning to Chaya's husband, who stood a head shorter and weighed several kilos less than his large wife, "go and find some planks. If you can't get them elsewhere, steal some from the town dump. Then go and get …" Amos slapped four fingers, one by one, into his palm as he rattled off a list of his needs.

Somewhat later, Shmuel returned with an armload of light planks, a hammer, a saw, a pocketful of nails, and jug of brandy.

"All right, Lev," Amos said, pouring a full mug of the foul-smelling stuff. "I want you to drink that entire cup down. It'll burn like hell and you'll feel like vomiting, but trust me, it'll make a big difference."

The boy glanced sidewise at the old man, then Chaya, who nodded. Holding his nose, Lev did as he was instructed. When the first drops hit his stomach, his body rebelled at the nauseating stuff, but Chaya kept urging him to drink. Meanwhile, Amos instructed Shmuel in the hurried construction of a shallow, narrow wooden trough with one end open, so Lev's leg could be laid in it and his foot pressed against the closed farther end. The box was just long enough to reach from the top of Lev's thigh to the sole of his foot.

Amos turned to Chaya, "Young lady, go to the commissary and fetch me a sack of bran, some carbolic acid, some long, thin sticks from the settlement's store of firewood, and some strips of cloth which I can use for tying." She did and was back less than five minutes later.

"Shmulik," he said, reverting to the man's nickname, "you hold the boy firm and steady while I pull on this leg and see if I can set the broken bone ends. And Lev, you're just going to have to whinny like a whole herd of horses, because this will hurt like hell."

Amos drank a long draught of brandy himself, and handed Chaya's husband what was left in the mug. Then the older man started pulling, just below the topmost break. Lev did more than whinny; he howled and screamed. Chaya grimaced and clapped her hands over her ears. But Amos felt one after another as the three bulges in Lev's leg diminished, and watched the jagged ends of bone slip back under the bloodied flesh and – he hoped – fit back where they belonged. Before the job was done, Lev had ceased screaming. Shmuel did not have to lean on him to hold him motionless; the boy had fainted dead away. Then Amos placed the sticks along the leg for splints, and with the cloth strips bound them tightly in place. He and Shmuel carefully laid the trussed leg in the newly built box and bound it firmly with cloth strips.

"Chaya," said Amos, turning to the rawboned woman, "before he wakes up, give his flesh a good burning dose of carbolic." While she did that, Amos ripped open the sack she had brought. He poured the bran into the box, packing it tightly under, around, and over the leg. "There," he said, wiping the sweat from his forehead. "That'll hold it pretty near immobile, but we need to let some air circulate around it. I'd appreciate it if you two could dig through the bran whenever you need to treat those wounds, about once a week – you know what to put on them and how to sew them shut – then pack the bran back tight again. The boy's going to have to lie as still as he can for about two months. With luck he'll come out of that box with a fairly usable leg. It worked with my horse anyway."

They propped Lev in a spare bed that night and promised they'd care for the boy until Amos returned.

❦

"Who is he, Chaya?" Lev asked.

"No one really knows," the woman replied. "I've lived my whole life, thirty-eight years, in Poland. He started coming around my parents' village when I was ten. He was a rogue, even then," she said, her eyes clouding over, taking her back to another time, another place – before the War. "He'd stay on in our settlement for a week or so. We never knew where he stayed. He probably spent most nights in that covered wagon of his, but there was plenty of talk around the village that he often spent the night with a young widow when he came through. He was about as old as I am now when I first laid eyes on him."

"What did he do?"

"What *didn't* he do? He could fix anything, from a sick cow to a leaky faucet. He could sharpen a knife like you wouldn't believe, and it stayed sharp 'til he came back a year later. He entertained our village with tales of faraway places, different worlds. Then he set up the gambling games…"

"Gambling games?"

"Every kind of game of chance you could think of."

"Did you ever find out where he went between his visits?"

"Oh, yes," Chaya said. "He always told us. He was the best 'newspaper' in Eastern Europe. I can't tell you how many Jews he saved by telling them in advance when and where the Nazis would strike next. Certainly more than fifty thousand, but if you ask him, he'd just say, 'a few here and there.'"

She paused for a moment, then said quietly, almost to herself, "I never knew anyone who *didn't* adore him. Men, women, it didn't matter. I don't think the men would have cared if he had slept with their wives – you don't need to blush, Lev, sooner or later you'll know all about that kind of thing. But Amos had his own sense of morals, and that did not include sleeping with a woman who was not 'available.' He introduced me to my Shmulik."

"Is Amos Jewish?"

"No one really knows. If he has any religion at all, he keeps it to himself, or he dismisses it with a joke."

❦

"My leg itches like there are a thousand flies attacking it."

"They probably are," Shmuel said, shrugging. "It's been close to sixty days. Perhaps we might have the camp doctor take a peek?"

"I don't know," Lev said uncertainly. "Amos said …"

"Amos can be a bag of wind," Chaya said. "Dr. Rubin is one of the finest, kindest men I've ever met."

"Bag of wind am I, you harlot?" The booming, unmistakable voice cut through their talk, the slamming of the front door sealing the speech with an exclamation point. "I'll have you know, I knew Hillel Rubin when he was sucking at his mama's tit. Don't trust me, do you? All right, let's get that young whelp over here."

❦

Hillel Rubin, in his early thirties, tall, cadaverously thin, with long, unruly black hair, a hooked nose, displayed a gentle manner. After his four visitors had told him the story, Rubin said, "Time to see what God – or God's anointed – has wrought."

He lifted the sheet of Lev's bed and saw the bran box. "What in God's name … ?!" Doctor Rubin exclaimed. The bran in the box had been replenished from time to time, as the marauding mice or rats, or both, had eaten at it. The bran was mixed with rodent droppings. Toward the bottom of the box, the bran had gone green with mold.

Lev's leg looked ghastly when Doctor Rubin lifted it from the box: shrunken, discolored by the bran, and wrinkled like a twig. The doctor continued to mutter imprecations as he swabbed the leg clean, then prodded, manipulated, and scrutinized it. Still, the leg was whole, it bent only in the places where it should, and its flesh wounds were now only scars.

Dr. Rubin looked around at the others in the room. His gaze turned into a glare when it stopped at the benignly smiling Amos. "Dare I ask who prescribed this lunatic treatment for the injuries? Surely not a physician."

"It was my idea," Amos responded proudly and, Lev thought, a bit arrogantly. "It worked once for a horse I was reluctant to shoot."

The doctor snorted and shot a gaze at Chaya. "Madame, you did not inform me that I was being called to examine a veterinary patient. May I ask, aside from this shit-filled box, what attentions you gave?"

"I cleaned the wounds with carbolic," Chaya said. "Afterward, I used a couple bottles of some nostrum Amos left with me."

Hillel Rubin shrugged his shoulders, looked around, and suddenly grinned broadly. "You realize, of course, none of this should have been done, none of it! Utter stupidity, peasant remedies, horse cures, unforgivable meddling." He lit a small clay pipe, then continued. "Nevertheless, it all worked. None of those ridiculous nostrums that grizzled old whitebeard gave you could have prevented the corruption from getting into the wounds. The boy should rightly have died of a fever. As for this – these dropping-mixed husks of grain – you might as well have packed the limb in sawdust *except*... The bran spontaneously generated these *fungi*." He fingered the nasty green mold in the box. "It is known to physicians – but *only* to *physicians* – that certain of these fungi have a subjugating effect on the disease. This green mold, this particular green mold, *this alone*, healed the patient's limb and preserved his life."

"Oh, my," Amos remarked innocently.

The doctor looked daggers at the older man. "How could you possibly have known…?"

"Peasant wisdom, conversations with people. As for old wives, young widows actually, they can be far more entertaining in different ways. Will he walk, Hillel?"

"Of course," the doctor said, realizing the humor of the situation in which he found himself. "But I suppose you knew that all along?"

"Not all along, Hillel. But the lad survived the murder of his family in the Tatras, He was the only one who survived *Selah Sholom*. That's two. They say a cat and a Jew each have nine lives. He's still got seven to go.

※

When the doctor had gone, Amos said, "You know, I never had a son of my own, and now I'm old enough to have a *grandson* of my own. You two have got each other and two sons who've made it to Palestine. I imagine you'll be going there when the War's over. The boy's got no one; I've got no one. Maybe we'll just keep each other company for awhile. Besides, he's got to learn a trade sooner or later."

"A *trade*?" Chaya asked, rolling her eyes.

"A living then," Amos replied.

"You want him to be like you? A *luftmensch*? Someone who lives off the air?"

"It can't hurt. He could afford to learn a few things about life. What do you say, lad?" he asked, turning to Lev.

After what had befallen him the past few months, Lev had not given a thought to what the future might hold. "Wh – when would you expect us to go?" he asked.

"Tomorrow morning at sunup," the whitebeard replied.

"Where to?"

"Like two birds. Wherever we happen to light."

3

"What am I supposed to call you?" Lev asked. "No one ever told me your last name. Pan …? Herr …?"

"Plain old Amos is good enough for me," the man said as he packed the bedding which he'd let air out overnight into the back of the wagon. "Haven't used my last name in so long I don't even remember what it is."

"My father told me it's a sign of respect to always call someone older by his last name."

"Might be for some. I imagine we'll be together long enough to end up calling each other what feels most comfortable. Might even use different names in different places."

"Different names?"

"Uh-huh," he said, turning to face the boy. "Some places they hate Hungarians, so we'll use Polish names, or Russian or German, depending on where we are. Sort of like that funny-looking lizard that changes colors to camouflage himself from enemies. Have you ever ridden a horse before?"

"No," Lev replied.

"No matter," Amos said. "You'll learn that among other things. Miss your family, do you?"

"Very much, Pan ... Amos. The last few months, no one gave me any time to really think about it. People were so busy trying to be kind and show me a new life that I never got over the shock of losing the old one."

The old man looked at one of the wagon's wheels, went into Shmulik's house, and came back with palm-size chunk of birch wood. He started whittling the wood into the shape of an egg, while he continued talking. "I can relate to that. You're eleven?"

"Just."

"Same age as me when I lost my parents. Cossacks came through our little *shtetl* one night during a wedding celebration. No sense to what they did, just got drunk and cut up the nearest Jews. When they woke up in their own camp the next day, they probably had no idea what they'd done. Just like that, ten people gone," he said, snapping his fingers.

"You're Jewish?"

"Born Jewish. Wasn't *Bar Mitzvah*. Haven't thought much about a God or religion since that time. If there's a God out there, He hasn't shown me much of that all-knowing, all-powerful stuff the rabbis always fill your head with. Why should I believe in anyone who lets a bunch of organized murderers kill off millions of people for no other reason than that they're a different religion?" Amos reached into a small cabinet in the wagon, drew out a heavy hammer, and drove the wooden plug into a hub which supported one of the wagon's wheels.

The boy looked down at the ground and kicked a few nearby pebbles.

"Wonderin' how you'll get over them?"

Lev hesitated a few moments, before he replied softly, "Yes."

"One day at a time. No one said it's gonna' be easy. No one said life's easy. You don't get a free pass to happiness. You know what it is to sit *shiva*, boy?"

"No."

"They didn't even have time to tell you that? Well, every Jew I've ever met, when someone near dies, the whole community gathers around the survivors. Different friends bring all kinds of meals for seven days. During that time, they sit around on low stools and simply do what comes naturally. They cry a lot, they talk about the deceased – mostly good things, but some bad, too. Some of 'em rip their shirts, some of 'em just wear a black ribbon. After seven days, they're through sitting *shiva* and they're ready to get on with life. Seems to work. In any case, life goes on and you can decide whether you want to join the dead or go on living. Most times you don't have much choice."

"But I don't have any friends to sit *shiva* with, Amos."

"Well, you got me and I got you, and maybe that'll have to do. Sometimes we'll be travelin' two, three days between villages and there ain't much to do *but* talk. And listen."

"Chaya told me you travel everywhere," the boy said, suddenly feeling a lightness he'd not felt since that evening in late January.

"'Everywhere's' a bit of an exaggeration. We'll see a pretty good piece of Eastern Europe, though."

At that moment, Chaya emerged from the house bearing a large platter with two mugs of tea and a number of poppy seed cakes. She handed a mug to Amos and one to Lev. "Can't let you get on the road with empty stomachs. Where're you boys headed, Amos?"

"East. Przemyśl, then Medyka, maybe as far as L'vov before we turn north."

"Not Kraków? That's one of the largest Jewish cities in Europe."

"Used to be. Now it's too close to the outskirts of …" His eyes hooded over, as though he didn't want the boy to hear.

"I've heard about it," Lev said. "Gabriel told me back in *Selah Sholom*. Auschwitz. Birkenau. The killing factory."

"I'd just as soon avoid it. Doesn't matter where you go, ain't gonna' be many Jews anywhere anymore. When the War started, one in every three who lived in Przemyśl was a Jew. Today, you'll be lucky to find two hundred still living in that town. It's the same everywhere. Worse in L'vov. That city had two hundred thousand Jews before the war, three hundred today."

"So why go there?" Lev asked.

"Jews aren't the only ones willing to pay for entertainment. Like I said before, we become like that little lizard, the chameleon, and change colors. They want Ukrainian, we'll be Ukrainian. Even have the right clothes for it. Well, my dear," he said embracing Chaya, "the sun's midway to the zenith. It's time we got on the road."

"You'll take care of him, Amos?" the woman said, choking up.

"Hell, yes. I told you I need a grandson. I won't let anything bad happen to him."

※

The first evening, Lev and Amos camped between Sanok and Przemyśl, on the bank of the San River. The late spring day had been warm and convivial. In virtually no time, Amos had taught his young charge how to bait a line with tied flies and cast out into the river. Less than half an hour later, they'd netted six river trout. After gutting them, Amos searched around for some wild onions and other herbs in the area, then brought out a large pan, started a small fire, and fried the evening's meal over the flames.

"I can't remember eating anything so delicious since Bratislava," the boy said. "Maybe not even then."

"You given much thought to your parents and sister?" the older man asked.

"Some. You said, 'one day at a time, one step at a time.' I'm trying hard to keep that in mind."

"Good for you," Amos said, crunching some of the crispy fish noisily. "It'll be easier if it comes out slowly."

"What do you do when you come to a village, Amos?"

"A little bit of everything. Chaya told you about the games of chance?"

"Uh-huh."

"And knife sharpening and handyman stuff?"

"Yes."

"Well, that's part of what I do. Of course, there's nothing to make a man welcome like the ability to tell a good story. I make it a point to have hundreds in my memory, and many times folks want to hear the old ones over and over again. Specially at night, before they go to sleep. Puts 'em in a mood to have good dreams."

After the sun went down, Amos suggested that since it was a warm, star-filled night, it might be just as well if they bedded down outside the wagon. "Get some more wood, though," Amos commanded. "It might get cold in the middle of the night."

While Lev was gathering wood, Amos attended to the horse, walking him to the river where he drank his fill, then making sure a trough filled with hay was close by and the animal had a blanket to keep him warm. After they were comfortably ensconced in their bedrolls, Lev ventured, "You said you had a whole storehouse of stories. If I'm going to be your apprentice, there's no time like now to start learning them."

4

"Wake up, boy! It's a new day and a new world!"

"Wha …?"

"Hitler's dead. It's all over the radio."

"You've got a radio, Amos?"

"Yep. Being a scavenger, going from place to place, I've managed to pick up a few things here and there. People seem to appreciate things I do for them, but lots of people don't have money in these parts. They'll trade anything they can for what they think they need." The old man pointed to a small receiver he'd placed atop the drover's seat. "Polish partisans gave me that two years back. It's been a life saver to me more than once."

"How?"

"The powerful stations operate out of big cities. But there are thousands of towns and villages all over Europe and thousands more amateur radio operators everywhere in the world. Most of 'em transmit by code, just a series of blips and beeps, but some of 'em transmit by voice, just like the big stations. I'll show you what I mean."

"Uh … Amos …?"

"Oh, right, you just woke up. Go piss over by yonder tree. When you come back we'll have a little of that fish from last night and listen in to Przemyśl."

The news was just as Amos had said, and it was repeated over and over every five minutes in Polish and Russian. Three days ago, Mussolini had been captured and executed and his body had been hung for public display in Milan. Last night, while the Battle for Berlin raged above him, the demon who'd confidently declared, "Today Germany, tomorrow the world!" had committed suicide in his bunker. At his direction, gasoline has been poured over his body and that of Eva Braun, his wife of a few hours. Their remains had been incinerated beyond recognition. Radio Przemyśl predicted the war in Europe would be over in a matter of hours, days at most.

"We'll have quite a time in Przemyśl tonight," Amos gloated. "People will be dancing in the streets and coming out of a six-year nightmare and we'll be there to help 'em wake up!"

"I don't think so," a ragged voice cut through Amos' reverie. Looking around, Lev and his mentor found themselves staring into the faces of three scrofulous looking peasants and down the barrels of two rifles that looked to be a hundred years old.

"You got any food, old man?" the leader asked harshly. Amos nodded toward the plate of fish he and Lev had been about to eat. "I mean *real* food."

Amos remained silent. Lev followed suit.

"If you're not gonna' answer, we'll answer for you," the leader said, turning to his two associates. "Ryszard, look into yonder wagon. Probably plenty there." He kept his gun trained on the man and boy.

A few moments later, the second man called out, "Nothing but a bunch of wooden stuff, a sack of rice, and some grain. Shit, they're as poor as we are."

"Is that true, old man?" the leader asked.

Amos replied, "Take whatever you can find. I don't own anything worth dying for."

"Smart old coot," the leader said. "Very well, we'll take the horse and the wagon. 'Course we don't want you following us too close. Off with your clothes!"

"What?" Lev blurted out.

"You heard me," the scruffy man continued. "It'll be hard for you to track us when you're too embarrassed to show yourselves to anyone. Go on now," he said, nudging the boy with his gun. "Be quick about it."

When Lev and Amos were naked, the third man, Bolek, came up with what, to him, was a bright idea. "Any rope in the wagon, Andrzej?" he asked, addressing the leader.

When Andrzej affirmed there was, Bolek said, "Let's tie them to two of yonder trees to slow 'em down a bit more."

Several minutes later, properly if not neatly trussed, Amos and Lev watched with dismay as horse and home moved down the road. Several hours later, they were still tied to the trees. As the spring sun warmed the land, Lev felt himself growing thirsty. As afternoon progressed and the shadows grew longer, he felt stabs of hunger as well. Was his life to be cut short now after so many narrow escapes?

He felt sharp pains radiating through his leg, which was still not back to its full strength. "Amos?" he called out. "Are we going to die?"

"I doubt it. It's not the best situation I've been in, but I've seen worse. We're not too far from the road, There's bound to be some folk comin' along sooner or later. I sure hope it's sooner, though."

"Are there wild animals in the woods?" Lev asked nervously.

"Bound to be, but not as many as there were. I'm sure people killed a lot of them for food. Even if there were wild animals, they wouldn't be interested in us unless they were starving."

"Why do you say that?"

"What's the worst thing you ever smelled, boy?"

"What kind of question is that?"

"Just answer it," the old man said gruffly.

"Limburger cheese, rotting vegetables … What does that have to do with wild animals?"

"Many years ago, a very wise man told me why human beings survived. They weren't fast like deer, they didn't have fangs or claws, and they were weaker than just about any large animal. They had brains and they could think, but I'm talking about way before they had knives or guns or even large sticks. The reason humans survived is that they had the most repulsive smell of any animal, so none of the other animals would think of coming near them, let alone eating them."

"That can't be true," Lev said. "Lots of people smell pretty bad when they haven't taken baths for awhile, but for the most part I don't find people disgusting."

"I didn't say *you*, lad. I said *other* animals found us dreadful. That's why I don't think you need to worry about wild animals. But being hungry and thirsty? *That's* what we should worry about. So let's just use our ears, and when we hear something, or hopefully someone, let's use our voices."

Sure enough, within the next hour, they heard the sound of footsteps and, even more welcome, the sound of singing coming from the direction of the road. "Help!" they called out in Polish. The singing continued. Soon the voices seemed to be drifting away. "How could they not have heard us?" Lev asked his companion.

"Probably too caught up in themselves to be interested." The old man made a sudden loud, strange sound, similar to the ambulance sirens Lev remembered from Bratislava, "Ooh-EE, ooh-EE, ooh-EE," followed by a harsh, strong command. "*Baczność! Baczność! Oto Amos! Baczność śpiew mężczyźni! Oto Amos! Pomocy!*" The old man repeated his siren-sound and his command, "Attention! Attention! This is Amos! Attention, singing men! This is Amos! Help!"

The singing stopped. The footsteps became louder.

"Amos? Old Amos? Is that you?" A solidly-built man of twenty-five, his blond hair in stylish ringlets was the first to approach them.

"No, it's not Amos. Of course it's Amos, you dolt. Does a bear shit in the woods?"

"You know, you'd be a bit more presentable if you were a bit more ... *presentable*."

"Very funny," the older man said, scowling. "If that's the kind of dialogue you write in your plays, you'd do better off becoming a monk and taking a vow of silence. Not that I'm particularly sorry to see you, young Karol."

"That young fellow with you is not dressed much better." The man named Karol removed his light outer jacket and put it over Lev's shoulders. "Hey, Filip, come over and help cut these guys loose. While you're at it, see if there's an extra cloak in the car."

Within a few moments, the four companions had freed and somewhat clothed Amos and Lev. "We're just about to have a light dinner," Karol said. "Why not join us? We've got plenty of sausage and some apples, and there's a river full of water close by."

As they sat companionably munching their meal, Amos explained what had befallen them.

"A shame," Karol sighed. "But you're well enough known in these parts that the locals would recognize your wagon anywhere. If they see you without that wagon, the peasants would put two and two together and probably come up with four. My friends and I will climb that hill up ahead and see if we can spot anything."

They did and they did. Returning to where Amos and Lev sat, the man named Filip said, "You're in luck. The highwaymen who attacked you got about five kilometers on the Przemyśl Road before one of the wagon axles cracked. I don't know how long it's been that way, but all three of them are yelling at one another, trying to decide whether to leave the horse and wagon and just walk to Przemyśl, kill the beast for meat, or somehow try to fix the axle."

"Dumb all right," Amos said sourly. "There's enough birch wood in these forests to make a dozen axles. Their leader is as strong as an ox and almost as smart as one. But if they'd rather spend their time cursing the darkness instead of lighting a candle, that's their business."

"The sun'll be going down in an hour or so," Karol said. "We could probably attack them and chase them off."

Amos looked thoughtful. "Thanks, fellows, but what I've got in mind will be much more fun." Amos looked toward Lev and said, "Seems I've forgotten what few manners I have. Karol, I'd like you to meet my young apprentice, Lev Arkady. Lev, this fellow's Karol Wojtyła. I wasn't kidding when I said he should become a monk. Did you ever follow through on your threat to become a priest?"

"I did, Amos. I'm studying with Cardinal Sapieha now. By this time next year …"

"Every young woman in Wadowice and Krakow will be moaning their loss. You know, Karol, once the Communists come to power the priesthood in Poland will be a one way trip to nowhere. I'm told you're a talented playwright …"

"Another great way to make a living under the Communists," Karol said, laughing genially. "Did you have any clothing in the wagon?"

"Everything I owned," the old man replied. "Clothes, shoes … I only hope they didn't throw out the wooden stuff. I need that to make a living."

"We've been hiking most of the day," Filip said. "It'd probably be quicker if we drove you closer to your wagon."

"Much obliged." Shortly thereafter, two of the men reappeared in what at one time had been a red, but was now a mostly rust-colored,

DKW F-9, its two stroke engine chugging noisily. It was twilight when Filip and his friend dropped Amos and Lev off half a kilometer from the wagon they'd lost that morning. After they'd moved to a small declivity under a hillock which shielded them from the wagon, Lev asked, "What do we do now?"

"We wait until it gets dark. Then we'll put our plan into play."

"Why do you have a chain?"

"Part of the game. I saw it on the back floor of the car and asked if I could 'borrow' it for a few days." During the next several minutes, Amos explained exactly what was going to happen. The boy considered the sheer audacity of what Amos proposed. Then, for the first time that day, he smiled at his mentor and said. "It should be fun!"

❧❦❧

The horse had survived because when one of the highwaymen had cut it loose to graze for a few moments, it had trotted off into the nearby forest.

"Just as well," Andrzej remarked. "You'd really have to be starving to want raw, freshly killed horsemeat."

"You ever eaten any, leader?" one of his two companions asked.

"Naww, but my daddy told me it tasted awful."

"Hell, he didn't have any teeth to gnaw with," the other guffawed.

"Maybe, but he told me some old farmer had told him and he wasn't about to take a chance."

The three filthy men swore as they looked at the crippled wagon. "A fine mess this is," the third man said. "Couldn't get more than a złoty for all that crap in the wagon, then the axle breaks in the middle of the road and the nearest food's twenty kilometers away."

"At least the old guy had some wine in the back."

"You call that wine?" Andrzej said. "Smells and tastes more like horse piss to me. Man, look at that moon. So big you could reach out and touch it."

"Guy working at my last job said the werewolves come out on a night like this."

"You believe that?" Andrzej raised his eyebrows.

"Might."

"Just as well we pack into the wagon, then. The earlier we get to sleep, the earlier we wake up to catch another pigeon. Like the story says, 'The early bird catches the worm.'"

※

The moon rose higher in the sky, cutting arcs of light through the trees and onto fields of young grain in the distance. A sharp wind rose. The sound coming from the grain fields emulated a groan. Then another sound issued from under the wagon.

"Do you hear that?" Ryszard asked nervously. Sleep had eluded him and he felt cranky, tired, and on edge.

"Hear what?" Andrzej mumbled.

"Wake up and listen!"

"I don't hear …"

But he did. The clanking of heavy chains and a high-pitched voice sent chills down his spine. "Mottthherrrr!"

Now all three men were awake. The clanking grew louder. The high-pitched voice continued its eerie whine. "Mottthherrr! Where's Amos?"

"Shit! That was the old man's name," Andrzej whispered. "Maybe I'm dreaming."

"Then we're dreaming the same dream," Ryszard replied. "This ain't good."

As the wavering voice continued its frightening plea, it was joined by a second, deeper voice. "They attacked him and left him for dead. Tied him to trees with some puny rope. Too stupid to know it was the night of the full moon. *Wilkołaks noc!*"

"Oh, Papa!" Ryszarc wailed from within the wagon. "Werewolves' night! And we're stuck in this God-cursed place!"

"Hush, coward! There are three of us and two of them."

"Yes, but we're only human beings, Andrzej," the man cried. "A werewolf is as strong as ten men!"

As if to underscore those words, the unwieldy wagon started rocking as though giants had grasped it and were getting ready to throw it into the nearby river. "*Wilkołaks noc! Wilkołaks noc!*" the voices and the chains chanted in unison.

"Where is blood to fill our belly?" the high voice screeched.

"In yonder wagon, shaking like jelly," the lower voice growled. "Three there are, and villains all."

"Eat them, Papa, make them fall!"

But the three men were not about to stick around and be gobbled up. Wearing nothing but their bedclothes, they tumbled one over the other, falling out of the wagon. Without so much as gathering their shoes, the three bolted in different directions. For the next few minutes, cries of "Ouch!" and "Damn!" and "Shit!" could be heard as each of them, barefoot, stepped on nettles or thorns or brambles in their panic to escape the haunted wagon.

❦

The following morning, still chuckling at a game he'd played before, Amos found the horse placidly grazing at the edge of the forest. With axe, hatchet, and a small, old-fashioned hand lathe which the old man had stored in a drawer under the wagon, man and boy chopped, fashioned, turned, and fitted a new axle onto the wagon by noon. Then they hitched the horse to their home on wheels and continued on to Przemyśl.

5

Lev's excitement mounted as they approached the outskirts of Przemyśl. He was eager to see a city of any size, and Amos had told him Przemyśl was the second largest city in southeastern Poland. As the boy asked question after question about their destination, Amos was uncharacteristically quiet, mumbling monosyllabic responses. For the next hour, they passed through fields of bombed-out rubble, half-standing ruins of buildings, and deeply pockmarked, potholed roads. As they continued toward what had been the center of the city, Lev's enthusiasm diminished. He looked questioningly at his mentor. "I thought this you said this is the second biggest city in the area," he ventured.

"Was," the older man replied.

"What happened?"

"The war."

As they plunged into the center of the town, where two dozen multistory buildings were still standing, the boy's eagerness evaporated with each step. "Is there a Jewish quarter?"

"Used to be. Before the war, twenty thousand people, one out of every three in Przemyśl was Jewish."

"Amos?" a voice issued from a one-story building adjacent to the town square.

"Boris," the old man beamed at a short, slight man of forty, who stood slightly taller than Lev. "So there're still a few Jews around here?"

"Three hundred-fifty, maybe a few more. How long since you've been here?"

"'Forty-one."

"A lot of blood has run under the bridge."

"I heard they sealed the ghetto in the summer of '42."

"They did. Destroyed the Tempel Synagogue and the Old Synagogue. Confiscated the New Synagogue, the Zasanie Synagogue and everything else owned by Jews. Almost everyone got sent to Auschwitz or Belzec. The Polish underground saved four hundred of us. The Nazis paid 'em back by executing six hundred Poles for 'treason.' You'll stay with us tonight?"

"Best invitation I've had. Your family survived?"

"God be thanked. Who's the youngster?"

"Lev Arkady. Orphaned. Bright fellow. He needs a grandfather, I need a grandson."

"Welcome, Lev!" Boris exclaimed. "Leah!" the man called into his house. "We've got guests for the night."

"Good thing I made extra *cholent*." A plump woman in early middle age emerged from the house. "Who is …? Amos!" she cried out. "My God, part of our world survived after all!"

"Takes more than a little war to kill this old bugger," Amos replied. "Hannah must be what, eleven, twelve?"

"Twelve next month."

"Got someone I think she'd like to meet." Lev stood quietly. "Is there a place I can leave the horse and wagon?"

"Out back," Boris said. "Don't think your horse will mind if the grass is a bit high."

Boris, who had been a butcher before the war, was delightful, courtly, charming and hospitable. At dinner, he, Leah, and Amos reminisced about times past. It had been several hours since Lev had eaten and he partook ravenously of the delicious stew made up of chunks of meat, carrots, and potatoes. After dinner, Leah served Hannah and Lev mint tea and opened a bottle of vodka for the menfolk.

Lev hardly heard any of the conversation between the adults. He was struck by the family's daughter, who had long-flowing, dark hair and sparkling brown eyes, a light complexion and the softest looking skin he'd ever seen. Beneath her modest dress, he made out the faint outlines of a budding young feminine figure. During the dinner, Hannah favored Lev with well-timed smiles. Lev found it hard to speak.

He was still thinking about Hannah when he and Amos retired to their wagon for the night. "New discovery?" Amos asked knowingly. Lev didn't know what to say. "Nothing to be ashamed of," the older man said. "It comes naturally and it starts at just about your age. Pretty little girl, that one. But we've got work to do before we turn in for the night. Tomorrow you start helping me earn a living. Now, this here's a mouse table…"

"First thing you do, catch a field mouse."

"Catch … a … field … mouse? I've never caught a small animal in my life."

"It's easier that catching a fish in the San. They've survived the war much better than human beings. Come on, I'll help you catch your first one."

In almost no time, Amos found a field that seemed to be teeming with the tiny rodents. He scooped two of them up and placed them in a cotton bag into which he'd thrown a few grains of dried rice. "They'll eat anything," he told his young charge. "Raw fruit and vegetables, hay, ham, cheese, even a boiled egg." As if to underscore his point, when Lev looked into the bag he saw the mice contentedly gnawing on the rice.

By nine the next morning, word had spread that the legendary Amos was back in town. Although the Jews, indeed most residents of the entire city, were impoverished, the promise of a day filled with Amos' entertainments was so enticing that within half an hour there were well over a hundred people in attendance. Amos did not disappoint. He started the day's events with a few jokes, followed by two or three of his tales. Soon a shout rang out from a man in the audience, "What game today?"

Amos pretended to ignore the man, knowing that once a few more took up the chant, the time for making money would begin. While he kept talking, Lev set up the table thirty feet behind where the crowd was standing. He placed a wooden board, 125 centimeters feet wide by 150 centimeters long – about four-by-five feet – on the table. The board had twenty-one holes, numbered from zero to twenty, each slightly less than four inches in diameter.

At a signal from Lev that all was ready, Amos called out, "Ladies and gentleman, it's time for you to make your fortune! Bet one *grosz*, win *twenty groszy*! Bet ten *groszy*, win *two złoty!* The most honest guessing game ever invented. Bet a *złoty*, win *twenty* of 'em! It's a game of human intuition versus animal instinct. Simply pick the hole that little *Mazel* the Mouse will run to," he said, holding up the cotton bag and taking a brown mouse out of the sack.

With that, Amos stepped off the raised platform and, followed by the already mesmerized crowd, carried Mazel to the board. The game consisted of putting the wee mouse in the middle of the board, and watching when it instantly scurried for one of the holes around it and ducked into the dark interior. There, Amos's hand was waiting to snatch it, bring it out, and set it on the board again.

A cluster of men quickly gathered. After they had amusedly watched the proceedings for a minute, they began to dig in their pockets and plunk down *groszy,* even a few larger coins, and one or two *złoty* bills, alongside one or another of the numbered holes. The mouse dutifully ran for a hole every time it was exposed to public gaze, and Amos directed Lev to pay off every winner, while he bellowed things like, "*Two złoty* to this clever fellow! Good going, Sir! A return of *two thousand percent* on your investment!"

The noise brought others crowding around. Soon, they had to reach over and under the tangle of arms to place their bets. Every couple of times, as he had been told to do, Lev wiped the whole board with a damp rag. Eventually, every time the mouse ran, almost every hole on the board bore a stake, and there were one or more winners almost every time, adding his own shout of "Whoopee!" to Amos' own congratulatory clamor: "Mind over mammal! Absolutely guaranteed to be the fairest game you'll ever play! And there's *another* winner! Don't crowd, gentlemen. Give the ladies a chance at instant fortune, too!"

The mouse never seemed to tire, but after each half-hour Amos' alternated one mouse with the other. The players never even noticed that the second mouse was grey instead of brown. It could have been white, red, or black, and it would have made no difference. As the day continued, Amos let Lev run the game, while he busily set up other gambling games and collected a small percentage from the foodsellers who had set up shop in the immediate vicinity. By four that afternoon the gamblers were either satisfied with their winnings or unable to go on losing.

"Two hundred *złoty* and eighty *groszy!*" the old man crowed happily. "And that's just from the mouse game. Another fifty *złoty* from the rest of the operation. Pure sweet profit! Lev, we must set up a second board tomorrow. Once word gets out, we ought to fetch *ten times* that much easily!"

Boris invited them back to his house for another fine dinner. On the way back home, he asked Amos confidentially, "Would you mind telling me what's the trick to the game?"

"Trick?" Amos looked inexpressibly wounded.

"Well, one simply assumes ... a game of chance ..."

"My mouse game doesn't have to be rigged in any way," Amos said. "Twenty-one holes to bet on, and I *say* I pay odds of twenty-to-one. Suppose twenty-one gamblers bet ten *groszy* apiece. I scoop in all the ten-*groszy* coins and give the winner two hundred *groszy*, two *złoty* bills. He's actually getting only one-hundred-ninety *groszy* profit and I'm richer by ten *groszy*. That extra hole, number *zero*, always gives the edge to the house."

"But that business of having the boy wipe the board with the rag. Perhaps some secret preparation ..."

"Only ammonia water. If a mouse runs to the same hole a couple of times, he might afterwards follow his own scent and go there repeatedly. Some players will be sharp enough to notice that and bet on it. So I wipe the board clean after every couple of plays. That's to keep *Mazel* honest."

At that moment, someone plucked at Amos' sleeve, saying in a frigid voice, "Sir, I am told that you are the proprietor of this enterprise."

Amos turned to face a gentleman with a doleful long jaw, stiffly fringed with a beard nearly half as long. "That I am, Sir. I trust you enjoyed the entertainment."

"Enjoyment is not our object in life, Sir," said the man, indicating the other people with him, three more men and several women, all wearing the same expression of pious woe. "We represent the Citizens' Crusade. It has been brought to our attention that your so-called entertainment includes a certain board of chance."

"The board is indeed mine," Amos said. "If you are here to complain, I can assure you the game is honest."

"Honesty or dishonesty is not our concern," said the man. "We are interested in protecting the innocent victim of this outrage and indignity."

Amos looked bewildered. "Well, some have lost money, I confess that. But outrage? Indignity? I don't – "

"We wish you to show us this game," said a flat-faced woman.

"I don't mind," said Amos." He brought the board and table, then reached into the sack and brought out one of the mice, which he had to disengage from a morsel of cheese it had been busy gnawing. "You interrupted Mazel's mealtime," he said, as he set the mouse on the board. "Now what happens – the players guess which hole he'll run to. And Mazel picks his own. No forcing, no trickery, see? Number fifteen this time. No earthly way this game can be diddled, doctored, or cheated."

"As we suspected," said a woman with tightly coiffed, iron-gray hair. "Cruelty to animals."

Prepared as he was to defend himself against charges of swindling, fraud, or flimflam, Amos was staggered by this unexpected accusation. He said with some heat, "Lady, you folks disturbed Mazel's mealtime rest. Do you see *me* being cruel to him?"

"If not overt cruelty," said one of the men, "certainly a perversion of the animal's natural behavior and a violation of its dignity."

"Dignity?" said Amos, unbelieving. "Man, this is a common, ordinary field mouse. Not some noble horse being mistreated. Just a *mouse*, doing what mice *do*, running for a hole."

"But at your bidding," one of the women said flintily. "Not of its own accord. The creature is being callously degraded."

"Madame," Amos said summoning as much diplomacy as his temper allowed him to muster, "perhaps you accord this mouse an undue amount of concern, because the mouse occupies, so to speak, the limelight of celebrity. But consider. If you were to find this rodent running about your kitchen, would you not regard it as unwelcome vermin? Would you not kill it, just as you would a cockroach?"

"Entirely different circumstances," said the woman, unswayed. "In that case, the animal would be pursuing its normal way of life, and taking its normal chances at survival. Here, it is being forced to perform unnatural acts."

"Unnatural acts?" Amos sputtered. "A field mouse?" Then he quickly regained his composure as he realized the idiocy of the situation. "I take it you object to the use of a *mammal*. A few moments ago, I mentioned a cockroach. Would you sensibilities be soothed if we substitute a cockroach for the mouse?"

Nobody laughed at this further descent into the ridiculous. The Citizens' Crusade exchanged inquiring glances. The man with the long beard murmured, "Hmmm…well… a cockroach *is* an invertebrate, certainly a being rather lower in the order of Creation …"

Amos said quickly, "Lev, a sturdy bull cockroach would serve as well, wouldn't it?" While the boy simply stared, amazed, Amos continued smoothly, "There we are, then. A cockroach it shall be. And we thank you folks for helping us mend our ways. Now, would you, ma'am, care to take possession of Mazel the Mouse?" The woman he addressed cringed away, aghast. "Would you prefer we set him free? Very well, Lev, let Mazel return to his, er, natural habitat." Slowly shaking his head in incredulity, Lev knelt and tenderly set the tiny creature on the ground. As Amos handed the boy the second mouse, he did the same. The two mice stood still for a moment, their whiskers twitching, looking for a last handout. Seeing none to be had, they scurried quickly away.

6

From Przemyśl, they turned east. Less than a day-and-a-half later, Lev's mouth dropped open and his eyes widened in wonder. "My God, this place must be twice as large as Bratislava!"

"That it is, boy," Amos remarked. "Did you see how many people were heading west as we approached the city?"

"Thousands."

"There'll be tens of thousands in the next few months. Welcome to Ukraine, or, as it's better known today, the Ukrainian Socialist Republic."

"Ukraine?" Lev asked. "I thought L'wów was in Poland."

"Was," the old man replied acerbically. "At least until a few months ago. It's also been part of Austria-Hungary and Russia. Even the Swedes and the Ottoman Turks tried to take a bite out of it."

"Jews?"

"The Jews were the one constant here before the most recent war. They actually had equal rights with other citizens and lived pretty well here."

"Now?"

"Same as everywhere else. Three, four hundred of 'em, maybe. They don't even call it Lwów anymore. It's been L'viv since last August, when the Ukrainians reclaimed it. The Russkies and what few Jews are left still call it L'vov. The Germans insist it's Lemberg."

"Are we headed anywhere in particular?" the boy asked.

"We are," Amos replied. "The larger cities always have a circus coming through. I always try to team up with whatever circus is around. Good for them and great for me because that's where the real money is."

As they moved deeper into the city, Lev observed, "L'viv seems to be in much better shape than what we've seen so far."

"Physically, yes. The old town's still intact. Sort of like Prague in Czechoslovakia. It was pretty enough that while they didn't mind killing the people, everyone wanted to keep the most attractive parts bomb-free."

"Not like Warsaw?" the boy asked.

"Nope," the older man said, taking out a carved wooden pipe and lighting up. "The Germans viewed the Jews as subhuman scum. The Poles weren't much higher on the ladder. But the Nazis looked at the Ukrainians in a different light. They weren't Russians. In fact, they've hated the Russians for hundreds of years. They were more like civilized folk, so the Nazis left the city untouched once they'd gotten rid of the Jews and most of the Poles. When the Soviets came back a year ago, they decided to finish mopping up what the Nazis had started. Those folks you saw heading west were Poles who've been sent packing by the present ownership. Ukraine is now part of the greater U.S.S.R."

As they walked through the Old Town, Amos said, "It's getting on to dinner time. I'm supposed to meet with an old friend, Albrecht Rittmeister at *Ratusha*, the town hall, at five."

"Rittmeister? A German?"

"Swiss. Like just about everyone else on a circus, he's a mongrel, comfortable anywhere he can put on a good show." As they strolled around the market area, Amos pointed out numerous tall, stately buildings. "All churches," he said, not without a hint of bitterness. "There's the Roman Catholic Cathedral. Took more than a hundred years to build. They had a lot of time on their hands back then. That's the Armenian Cathedral. Over there's the Ukrainian Catholic Church."

"Was there a Jewish section?"

"*Two*," the old man replied. "One within the city walls and one on the outskirts. Lots of synagogues. There were a hundred thousand Jews at the outbreak of the war. Today …" Amos said no more.

No sooner had they come in sight of the town hall, which dominated Market Square, then a man of indeterminate middle age, five feet tall and four feet wide, whose tight suit accentuated his boxlike physique, approached them. "Amos! If you get any older we'll put you in the main show as a mummy!"

"If you get any wider, 'Brecht, you won't be able to fit through the cathedral door!" The two men laughed and hugged each other, comrades who'd come a long way down the trail of life, frequently running into each other along the way.

"I'm glad you noticed that, *alte*," Rittmeister replied. "I don't know about you, but I need something to eat to keep myself in shape, a proper *pear* shape," he said, guffawing. "I'm sorry," he said, turning to Lev. "Neither Amos nor I have any manners. I'm Albrecht Rittmeister. You must be my friend's grandson?"

"Close enough," Amos said. "His name's Lev Arkady," he continued, putting his arm around the boy's shoulder. "Got quite a history. I'll tell you more over dinner."

The three of them enjoyed a huge repast of *borscht,* beet soup, followed by stuffed cabbage, and Chicken Kiev, a deep-fried butter-stuffed ball of chicken, at a small restaurant on Prospekt Svobody.

"So you've already survived two lives, Lev, and now you're apprenticed to my old friend," Rittmeister said, after he'd heard the boy's tale. "You could do far worse. Amos. Between us have seen …"

"More countries than most people have seen *counties,* the old man replied. "Been awhile since we've seen one another, though."

"Five years. Thank God I had a Swiss passport during the troubles. How'd you manage to survive?"

Amos dug into his pocket and produced five passports of his own: Swiss, German, Hungarian, Romanian, and Italian. "Greatest forger I ever knew," he said wistfully. "Shame he got sent to Auschwitz. Thank God he left me a dozen others, all passably good, all with different names. All I have to do is insert a photograph when I need to. I was able to get his son out of harm's way."

"How often do you need those *cartes de visite*?"

"Hardly ever. Mostly, the authorities think I'm a harmless old coot, or, if they know me, they know my kind of entertainment soothes the locals and keep them from rebelling against their overlords. They look the other way when I cross borders. How about you, Albrecht? Where were you during the war?"

"Turkey, Persia, Egypt, far enough away from the action. Long ago, we Swiss learned not to make war but to profit from the wars of others."

"How'd you end up with the Zaƚewski?" Amos asked.

"They needed a governor and I was 'between engagements.' The show's as good a circus as any in Eastern Europe for the time being. Won't be that way much longer."

"The Communists?"

"Uh-huh. They're disguising that name for now, using 'Popular Front' or 'Peoples' Democratic Republic.' They've convinced the West that since they bore the brunt of the war on the Eastern Front this is their sphere of influence and they deserve to run it. By this time next year the Zaƚewski'll be State-owned."

A bearded waiter approached and inquired if they'd like some dessert. Rittmeister ordered a piece of *apfelstrudel* for each of them, two for himself, and a bottle of Crimean sweet red wine.

"Probably not the best time for a Polish show to be in Ukraine, Albrecht."

"It's not, but L'wow, sorry, *Lviv*, was on the schedule before the war shut down. We'll play here for two more weeks, then back to Poland for the rest of the season. Why not tag along with us? We can always use entertainers who pay their own way."

"If that's all right with you."

"Of course, my friend. Lev, would you like to learn what circus life is like?"

Trying to mask the excitement he felt, the boy looked toward his mentor. When the old man nodded, he said, "I'll go wherever Amos goes."

"Wonderful. We'll carry your horse and wagon on our train between the large cities. There'll be plenty food for all three of you. For now, why don't you just camp out on our *tober*? It's south of the city, plenty of room, and the weather's warm."

⁂

During the next several months, Lev concentrated on learning everything he could, both about the circus and, more importantly, about how to deal with the foibles of his fellow human beings. He found Albrecht Rittmeister knowledgeable about the former, but it was Old Amos who knew precisely how to deal with poets and peasants, princes and paupers, and government functionaries.

Lev had been tongue-tied when he first saw Maximus, "the biggest brute that breathes," an elephant of impressive, but not particularly gargantuan, size. Rittmeister remarked, "You'll find at least one bull in every circus of any size in Europe."

"A bull, Herr Rittmeister?"

"That's what they call an elephant in the circus, Lev. A double misnomer. First, because she's not cattle, and second …"

"She?"

"That's the second thing. Every circus elephant I've ever seen is a female, a *cow*. They've got a much milder temperament and they're easier to train than a male. They still call 'em bulls, though, I suppose to make the jossers, the audiences, think of them as both huge and aggressive."

"His, er, *her* name is Maximus, though."

"In the show ring. Her real name's Marthe."

"Not a very impressive name," Amos said, coming up to them. "Of course, I've seen much larger bulls."

"Ah, but you won't find any smarter or gentler in all of Eastern Europe."

One of Lev's lessons in how masterfully Amos handled people, and what incredible nerve, *chutzpah,* the old man had, came a month later. The train had dropped the circus off in Lublin. For the next couple of weeks, the show played in smaller venues, from Lublin to Terespol, to Chelm, and back to Lublin, from whence it would travel northwest to the capital. The countryside, rolling hills interspersed with patches of forest, showed off the beauty of eastern Poland in autumn. The circus arrived at one of hundreds of small villages along the route one Saturday evening. Management decided the Załewski would take a day off before moving on to its next venue. Since many of the performers were nominally Roman Catholic, they attended next morning's Mass in the small country church. Those who professed other religions or no religion at all either slept in late or stretched their legs hiking through the meadows.

Lev, who'd become quite enamored of Marthe the elephant, begged Rittmeister to allow him to take the pachyderm on a walk around the village. The circus director assented. Later that morning, Rittmeister and Amos, who were not inclined toward walking about, sat contentedly smoking pipes and jawing about old days, when they were approached by an officious-looking man wearing a Sunday go-to-church suit with a tin star in its lapel. He sternly introduced himself as the county constable.

"I'm happy to make your acquaintance, Constable," Rittmeister said respectfully. "Is there a problem?" He started to extract a paper from his pocket. "We have all of the required permits to perform in the province, and …"

"I'm not concerned with that, Sir," he said, pointing to a spot several yards away. "Is your establishment the owner of that … that beast?" he continued, pointing to Marthe and an embarrassed-looking Lev. It was difficult to determine which of the two looked more shamefaced.

"Why, yes, Officer, that elephant is the star of our show."

"Whether he's a star or not doesn't concern me," the constable said. "That big critter frisked like a goat through half the backyards in our village and plucked up every green sprout from the kitchen gardens, and turned over just about every outhouse. I'm here to inform you that you are responsible for the damages. I wouldn't be so upset, but *my own privy* was one of the ones he overturned!"

At this point, Amos stood up. "I am terribly sorry, Your Lordship," he said, elevating the constable's rank by several degrees. "Lev, my boy, I apologize to you as well. We all stand convicted as charged. It is no excuse that we had quite a few other matters to occupy our attention here. Lev, go and stake Maximus where she belongs and give her a plug of tobacco to settle her nerves."

While Lev stood watching uncertainly, Amos continued smoothly. "Shades of Mary and her little lamb, eh, Your Lordship? Well …" he squared his shoulders. "Can you tell me what the damages are likely to amount to?"

"No, sir, not yet I can't. Practically the whole town was in church during that animal's foray. Half the town probably still is.

I won't know the total extent until everybody gets home and starts raising all kinds of …"

"At least let us begin by paying for your own, er, outbuilding," Amos said, reaching into his pocket.

The officer dismissed that with a wave of his hand. "Never mind. No real damage to speak of, except that my wife was inside it at the time. No, what I want to say is that the property damage is the least of your problems. I could swear out a criminal warrant for you letting a dangerous beast like that run loose."

Amos chuckled. "That mild-mannered old pachyderm? Why a cow elephant is no more of a menace than a cow *cow*." At that remark, Amos got a sharp sidewise glance from Rittmeister. "You observed, Your Lordship, that the animal is a vegetarian. Clumsy and awkward, yes. But vicious? Tut tut."

"Well …," said the constable. "There's still the matter of it committing a public nuisance. After eating up them gardens, the critter – if you'll excuse my vulgarity – the critter emptied its bowels all over them gardens."

"*What*? *God help us all!*" blurted Amos. He whirled to Rittmeister. "Governor, get every man you can! Pull them all out of church if necessary! And get shovels! *Immediately!*"

The constable blinked. "Is that stuff dangerous?"

"Dangerous, sir? Elephant dung is the most potent fertilizer in all Creation. Your village would be a jungle of vegetable produce. Cucumbers climbing in your windows! You'd need two hands to lift the corn cobs! Melons would block every meter of the road between here and Warsaw! We must scoop it up, and quickly! It is, after all, our property. Whatever we are fined for the damage done here, we can sell that rich manure to any knowledgeable farmer along our way for fifty times what we have to pay your citizens!"

"It's that valuable, eh? Well, then, wait a minute, Sir. Consider. You'll have to send your men all over to find the sh— the stuff, and shovel it up, and fetch it back. Then you'll be detained while all the folks' damages are assessed and then you'll have to pay. How about we settle for an even swap? Leave the elephant droppings. I'll explain to the people. Those who don't want to use it themselves can sell it to Wielocki's greenhouse, and we'll call everything square."

"We-ell ..." said Amos. "It's noble of you to save us work and time and penalties. I think we'd do better by peddling the manure, but ..." Amos took the man's hand and pumped it, "I'll accede to the agreement. And here, sir, tickets to tomorrow's performance in Małopolskaya Vitebsk. For you and Mrs. Constable, if she has recovered from her, er, discomfiture by then ... and for any little constables ..."

The man went away happy and Amos took out a handkerchief and patted his brow. Rittmeister and Lev looked at him with mixed expressions.

"I've known you to tell some Christly lies before, Amos," Rittmeister said. "But making Marthe out to be a cuddlesome pet lamb? If some peasant had poked her with a pitchfork or some brat had thrown a stone, you know damned well she'd have done a headstand on him. Then we'd have needed a shovel for sure."

"Of course I know that," snapped Amos, "and I am sincerely thankful that no such thing happened. But I refuse to fret over every *what if?* until I have to.

Either there were not too many peasants fearful of the marauding beast of the day before or else the constable had spread the word that the circus folk were decent, because the people from the village and over fifty others within a ten kilometer radius came to Małopolskaya Vitebsk the next day to attend the performance. The crowd may not have seemed numerically great, but they filled all the available seats.

At the end of the day, Rittmeister and Amos sat around, counting the take. "Most of 'em paid in fairly worthless złoty," Amos said, "but some seemed to realize that we fleshly mortals require more tangible payment than their spiritual clergy, so a fair number paid in silver, and the rest brought good edible or usable barter. I even had one young lad offer me a handful of Marthe's droppings."

Rittmeister laughed. "Did you turn him away?"

"Hell, no. I told him a mere pinch of the stuff was worth a ticket and let him keep the rest. A good lie is always worth the effort of sustaining it."

7

"Ana! As I live and breathe! What are you doing so far from home?"

"Thirty kilometers is not that far, Amos. Besides, it's much easier to be anonymous in Iași than in *Codăești*." She pronounced the city's name in the Romanian manner, "*Yahsh.*"

"True. Three hundred thousand's a few more than three thousand. Nice to see you in the lobby of the Grand Hotel Traian. Of course this is anything but anonymity. A bit sumptuous for a committed Communist, wouldn't you say?"

"All the more reason to meet here." The round-faced woman reached up with her right hand and stroked her hair, now stylishly short and graying, with a part in the center of her high waves. "Besides, I blend into the scenery, a chunky Jewish middle-aged woman."

"Still lovely," Amos said gallantly. "Marcel would have been proud."

"It's been eight years. Ioseb Besarionis would never have sanctioned it."

Amos said nothing. He did not share his friend's trust in the Soviet leader, nor did he believe that Besarionis, who'd conveniently changed his name to Joseph Stalin when he'd assumed Lenin's mantle on the great man's death, did not know of the 1938 purges carried out in his name by his closest associates. Ana, too, might have been a victim of Stalin's axe had she not been serving a ten year sentence in Văcărești Monastery Prison, southeast of Bucharest at the time.

"If he was as anti-Semitic as they say, why would he have protected me by trading me for Codreanu and letting me sit out the war safely in Moscow?"

"Safely?" Amos raised his eyebrows.

"Except for the German offensive two months after I arrived. By November 27, they'd gotten within thirty kilometers of the Kremlin, Khimki, the last tram stop on the Moscow line. The boy your grandson?" she asked, looking directly at Lev.

"To all intents and purposes. Lev Arkady, orphaned in forty-five."

She reached her hand and shook Lev's warmly. "Ana Pauker," she said. "You're what, thirteen?"

"Twelve, ma'am."

"Almost time for your *Bar Mitzvah*. Have you given it much thought?"

"No, ma'am. I've been on the road with Amos for a year-and-a-half."

"I'd wager you've already gotten the equivalent of a college education in life. Have you ever thought of leaving *shtetl Europe,* what's left of it anyway?"

"To where, Mrs. Pauker?"

"Palestine. There are probably more Jews there already than there are Jews left in the whole of Eastern Europe, which has become a relic of the Jewish past. Palestine's its future."

"I've never thought about it that way," the boy said.

"You've heard about *Eretz Israel?*"

"Of course."

Turning to Amos, she said, "I could easily get him to Constantia. It's not that far from there to Kilyos."

"He might be happier here in Eastern Europe," Amos said gruffly. "Not a bad place for a Jewish Communist to be."

"You think so, Amos?" She looked at him strangely.

"Well, you've certainly climbed the ladder."

"Because they can use me. Marcel was Jewish. So was Maxim Litvinov and dozens of others that didn't survive the purge of '38. They're cozying up to us because we're convenient, intelligent, and 'oppressed,' not to mention mostly dead."

"I thought you and Stalin were such close comrades."

"As long as it suits his purpose. The cat and mouse in partnership. Don't get me wrong, Amos, I genuinely like Josef and I think he likes me as well, but if I ever became a political liability, 'Bye 'bye Ana Pauker.' Shall we look for a place where we can have a quiet cup of tea and some pastry?"

"Why not?" the man said. "I'm feeling flush this week. I'll even pay."

The three of them left the hotel and headed across Piaţa Unirii toward Cuza Vodă Street. Just before they reached the southeast corner of the square, Ana's right hand flew to her mouth as she looked at the side street, then at Amos, then back to the street. Recovering her composure, she stared at what could charitably be called a 'strange' vehicle parked on the street, then turned to Amos, the unasked question in her eyes.

"As I said, business has been very good and I am flush this week."

"What profoundly good taste," Ana remarked tartly. "Red, white, blue, purple orange, violet, red, yellow, green, and mud color go so well together, particularly when they're arranged in stripes, waves, dots ... And such modesty. 'Amos's World Renowned Miracle Shows and Medicines,'" she said, emphasizing the final "s."

"The horse died and the wagon got old. I didn't want people to think I was behind the times."

"Lev...?"

"He saved my life, Mrs. Pauker. Like you said, he's been a good teacher. He even let me paint some of those swirls," Lev said, pointing proudly to his handiwork.

"My God, Amos! Don't you feel ashamed! You're making him into a copy of you!"

"God?" the old man replied? "Did I hear the word 'God' coming from the lips of an avowed Communist?"

"You know I've never abandoned my religious beliefs," she rejoined. "And despite your ambiguous statements, neither have you. If you'll excuse my rudeness in asking, exactly what *is* it?"

"It's called a van," Amos replied. "A friend in Warsaw, or was it Bratislava ...?"

"Vienna," Lev supplied.

"Got hold of an old Citroën ..."

"Daimler..." the boy interjected.

"Ambulance and raised the roof, added some living space and some storage ..."

"Not to take God's name in vain," Ana said, "but if I may be blunt, it's the godawful ugliest thing I've ever seen. If it rides as bad as it looks ..."

"Silence, woman!" Amos thundered with mock gravity. "Unless you want me to revoke my invitation for you to ride in it and let you walk to the Great Synagogue on your own."

"You'd let an old woman walk three kilometers? Not even you would invite the wrath of God by doing that."

They reached the vehicle. Amos gallantly held the door open. Ana Pauker got in first, followed by Lev. Despite its appearance, the former ambulance was solidly built and its engine turned over smoothly as the old man turned the key in the ignition. The ride was surprisingly pleasant as they entered Cuza Vodă, turned right six blocks later, then turned left onto Anastasie Panu. When they arrived at Sinagogilar Street, Amos said, more to Lev than to Ana, "Behold the Great Synagogue of Iași!"

"Looks pretty modest to me," Lev remarked.

"The floor is located below street level," Amos replied. "Jewish tradition says the synagogue should be the highest building in the neighborhood, but because Jews weren't allowed to build high structures by the Romanian authorities, they got around the restriction by lowering the floor of synagogue, so the interior is actually higher than the exterior elevation of the building."

"Why bring us here?"

"First, because it's the oldest Jewish prayer house in Romania and one of the oldest synagogues in all of Europe, and second, there's a restaurant next door that has the best Kosher food in the city, maybe in the whole country."

⸙

"So you're still traveling from place to place without borders, Amos?"

"That I am."

"Still operating on the edge of the law? Sometimes over the edge?"

"I prefer to call it entertainment."

"Like peddling your old wives' nostrums?"

"I'll have you know that Doctor Rumphius's …"

"Or Doctor Feelgood's, or Doctor Quack's or whatever you call it this week …" the woman interrupted.

Lev coughed to suppress a giggle. In his time with Amos, he'd learned firsthand exactly what Ana Pauker was talking about, but like everything else about Amos, there was a new-old story around every corner, and the boy was eager for the entertainment these stories provided. The woman turned her gaze toward the boy.

"You say he's taught you a lot, boy? What's his latest fraud?"

"I wouldn't call it a fraud exactly, Mrs. Pauker. When we go to a town or village of any size, he says I am a clair – clair - … Someone who can predict when something's going to happen."

"A clairvoyant," the woman said. "The pregnancy game?"

"How did you know that?" Lev asked.

"Amos and I go back a few years. He, my late husband, and I shared a few meals and a few evenings together and he actually told me about it. Of course, he's got to mix his tricks up from time to time, so he doesn't get caught and get run out of town or worse."

"It's not a trick," Amos said adamantly. "It's sheer prognostication."

"Sheer toot is what it is," Ana remarked. "Let's see if I can get it right. He takes you with him into the village. He claims you can see the future, that you can accurately predict whether a pregnant woman will have a boy or a girl."

"That's right," Lev said. "He makes sure I take a little notebook and write the woman's name and town in it, so I won't forget …"

"Nine out of every ten women want a boy. If it's what you predict, they're so happy you either never see them again or they might give you a gift. If not, they might be angry at you, so you cover yourself by writing down 'boy' or 'girl' in your notebook. Only you always *write* the exact reverse of what you *said*. If you tell a woman a boy is coming, you write 'girl' in your book. If you tell a woman a girl is coming, you write 'boy.' So either way you're always right."

"You know the trick?"

"I've known Amos long enough. And I am a politician, so I've learned one of the oldest politician's tricks in the world: Promise the voters what you must, deliver whatever you can, and pray they forget most of what you said as soon as the election results are in. Where are you boys going from here?"

"Next country down the road."

"Hitler's allies during the late war."

"Yes," Amos replied, slowly lighting one of his never-ending, foul-smelling pipes. "If only all our enemies had been like the Bulgarians. Bulgaria was one of only three countries in the world that saved its entire Jewish population from the Nazi camps, even though the Nazis deported almost the entire Jewish population of the Bulgarian-occupied Yugoslav and Greek territories to Treblinka.

"Dimitrov's a truly popular man," Amos continued. "If we've got to winter someplace, Bulgaria's as good a place as any. October's still tolerable in the mountains and we can camp on the Black Sea coast or trundle down to Thrace if we get too cold."

"What about Turkey?"

"Certainly a possibility. The Jewish community in Istanbul has been strong since the days of the Spanish Inquisition and that's one of the grandest cities I've ever seen. The 'Whore of the Ages,' they call it. Maybe even give the boy some more of life's lessons."

"Why you old reprobate. You are truly beyond ..."

"Ah, ah, ah," he waggled his right index finger playfully at his friend. "You're the one suggested *Bar Mitzvah*. When a boy becomes a *Bar Mitzvah* be becomes a *man* ..."

"Just don't have him bring home a loathsome disease," Ana snapped. The boy looked at both of them in surprise and utter ignorance. After a few minutes, Ana suggested she take leave of Amos and Lev.

"But just think," Amos said, "what people would think if they saw you in my beautiful new conveyance."

"I *am* thinking," Ana replied. "Which is exactly why I'd like to part company while I still have a semblance of dignity left."

When she had gone Lev said, "She's really serious about my becoming a *Bar Mitzvah*. But you told me she's a confirmed Communist, part of the new godless elite."

"That she may be," Amos replied. The old man brushed a flyspeck off the windshield off what Lev called the Amosmobile. "Lev, have you ever heard the saying, 'The child is the father of the man?'"

"I've heard you use it on occasion, but I never thought to ask you what it meant."

"It means," he said seriously, "that lessons we learn very early in life are the most powerful ones and they never leave us."

"Like my memories of my parents?"

"That, of course. Damn, that fly must've been made of glue. It won't come off."

"You might try a little water and a brush. Sometimes your fingernail might not be enough."

"Smarty! Where was I?"

"The child is the father of the man – "

"Oh, yes. Ana Pauker's very big in the Communist world. She could be in line to be the next ruler of this country. Although you haven't been to the West – "

"I've been to Bratislava, Budapest, even Vienna while we've been together."

Amos patted the boy's knee and said kindly, "I don't mean the western part of Central Europe. I mean places like England, France …"

"Like I heard on the shortwave before my parents were killed?"

"Yes. They're saying an Iron Curtain has descended over Europe and we're on the wrong side of that Curtain. People may tell you that big things separate us from the West. Political systems, economic beliefs … But it's the little things that join us – what we eat, our old songs. The mothers in the West tell their children the same fairy tales your mother told you at night. Fathers talk about wars that were fought more than a hundred years ago. Little things, maybe, but in my experience the little things outlast the big things. We Jews are a tribe, Lev. Maybe that's the best thing about us and the worst. You'll spend a good part of your life trying to find out which is the greater truth."

8

"It's time we thought seriously about moving West," Amos announced one evening in the spring of 1948. Lev was now fully a head taller than his mentor. Indeed, he was larger than most men in the villages where he and Amos found themselves.

"Why? We've made more money than ever during the past year. People seem happy with us wherever we go."

"Yes, but have you noticed how everyone seems almost too happy to see us? The peasant dances are always vigorous and the people are always smiling."

"So?" Lev replied. "I've never known folk not to be happy when you're around. The old tales and stories …"

"Yes, but I've told those same stories a thousand times or more. Used to be I could always count on at least some groans from the audience. Or someone accusing me of rigging the games of chance. But not this year. It's as if whole villages have become like Theresienstadt during the war. Like these people were being *ordered* to enjoy themselves – or else."

They'd put down overnight in a meadow just east of Szczecin, a few kilometers from the German frontier. While the Amosmobile gave them great notoriety, it also provided privacy and they paid nothing for their nightly accommodations. Lev had noticed that during the past year Amos evinced less and less interest in visiting his women friends in the towns and villages and that he fell asleep much earlier than in the past. While he still put on a good show in public, he'd become quieter, and more pessimistic when night came.

"Jewish men become adults when they become *Bar Mitzvah*. They're usually thirteen. You're already a year older than that. Maybe Ana was right. It wouldn't hurt you to become a *Bar Mitzvah*. Besides, when it's my time to go, it would be nice if I had someone to say *Kaddish* over me. Never had a son of my own, but you're as close as I've come. Other things you can do besides saying *Kaddish* when you're a man."

Lev blushed. They'd had this conversation an increasing number of times during the past several months. The boy always knew where such talks led. Lev had heard Amos referred to as an old reprobate. He never pretended he didn't know *why* Amos used to absent himself so often at night. But nowadays, Amos seemed to delight more in *talking* about such things than in doing them. Lev felt uncomfortable when these talks started. While he knew, more or less, the mechanics of sex and its sometime consequences, intended or not, he doubted he'd ever crow about such things like this old rooster.

"How do you expect me to become *Bar Mitzvah* when we've never settled down in one place long enough for me to learn what I need to know?" Lev asked.

"No time like the present to start," Amos said, extracting a well-thumbed volume written in Hebrew. "I figure in two or three months you should be ready."

"But won't I need to learn my *Parsha*?"

"The weekly Torah portion? Of course."

"So where do you propose to find a Torah? I haven't seen more than half a dozen synagogues still functioning in this part of the world, and we don't stay in one place long enough that even if we were to find a Torah scroll I'd have time to learn the portion."

"You read Hebrew?"

"Of course."

"All right, Smarty Pants," Amos said, bending down and opening a small drawer near the floor of the vehicle. "Here's a book with all the weekly portions. The synagogues might be bombed out and the Torah scrolls no more, but if you have to read your *Parsha* from a book, God will simply have to understand."

During the next few months, as Lev studied diligently each night, the old man seemed to become more dour and withdrawn. More alarming, Amos's usual sprightly walk had become a stumbling shuffle. He often hesitated and fumbled for the right words in the midst of an old story, and his skin had taken on the crepecious pallor of an unknown illness. Amos greeted Lev's attempt to become more solicitous either with disdain, or, more frequently, with an empty, questioning stare. One evening, in an attempt to reignite the old man's spirit, Lev suggested, "Amos, May 15 is a Saturday. We'll be close enough to Warsaw" – he pronounced the name of the capital in the Polish-Jewish manner, *Var-SHA-va* – "that we might ask that I be called to the Torah that day. Afterward, if you'd like, we can make our way west, maybe to Berlin. It shouldn't take more than a couple of days to get there."

The old man perked up, as though he were giving the idea serious thought. Then, his eyes downcast, he mumbled, "Not far enough west. The old capital's still on this side of the Curtain and I smell trouble brewing ahead. Last month America, England, and France agreed to establish a West German republic. That means the Soviets will create an East German state and Berlin will be deep inside that state."

"But Berlin's an international city," Lev persisted. "We could make it to the British or French sector, maybe even to the American sector."

"Berlin will still be an island. It's two hundred kilometers to the British area."

"No reason we couldn't try, if that's what you want."

"I'm not thinking about me, Lev. My time's pretty much over. I'm thinking of you."

"Don't talk like that," the boy responded more sharply than he'd intended. "We'll be together a good twenty or thirty years." Amos made no reply.

⁂

During their three years together, Amos and Lev had been to the Polish capital twice. The first time, in 1946, Warsaw had consisted mostly of bombed-out rubble. With the exception of a couple of tenements and a tiny remnant of what had been the Ghetto Wall, the Jewish area had been leveled. When next they'd stopped overnight in Warsaw, eight months ago, dramatic changes had come to the city. After Operation Vistula, fostered by Poland's Soviet overlords, the capital now had a distinctively *Polish* flavor. More than ninety percent of the few surviving Jews had emigrated to Palestine. Of ten million Germans who'd been in Poland during the war, less than fifty thousand remained. They'd been expelled or had fled back to their own country. The exchange of populations between Ukraine and Poland had been completed.

On September 1, 1947, under Prime Minister Boleslaw Bierut's urging, the Warsaw population turned out en masse for the beginning of the drive to rebuild the capital stone by stone, brick by brick, mostly by hand.

"Should be moving right along when we get there," Amos remarked at the beginning of May. "The Nožyk Synagogue survived the war only because the Germans needed a stable and because the Nazis moved the line so it was outside the Ghetto. It's still not in regular use as a synagogue and there's no *Rebbe*, but it *is* a legitimate *Shul.* I've contacted Esther Meyerson, an old friend. She's arranged for a *Minyan* on the fifteenth."

"Is she a Board member of the *shul*? An elder? A higher-up?"

"Well … not exactly. Let's just say she's familiar with the Synagogue."

◈

Although there had been lots of work done, most of the city still had a woebegone, ruined look about it. As they approached Twarda Street from the Grzybówski neighborhood, where they'd spent the last night, Lev saw a mostly demolished building.

"Not a pretty face, but the heart's still beating, Lev. Always remember, something does not have to be pretty to be beautiful. Today you'll be adding to its heartbeat and kicking Hitler and his millions right in the arse." The old man coughed and spat phlegm into the street just before they turned into an empty lot adjacent to the synagogue. He glanced at his watch. "Half an hour to go. Ah, there's Esther now," he said, honking the van's horn at a garishly attired, hefty, sixtyish woman with blue-dyed-gray hair.

"Amos!" the woman called out. "Leave it to you to make a grand entrance! "You'll excuse my saying so, but you look like shit and older than dirt. At least you've put on your best clothing. How stylish you'd have looked in the thirties! I trust this handsome young fellow is the *Bar Mitzvah*? Good morning and *Mazel Tov,* Lev, I'm Esther Meyerson."

"It was very thoughtful of you to arrange this Mrs. … Miss …?"

"Esther will be fine. Actually, it's you who's doing the Jewish community an honor, Lev. Yours will be the first *Bar Mitzvah* in more than a year. The last fellow emigrated to Eretz Israel right after, so he won't be here today. We've barely got a *minyan*. If the tenth man doesn't show up, we'll simply haul someone off the street."

"How very refined you've become, my dear," Amos wheezed.

"I count fourteen people waiting outside the door, Mrs. ... Esther," Lev said.

"Yes, but you need ten *men* to make it a legitimate prayer meeting. Let me show you around the *shul*. Amos, you stand watch for the tenth man. Thank you, Darling."

Once inside the building, Lev looked in awe at the walls, which were not covered by wallpaper or lined with bookcases, but rather held grainy black-and-white photographs of old men and women, small babes, and young couples standing apart from one another in the traditional Jewish manner. The men wore *payess,* the earlocks all Orthodox Jewish men wore, which blended into their full beards, *yarmulkes,* the traditional Jewish skullcaps, and long gabardines. The people in the pictures had dark eyes, some filled with hope, others with fear, as though they knew what lay in store for them – the ovens of Treblinka, Majdanek, Belzec, Auschwitz-Birkenau. The photos were haunting, a view into a world that was no more and would never be again. Lev silently mouthed the words of the *Kaddish,* the prayer for the dead. His reverie was interrupted by Esther Meyerson's quiet voice.

"How is he ... really?" she asked.

"Not the same as he was," Lev replied. "He seems sadder, changed."

"It's finally caught up with him, then."

"What?"

"His age. His life. He traveled the length and breadth of the *Pale* during the war, witnessed more destruction than most, and managed somehow to survive. Does he still smoke?"

"Always."

"And you?"

"Only to humor him."

"Stop doing it when he's gone."

"Gone?" the boy exclaimed, alarmed. "But ..."

"He's coughing a lot more now. He looks like hell."

"He doesn't look that much different to me."

"You wouldn't notice. You see him every day. It's been a year-and-a-half since I've seen him. He looks ten years older. Promise me you'll watch out for him. Make it easier when ..." Lev felt a sudden premonitory chill. He didn't want to admit to himself that Amos *did* look older, and the pallor seemed to have become more noticeable each day. "Come," Esther said, "let's get you tarted up. Do you have a necktie? A coat?"

"No."

"Not even a gabardine?"

"Uh-uh."

"Fortunately, Amos wrote me about how tall you were and how much you weigh. I was able to borrow an outfit from a friend." She opened a hall closet and took out a few-years-old sport coat and a black tie. Correctly concluding he'd never worn a tie in his life, she tied it in a Windsor knot and slipped it over his head. "Now, let's gather the *minyan*."

By the time they returned to the outside, there were twenty people, twelve of them men, waiting for them. They pushed and shoved Lev and Amos to the front of the line. Lev noticed that Amos was visibly panting after they'd negotiated the eight steps up to the front door of the house of worship. Inside, a small man of late middle age, no doubt the leader of the congregation, led them to the sanctuary, a gray-walled, high-ceilinged room no larger than twenty-by-thirty feet. The *Ner Tamid,* the everlasting light, hung at the eastern end of the room. Immediately under it stood the Ark of the Covenant which had housed three Torah scrolls in the days before the War. Today the single remaining remnant of a Torah was ensconced in the Ark, hidden from view by a shabby, worn felt curtain.

A *bimah*, a raised wooden platform from which the *Rebbe,* had there been one, would have conducted services, occupied the center of the room. It appeared to have been hastily hammered together. The lectern on which a large, open book sat, didn't quite match the platform. Thirty cheap wooden folding chairs, none of which matched, surrounded the *Bimah* in the men's section. Another twenty chairs had been placed beyond the *mechitsa,* in the women's section. Men and women prayed in separate areas of the sanctuary. Usually the women's section was in the upper balcony or off to one side of the room, divided from the men's section by a railing and curtains. Today, since the only place left to pray in the Nożyk Synagogue was a small, unadorned and unpartitioned room, the *mechitsa* dividing men from women, consisted of a series of covered coat racks. God would have to understand that this tiny remnant of a Jewish population that had once numbered over three hundred fifty thousand in Warsaw was doing the best it could.

As Lev ascended the *Bimah* to lead the minuscule congregation, he soon became so involved in the order of prayers, the *Borchu,* the *Shema,* the *Amidah,* which he murmured in near silence, and, ultimately, the Torah service itself, that he took no notice of his surroundings. A Torah, or at least part of a Torah, had survived the war. Somehow, when he marched around the *Shul* holding the Torah on his shoulder as the congregation lustily chanted thousand-year-old melodies, he felt at one with those who had gone before him for more than three thousand years. And – surprise of surprises! – when he concluded his reading and gave his traditional speech, the poverty-stricken Jews who had somehow survived the Holocaust had found the money to buy hard candies and pelt him with them, a tradition which went back hundreds of years.

"*Mazel tov! Mazel tov!*" rang out from the audience as Lev concluded. Lev grinned proudly. Esther Meyerson was the first to burst from behind the *mechitsa* and hug him. "A fine job!" she cried. "Your parents would have been so proud!"

After the *Kiddush,* the blessing over the wine and bread, and an abbreviated *Oneg Shabbat* consisting of sugar cookies and grape juice, the assembly headed toward the exit of the building.

As the happy little group exited, it was their misfortune to get caught in the crossfire between competing neighborhood gangs, which had proliferated despite the iron fist of the Soviet-backed Warsaw police force. Amos became the first of three men and one woman to be shot. As Lev screamed and ran over to where he lay, face down, in a widening pool of blood, it quickly became apparent that the old man was not going to survive. Moments later, Lev Arkady's greatest hero, mentor, and savior was no more.

Lev tore his shirt off to stanch the old man's blood. As he realized his efforts would have no effect whatever on what had happened, the wracking sobs came and he cried out his frustrated fury at everything – God, the world, and Warsaw – until his voice was a scratchy rictus and there was nothing more to be done. Within half an hour, those who had survived this latest tragedy dispersed, leaving a grieving boy, a dead old man, and one other in the dry, weed-filled lot adjacent the *shul.*

Esther Meyerson, waited in silence for another quarter hour, then approached Lev. As tenderly as a mother, she said, softly, "You'll live with me for a while." It was not a question. It was a simple statement.

9

"When did you learn to drive that monstrosity?" Esther asked.

"Back when Amos got it, two years ago."

"When you were twelve years old?"

"About."

"Now that you've been living with me for two weeks, are you shocked?"

"Not really. When I asked Amos if you were an elder in the temple or a board member, he said 'Not exactly.' By the way he said it, I gathered there was something he wasn't telling me and it might be better not to ask."

As noon approached, they drove into town from Esther's residence on the outskirts of Warsaw. The day after Amos died, they'd started sitting *shiva*. During the funeral, Esther told Lev that Amos had disclosed to her six months ago that the cancer had progressed, but he didn't know how to tell the young man. "He would have died within the year anyway. God simply spared him unnecessary suffering, probably because he'd given the Lord such a good time while he was on earth or because God simply needed some entertainment up in heaven. I noticed you haven't smoked once since the day he died."

"Any special reason we're going into Warsaw today?" Lev asked.

"I'll be talking with a new prospect and thought you might like to go for a ride."

Lev's eyebrows arched. "Let me get this straight, Esther. You're interviewing someone to become a … a …"

"Please, no lectures. I do *not* employ common streetwalkers. I find a poor but promising uneducated girl who would have no future except to marry some low-life who'd leave her at home with a basketful of brats while he went out spending what little they had on beer, cheap vodka, or streetwalkers. Then, when he found someone younger, off he'd go and she'd probably end up in the gutter."

"And with you she learns to earn money …?"

"No, my young friend. That's not all she learns. Any woman can lie there like a sack of potatoes and *some* man would be interested. They learn a lot more while they're with me. You'll see after you've lived with me for awhile that my house is as different from a common brothel as Chopin is from a grind-organ. When I'm through with them, they're fit to be court favorites, diplomats' wives, countesses, even royalty. And while they're with me, it's an honest living."

He turned the van left onto Aleje Jerozolimskie, Jerusalem Street, and started looking for parking. "She said she'd meet us at the corner of Jerozolimskie and Marszałowska, and – there she is now! Agata! Agata!" she called out through the passenger side window.

The young woman, who looked to be in her early twenties, stared uncertainly toward the rather unique conveyance in which they rode, then waved back and signaled them to a parking space half a block down the street. When Lev and Esther alighted from the Amosmobile and Lev got his first close-up view of the young woman Esther had called Agata, he was stunned. She was small and wore her long blonde hair in a ponytail. Her eyes were an intense green. She had a slender waist and high, jutting breasts. He felt a flush suffuse his cheeks and run up and down his body.

"I'm so damned tired of this new Communist invention, the *bar mlezny*, the milk bar," Esther said derisively, once they were on the street. "Steamed vegetables each day is for cattle, not for human beings. I say we go to the *Przy Zamku*."

The girl's hand flew to her mouth. "But, but ... a meal there costs more money than I see in a month!"

"Yes, and you must learn, my dear, that if you don't develop a taste for champagne you will seldom be offered champagne. Besides, no one's asking you to pay." She took the girl by the arm and propelled her into the famed restaurant and into an understated elegance of a time long past. Hunting trophies appeared in nearly every alcove. Old paintings of the hunt and of Polish royalty hung from the walls. The dimly lit restaurant turned the bright sunshine outside to a cool muted, prewar Warsaw evening.

Lev was by no means as overwhelmed as Agata. Amos had said much the same thing, albeit in different words, during the time they'd been together, and every town of size from Lithuania to the Turkish border had at least one restaurant that catered to the well-heeled. Still, the boy maintained his silence, first because he had no wish to embarrass this apparition of beauty, and second because this was Esther's appointment, not his, and he had simply come along because she'd suggested it.

Esther knew the waiter well. Without waiting for a menu, she peremptorily ordered an appetizer of hare paté with pickles and cranberry sauce, a basket of freshly-baked French bread, and a bottle of Moët et Chandon White Star champagne. The waiter, who was clad in dark slacks, white shirt, maroon bow tie, and waistcoat, nodded, clicked his heels smartly together, and departed.

During the next few minutes, while they nibbled at the delicious appetizer and sipped from half-flutes of champagne, the three of them engaged in small talk. Agata revealed she'd come from a small town fifteen kilometers west of the capital, "but a world away. The most exciting thing to do there was to watch the grass grow." Her family "was so poor we couldn't pay attention." Four months ago, she'd left the smallholding for the hope of a better life in the big city. Thus far, the "better life" was work as a part-time shop girl in a second-hand clothing store, a one-room walk-up flat on the fifth floor of a prewar tenement building, and dark bread and water. She'd had no time for the "attention" lavished on her by neighborhood workmen who had but one thing on their minds.

"It was lucky for both of us that I walked into that little shop on a day you happened to be working," Esther said.

"Is that how you find …?"

"For the most part, yes," the older woman replied without embarrassment or false pretense. "M'sieu," she continued, addressing the waiter, "I'd like the haunch of venison, and my friends would like …"

"Roast chicken," Agata ventured, selecting the cheapest item on the menu.

"Nonsense," the older woman said. "My daughter will have the duck flambé with string beans almandine, whipped potatoes, and pickled cabbage." The girl's eyes widened. Esther said firmly, "Remember, my girl, develop a champagne taste. Lev?"

"Broiled trout stuffed with shrimp, liver *knödl*, and mixed greens."

"An excellent choice," Esther said approvingly. "You see, Agata, the young man already has an eye for quality. I could tell that when he first looked at you." Both young people reddened perceptibly. She continued, "I noticed when you first walked over to us that you had a slight limp."

"That's so," she said with no apparent embarrassment or offense. "Our family doctor told me the limp comes from the fact that my right leg is slightly shorter than the left, and that the twitching is some kind of inherited symptom. I hope those things don't disturb you."

"Of course not," Esther replied. "It's the small imperfections that make a woman so much more appealing. Thank you for being so candid. Now let's talk about other things." Over the next quarter hour, Agata and Esther spoke so matter-of-factly about their proposed business arrangement that it significantly lessened Lev's embarrassment. The beautiful young girl was no more uncomfortable than she would be discussing the purchase and sale of a piece of furniture, a coat, or a kilo of sausage.

"While your physical beauty certainly had something to do with my selecting you to join us for a while, there is much more to being an accomplished courtesan than simply spreading your legs and looking lovely. Once you've been prepared to meet and capture the man of your dreams, you must use every available weapon in your arsenal of charms to constantly tantalize and ultimately keep him interested in you, and only you."

"Let me understand your proposition, Madame Meyerson. You will purchase a wardrobe for me, tutor me in French, English, table manners, current events, and polished conversation …"

"As well as private instruction in …"

"Of course, that goes without saying."

"No, my dear, that most certainly does *not* go 'without saying,'" Esther said sternly. "Everything else is elegant, magnetic window dressing, but it is *window dressing*, nothing more. Above all, you must learn to give and receive the greatest pleasure a man and woman can share together, the right way, and you must learn to do *everything* necessary to attain this goal with the maximum degree of pleasure for yourself. If a woman makes a man happy, he will make her *very* happy indeed, and, of course, the reverse is true. Further," she gazed over at Lev, "you must pardon what I say, dear Lev, men are such simple beings who really have one single, urgent need in life. Agata," she said, returning her focus to the girl, "just remember a woman has something a man wants much more than a man has something a woman wants."

Lev looked around the restaurant uncomfortably. At that moment, the waiter appeared with their lunch. It was a memorable repast, even for Lev, who'd eaten in such places before. He was just taking his second bite of the succulent fish when Esther Meyerson continued, "Are you a virgin, Agata?"

Lev choked on his fish in mid-bite and started coughing uncontrollably. Esther passed him a glass of ice water. When the boy had quieted down, Esther repeated her earlier question.

"There've been one or two," the girl said without emotion.

"The way you say that, these were most likely clumsy oafs. I trust you've never come, except perhaps when you masturbated?"

"That's true, Madame Meyerson."

"Those sorry excuses for men probably couldn't wait to pinch your titties and jump on your bones?"

"Also correct."

"No harm done," the older woman said. "You see, we not only train you to bring a man the greatest pleasure, we also train you how to teach a man to become a more adept lover."

"Even though they're paying for it?"

"*Especially* if they're paying for it. It'll make them more appreciated when they return home to their wives or mistresses, so you'll be providing a service not only for the customer but for other women as well. Have you never noticed that the doctor or lawyer who's most successful is the one who convinces you that you are the single most important patient or client he's ever had?"

"No," the girl said. "The only doctor I saw was grizzled old man who smelled of stale tobacco and sweat. I've never even met a lawyer."

"Pray God you never have to, except when he's *your* client," Esther said. "They are among the most pernicious of vermin. However, they're far better tippers than doctors, who are so notoriously stingy they'll squeeze a złoty until it bleeds." She guffawed at her own joke. "Oh, and we should talk about financial arrangements. I set the price and manage the business end and we'll divide the proceeds equitably. You'll find me scrupulously honest. Although I don't expect you to question my books, you are always free to look at them. One more thing. You work *only* for me, is that understood?"

"Of course."

"Not always 'of course,' my dear. Some of my associates have conducted their own business on the side. When they try that, they're out of my house with no notice, one outfit, and nothing else."

Both women noticed Lev unabashedly staring at Agata during their conversation. "Look at young Lev," Esther said. "He's a virgin, but he's been undressing you with his eyes when he thinks you're not looking. That's the kind of thing I'd expect from an American or a German. A Frenchman will always be much more open about the way he admires a beautiful woman, even a not-so-beautiful woman. He celebrates each woman for her own particular beauty, undressing her slowly, deliberately, drinking in her every curve as though she were a fine vintage wine. Americans are prudes, Germans act like they own the world. They make a woman feel dirty or abased. A Frenchman or an Italian makes that same woman feel lusted after and treasured. Do you hear me, Lev?"

"What about Poles?" Agata asked demurely.

"What *about* Poles?" Esther replied, raising her eyebrows. "Most of them are better at milking cows than fondling a woman. Of course, most of them are like most men everywhere, smelly, disgusting animals who want to get in and out as quickly as possible, pleasuring only themselves."

Lev said nothing. His face betrayed discomfort, embarrassment, and not a little lust. Amos had spoken vaguely to him about sex, but seeing this astonishing young girl, who, wearing a light, open-necked sun dress, exuded sensuality, stirred him more than anyone he'd ever seen.

"There's no time limit?" This from Agata.

"None. You're free to leave at any time. It's entirely up to you. Most girls stay a year, some longer. The majority of them meet someone, not always but many times, at my home, fall in love, and off they go. I'm sure you'd recognize the names of many of our 'alumna' who've done quite well for themselves, but we subscribe to a strict code of privacy and propriety, so I'll mention no names."

"What about disease?"

"Nothing would kill my business more quickly than an unsafe house. Every young woman is checked by an internist each week. Each of my associates undergoes a thorough gynecological examination at least once a month. We make every effort to protect our young ladies from other unwanted, er, complications, even in this Roman Catholic bastion of hypocrisy."

"Not to pry, Madame," she said, nodding in Lev's direction, "but is the boy your, umm, son?"

"I don't consider it prying, Agata. He's the protégé of an old friend who was tragically killed in a recent battle among some unruly political factions."

"Amos?"

"How did you know that?" Of a moment, the older woman smiled. "Very adept. You read the side of the van. Amos was truly one-of-a-kind, and they say the chestnut does not fall very far from the tree."

"How old are you, Lev?" Agata asked. "Sixteen?"

"Fourteen, Miss … Miss …"

"Agata will do. Since we'll be living together for the foreseeable future, we may as well use first names." She addressed him as a colleague, not as a child. He appreciated that.

"You'll find Lev very astute at other forms of entertainment," Esther continued. Shortly after he moved in, Lev and I concocted an idea that allowed him to capitalize on his relationship with his mentor."

"When gentlemen callers come by, I engage them in various games of chance, mostly card games, while they wait their turns for other ... entertainment," Lev said. "Madame Meyerson and I divide the take. She tells me that in the week since we've started this, I've already earned more than my keep."

"He's a shrewd young man, my dear," Esther addressed the girl. "You'll find that everyone learns and everyone develops their own best talents in my home."

"When would you expect me to start?"

"How long would it take you to pack out your belongings?"

"A minute-and-a-half," the girl replied. "I've got two other outfits, a few cosmetics, and a bar of soap. I'd have to give notice to my employer and my landlord."

"That will be unnecessary," the older woman replied. "I'll make the arrangements with both. I'll take your measurements while we're clearing your quarters," she added. "That way I can purchase the beginnings of your wardrobe this afternoon and tonight we can ceremonially burn your old clothes and your old life. You should keep the sun dress, though. From the way young Lev has been staring at you, I think other men will enjoy that outfit as well. Of course, you'll look even more enticing with a bra that fits properly."

10

"I hope you enjoyed your holiday," Esther remarked sourly in January of 1949. "You were gone six weeks. During that time I made almost no money."

"Isn't Christmas a time when men stay home with their families anyway?" he retorted. "I notice that all of the ladies got time off for the holidays. Besides, if you are to be believed, you crowed about having the most profitable year ever and even gave everyone bonuses."

"You truly have inherited Amos' ways," Esther said. "All the charm and *chutzpah* the old man had, and you're less than a quarter of his age when he died. I suppose you have the same lack of *sitzfleisch*, so I might have expected you'd go out of the country. Your friend Ana's certainly had a memorable year."

"I'll say." He handed her two small packages. "Two gifts for you. One from me and one from Mrs. Pauker. Happy whatever-it-is you celebrate."

Esther opened the smaller packet first. "How thoughtful of you, Lev!" she exclaimed, examining the diamond brooch with a practiced eye. "I'd lecture you that you shouldn't have spent so much money, but I'd estimate this cost you only a fifth of the bonus I gave you." He arched his eyebrows. "Still," she said, hugging him to her ample bosom, "you are proving yourself to be a *mensch*. Now let's see what our Romanian friend sent."

Opening the second package, she extracted a copy of *Time* magazine, America's weekly contribution to world culture. A flattering photograph of Ana Pauker graced the cover and splashed across the picture in prominent type were the words, "The most powerful woman alive." Immediately inside the cover, Ana had personally penned, "To Esther Meyerson, who, according to Lev Arkady, may make me the <u>second</u> most powerful woman alive," with a smiling cartoon face.

"Hoo-*hoo*!" Esther said. "You are really traveling in high company. I'm impressed. Stalin's 'man in Bucharest,' Romania's foreign minister, and number two in the Party. She's still a practicing Jew?"

"Uh-huh. She still wants to get as many Jews to *Eretz Israel* as possible. What a marvelous year it's been" he continued. "A country of our very own."

"But for how long? The Arabs never accepted the U.N. declaration. Even now they're trying to push the Jews into the sea."

"It'll never happen," Lev predicted confidently. "How's Agata?"

"Why am I not surprised you'd ask? You've been making calf-eyes at her ever since she came here eight months ago. I see your face when she has a gentleman caller, yet you've never even told her how you feel."

"How could I, Aunt Esther?" he asked, reverting to a name he'd recently coined for his relationship with her. "She's so far beyond me, so much older than me. I'll never be more than a boy to her."

"Nonsense, Lev Arkady, how dare you say such a thing! You've shot up another hand's height since last May, and, if I may say so, from a woman's standpoint you are a very handsome young man. Blushing, by the way, is not your most flattering attribute. A woman wants a man to be strong, to take control of every situation. You sat at the feet of a master for three years. I'd have thought he taught you something about being confident in yourself. Now that you're back, you can help me shovel some snow and we'll talk outside. We may even be able to see a sliver of sunlight today."

An hour later, with Lev doing most of the shoveling, the entry to Esther's house was sufficiently cleared that four cars could park in the driveway and any expected 'company' could negotiate the front walkway without slipping on ice and risking serious injury.

"You'll be fifteen next month and you've still never been with a woman?"

"Uh-huh."

"I told you blushing's not your strong suit. Every human being starts out life as a virgin. But if they stayed virgins, we'd be back to Adam and Eve within two generations, and it would be a damned lonely and boring world."

"Aunt Esther, before Amos died, I could always turn to him for wise advice. When he died, you became his replacement, and – "

"Why thank you, Lev. I appreciate that, even though I know no one could ever replace Amos. As for my being 'wise,' when you get to be my age, there's nothing much you can do anymore *but* be wise. Ahh…" she said, thinking back. "There was a time when I was young and even quite attractive to men. Many years and thirty kilos ago. Might I try and guess what this conversation's going to be about? And no blushing this time?"

"I can't help myself."

"Why? Because you want to learn everything there is to know and at the same time you know almost nothing about it?"

"Well, yes."

"I thought as much. Remember last year when we met Agata for the first time and I was so amazed that you'd learned to drive the van when you were twelve?"

"Yes. So?"

"You've just come back from Romania. You drove down there just like that, like it was nothing."

"No great trick to that, Aunt Esther."

"Maybe not for you, but I'd be surprised if one in ten thousand Poles have ever driven a car. That's something you didn't know how to do when you were eleven. You can read and speak English, French, German, Hungarian, Polish, Hebrew, Yiddish, and God knows how many other languages. Did you know how to do that when you ten?"

"Of course not."

"You can tell almost as many stories as Amos and you know almost as many ways of winning at cards."

"Where is this leading us, Aunt Esther?"

"Do you think that learning how to make love – I didn't say learning how to fuck a woman –." He held up his right hand, palm forward, to put an exclamation point to his shock at her language. "Don't try to stop me, boy. You heard the talk I had with Agata on the day we first met. Don't pretend you didn't. I say exactly what I mean. There's such a thing as *fucking* a woman, which is what too many men do, and there's such a thing a *making love* to a woman, which will, if you'll forgive my being entirely blunt, allow you to 'see more arse than a toilet seat' and enjoy it a helluva lot more. Like anything else, whether it's music, politics, or whatever, it's an *acquired skill*, something you learn. If you go into it with that attitude, you'll do as well in that department as you've done with the rest of your life."

Lev forced himself to concentrate on Esther's words, while he felt a chill go up his spine which was not caused by the inclement weather. "How does one …?" he began.

"Don't expect me to answer that, Lev. I'm a woman, not a man. The first introduction I had was with an older man."

Lev blanched. "Amos?" he almost whispered.

"No. Amos came quite a bit later. But he'd been well-schooled in what makes a woman happy. No, this was much earlier. I was a little older than you and he was a Hungarian diplomat. Quite old, maybe even thirty-five. My parents had taken me down to Lake Balaton on holiday and …" Her eyes took on a faraway, dreamy look. "I had no idea what to do, but he certainly taught me. He was so very slow and so very patient with me. His hands … his tongue …"

"Did you find it disgusting when he put his … you know … in your …?"

"Not at all," Esther said, then more emphatically, "*Not at all*. It was the most pleasurable experience I'd ever had. Afterward, my life seemed to revolve around when I was next going to get it."

"I've heard that sometimes men and men … and women and women …"

"Oh, yes, that happens. Mind you, I've never had that experience. Some people find *that* disgusting, but I say live and let live."

"Do you feel uncomfortable that I'm asking you these things?"

"Absolutely not," Esther replied. "I feel good that you trust me enough to ask me. There are lots of fellows your age, or a little older than you – or even a lot older than you – who brag a lot, especially when they *haven't* done anything. They snicker and preen like roosters, but it's all for show. A man who's a caring, adept lover is restrained. Once a man has the real goods, he doesn't have to do empty bragging. Leave that to the would-be's and the has-beens and the never-will-be's. Remember this, Lev, if you kiss-and-tell, and if you name names, word gets around. Be discreet."

"Can … can I ask you something *really* confidential, Aunt Esther?"

"I don't see why not, but would you mind if we go inside – and bring a couple of large logs with you? You strong, virile young men might be able to stand out in Warsaw's January weather all day and all night, but when you get to be my age, heaven means standing with your backside to a warm fire."

❦

"Sto lat, sto lat,
Niech żyje, żyje nam.
Sto lat, sto lat,
Niech żyje, żyje nam,
Jeszcze raz, jeszcze raz, niech żyje, żyje nam,
Niech żyje nam!"

Seven very attractive young women and one hefty older matron belted out the traditional Polish birthday song. Then, in a lovely alto voice, Agata re-sang the song in her newly acquired English:

"A hundred years, a hundred years,
May you live for us.
A hundred years, a hundred years,
May you live for us.
Once again, once again, may you live, live for us,
May you live for us!"

Afterward, Esther rolled out a large birthday cake, Lev's favorite, a chocolate layer cake with strawberry jam in between the two layers. Amid cheers, he blew out the fifteen candles, "plus one to grow on," in one breath. Then everyone except Agata presented Lev with a small gift. As he looked toward her, she said softly, "I haven't had time to buy it yet, so I'll give you my gift a little later."

"That's all right, Agata," Lev said. "Just your being part of my birthday celebration is gift enough for me. What would really make my birthday complete is if you'd allow me to take you to dinner tonight."

She looked questioningly at Esther Meyerson, who nodded.

The trip into downtown Warsaw took less than half an hour, even though Lev drove slowly and carefully to avoid the snow and ice which clogged the two-lane road into the city. Agata was surprised when Lev pulled up outside the *Przy Zamku*. "My God, Lev, I haven't been here since the day we met. Are you sure …?"

"Yes, and yes, I can certainly afford it. Tonight's my birthday and I'm with the most beautiful girl in all of Poland, maybe all the world," he said. He was surprised at how smoothly the phrase came out, perhaps because he really meant it.

That evening, they talked of everything and nothing – where their lives had taken them in the nine months since they'd met. Agata carefully avoided any talk of her manner of earning a living or her clientele, concentrating instead on the success of Lev's enterprise in Esther's house, his infrequent travels, and how he'd grown and matured. Agata was radiant that evening. Although it was mid-winter, she had worn his favorite sun dress under a sweater and a heavy overcoat. Dinner was as robust and delicious as he remembered from his first meal at *Przy Zamku*, and the champagne left him lightheaded.

Lev was surprised at how natural the next words came to him. "It's a long, dangerous drive home. Might I suggest we stay in town tonight?"

"But where?" she asked. There was no hint of coyness in her tone.

"It's not every day that one has a birthday in the company of a woman such as you. Might I suggest the Le Regina?"

"The La Regina? The one in the Morowski Palace?"

"The very one."

"Lev? Never in a million years …"

"Sshh," he said, putting his fingers to her lips. "And if you don't mind, I'd like to turn the tables by giving *you* a small present on my birthday." Now it was Agata's turn to blush as he handed her a small jewelry box. Her eyes widened as she opened it and saw a graceful heart-shaped pendant with a single small diamond in the middle. "It's beautiful, Lev. I will wear it proudly," she said. "Would you help me put it on?"

He did, with trembling hands. He thought he felt the slightest tremor at her throat.

When he'd checked them into the hotel, Agata said, almost casually, "I have a birthday present for you, too. I'll give it to you in the room."

When they entered the enormous room, Lev saw a huge matrimonial bed with timbered floors, a chest of drawers, and a nightstand with a large, wide candle, which provided soft light for the room. He gently closed the door to the room. The candlelight caught the diamond at Agata's throat and reflected the glow in her eyes.

"I'd like ... that is ... might I kiss you just this once?" Lev choked out. Suddenly, he was no longer the suave man of the world. He was a fifteen-year-old boy who had never even dated a woman before.

"All right," she said softly. She figured she'd let him kiss her, count to five, and it would be done. His kiss was almost innocent in its intensity and she mentally counted to three before she found that her eyes had closed and she was kissing him back, her tongue willfully flicking in and out of her mouth, caressing his.

She had no idea how long the kiss lasted, but they were both shaking when it was over. "Shall we try that again?" she said. The second kiss was more passionate and lasted even longer than the first. While her eyes were closed, she felt his hand fumble at the top of her dress. "Lev?" she breathed huskily.

"Yes?"

"You're so young. ... but handsome, strong ..." She relaxed, closed her eyes, and said, "and it feels so good."

His response was to remove her coat, then her sweater. His hand insinuated itself slowly, gently into the top of her sun dress. He felt the intoxicating softness of first one breast, then the other, straining to be released from their binding.

She gently took his hands in hers, then put her index finger to his lips. He stood transfixed, not knowing what to do or say as she removed first the sun dress, then her underclothing. Her small, pink-tipped breasts stood out proudly, beckoning his hands to touch, to squeeze their nipples, to enjoy the greatest intimacy a man and woman can share. While he stood there, she took his hands in each of hers and moved them to her breasts. He did not need further coaxing and his hands, then his lips, moved of their own accord. As she felt the chilly warmth assaulting her, she started moaning softly.

They went on this way for some while before Lev said, somewhat ashamedly, "I … I don't know what to do from here. You are the first … ever …"

That knowledge seemed to excite Agata yet more, and she tugged at his belt, loosening it before lowering his trousers and after that his drawers. Now *her* hands and lips found what they were looking for. He may have been only fifteen, but he was certainly of sufficient size that she knew that once they lay in the large bed together, it would be a field of battle on which both sides would emerge victorious.

With a *whoosh* of breath, he climaxed in her mouth so quickly it surprised her. "Now you do the same for me," she said breathlessly, reaching down and removing the rest of her clothing, but for the single-diamond pendant which she still wore around her neck. She lay back on the bed. Lev unbuttoned his own shirt and when he was naked, she pulled him to her. His fingers and tongue were quickly and naturally adept, and now her moaning rose to a shrill crescendo as her spasms came stronger and faster.

For the briefest moment, she thought about how *young* he was, but then she became a mindless, demanding female animal. "My

God, I'm coming, I'm coming, I'm *coming!*" The last was a mingled scream and moan as she thrashed madly on the bed, her nether parts hot and wet, soaked with the paroxysm of their passion.

They lay side by side, breathing softly for only a few minutes before he felt himself growing rock hard under the ministrations of her fingers. Unable to comprehend what was happening, he reached for her breasts again. This time, she couldn't wait and pulled him on top of her. He entered her tight, slippery cavity and for the second time in a brief period, he could not help himself as he shot his fluid into her. Moments later, she erupted with the same gasping scream-moan as she had before.

Afterward, they slept, but not for a long time, and when they awoke, they made love again, and after they had slept awhile longer, yet again, until, by next morning, they were both sated and exhausted, as well as exhilarated. When they awoke, Agata raised up on one elbow. Her breasts seemed larger in that posture. His eyes lit up again, as he looked into her green eyes, which were now suffused with the embers of a distant, simmering fire.

"I love you, Agata," he said dreamily.

"To be more accurate, you love what we *did*," she said in a voice still half-asleep.

"No, I love *you*. I'll always love you."

"And I you, Lev. For letting me be your first, and for pleasuring this woman more than you know. Now, do you want to keep talking or do you want to do something else before we have to get up and go downstairs for breakfast?"

When, after breakfast, they drove back to Esther Meyerson's, she squeezed his hand and said softly, "Happy Birthday, Lev Arkady."

11

"Well, Lev, you've certainly had an 'interesting' six months," Esther said.

"Are you being sardonic, sarcastic, or simply worldly-wise?"

"A little of each," she answered. "In the time since your first experience with Agata, word got around quickly. It seems all of our little dumplings considered you not only their pet, but a *trainable* pet."

"I'm certainly not complaining," he grinned.

"You shouldn't be," she said archly. "Don't let it go to your head, but each of the ladies has told me, privately of course, that you learn very quickly and you've become quite a proficient lover. Tea?"

"Please."

"I might even be a bit envious," she continued. "No, Lev, I'm not interested in robbing the cradle, any more than you'd want to rob the graveyard."

"I'd hardly call you ready for the graveyard, Aunt Esther." During their time together, Esther Meyerson had assumed Amos's mantle of parent, mentor, and friend. He trusted her implicitly because she allowed him to initiate conversations rather than prodding him, and she was rarely, if ever, judgmental. More important, he knew that if he asked her opinion, she gave it honestly and without pretense or reservation.

"Maybe I'm not ready for burial, but when I see what the world is coming to ..." She sighed. "Now I'm starting to sound like my own parents."

"The world is going to hell and we young people are driving it there with our awful music, our scandalous behavior, our loose morals?"

She handed him a cup of tea, black the way he liked it, and poured some milk into her own cup. "Given my profession, I'd hardly qualify to give lessons in morals. No, Lev, the world I knew as a young woman ended on September 1, 1939. I'm talking about, for want of a better word, the *dehumanization* of things. The new regimes everywhere, not just in Eastern Europe, want everyone to be the same, even though that 'sameness' varies from country to country."

"The difference between Socialism and Capitalism?"

"It doesn't matter what they call the system. If your on 'our' side of the so-called Iron Curtain and you want to survive, you go along with collectivized farms, everything for the state, very little for ordinary men and women, and everyone 'doing without' to the same degree, except for our gracious and glorious leaders. If you're in the capitalist world of the West and you want to survive, you climb over the shoulders of ordinary men and women and trample them economically so you can be the king of the hill. Neither system seems to realize that most people simply want to have enough to eat, clothing to wear, a place to live, and the small everyday pleasures."

"Like what you offer here?" Lev asked.

"For some, if that's what they want. But for most, simply the ability to feed and educate your children so that they might, I say *might,* have a better chance at life than you had. And so that your children might even be a little bit happier."

"You're quite the philosopher, Aunt Esther."

"Not really, Lev. Just an old woman rattling her cage and – "

Their conversation was interrupted by a sudden high, piercing scream from upstairs. Not an animal scream of lust, but rather a wail of terror.

"What the …?" Lev shouted, jumping up. "That's coming from Agata's room." He grabbed the closest thing to hand, a broom, and took the stairs two at a time to the second floor. The screaming got louder as he got closer and it was joined by a harsh, guttural man's voice and what sounded like slapping.

When he reached Agata's door, he found it locked. The screaming had become a low howl. Lev shook the door. "Go away!" the man's voice shouted.

Lev tried the wooden door. Locked. He pushed at it with his foot. It did not budge. He lifted his right leg and kicked with the bottom of his heel. The door started to give way. The guttural voice from inside shouted harshly, "I said go away! Beat it!" More sounds of slapping and moaning. "Fucking bitch!" the man's voice growled. I'll teach you to – "

At that moment the door shattered and Lev peered into the room. Agata, unclad, was on the floor writhing in apparent agony. Lev found himself facing the furious scowl of a man his own height, about forty, barrel-chested and fifteen kilos heavier than he was.

"Fucking sick cripple!" he raged.

"Don't you dare say that!" Lev exclaimed. "She's a beautiful woman. Animals like you – "

"Animal am I?" The older didn't seem to realize he was as naked as the girl. Lev noticed the man's belly was larger even than his chest. "Just who the fuck do you think you are, breaking in on me like this?"

He reached for the closest thing to the bed, a heavy lamp. Without thinking, he hurled it at Lev, who deflected it with the broom. The boy advanced on the older man, consumed with a rage of his own, thinking only of protecting the young woman who lay cowering on the floor, her arms covering her breasts.

The large man kicked at Lev, then lunged at him, his huge, hairy arms punching and grabbing for Lev's neck. The boy may have been slighter than his attacker, but he had speed and agility which enabled him to bob and weave, avoiding the pummeling fists. Suddenly, Lev felt an explosion of pain as his assailant landed a well-placed kick between his legs. The boy screamed out in agony and went down.

The man followed up his advantage by grabbing the heavy lamp. Just as he was bringing it down on the boy's head, Lev pivoted to his right at the last possible moment, seized the broom and swung wildly, hitting the side of the man's head. With a scream, the man fell to the floor and lay still.

Agata, sobbing and moaning, reached for the mattress and tried to in vain to pull herself up. Esther and two of her other girls had entered the room and stood gaping at the grisly sight. The older man was not breathing. A slow stream of blood dribbled from his ear. A large, bluish welt was rising at the side of his skull. Esther had the presence of mind to feel for his pulse. After several moments, she raised her head, he face pale, her hands shaking.

"Dead," she said. "Oh, my God, he's dead."

"I … I didn't think I hit him that hard. He was about to …"

"I'm sure you were defending the lady as well as yourself. But that's not our real problem," Esther said, recovering her composure. "Do you have any idea who he is?"

"A depraved brute," Lev said. "Can you imagine, he called her a sick cripple?"

"No question he's an evil man. This was his first time here," Esther continued. "I recognized him when he came in. And *that's* where the problem lies."

"Why?" Agata asked in a high, thin voice.

"It's not *what* he is, it's *who* he is. We have a dead man on our hands who just happens to be Abel Warshawski."

"The name means nothing to me." This from Lev.

"You might think otherwise all too soon," Esther replied. "He's the minister of transportation. But much scarier, he's Boleslaw Bierut's brother-in-law."

"You mean?"

"Yes. *That* Bierut. Our Prime Minister, the head of the Polish state."

Immediately after his arrest, Lev was subjected to three hours of vicious beatings, all done in absolute silence. After the first hour, he never believed he would survive the pain. Shortly thereafter, he lost consciousness. The following day, he was tied to an upright, wooden chair, and left to sit for several hours. He'd not been asked so much as one question. On the third day, he was moved to a jail in a small town outside the city.

After he'd been escorted into a nondescript office and the guards left, a short, middle-aged man dressed in clothing a size too small for him appeared. "Lev Arkady," the man read from a single sheet. "Fifteen years of age. Charged with the brutal murder of our transportation minister. I see they've given you the royal treatment," he continued neutrally. "I haven't seen so many security types around here since the war ended."

Lev sat silently, not knowing what to say.

"A *zid?*" the man continued. "I thought they got rid of all *zids* during the war."

"You have a problem with that?" Lev croaked, his throat dry and parched.

"It's not something I'd broadcast to the world. Our friend, the Soviet bear next door has placed a lot of *zids* who survived into the current government. Most Poles have never been crazy about the Jews. Hard to tell who they despised more, the *boches,* the *zids,* or the Russkies. Many of my countrymen were pleased that Hitler and his gang got rid of the foreign element, made it a more *Polish* Poland. Would you like some water?"

"Yes, please."

The man walked over to a nearby bureau which held a pitcher and six glasses. Filling one with water, he returned and handed it to Lev. The boy had not realized how thirsty he was. He downed two full glasses so quickly he felt a bubbling in his stomach. "You're here to question me?" he asked.

"No, that's for the detectives."

"But you are a servant of the state? You obviously have a dossier on me."

"I'd hardly call a single page a dossier."

"You're in charge here?"

"I'm the warden, not that that's saying much. Brzezinska's a pimple on the arse of the Polish prison system. A holding jail for twenty-four inmates. The State could care less. You look like they've taken good care of you, black eyes and welts. I trust you didn't break your arms by falling against a wall? What a surprise. They'd never stoop to doing such things in civilized Poland."

"Sorry, I haven't been able to clean myself up for you," Lev replied acidly. "You're at an advantage here. You know my name. I have no idea of yours. I suppose that's the way it's supposed to be."

"It is. You worked for Esther Meyerson?"

"Yes."

Neither of them said anything for several moments. The warden was the first to break the silence. "My name is Jan Kalman." At that moment, two heavily armed guards knocked. "Come in," Kalman said.

"Warden," one of the men said. "Is this man giving you any trouble?"

"No, why?" the warden asked.

"We're told he's part of an extremist group and that Minister Warshawski's murder may not be an isolated act. You know how these Jewish gangs are."

"Indeed," Kalman said. "Is that so, Arkady?" he asked, turning to his prisoner. Lev remained mute. "Speak when spoken to!" the warden commanded. When Lev still said nothing, Kalman approached Lev and slapped him, not particularly hard, Lev noticed. "Did you hear me, Jew?"

"Yes, Sir," Lev said.

"Good." Turning to the two guards he said, "I think I can manage this one just fine. I much appreciate your checking on my safety. Take him to the cell in 'C' block. There's no one else there, He may as well have time to be alone and consider who he's messed with."

※

Lev didn't know what time it was. He could tell it was night because the high transom windows across from his cell were devoid of light. He'd lain down on the thin, lumpy cot. The springs felt as though they were poking crisscross marks on his already bruised back. He heard two voices, a man and a woman, speaking outside the block. The woman's voice sounded startlingly familiar, but it couldn't be. The events of the past few days must have addled his brain.

"You're sure, Chaim?" the woman asked.

"Positive. You know what's necessary to survive in this atmosphere."

The voices came closer. Suddenly the male voice barked out, "Wake up, *zid!* Wake up, do you hear me? If you don't, I'll ..."

"I'm up, Warden, Sir!" the boy said crisply. He'd heard of nighttime beatings and he did not want to risk more pain at this moment.

"Good. So …" he said, turning to the woman. "Is this the right one?"

"It looks to be him," she said. Lev found himself staring into the eyes of Esther Meyerson. "And boy, when we are alone together, you may as well call Warden Kalman by his proper name, Chaim Yankel Kalmanovitz."

❦

"But how did …?"

"A Jew become the warden? How did I know you worked for Esther Meyerson? Why of all the possible jails in Poland did you happen to land here?"

"Well … yes. And a thousand more questions."

"First, Esther knew I was here. She's responsible for my getting this job. Second, she has connections most people don't know about, 'dossiers' of her own, client lists … She's not simply a 'Madame.' She knows they never bother to ask what goes on here."

"Our meetings must take place late at night, Lev," the woman replied. "After all, I have a business to run."

"Agata?"

"As well as can be expected."

"What do you mean 'as well as can be expected?'" A note of urgency came into his voice.

"We'll discuss it later. She's no worse than she would have been had he not knocked her about. Right now, our first concern is dealing with your problem. We've spoken with Marvin Zuckerman, through an intermediary, of course."

"Who's he?"

"A Jewish American colonel attached to Operation Overlook. He was one of the prosecutors in the Nürnberg trials and became quite friendly with his Soviet counterparts. One of a few of those provincials who's fluent in German, Russian, and Polish."

"A lawyer?" Lev asked.

"Yes, but not admitted to practice in Poland. It would be better handled through political back channels rather than the court system. Talks have already started. Not publicly, of course. ... My friends in positions of some ... influence."

⁂

"It's not that the Prime Minister has any personal stake in this, Colonel," Bierut's emissary said to Zuckerman. They were sitting in an ill-lit back corner of a Turkish coffee house in the Soviet sector of Berlin. "God knows ... oops, I misspoke, our people's paradise no longer officially recognizes God ..." There was comradely laughter between the two men. "As I was starting to say, Bierut knew Abel Warshawski for exactly what he was. He hated his brother-in-law from the beginning. Your American colleagues know the story."

"A pederast. Little girls, little boys, it made no difference. But why a brothel?"

"Bierut laid down the law in no uncertain terms. If his dear brother-in-law wanted to screw his brains out, he'd better do so in a private, socially acceptable manner, and *only* in a socially acceptable manner, and particularly in a very discreet establishment."

"Esther Meyerson's house?"

"You'd be surprised how many politicians, diplomats, famous actors, the crème de la crème, frequent it. And Esther, God love her – Damn! There I go again – is a classy lady who knows how to keep her mouth shut."

"And her girls' legs open?" Zuckerman said sardonically. The two men sipped their tea quietly. "Warshawski's demise was an accident. I've provided you with the declarations of the witnesses. The boy's fifteen, no record at all."

"And a Jew," Yablonsky added.

"Like me, if you want to take that road."

"No, Colonel, I don't. No offense intended, of course."

"None taken."

"It's just a matter of how we can manage it. I'll admit the situation stinks. On the one hand, a cabinet minister who's as well connected as anyone in Poland, on the other, a young hooligan working in a brothel, and a Jew to boot – not the most popular race in Catholic Poland."

"The boy's originally from Bratislava. Before he settled down in the whorehouse, he'd traveled quite a bit on the underground circuit, from village to village with an old Jew who'd more-or-less adopted him. A very small fish, and small fish have always found a way of slipping through the net."

"But there could be unfavorable publicity, Colonel."

"Or no publicity at all, Pan Yablonsky. Let's talk realities here. I don't think your boss believes his tenure is long-term. Ten thousand in a Swiss account …"

"Złoty?"

"Dollars. Or Swiss francs if he prefers. But he'd have to state publicly that after investigation they'd concluded this was a tragic accident and there was absolutely no fault on anyone's part. The boy needs a clean reputation."

"And you Jews have to stick together?" Yablonsky said, his eyebrows arching.

"You want me to start taking offense, 'Ivan?'"

"No, Yank, I don't."

12

Over the next few months, Lev watched Agata more carefully than ever. He was as solicitous toward her as though she was his affianced. Once he'd returned to being with Agata, he had no need for any of the others. However, he learned that being open with them about how he felt toward Agata and reassuring each in turn that but for his feeling toward their resident-sister he'd want any of them in a heartbeat, deflected their sense of rejection.

Yet he could not deny that there was something different about Agata. The invariably good-natured girl he'd known had turned moody and unpredictable. While she never flagged in her sexual desire for him, her mood swings were troubling. Often, while they were in the foreplay leading up to lovemaking, she'd spasm in her arms or legs, ill-controlled and not a part of normal passion.

One night, after they'd finished making love, he felt a sudden warm moisture in bed and realized she'd lost control and wet the bed before she'd fallen asleep. When she awakened, she did not seem as surprised as she did sad. "This has happened to me more and more often," she confided in him. "I fear that soon no man, not even you, will want me."

"I don't know what you mean, darling," he replied. "How could anyone not want to give his very life to be with you?"

◆

"When did she first know?"

"She's known *something* was amiss from the day we met. Remember when I asked her about her limp and she told me about a shortened leg and seizures."

"Vaguely. I remember you saying that a woman's imperfections make her more attractive. But this other?"

"It started getting worse three months ago," Esther said. "She tried to hide it from you because she felt so protective of you. But when it got to where she couldn't control it, she came to me. When I took her to the specialist … The doctor was very gentle. He's told her it's a long-term thing that might get better or might get worse as time goes on."

"So basically he told her nothing?"

"Neither entirely truthful nor entirely untruthful."

"How old is she?"

"Twenty-four."

"And the doctor told you …?"

"She'll most likely be dead before she reaches thirty."

He gasped. "But she's so young … so beautiful … so full of life."

"If she was a vicious old woman, or even a beast like Warshawski, would that make it any different?"

"It would be so much better for all concerned."

"Did the six million Jews have a choice?"

"N-no."

Esther Myerson moved slowly over to the sideboard, poured him a cup of tea and one for herself. "Milk?" she asked.

"I don't think I want anything just now. If only it were me," he said. "Are there no other doctors?"

"Von Murtasser is the best in Warsaw, probably in all of Eastern Europe."

⚜

Yevgeny von Murtasser was a tall, thin, studious-looking man in his mid-forties, who exuded competence and genuine concern when he met Lev. "Despite the name, I'm neither Russian, German, nor even Polish," he said.

"Hungarian, I'd wager."

"How could you know that?"

"A long time traveling through Eastern Europe. I was born within sight of the Hungarian frontier.

"How much do you want to know?"

"All of it, Doctor von Murtasser."

"It might be ugly."

"My life has not been pretty, Doctor."

"Very well," the neurologist said, extracting two packets of paper from a manila folder. He handed one to Lev.

"Huntington's Disease," he said simply. In answer to Lev's questioning look, von Murtasser continued. "It's well-known in the medical community, but unlike diseases that get a great deal of publicity, heart attacks, cancer, strokes, and such, the public doesn't know much about it."

"Mrs. Meyerson said she'd be dead before she reaches thirty." There was a lump in his throat as he said that.

"If she's fortunate. I see from the look on your face you find it shocking that someone who's trained to believe in the sanctity of life would say such a thing?"

"Yes."

"If she's unfortunate, she could live for twenty years or even more and get worse every year. Your hand is shaking, son. Are you sure you want to hear this?"

"Y- yes," Lev stammered.

"Very well, then. Let's look at this diagram," he continued, thumbing through the pages he'd given to Lev. "All human beings have a certain gene called the Huntingtin gene. No, I didn't spell it wrong, the disease was first described by a man named Huntington with an 'o' but the gene is with an 'i.' On very rare occasions, this gene mutates and causes pathological changes. You've already observed some of them."

"Limping? Seizures?"

"Jerky, random, uncontrollable movements called *chorea*. You've seen those?"

"Yes."

"As the disease progresses, things get progressively worse. Might I suggest you use the lavatory. Your face is turning white and your breathing tells me this is hard for you to take."

The boy barely made it to the bathroom. When he returned, ten minutes later, Doctor von Murtasser applied a cold, wet compress to the back of his neck. "I suggest you lie down for several minutes. I told you this would not be easy."

When Lev had recovered to where he thought he could listen to whatever else the doctor had to say, he followed with increasing dread as von Murtasser recited the litany of what would most likely occur in a voice that was clinically flat, but even more frightening because of the lack of emotion when he spoke. Lev caught only snatches of the doctor's words. "Short-term memory deficits, which become long-term memory difficulties … dementia … often insanity."

"Is there no cure?" the boy asked huskily.

"None."

"Mrs. Meyerson said …"

"We could perform tests to prove conclusively, but I've seen enough of these cases to confirm my diagnosis. Because she's much younger than most, her symptoms will move much more quickly. God willing, she'll perish before she knows everything."

"I see," Lev said stonily.

"Was she your first experience, son?"

"Yes."

"Then we can only hope she will live on in your memory, hopefully as you knew her then, not as she will be."

The dismissal of all charges against Lev brought him no consolation. He found it increasingly difficult to remain in Esther Meyerson's house, seeing his beautiful young Agata daily, having to speak with her daily, living a lie while knowing … knowing …

Six months after his initial visit, Lev found himself in Doctor von Murtasser's office. The doctor was as gentle as he'd been when they'd first met. "Doctor …?"

"It's getting worse?"

"Much. How quickly will it progress?"

"I cannot predict."

"Is there any way …?"

"Are you saying what I think you want to say, Lev?"

The younger man looked down at the floor. He refused to meet Doctor von Murtasser's level gaze. "The suffering … the suffering …"

"You realize there's absolutely nothing I can do, legally or ethically."

"I didn't ask you to …"

"Are you asking my permission to be the Angel of Death?"

Lev said nothing. His hands were clenched and he was rubbing both thumbs against his forefingers.

"Sometimes the greatest cruelty can be the greatest kindness, young man. And vice versa. The decision to play God is the hardest one of all, for only God can play God. You realize this may be on your conscience as long as you live?" Still nothing from Lev. "Very well," von Murtasser finally said. "As I said, there is nothing I can do to help you. Nothing at all." He wrote something indecipherable on a small, blank prescription form. On a separate piece of paper, he wrote an address in clear, legible hand. He handed both pieces of paper to Lev. "Goodbye, Lev Arkady," he said sadly. "And whatever you decide, may God bless you."

After he returned from his errand, he thought long and hard about what he proposed to do for a week. At the end of that time, he made love to Agata for the first time since he could remember, gently, hoping it would never end. He was astonished by her beauty as never before. When it was over he returned to his room and cried the entire night.

Next morning, he brought her a cup of hot coffee and a sweet pastry.

"For me, darling?" She sighed contentedly. "I never thought I'd say this, Lev, and I hope you don't feel offended. No matter I'm older than you, I believe I'm falling in love for the very first time. Might we get away from this place? Just the two of us? It doesn't matter where, just so long as we are together."

Lev felt hot tears forming just behind his eyes. "Agata ...."

"How do you feel about me?"

"I don't *believe* I'm falling in love with you, Agata. I know I *am* in love with you. Age makes no difference. I'll love you for ..." he choked on the words.

"And you brought me a pastry to seal the sweetness of our love," she said. "I don't know if I can eat it all just yet. Perhaps a few bites, though …"

Shortly afterward, he watched her body relax. "I don't know why I'm so sleepy," she said. "Perhaps it's because I know … Promise me you'll be here when I awake, my darling. It will only be a few minutes."

"I …"

"Come to bed with me, darling. And hold me, just hold me …" He climbed into bed and wrapped his arms gently, so gently, around her. The tears began to come as he watched helplessly while she accepted the greatest gift he could ever give. She drifted into peaceful sleep and then passed softly, softly into the valley of the shadow of death, her serenely beautiful face in perfect repose. And it was thus that Lev Arkady became responsible for the second death of another human being in less than a year.

BOOK II

PENNY

13

Penny's mother died at their home in the Rancho Park section of West Los Angeles on Saturday, March 21, 1953 when Penny was twelve. Lung cancer. As long as Penny could remember, her mom had smoked Philip Morris unfiltered. She'd never counted how many cigarettes her mother smoked a day, but every time Penny looked, mom was puffing away. When her mother got down to the nub of a cigarette, she'd usually light up a new one, using the ash from the older one. She always smelled of tobacco, but lots of houses smelled of tobacco smoke, so Penny hardly ever noticed.

"Coffin nails," her dad used to call them. "A one way ticket to tuberculosis." Although he didn't smoke cigarettes, he'd occasionally light up a pipe, which smelled much different from mom's cigarettes, a sweet, cherrywood aroma Penny associated with her dad until the day he died.

"Nonsense," his wife would reply. "They're good for your nerves. Even the doctors in the newspaper ads say so. And that good-looking fellow on the TV, Ronald Reagan – she pronounced the name *Ree*-gan – he sure seems to know what he's talking about and they wouldn't let him say those things if they weren't true."

ARCADE

After Penny's mom had passed, she thanked God for her dad and her brother Jack. Jack was fourteen years older than Penny. He'd gone into the army in '46, when he was nineteen and she was four-and-a-half. They'd sent him over to Germany and then to Korea. Penny didn't see him but maybe once a year until she was in fifth grade and he'd gotten out of the service.

For the past two years he'd had the same girlfriend, Mitzi, and he rented his own apartment near Sepulveda and National. He worked at Norty's Records on Pico Boulevard, next to the Security First National Bank, where Penny's dad had opened a Hopalong Cassidy savings account for her. Jack had a really great job, because when she visited the store it had all the latest records, half 78s and half the new 45s, in stock, and she got to listen to them in the back room whenever she wanted.

A few weeks after her mom died, Penny's father took her fishing at the Santa Monica Pier. Halfway down the pier, on the left, there was a huge, noisy place, from which came the sounds of the same kind of music Penny had heard on the merry-go-round when the Clyde Beatty Circus had come to town.

"Arcade," her dad remarked. "Maybe we'll stop by on our way back."

At first, fishing off the pier seemed exciting, just because it was different and because she had some time alone with her dad, but by two-thirty that afternoon, when her dad said, "Time to call it a day," and when he cut the heads and tails off the eight perch they'd caught and wrapped them in butcher paper the day's catch looked pathetic. Penny's hands felt grimy and smelled fishy. Not the most fun she'd ever had.

Dad looked at the big Benrus wristwatch he always wore on his left arm. "Almost three o'clock. Should we stop at the arcade?" She shrugged. The day which had started out so full of promise had fizzled, but her father took Penny's hand and that made things all right.

The Playland Arcade was warm inside, not like the fishing rail, where a cold wind had blown most of the day. Penny had never seen so many lights flashing at one time. There must have been fifty games. She saw eight people seated at pinball machines where you pulled back a knob and shot a ball forward. When the metal ball hit a light or rolled through a narrow track space, wooden horses on a track moved forward, one for each machine. When the next seat came vacant, dad invited her to sit down and play. Penny didn't win, but her "horse" came in third, and the attendant handed her a token allowing her to play the next game for free.

After two more tries, when her horse did not do any better, Penny's father propelled her toward a bank of different kinds of pinball machines. If you got 50,000 points you could win a small stuffed teddy bear. Although Penny scored only 40,000 points, the attendant told her she'd won a goldfish in a small glass bowl. The fish survived for six months. Penny never got over the thrill of the place.

❦

By her second year at Palms Junior High, Penny was taller than most girls. She was on the girls' track team and the girls' softball team.

One Sunday, for no reason at all, Penny decided to go for a walk on Santa Monica Pier, just to be by herself. After showering, brushing out her hair, and getting dressed, she'd gulped down a bowl of Nabisco Shredded Wheat and walked up to Pico Boulevard. It took ten minutes for the bus to arrive.

When she got off at the end of the line, several kids her own age were headed toward the beach. Some had heavy portable radios, the kind with huge batteries that ran down after about thirty minutes. KFWB, Channel 98, played *I'm Walking Behind You* by Eddie Fisher.

Penny's heart did flip-flops just thinking about him. She'd seen him on the cover of both *Hit Parader* and *Song Hits*. What a dreamboat!

She savored the salty, slightly rank smell of the sea and enjoyed the look of the small waves as they broke on the sandy beach. She'd saved up three dollars from her allowance, which would easily get her through the day. The bus fare had cost ten cents. She'd taken a Mounds bar and an apple from home. Her goal was the Playland Arcade, where she won the pinball horse race three times in a row and *almost* beat the day's high score on the ski-ball apparatus. She jumped around on the trampoline and fell on her rear end a couple of times, but it didn't hurt. They had a hall of mirrors in the back of the arcade with a shaky bridge. One of the mirrors made Penny look short and squat, with a pinhead. Another made her appear much taller and skinnier. One of the mirrors even divided her in two, with the bottom half being short and fat and the top half making her look like a giant. Penny felt dizzy after getting off the shaky bridge and went outside for a few minutes just to sit on a bench and breathe in the salt air.

As soon as she felt better, Penny went to a booth in the back, bought several ping pong balls for a nickel apiece, and tried to pitch a ball into one of fifty tiny fishbowls, each with a goldfish that sat on a rectangular table ten feet away. On her tenth ping pong ball, fifty cents later, she won a bowl with a bright orange goldfish, which probably would have cost twenty cents at the pet shop. By one o'clock, she was happily exhausted and wondered, for the first time, what it would be like to work in a penny arcade all day every day. To get to play all the games for free. Maybe even to own an arcade some day.

February 25, 1956. Three weeks since Penny had started Hamilton High. Two months ago her brother Jack had borrowed a thousand dollars from their dad and bought Norty's record shop.

Hamilton High – Hami – had twenty-five hundred kids, six times more than Palms Junior High, and the buildings were *old*, like from the nineteen-thirties. The main building had age-blackened bricks and a big bell tower in the center, but no bell. Penny had never seen so many kids in one place at the same time. The first day was really scary. Out of every fifty people she knew two. The teachers piled you up with lots of homework, and it seemed that every second kid was named Goldstein or Goldberg or Cohen or Levy. Penny had nothing against Jews. She'd been to church only a few times in her life, so she couldn't say she practiced *any* religion.

Penny had always thought Jews were a minority. Not at Hami. And of course with a name like Penny Jo Fullerton, five-feet-seven, with straight blonde hair, no one was going to mistake her for a Jewish girl.

By the time three weeks had gone by, Penny found high school to be *fun*. Hami had tremendous school spirit. Eighty percent of the school turned out for the first pep rally, which took place on the football field. Cheerleaders danced and jumped around, and the student body made so much noise Penny thought they could hear the cheers all the way to University High, five miles away!

A month into the school year, Hami held its first sock hop. The dance was really a blast. Great music, *Memories are Made of This, Rock and Roll Waltz, Sh-Boom,* and some absolutely dreamboat guys. The Mandarins, the Senior "A" class with their yellow class sweaters, looked so cool.

Some girls had already paired off with guys. When they started dancing, they were all over each other, practically making out on the dance floor. Penny guessed that a lot of them were getting ready to play back seat bingo in the guys' cars later that evening. While Penny didn't know how many girls were fast, they sure dressed like they were: tight sweaters and bullet bras like the movie stars wore.

Penny, one of the tallest girls in school, confided to one of her friends, "As tall as I am, you'd think I'd have grown a good set of boobs already, but when I look in the mirror after I take a shower, there's not much there. It kind of frosts me when I see some guy going ape after someone who's stacked, like Sherry Dickman, who's maybe half my size except in the bazoom department." On the plus side, Penny wasn't exactly flat chested, and she didn't have acne anymore.

Some of Hamilton's teachers were way cool. Mrs. Bettington, who looked to be about a hundred, had been teaching American History and Civics *forever*. First day out, Mrs. Bettington had said, "Don't you believe a damn thing the history books tell you (she actually used the "d" word, can you believe it?). In this class you're going to find out who's lying and who's telling the truth by doing your own research, and you're going to find that what we call 'history' is always written by the winners. Cowboys and Indians … have you ever wondered why the Indians are called the 'bad guys?' Every generation manages to screw things up, and when you're grown up, you'll screw things up just as badly, but at least you'll be able to say someone in high school tried to get you to really *think*, not just repeat something you were told so might get an 'A.'"

Penny's schedule was pretty much what all first year students took: Homeroom, English, U.S. History, Math, and Phys Ed. They got a choice of Latin, French, or Spanish. Penny signed up for Latin because she knew there were a couple of really cute guys in that class. As for which science she'd take, either Chemistry, Physics, or Physiology, Penny took Physiology because everyone said it was easiest.

School let out at three every afternoon. Penny thought she'd go deaf listening to the noise from all the cars rumbling up the side streets. Life was good, really good. Penny couldn't imagine life being any better. Except maybe if she had a steady boyfriend.

14

One Saturday in October 1957 Penny decided to visit the Playland Arcade. Although she'd heard that a rough crowd from Venice High hung out there, she wasn't worried, since it was a weekend and broad daylight. She spent two hours at the Arcade having a ball. Afterward, she headed back toward the bus stop. She'd gotten about twenty feet down the walk when two heavyset Mexicans accosted her. "Hey, white chick, where you think you're goin'?"

"Hey, honey, you think you're too good for the likes of us?"

Penny walked faster to get away from them as quickly as possible.

"Hey, seester, you *no comprende?* Are you pickin' up what we're puttin' down?"

The larger one shoved Penny hard and she found herself off balance, pushed into the other fellow.

"Gentlemen," a cultured voice suddenly said commandingly, "that's no way to treat a lady. I suggest you might want to act with more respect."

"Who the hell you talkin' to, Nigger?" Penny's assailant asked. His accomplice withdrew a switchblade knife, prepared to show who was boss.

What occurred next happened so fast Penny didn't have time to comprehend it. The cultured voice whipped switchblade knife's arm in a hammerlock, then shoved him against his friend. Before they knew what was happening, he grabbed each one's head and cracked it against the other's. They staggered away, mouthing obscenities. Penny looked over at the guy who'd saved her from ... what, she didn't know, but she surmised it would not have been pleasant.

The fellow looked like a senior, maybe even in college, tall, six-foot-two, dark, and very fit-looking, with wide shoulders tapering to a narrow waist. His facial features were not what she associated with Negroes. He looked like a young Harry Belafonte. *Café au lait* coloring and short-cut hair, immaculately dressed in casual pants and a cardigan sweater.

"Is this pier neutral territory for a Marshall High defensive back and the most attractive Hamilton cheerleader?" His voice was gentle, his question framed so simply. Penny said nothing for a few moments and kept walking. The young man made no move to rush her.

"How long have you been here?" she finally asked.

"Five minutes or so, before those hoods started in on you. I saw them looking you over and thought there might be trouble. Where're you headed?"

"The Santa Monica Muni bus."

"Would you mind if I walked you there? Just in case these guys decide they'd like another round? "

"You can walk anywhere you want. It's a free country."

"Not for everyone."

"You're talking in riddles." Penny smiled, stunned that she found him so attractive. There were no Negroes at Hami. She felt the thrill of forbidden fruit. She knew that if she were seen even walking with him, tongues would start to wag.

"My name's Andy, Andy Burgess," he said, as they headed inland off the pier. "I thought you'd best know that before you continued walking with a strange guy, undoubtedly one who looks *very* strange in these parts."

"Hi, Andy. I'm Penny Fullerton. You said Marshall High. Now I recognize you. You're the guy who intercepted Bill Tennant's long pass and ran it back for a touchdown last week. You're not from around here?"

"You mean Marshall High or Los Angeles?"

"Either or both. Your choice."

"*Down de the way where the nights are gay and the sun shines daily on the mountain top* …" he started singing in a light tenor voice."

"You're kidding," she said.

"I wasn't born in Jamaica, if that's what you mean. Barbados. But it's in the same neighborhood. Before you say, 'Funny, you don't look like a Negro,' I'm not, at least not totally. Mom's dark but dad's an Englishman who was BOAC's resident manager on the island until I was twelve. They promoted him to L.A.X., and here I am, five years later."

They continued walking toward the parking lot as naturally as though they'd known each other for years. "You have your own wheels?" she asked.

"Actually, no. Dad lets me borrow one of the cars when I need it. How about you, Penny?"

"I usually hitch a ride with friends or catch a Muni bus. You said '*One* of the cars?'" Her eyebrows rose.

"The spare one. BOAC lets him use a company car, so we've got two at home. I use the older one. If you've got time, we could drive to DL's. They've got great burgers, fries, and milkshakes, and I could still get you home before seven."

Penny thought for several moments before she answered. He was Negro – well, not really Negro. She didn't want him to think she was a cheap pickup. And if they were seen together, people *would* talk.

On the other hand, Andy Burgess was obviously intelligent and more sophisticated than most boys she knew at Hami. Once he opened his mouth, no one would ever equate him with Jefferson High, where there were a lot of Negroes. U.C.L.A. would be more like it.

"O.K.," Penny said. "Is your car parked in the lot?"

"Uh-huh."

She didn't know what she'd been expecting when he said he was driving the 'older' car, but she certainly knew what she did *not* expect, a white '53 MG-TD convertible. There were maybe a hundred of them in the whole city. Penny looked questioningly at Andy.

"It's tiny, but the seats scoot way back, so we'll have plenty of room. I'll put the top up 'cause even L.A. gets chilly in October when the sun goes down." He actually held the passenger side door open while she got in.

And that was how Andy Burgess and Penny Fullerton began their first conversation.

During the next month, Andy and Penny kept their growing relationship very private. She'd meet him twice a week, usually on Wednesdays after school, and on Saturdays. On Saturdays, Andy picked her up at Westwood and Exposition at ten, and they'd spend a much longer time together. Sometimes they'd drive over to the Self Realization Fellowship Lake Shrine at the western end of Sunset Boulevard. Other times, they'd drive up or down the Pacific Coast Highway.

A month-and-a-half after they'd started seeing each other, they drifted into making out, on a side street near Manhattan Beach. It was unlike it had been with any other boy, not that Penny'd had much experience. For the first time she learned what a real French kiss felt like. She got all trembly when he softly ran his hand up her arm.

When she got home that night, she looked at herself in the mirror. Damn! She really *was* pretty. The fact that she was five-seven didn't bother her at all. She'd finally developed curves in all the right places, just like she'd yearned for all along.

By their third month, Penny knew kissing wouldn't be enough. She'd touched herself enough when she was home alone in her own bed to know how good certain things could feel, and she daydreamed about what it would be like with a boy ... No, not with just *a* boy, with Andy Burgess.

In February '58, a month before Penny's seventeenth birthday, Los Angeles experienced a week of balmy spring weather. On past walks, she and Andy had explored Paradise Cove, just north of Zuma Beach. They knew there were lots of small coves hidden from sight. In conversations at school, some of the girls had mentioned it was the place to go if you *really* wanted to make out heavy duty. Penny suggested to Andy that they take advantage of the thaw to spend the day at Paradise Cove. She'd recently purchased a figure-hugging two-piece bathing suit, one he'd never seen. They got to the beach around eleven-thirty. Penny had packed a picnic lunch for them. After he'd parked in the guarded parking lot, they walked north, away from the crowds. When they came to the cove Penny had in mind, she said, "This is as good a place as any to eat lunch. O.K. with you?"

"Sure."

"Spread out the blanket and unpack, but close your eyes 'til I tell you to open them. I want to see how you like my new bathing suit."

"They're closed. Scout's honor," he said, laughing.

As Penny stepped behind a large rock, she suddenly felt like doing something totally wicked. *Bathing suit be damned! Let him see it all.* When she was appropriately attired, or, to be honest, when she was not attired in anything at all, she said, "You can look now."

When Andy saw Penny, he practically choked on the Coke he was drinking. He stood up like he was in a trance, and made no attempt to hide the huge bulge in his bathing trunks.

"Penny … uh … uh … you're … you're …"

"Beautiful?"

"More than that. Stunning. I … I don't know what to say."

"Well, it seems your little friend is doing a lot of talking." Making sure there was no one in seeing distance, she moved closer. "Want to touch them?"

He was speechless. He reached out, gripped her breasts, and squeezed her nipples very gently. "Penny?"

"Uh-uh. You can look and you can touch, but that's all for now."

And that's what they did for the next quarter hour, before Penny went back behind the rock and got into her two-piece. She noticed when she was putting on the bottom half of the bathing suit, she was wet down there.

❧

Dear Diary –

How do I begin this entry? No one must ever, ever, ever see it or I'm dead.

I'd always been very popular as a babysitter. I was prompt, dependable, respectful, and inexpensive, fifty cents an hour, a dollar an hour after 11:00 p.m. Weekends only. Dad would almost always let me drive his Pontiac to and from my babysitting jobs, since he was usually asleep by nine o'clock, unless there was something really good on the boob tube.

Not long after that day at Zuma Beach, I suggested to Andy that he come over for a little while when I was sitting. The kids would be in bed by eight or eight-thirty and I knew their parents wouldn't be home much before ten, so that would leave us about an hour to make out and he could be long gone by the time the folks came back.

It worked out fine the first time he visited. Then we drifted into more than making out. We didn't go "all the way," but we came pretty close. Let's just say that within a couple weeks we were very familiar with one another's bodies. We'd lay on top of the big double bed, making sure not to mess it up. I remember the first time he touched me down there. It was so much different from when I'd touched myself, and when I came, which took about a second-and-a-half, there were shooting stars everywhere. I started screaming and Andy had to cover my mouth with a pillow or the kids would've woken up and thought someone was committing a murder or hurting someone pretty bad. And Andy was by no means 'Silent Sam' when he came.

Maybe we were lucky what happened happened, before something could have happened. Two of my "regulars," Art and Janice Dunn, called me in early June to ask me to sit on Friday night. They told me they were going to a double feature at the Picwood that started at 8:30 and didn't let out 'til nearly midnight. When they asked if I minded staying late, I replied that of course I didn't. What an opportunity for a long, long evening of messing around!

That evening, I put on the sexiest black half-bra and the scantiest panties I owned. I'd bought them a few weeks before and made sure they were well hidden in my bottom drawer beneath lots of other stuff. My nylon blouse had large buttons and the neckline plunged so deeply it left almost nothing to the imagination. Of course, when I greeted the Dunns, I wore a bulky cardigan over the blouse so I looked prim and demure.

Andy came over a little before nine, forty minutes after the kids had gone to bed. By that time, I'd taken off the cardigan so when he came in I was dressed to go. By nine-thirty, we'd both come once and were just lying on the bed, stark naked, watching TV quietly, when Andy reached over and started me squirming and spasming really hard. I was just about to climax and it was going to be a big one, when all of a sudden I heard the front door slam. Through a fog, I heard Mr. Dunn say, "That was one of the worst movies I ever saw! Penny'll miss the money but she'll be glad we got ho ..."

He didn't finish the sentence. It was punctuated by an animal scream when his wife walked into the bedroom and saw ...

There was no way to even try to explain. Mrs. Dunn was hyperventilating like she was going to faint. Mr. Dunn's eyes riveted on my body. Simultaneously I saw by the widening of his irises that he was not the least bit disgusted by what he saw. I felt really strange, terror, sure, but also a fierce pride at the fact that he really, truly was looking at me, and was transfixed by what he saw.

Andy had quickly jumped from the bed and had his trousers on within a few moments. I didn't know what to say. There's nothing I could have said. Although it didn't make the minutes that passed any easier, Andy said, "I'm sorry you had to see this, Sir, Ma'am. We'll be out of here and we won't bother you again."

The Dunns didn't say a word, nor did I, and we left rapidly. I didn't even stop to collect my money. Thank God they didn't call my dad. They never called me again.

By July of 1958, Penny's father and brother had met Andy and had accepted him. A few of Penny's closest friends knew what was going on, but they were more concerned with their own lives, so the underground whispering never got started.

On Friday, July 17, Penny and Andy planned to go to a party at Malibu Beach. It promised to be a fabulous midsummer sing-along night. Sheb Wooley's *Flyin' Purple People Eater* was still number one on KFWB, but Elvis' *Hard Headed Woman* looked like it would knock the novelty record out of the top spot within a week. Gone were the bulky, unwieldy portable radios of only a few years ago. Today, almost everyone had a transistor radio that weighed only a few ounces, one that you could carry anywhere, and that stayed on the whole evening.

When Andy picked her up at five that afternoon, Penny could tell by the look on his face that something was dreadfully wrong. He couldn't look her in the eye and when he spoke it was in dull monosyllables.

At first, Penny didn't say anything, thinking it was just a mood and it would pass. She couldn't think of anything she'd done or said, and the night before he'd been an eager, ardent lover. In fact, lately the word "love" had crept more and more into their vocabulary.

When he pulled over on a side street off Santa Monica Boulevard, he looked at her, his eyes teared up, and he put his head in his hands, sobbing.

"What is it, darling?" she asked gently.

"It's my parents."

"Are they O.K.? Is everything all right between them?"

"Oh, *they're* fine, just peachy keen," he replied.

"What then?"

"It's *me*."

"Are you all right?"

"No."

Penny shivered involuntarily, feeling a rising sense of terror. Did he have some sort of disease? Had he suffered a calamity? She didn't want to ask. Perhaps it was best to let him reveal what was so horrible at his own pace. The silence between them didn't last long.

"Penny, this afternoon my dad told me he's being transferred to Nairobi. It's a promotion he simply can't pass up."

"Nairobi? Where's that?"

"Africa. He'll be regional head of the whole eastern part of Africa, all the way from Khartoum to Johannesburg. It's …"

"What does that have to do with us?"

"Everything. He expects my brother and me to go with him."

"But you're supposed to start U.C.L.A. in September. And *we've* got plans …" Her voice had risen several decibels.

"I know," he said miserably. "I told him all those things. All he said was 'Plans change.' My mom didn't raise her voice against him. Just listened."

"And you?"

"Penny, I can't ask you to understand my culture. The father's voice is the law and I just can't disobey him. He'd lose a tremendous amount of face."

"What about *us*?" Penny almost shouted.

Andy sat wordless. He had no response.

Finally, it was Penny who broke the silence. "I don't feel very much like going to the beach tonight. Please take me home."

"Penny, darling, it doesn't have to end."

"And how, exactly, are we supposed to continue? Do you intend to fly back every weekend from mumbo-jumbo Africa or wherever it is? Or do you think I'm made of money and I can afford to fly back and forth for forty or fifty hours at a time?" Now Penny's hurt was turning to anger. Her cheeks bore a high color and she started to express the frustrated rage she felt.

Andy waited until her weeping let up a bit. "Can't we remember the good times and put them away for a little while 'til we're together again? I'll be eighteen in three months …"

"Big deal. That means three years to go until you're twenty-one. And you expect me to sit around waiting for you all that time? For all I know, you'll be screwing your goddam brains out over there."

"Penny!" he said, shocked.

"Don't 'Penny' me, Andy. It's the way of the world," she said, her head lifted high. "When are you supposed to leave?"

"Next Friday."

"Well at least you gave me a week's notice."

"No more than me, Penny. Are you …?"

"No, Andy, thank God I'm not. I had my period last week, so you don't have to worry about *that*."

"Penny, don't let it end like this. I love you."

"I'm sure you do, Andy. It's just that we'll both have to go on living. Take me home, please."

There was nothing more to say. More words would only have made the burden heavier. When she arrived back home, Penny's father knew enough not to say a word as she went straight to her room, lay on her bed, and cried for most of the night.

Andy left Los Angeles on July 24. Over the next month, he wrote Penny a dozen letters. While she never answered them, she kept them all, hoping against hope that someday soon … But the "someday soon" didn't come.

In August, Red Sanders, U.C.L.A.'s legendary football coach, dropped dead of a heart attack. U.C.L.A.'s first football game of the season was September 20 against Pittsburgh. Penny thought she might help heal her own broken heart by losing herself in the biggest crowd she could find. The Bruins were playing on their own turf. Home field or not, despite Billy Kilmer's 58-yeard-pass, U.C.L.A. lost 27 to 6, so it wasn't the most auspicious beginning to the season. As Penny was driving her dad's Pontiac home on Westwood Boulevard, she'd just entered a nearby intersection when a man in a truck ran a red light and creamed her car. She never even knew it happened. When Penny woke up at U.C.L.A. Medical Center two days later, she was told she had suffered a broken neck.

15

The next four months went by in a blur. The doctors who performed the surgery said she was incredibly lucky, no damage to the spinal cord, no shattered vertebrae, and they expected an excellent recovery. Easy for them to say.

Penny's dad and brother Jack came to visit the third day out. They stood directly in front of her, since her neck and head were totally immobilized. Penny could hardly speak, not that she wanted to. What could she say? At the end of the second week, Penny began a program of physical therapy. She had always been a fighter, and if the therapists told her to do a certain exercise once or twice, she'd do it five times. Penny was determined to achieve one goal if it was the last thing she did in her life. She would graduate with her senior class, the Heiwans, and she would walk down the aisle and sit with all the other graduates.

After the fifth week Penny started regaining some motion in her legs and even in her neck. As October slid into November she was actually able to take a few halting steps. A week later, with an orderly holding onto her just in case, Penny navigated all the way from one end of the corridor outside her room to the other.

Some girlfriends from Hami dropped by a few times during Penny's convalescence. She was truly shocked when the legendary Blanche Bettington visited. As no-nonsense as ever, she asked Penny where she intended to go to university and what she proposed to study. Penny hadn't given it much thought. Most of her friends either planned to go to U.C.L.A., which was cheap, or, if their grades weren't good enough, to Santa Monica City College. The really adventurous students went to U.C. Berkeley and one or two "eggheads" got into Stanford, but for the most part kids from Hami stayed in L.A.

"You know, Penny, you might think about Cal Poly up in San Luis Obispo."

"Never heard of it."

"It's no more expensive than U.C.L.A. and it's a much more practical school. You always seemed to me to be a learn-by-doing kind. Plus, it might do you good to get away from L.A. for awhile."

"I've never been out of L.A. Why do you think it would be good for me? If you mean my mechanical ability …?" Penny had done a lot of stage sets for the school plays. While she'd never gotten a reputation as a tomboy, she had found it easy to work on engines when she'd visited the machine shop. She wasn't surprised that Mrs. Bettington knew about that part of her life. Mrs. Bettington knew everything about everybody.

"Someone like you would be a natural to take engineering courses," Mrs. Bettington continued.

"Like driving a train?" Penny said jokingly.

"Like driving this country forward," Mrs. Bettington said, without missing a beat. "We've got enough psychologists and high school teachers and lawyers coming out of Hami. Technology will be the wave of the future. You could do worse than being one of the first passengers on that 'train.'"

When she departed, Mrs. Bettington left a Cal Poly catalogue on Penny's bedstead.

During the latter part of her stay at U.C.L.A. Med Center, Penny worked on school assignments to ensure her graduation. Not that there was any worry about her graduating. By the time she had gotten to Senior-A class at Hami, she'd completed all the units she needed to graduate. Those left were Phys Ed, Home Economics, Introduction to College, Senior Problems. Penny thought, "Boy, with what had happened to me since July, I could've taught that class."

In December, she returned home to a house that seemed smaller than she'd remembered it. Three bedrooms, one bath, eight hundred square feet, pretty standard for those days. The area where Penny lived was flat and ideal for walking. During that month Penny traipsed all over the neighborhood. She walked a mile-and-a-half every day and continued doing the bending and stretching exercises the physical therapist has assigned her. By the first of the year, she was pretty much back to normal. Penny had made good on her promise to herself that she'd be able to walk down the aisle with her graduating class. On January 12, she returned to Hamilton.

Penny was overwhelmed when she arrived. The graduating class had declared the 12th to be "Penny Fullerton Day," complete with balloons, cake, tee-shirts that said, "Welcome Back, Penny!," party favors, and even a sort of ragtag band to "serenade" her.

School was over by three. Penny was just about to hop on the bus and head for home when she heard a sharp beep. Turning to look, she saw it was her brother Jack. Penny was surprised to see him, because Monday was a workday for him. There was something about the way he looked which was not quite right, kind of a pallor.

"Jack? What's up?"

"Get in the car, Penny. Dad's had a heart attack. They've taken him over to Beverly Glen Hospital."

"Oh, my God!" I gasped. "Is he …?"

"He's alive. But no one seems to know for how long."

When they got to the hospital, their father had wires coming out of his wrists and arms. A saline drip hung by his bedstead and there were electrodes attached to his arms, chest, and other areas. His breathing was shallow and rapid. He went into and out of consciousness. A tall man of thirty-five, wearing a white lab coat, approached them.

"Are you his immediate family?"

"Yes, sir," Jack replied. "Is there anything we can do?"

"Nothing we're not trying to do already. He's suffered a massive heart attack. Can you tell us anything about his past recent history? Smoking? Alcohol? Fried foods?"

"He occasionally smoked a pipe," Penny responded. "He had a martini every night when he came home, but I never saw him drunk. For the last couple of years I've seen him twice a week for dinner, and it was pretty much on the run."

"Same here," her brother added. "Dad seemed more stressed than usual these past few weeks. Something about layoffs at the plant where he's been shift supervisor for thirty years. He had just turned fifty-eight. He said they were trying to push the older guys out. Then there was Penny's accident in September. That took a lot out of us."

"Any female friends?" the doctor asked.

"He and a neighbor woman down the street, a widow, would go to the movies occasionally. She'd have him over for dinner."

The doctor wrote Penny's and Jack's responses on a notepad, mumbling a noncommittal "Mm-hmm," "I understand," and asking a few more penetrating questions.

"What have you found, doctor?" Penny asked.

"Too early to tell," he replied. "We're waiting for him to stabilize. It will be a day, maybe two, before we know much more than we do now."

The doctor's prognosis was "Guarded." That was as vague an answer as medical science knew how to use. "Critical," she understood.

"Grave" she understood. "Guarded" was essentially meaningless. During the next days, Jack and his younger sister took turns at the hospital. The staff was kind enough to bring in a small cot, and they spelled one another, sleeping alternate nights in their father's room. For the first week, the elder Fullerton seemed to rally. Mostly he was pale and lethargic, but there were times when color returned to his cheeks and he became talkative. By the beginning of the second week, Dr. Block, reputed to be one of L.A.'s top cardiologists, came over from Queen of Angels, a large hospital downtown. He was Penny's height, trim, with iron gray hair, in his late 40s. Despite his reputation of being all business, he was friendly and forthcoming to Penny. She felt comfortable in his presence.

"Penny, today we're going to perform an angiogram on your father. We'll be putting a long, thin, flexible tube, a catheter, directly into your dad's coronary artery. We'll shoot some x-ray contrast agent into the same area and take images to see exactly what's going on inside his heart."

"Is that dangerous, Dr. Block?"

"Like anything else in medicine, nothing's foolproof. A lot depends on the patient's condition."

"Couldn't you wait to do it 'til he's stronger?"

"It's kind of a judgment call. If we wait too long, there's a chance that scar tissue might obliterate what we're trying to see. If we do it too soon …" He didn't finish the sentence. "Your dad wanted the most aggressive treatment we could give."

"You think it'll be O.K.?"

"As I said, there's no way of knowing."

Jack and Penny remained in the hospital when they wheeled their father into the cardio unit. Two hours later, Dr. Block emerged. "He seems to have made it through all right," he said, smiling at brother and sister. "We'll do a complete workup and analysis later today and we should have the results by tomorrow morning. It'll take the better part of two hours before he's conscious. You may as well take a break for a couple of hours."

"The record shop's a mile away. We'll be there waiting to hear from you. Here's the phone number," Jack said.

An hour went by. Two. They were just about to call the hospital when a call came in to the store.

"Hello?" Jack answered on the first ring.

"Jack Fullerton?"

"That's me."

"Mr. Fullerton, this is Trudy at Beverly Glen Hospital. I don't know how to tell you this but …"

◈

"It wasn't the angiogram," Dr. Block said, his face sympathetic. "It was a second myocardial infarct. Mercifully, he never fully regained consciousness."

The rest of his words were a blur, filtered through Penny's tears. The next week was hellish. In the week after the funeral, in the curiously grisly humor that somehow makes people feel a little better when they're at their lowest ebb and can't take any more, Jack remarked that now he and Penny were orphans with only themselves in the whole wide world to take care of one another.

"You have Mitzi," Penny said. "That's one more person than I have."

"Yeah, but if I don't finally put an engagement ring on her finger, I won't have her for long. Seriously, Sis, do you have any plans?"

"Don't know. Maybe Mrs. Bettington was right. She suggested San Luis Obispo. Cal Poly. Of course I'd need money to tide me over. I could probably earn that between now and the end of summer. Do you need help in the store?"

"Why not? I can use a break from work now and then. Even without you working, Dad's insurance should get you through the first two years with no problem. The house is paid for, and we might think about renting it out or selling it after you go."

And thus it was that Penny entered the next phase of her life.

16

A Korean man had opened a small martial arts training facility in a previously empty storefront on Westwood Boulevard, three blocks from Jack's record shop. It didn't take long before Jack and the Korean discovered one another. Soon, each started visiting the other's businessplace, spending an hour here, an hour there, sharing tea, Asiatic pastries, and conversation. One day in late February, Jack mentioned in passing, "Sis, in a few months you'll be going up north. I'm not saying you won't be perfectly safe, but you'll still be a girl alone, and the occasional date may turn out to be, well, uh …"

"Dating's the last thing on my mind. I'll be living in the dorms for the first year."

"It's not only that, Penny. If you could defend yourself, you'd feel more confident, more in control."

"Of what? Beating up on people?"

"No, no," he said. "It's just that if there's ever an emergency, I'd feel better knowing my baby sister could handle the situation."

"Baby sister?" Penny bristled.

"Open mouth, insert foot," he said, reddening. "Let me start over. I've got a friend, Harkjoon Paik, who started a martial arts studio. He's halfway between your age and mine, twenty-five. He opened a couple of months ago. His business isn't great, but he needs someone to help with the bookkeeping and greet people when they come in the front door. He can't afford to pay anyone, and he can't run the place by himself. It'd be a shame if someone who works as hard as he does failed. He asked me if I knew anyone who'd be willing to trade off a little work for learning Oriental self-defense. He'd said he'd be able to pay something when he got on his feet."

"And you volunteered me?"

"Well ... not exactly *volunteered* you. I said I'd ask."

"Why would you think I'd even be interested?"

"First, you're bored out of your mind. Second, no boyfriends that I know of. Third, how often can you walk the same two miles every day? Finally, my beloved little sister, it might be good for you to learn something new, something that will give you a good physical workout and something that may teach you about a different culture."

"Meaning?"

"Why don't you come over to Mr. Paik's studio and take a look. If you like what you see ..."

Penny did not know what to expect when she entered the martial arts studio. The handwritten signs in the plate glass window read *Taekwondo, Karate, Judo* in black letters that had been written with a felt-tipped pen. Below that, there were a bunch of squiggly symbols she couldn't make out. In bright red felt-pen letters below that, "Learn to defend yourself! Men, women, children welcome."

The place was fifteen feet wide by thirty feet deep. Four walls and a few mats scattered around the room. Harkjoon Paik stood five foot three inches tall. Penny guessed he couldn't have weighed more than a hundred pounds.

"Harkjoon, this is my sister, Penny."

"Ah, Miss Fullerton," the man said, bowing slightly. "I am delighted to meet you, although I feel I know you already. You are a brave woman, who's shown great courage in the face of adversity. The loss of a first love, the loss of a father, and a potentially paralyzing injury." Although he had a strong accent, he did not mispronounce his "l's" or "r's" like Orientals did in the movies. His voice was soft, gentle, and well-modulated. "You and I are bonded by a mutual loss. My mother and sister …" He looked down at the ground. "I was in my second year at the university at the time."

"I'm so sorry, Mr. Paik. Was it during the war?"

"Yes. An American soldier knew what had happened, took pity on me, and sponsored me into this country."

"You were going to college at the time?"

"I was studying law. Not much call for Korean law in the United States, so I use something I learned when I was much younger to try to make a living here. Your face registers surprise, no doubt because of my size," he said.

"Well … yes," she replied.

He glanced at his wristwatch. "You came at a very propitious time, Miss Fullerton. Ah, here comes my two-thirty student now."

As Penny looked toward the door a man in his early twenties, six-foot three and muscular approached. "Good afternoon, Master," he said respectfully, bowing to Mr. Paik. "I apologize if I interrupted you."

"Not an interruption at all. Karl Holzer, this is Penny Fullerton. You've met her brother," he said, nodding at Jack.

"Of course. Jack's record shop. I've seen Miss Fullerton once or twice when Jack wasn't there.

"Miss Fullerton may be thinking of joining us. I would like to perform a small demonstration for her. May I ask you, please, to come at me with a full force attack? Everything you knew before you came here, everything you've learned while you've been here, and," he said, walking over to a wall, picking up a two-by-four board, and handing it to the much larger man, "I'd like to give you the advantage of a weapon."

Penny glanced balefully at Jack, not knowing what to expect. If this was some sort of game, it was one which made her uncomfortable. "Don't worry, Sis," he said *sotto voce*. "I don't think Mr. Paik would have asked Karl to do this if he felt he was in any danger."

"Karl or Harkjoon?"

"Take your choice," he said, smiling inscrutably.

The two men went behind one of the doors in the far wall and emerged a short time later, each clad in a robe. They stood at opposite ends of one of the mats and bowed to one another. Each removed his robe. The two men wore shorts and nothing else. At a nod from Mr. Paik, the larger man grabbed hold of the two-by-four and approached him.

"*Jun-bi?*" Paik asked. The larger man nodded. "*Shi-jak!*"

Holzer, the two-by-four raised menacingly, circled to the left. The much smaller teacher, moved left as well. They continued circling one another for a few seconds. Then, Holzer feinted, thrusting the wooden weapon forward. Paik kept his eyes on the two-by-four, seemingly ignoring Holzer. He bent right, then left, never losing his concentration.

Penny felt a shiver of alarm go up her neck as Holzer, his eyes never leaving Paik's body, poked at the smaller man, then suddenly raised the piece of wood and prepared to bring it down on his opponent's head. Paik anticipated the strike and ducked sharply to his left, but Holzer was not fooled. Almost in midstroke, the big man ceased the downward motion, and with both hands, swung the two-by-four like a baseball bat toward Paik's midsection.

In what appeared to Penny to be slow motion, but probably took less than two seconds, Paik's bare foot connected with the board, shattering it. He jumped up and drop-kicked Holzer on the chin. While the large man started to go down like a bludgeoned ox, Paik somehow used his feet and hands to totally flip Holzer and brace the muscular giant, who landed remarkably gently on his back.

Alarmed, Penny approached the two men. Paik said,"

Geu-man, finished." He was not breathing hard, nor had he worked up a sweat of any kind.

"Is he …?"

"All right? Certainly." Paik smiled. "Fortunately, he knew how to fall. Dramatic, but not so much as a bruised fingernail." As if to punctuate the teacher's statement, Holzer stood up and brushed his shorts. "My next lesson, Master?"

"Indeed. Let's start by critiquing what you did that was right, and what you did that was *less* right."

Penny stood by, mesmerized, as the master and his student went through a series of moves in which both of them demonstrated grace and agility. When, an hour later, Holzer left, he said, "I'm glad you had a chance to observe this, Miss Fullerton. Are you thinking of taking lessons from Mr. Paik?"

"I hadn't given it any thought until today."

"It's something you should seriously consider. As you can see, size and brute strength doesn't always mean control. Might does not always make right."

⁂

For the next three months, until the end of May, she worked her butt off, literally and figuratively. She wanted to prove not only that she was the best bookkeeper-receptionist Mr. Paik had ever had, but also the best student. The latter was far more difficult and more frustrating, but Harkjoon Paik had enduring patience, and as summer began, Penny finally felt she was getting the hang of what he was trying to teach.

When Penny first started working with Mr. Paik, there were very few students, but each month, as word got out in the community, at least ten new students appeared. By May, there were eight women, most older than Penny, but two were her age. Mr. Paik approached her one day while she was at work.

"You know, Miss Fullerton" – he always called her that, although she'd told him a dozen times to call her Penny – "I cannot begin to tell you how much it has meant to me to have you here. You are the glue which holds my whole business together. I have not been able to pay you until now, but I would like to start to do so. Would you feel insulted if I offered you two dollars an hour, and continued with your lessons of course?"

"Mr. Paik, my lessons are more than payment enough. You're offering to pay me eight cents an hour more than an average worker makes, plus giving me the added bonus of your knowledge. I feel that would be unfair to you, particularly since we both know I'll be leaving for school in only a few months. Perhaps we could work out a deal where I'd help train my replacement. You pay me the two dollars an hour but only for the time I spend training him or her." Harkjoon Paik smiled, then blushed. "What is it? Did I say something wrong?"

"No, Miss Fullerton," he replied softly. "You said something very right and very generous. Back in my country I fell in love with a girl from my village. She's three years younger than me. Thanks to your help, I have been able to bring her to Los Angeles. She speaks some English, not much. I was worried that the cost would overwhelm me. Now you have provided me with the answer."

Chang Mi-Ra was smaller than Harkjoon Paik, with long, coal-black hair and skin the color of fresh peaches. She spoke softly, with a musical voice, and proved to be a very rapid learner, whose determination matched Paik's and Penny's. Her natural charm and delicacy provided a perfect contrast to Mr. Paik's more forceful personality. During the month-and-a-half Penny spent with her, Mi-Ra's English multiplied severalfold. She became adept at the business end of the studio so quickly that by early June Penny felt she'd be wasting Mr. Paik's money if she stayed on. Penny suggested Paik might do better if he and Mi-Ra saved their money for a life together.

Disneyland had opened in the summer of '55. Everyone wanted to work there, but Anaheim was a long way out, forty-five minutes south on the crowded, dangerous Santa Ana Freeway. Gas was only twenty-three cents a gallon, but parking cost money, so at the end of the day she wouldn't net that much, even if she *could* land a job at the Magic Kingdom. There was another alternative.

Pacific Ocean Park, which most young people on the west side of Los Angeles called P.O.P., was a Disneyland copycat that had opened on the old Lick Pier, half a mile south of the Santa Monica Pier in summer of '58. It was not so much a theme park as a combination of an old-time amusement park with a few special exhibits like the Nautilus, the House of Tomorrow, and Neptune's Kingdom. Penny found it more "hokey" than "magic."

A lot of kids from West L.A. got jobs there, especially if you were white and clean-cut looking. Like Disneyland, there was a dress code: black pants, white shirt or blouse, black bow tie, red-and-white candy striped cotton coat, and a straw-boater hat. Shades of *The Music Man*! Penny knew a couple of friends from Hami who worked there and they said she'd be perfect for P.O.P. The only drawback was that while Disneyland was in a safe area, P.O.P. was adjacent to Venice Beach, which was slummy and said to be dangerous at night. Girls were either restricted to working during daylight hours, or, if their shift was finished after sunset, at least three male employees had to escort them out of the park to their own cars.

Penny's mind drifted back to what had happened on nearby Santa Monica Pier a couple of years back, when she'd met Andy. While she'd never lost her intrigue for the Playland Arcade, which was ho-hum and old-fashioned compared with the much louder and more honky-tonk P.O.P., the atmosphere was forbidding. Two openings came up; since the attractions were owned by the same company, she could be scheduled to work at one or the other.

The following week, Penny interviewed two men. The first was a regular-looking guy of thirty, who wore an open-necked shirt and denims, Ray Blanding. The second was a much more forbidding-looking man ten or fifteen years older than Ray, John Hutchins. Mr. Hutchins was a "suit," stocky, with graying hair, a thick moustache, and a gruff manner. Penny felt much more comfortable with Ray. Within ten minutes of her interview she was hired as a "red button," at two dollars an hour.

P.O.P. had two classes of workers. Red buttons were kids Penny's age who were summer hires, ride attendants, clean-up crew, the worker bees of the park. You could always tell management because they wore the "gold buttons." They got paid three dollars an hour, *real* money, and they had a lot more benefits. Longer lunch hours, less grunt work, and the red buttons who let you in when you came to the park were always a lot more respectful. None of that mattered to Penny. She was not looking for responsibility. She was glad to have a job.

17

Everything went well for the first week. Most of Penny's job consisted of riding in the Sea Tubs to make sure the area around the churning water was clean of debris and safe in the event an emergency, or walking through the Davy Jones' Fun Locker, policing the cleanliness of the place. Knowing of her bookkeeping experience, Ray asked if Penny would check the receipt books and make sure they matched up against the paid admissions. Penny was eager to be as diligent an employee as she could. She even volunteered to throw in a few hours of bookkeeping for free.

Thus, she was quite surprised when she was called into Ray's small office mid-way through her second week. "Sit down, Penny," he said. "I'm afraid I've got some rather bad news."

Penny frowned, not knowing what to expect. "It seems that the books don't match up. There's been a hundred dollars a day missing from the till."

"The books seemed O.K. to me," Penny said.

"That's what I told Mr. Hutchins, but he told me there'd be no time to do a full audit. He's said there was no problem until a week ago, just about the time you were hired. So I'm afraid I've got to let you go."

Penny turned pale. No one had ever accused her of dishonesty. She was tongue-tied with a combination of anger and hurt. "I'd like to talk to him," she finally blurted out. "That's so unfair. I've done nothing wrong."

"He doesn't want to talk to you. My hands are tied. Word came from above, and I need this job." There was something in the way he said this which sounded suspicious to Penny. While she realized there was no need for him to have any loyalty to her, she felt it was wrong that he hadn't even tried to come to her defense.

"Is there no one I can talk to?" Penny felt herself choking up, but she'd be damned if she'd let anyone in that company see her cry. Now anger got the better of hurt.

"Nope," he said. Somehow Penny felt his tone was more relieved than helpful. He reached in his pocket and extracted a small stack of money. Counting it out, he said, "Here's your pay through tonight." Penny felt like tossing it in his face, but she wouldn't give him the satisfaction of seeing her break down. Without a word, she took off her striped coat, bow tie, and straw hat, folded her outfit neatly, placed it on the table in front of her, and left without saying another word.

As she walked miserably out of the P.O.P. gate, Penny forgot, or ignored, the admonition that a girl should never walk alone at night in this area. She didn't really care. Once again, the rug had been yanked out from under her world. As she headed toward the parking lot, the bright lights of P.O.P. receded in the distance. Penny sensed rather than saw a sinister presence behind her. As the footsteps became closer, louder, she walked faster. Then she heard a snarling, vaguely familiar voice.

"Hey, Chuey, look what we got here. The nigger-loving bitch from a coupla' years back."

"Yeah, and no one to interfere with us this time."

"Hey, poosy, poosy, poosy."

"Meow! How'd'jou like some Mexican cock. Or are you still bangin' the nigger?" Penny tried to ignore them, but she could feel them gaining on her.

"Hey, mamacita, *donde esta Santa Claus?*" the first one taunted.

"He's right here, baby," the one called Chuey called out.

"Why don't you two crawl back into the hole you came from?" Penny snarled. She was surprised at how calm she felt, notwithstanding she was alone.

"Hey, bitch, you talk big, but it's just you and us this time around." He grabbed Penny's arm and spun her around.

In that instant everything came together in her head: anger at the injustice of what had taken place several minutes earlier and a hot rage; oddly enough not fear at what they might try to do to her. In the midst of it all, Harkjoon Paik's calm voice came to her. "*Karate-do* teaches ethical principles. *Judo* means 'the gentle way.' You must always be in control of your inner self to prevail against the savage onslaught."

Penny started to feel almost sorry for the thugs who had assaulted her as she realized that unless they knew more than she did, something she sincerely doubted, neither of them stood a chance. Penny thanked God she was wearing loose-fitting pants rather than a more restrictive shirt. She reared back, stiffened the index and middle fingers of her right hand, and jabbed them hard into the first tough's carotid artery. He hadn't even collapsed to the ground when I she drop-kicked her attacker's companion in the groin. The second guy fell to his knees, clutching desperately at his crotch.

The first man was conscious, but gasping for breath and crying. The second was in too much pain even to do that.

At that moment, Penny heard heavy footsteps running toward her, and the sound of labored breathing. "Miss Fullerton! Wait! Stop! Please!"

Penny turned, ready to face a third potential attacker. She saw to her shock it was Mr. Hutchins, the general manager of the attractions from which she'd just been fired.

"Mr. Hutchins? What do you have to say that I'd even want listen to?" Penny's anger and vitriol were evident in the tone of her voice.

"Can we … can we talk for a moment?" When he saw Penny had stopped walking toward the car, he stood in place. His breathing became more regular.

"I'm listening."

"What happened tonight was … a mistake. Please, just hear me out." He looked beyond Penny to where her two erstwhile attackers were writhing. "Who are those …?"

"Fucking bitch almost killed us, Mister," one of the hoodlums moaned. "Better call the cops if you want to survive. Better still, get the fuck away from her while you can."

Hutchins glared at them for a moment. "You expect me to believe this young lady set out to attack *you*? Is that what you're telling me? I think you're right. I *will* call the cops."

"Wait, Mister," the second man pleaded. "We didn't exactly mean call the cops. We …"

"What exactly *did* you mean?" Hutchins growled. He reached into his pocket, drew out a police whistle, and blew it hard and long. It took less than a minute for P.O.P.'s security forces to respond. Minutes later, a police cruiser arrived.

The policemen listened to Penny's story. Her assailants were unable to answer the officers' questions. Next thing she knew they were handcuffed and shoved roughly into the back of the cruiser. As the police car drove away, Hutchins took her gently by the arm. "Might we talk now, Miss Fullerton? There's a decent coffee shop a few blocks from here. If nothing else, I think we could both do with some quiet time."

Penny didn't disagree. Soon they were seated in Denny's. "You wanted to talk?" she said noncommittally.

"I understand Ray Blanding fired you earlier tonight."

"You should know that. He told me you said there were discrepancies in the books and that there'd been no problems before I came."

"Partly right and partly wrong," he said, lifting the cup of black coffee to his lips. "We hadn't discovered anything until a week-and-a-half ago, about the time he asked you to help him with the books." Penny nodded. "A couple of days before you started work, our accountants conducted an audit when he wasn't working and found some very suspicious numbers. They replaced a few pages of the accounts with some that looked almost exactly the same as the books Ray kept. The only difference was that Ray's books didn't balance and these did."

"And when I found the books balanced he became suspicious?"

"Correct. He thought you were a plant placed at P.O.P. by management. He believed he could cover his tracks if he blamed you for the discrepancies. I never for a moment suspected you of any wrongdoing, nor did I direct that you be terminated. Quite the contrary. It didn't escape my notice that you always came to work early and didn't hesitate to put in extra time if it was needed. Like tonight, as a matter of fact."

"So the whole thing was Ray's idea?"

"Like he told you, he needed the job. But orders never came down from above to fire you or anyone else working at our rides. We've got a good group. All of 'em are putting in maximum effort."

"Why are you telling me all this now?"

"Within ten minutes after you left – and I heard the whole thing, by the way – I fired Ray Blanding. That leaves me without an assistant manager." He smiled and for the first time since Penny had known him his face did not look nearly so severe. "Penny ... may I call you that?"

"You're the adult. You can call me whatever you like, Mr. Hutchins."

"John."

"John?"

"Mr. Hutchins while you're working. My friends and my wife have always called me John."

"But I'm not working for you. Not at P.O.P. and not after tonight."

"That's what I wanted to talk about with you, Miss Fullerton, uh, Penny. I'd consider it a personal favor to me if you'd consider coming back to work as my assistant manager. A gold button, of course, and what would you say to four dollars an hour?"

"Four dollars? That's more than most of the gold buttons at the Park."

"It's the same as Ray Blanding was making. Of course, there'd be a change in your duties and your hours. Although you proved you could handle yourself very well at night with two completely different sets of confrontations, I think I'd like to start you as day manager, ten-to-six with an hour off for lunch."

Penny had been sipping so vigorously at her chocolate shake that she was a little embarrassed when she sipped air and their conversation was punctuated by a loud Sssllpp, sssllpp. "How long do I have to think about it, Mister ... John?"

"I'll hold the offer open for a week. You can start tomorrow if you'd like."

Sometimes you never can tell where life's going to take you and appearances can be deceiving, Penny thought. What had started out as a horrible night turned out to be a good one after all. During the two-and-a-half months Penny worked at P.O.P. John Hutchins turned out to be a great boss, thoughtful, kind, and always supportive. When Penny announced that she was leaving for San Luis Obispo, he gave her a goodbye party, a fabulous recommendation letter to put in her resume, and a hundred dollar bonus.

Just before Penny left, she received one more bit of good news. Harkjoon Paik told her he had asked Mi-Ra for her hand in marriage and they'd be getting married during Cal Poly's winter break. Mi-Ra asked that Penny serve as her maid of honor.

18

San Luis Obispo was one one-hundredth the size of L.A., with a much slower pace than her sprawling hometown two hundred miles to the south. There were no strings to tie her down, and her schedule was her own. Penny Fullerton truly felt like a grownup for the first time in her life. Jack had driven her up, clothes, English touring bike, old teddy bear, and all, had dropped his little sister off at the dorm, and helped her unload.

Penny's roommate had arrived a couple of days before. Birgit Petersen, who was her own age, spoke with an accent and told Penny she was here from Denmark on a student visa. They made a striking pair of roomies, Penny tall and robust with dishwater blonde hair and brown eyes, Birgit five feet tall, slender, with straight, white-blonde hair that hung down below her shoulders, and blue-grey eyes. Soon the two of them became inseparable. They rode bikes, bused, or walked everywhere, exploring the campus and the downtown area of SLO-town.

Penny signed up for a year's worth of Freshman classes at Cal Poly that everyone had to take. She signed up for French because during the sign-in week two particularly cute guys also enrolled in French class, as well as English 101, a basic engineering course, and what soon became her favorite class of all, European History. Professor Hoxie was the funniest and cleverest teacher on campus. It didn't take long for Penny to find out that the reason his class was so popular was that his view of Europe was a series of bed-to-bed misadventures among high-class miscreants. He was quick with the *bon mots* and wisecracks designed to titillate his sexually curious students.

"Before you start snickering and thinking all kinds of thoughts I know you're thinking," he said one day, "just remember these people only bathed once a month or so, and when they had fun it could get pretty ripe and smelly. Ooooh! Ugghh!"

Professor Hoxie, a tall, balding man, with a pencil-thin moustache, almost always wore a purple smoking jacket and light tan pants to class. He only lectured twice a week. Since there were three *hundred* students enrolled in his class, he conducted his lectures in a large lecture hall on Monday and Wednesday. On Tuesday and Thursday, the class was divided into eleven smaller units, arranged alphabetically by last name, and taught by graduate student teaching assistants who got paid very little, but who felt honored to work for the great man.

When it came to both European History and French, Birgit was a godsend. She'd grown up in Europe, so it was a given she'd know a lot of its history, and her French was flawless. "How many languages do you speak?" Penny asked her.

"Danish, English, French, German, and a tiny bit of Italian."

"*Five* languages? I never knew I was rooming with a genius."

Birgit laughed. "That I'm certainly not, Penny. I've never met anyone in Europe who doesn't know at least three languages. Once you've learned two, it's much easier to learn a new one after that."

During winter break, Penny invited Birgit to Los Angeles. When some of her old buddies in West Los Angeles, especially her "friend-boys," first met Birgit, they started hanging around Penny's house in droves. Both girls got asked out a lot, and they always double dated, so each could chaperone the other. They didn't go "all the way," at least Penny didn't, but there were nights when she went pretty far. And *that* led to some interesting conversations when the two roommates were alone.

"Europeans have a much more tolerant outlook on sex than Americans," Birgit told Penny one afternoon. Penny blushed, not because she considered herself a prude, but because she'd never heard a girl her age just come right out and start *talking* about things like that. "I've noticed it's so different in the United States than in Denmark. To us, making love is as natural as breathing, but I've noticed that in America men don't look you in the eye, or if you catch them undressing you with their eyes, they immediately turn away. Sex is dirty but violence is perfectly all right."

"Why do you say that?"

"Western movies, gang movies, even cartoons between the double features. People laugh when the bad guy gets hurt. The more brutal, the more people laugh. And these movies are perfectly acceptable. On the other hand, have you ever seen the French movie *The Lovers*?"

"Mm-hmm."

"That's all you have to say?"

"It was one of those movies you never talked about seeing. It was at the Beverly Canon earlier this year. Can you believe they could show such a movie?"

"Why? Because they portrayed Jeanne Moreau making love? Because they showed her body? Jeanne Moreau is one of the most respected actresses in Europe. She's with the *Comedie Francaise*. *Les Amants*, that's the original French name of the film, was a serious movie, not like something you'd see at a fraternity stag night. America seems so hypocritical to me."

"Tell me, Birgit, have you ever …?"

"Of course."

"Just like that. You sound so casual about it."

"Have you?"

"Not exactly."

"What do you mean 'not exactly' Penny?"

Penny told Birgit about Andy, even about the babysitting episode.

"Did you ever think you'd marry him?"

"We never talked about it. We both thought about it, and maybe if we'd gone all the way, we might have *had* to talk about it. How about you, Birgit?"

"I've grown up believing that if you waited to make love until you got married, then found out you weren't sexually on the same channel as the guy, the two of you would have a pretty miserable marriage. In Denmark lots of girls live with a man before they get married, sometimes for years, and it's perfectly O.K."

"But that's … that's *immoral.*"

"You think so?"

"That's what I've been taught."

"Maybe you should travel in Europe, if for no other reason than to see how the rest of the world lives."

❧

In February, Jack sold the family home. Suddenly Penny found she had more money in a bank account than she ever knew existed. She became increasingly eager to visit Europe. Several things motivated her. First there was Birgit, who'd be going back to Denmark for the summer. What she'd told Penny about the Continent tantalized her.

Penny managed to get a few minutes in private with Professor Hoxie in his office to ask his opinion. He said candidly "How could you *not* go to Europe and still believe you'd completed your education?"

Two things sealed the deal for Penny. One day, Mademoiselle Soulé, the French teacher, who was half a dozen years older than Penny and one of the most beautiful women Penny had met anywhere, showed the class a travelogue. If Penny had had any hesitation about going to Europe before, that film erased all her doubts. Even though the movie was in black-and-white, Penny's heart saw it in color. The Riviera, men and women on the beach dressed in bathing attire that left nothing to the imagination, the Alps. And Paris. *My God, I've never seen a city so captivating, and the people, every single one of them, was so ... so alive and beautiful.*

The final exclamation point to "I've simply got to go!" came in early March, when Penny attended a lecture given by a visiting professor from U.C.L.A., Pier-Maria Pasinetti. From the first words out of his mouth Penny was dumbstruck. He projected urbanity and charm in a way she'd never known before. When he spoke, he caressed the English language with an accent so musical Penny could have gone on listening for days. He expressed thoughts she was unaware that anyone, particularly a professor, could say in public, but he said them so easily, so naturally, that they didn't sound at all irreverent.

"No matter what anyone tells you to the contrary, *all* women of *every* age are beautiful and desirable. There is no such thing as an 'old woman.' There are young women and some that are not so young. Sexual love is the supreme experience. But I fear I digress. I'm here tonight to talk with you about the Continent, *my* Continent, my Europe, and mostly about *Bella Italia*, my homeland.

"You need not worry about money once you get there," Doctor Pasinetti continued. "There are student hostels everywhere, perfectly respectable, for less than two U.S. dollars a night. Food, the equal of which you've never tasted in your life. And *romance* – ah, yes, you

Americans have such a Puritanical view of life. I have brought with me some color slides of Europe. Let me start with one of my favorite cities in the world, Venice ..."

U.C.L.A. announced a student charter flight to Europe in summer, two hundred-fifty dollars round trip. The flight would leave New York June 20 and fly to London, returning from Paris to New York on August 15, nearly two months later. *Paris? Oh, my God*, Penny thought. She signed up to get more information about the charter flight that very night.

For the next two weeks, she couldn't think or talk of anything but Europe. "Please, please, please, Birgit," Penny begged her roommate. "I've never been *anywhere*. I'm afraid to go to Europe alone. I don't know the languages. I don't know *anything*. But I want to go, worse than I've ever wanted anything in my life. Could you travel with me?"

Birgit thought several moments, then said, "I'm scheduled to fly back to Stockholm on the June 4. I could renew my student visa during that time. I've lived in Scandinavia and been to Belgium, the Netherlands, Germany, and a small part of northern France, but there are many parts of Europe I haven't seen before. Last year, European railroads introduced the Eurailpass, unlimited travel through thirteen countries during a two-month period for a single cheap fare. Next year's classes begin September 5. I'd have two more weeks at home after we get back. Let's do it!"

19

On Friday, June 10, 1960, Penny piled into a black 1949 Mercury with three other young people, two men and one woman, and four soft-sided suitcases. They left Los Angeles at ten at night and headed east on Highway 66. A month before, Penny had gotten her passport and her International Youth Hostel Association guidebook, and had visited U.C.L.A., where she'd found ads for hitching a ride from L.A. to New York for twenty-five dollars. She'd met the car's owner and he'd approved of her.

There were few freeways going cross-country in those days. They'd planned to drive straight through to Gotham, via Albuquerque, Amarillo, Oklahoma, and points east. The group took turns sleeping in shifts, two at a time, as the big car barreled across the country, stopping at grocery stores to load up on food and drinks, and at gas stations to tank up and perform bodily functions. No showers. They all knew they'd smell pretty rank at the end of the five-day journey. The two people whose turn it was to sleep would go to the back of the car, while the driver and "shotgun passenger" remained up front.

They reached New York City at 3:00 a.m. five days after they'd started. The owner of the car dropped Penny off at a student hostel in midtown Manhattan. It was 85° with 90% humidity in the City. The hostel didn't have air conditioning. As tired, sweaty, and undoubtedly smelly as she was, Penny didn't get much sleep that night, but she wasn't the least bit fazed. She had reached the center of the Earth, the largest, most impressive city in the universe. She would make the most of her four days here!

During the time Penny was in New York City, she walked and gawked at everything in mid-town Manhattan. Walking in the flat city was easy. The Big Apple presented amazing sights on every street corner from Central Park all the way down to The Battery. And "Broadway" was a world apart, the center of the entertainment universe, the center of the broadcast universe, and the center of the publishing universe. Penny found herself singing the words of the number one record of the day, Good Timin'.

At noon on the twentieth, Penny took the airport bus from the transit terminal to Idyllwild Airport. She got there three hours before her flight was to leave. When she checked in at the British Overseas Airways Corporation terminal, she received a large plastic BOAC traveling bag, which would fit under the seat in front of her. Inside the bag she found soap, a toothbrush and toothpaste, a fingernail clipper, and a comb. The overnight flight to London would take ten hours in the DC-7C, a modern propeller-driven aircraft. Penny had never flown in an airplane before, so she had no idea what to expect.

After the plane took off, the sky darkened. When the aircraft reached its assigned altitude, Penny became unnerved, seeing orange flames erupting from all four engines. The stewardess assured her the aircraft wasn't on fire, it simply looked that way at night.

Every one of the aircraft's seats was filled with a college student. Penny thought she'd died and gone to heaven when they circled over the city of London on an early gray morning, gaping at the well-tended fields of the English countryside, and landing at what was then called London North Airport.

She found her introduction to England laced with typical dry English humor. After she'd landed and was preparing to cross the road, she became confused. The cars drove on the left hand side of the road. Seeing her consternation, a cabby came up, looked sympathetically at her, and said, "You're in England now, Miss. Look a'*right*, look a'*left*, and run like 'ell!"

❦

The hostel where Penny stayed smelled of mutton. It had a small library adjacent to the dorm, where she found a book, *Europe on Five Dollars a Day*, by someone named Arthur Frommer. She took copious notes until the proprietor took pity on her and asked, "First time in Europe?"

"Uh-huh,"

"Why don't you just 'borrow' the book?"

"Could I? Really?"

"Why not? Someone else left it here a week ago, so it didn't cost me a farthing."

"A farthing?"

"Here," he said, digging in his pocket and coming up with a tiny copper coin. "It's an old-time coin, worth a quarter of a penny. You can return the book whenever you're done with it, or you can send me a farthing by post. Either way's fine with me."

Penny felt like a tropical fish that had just been thrown into a new tank. London seemed so big and she felt so small. Still, she managed to find her way around the city. Large red double-decker buses traveled everywhere. She ate foods she'd never tasted before: fried plaice and chips with malt vinegar, wrapped in newspaper. Indian food, curry, hot and sweet, not like chili at all. On her third day in London, Penny's joy knew no bounds when Birgit appeared.

That night, the two girls went to SoHo, a great place to dance, party, and meet guys. Birgit had no problem with that, but Penny hung back. Her Puritanical streak hadn't let go yet. Next day, they took the train to West Malling, Kent, less than an hour from London. West Malling had one long main street which intersected London Road, the highway that connected London to Dover on the English Channel. Tudor, Edwardian, and Georgian-style houses and shops lined both sides of High Street and the south side of London Road. Penny had studied English architecture in her engineering class, so she wasn't completely unfamiliar with English buildings.

A large wood spread north of London Road, far enough away from the main thoroughfare that when Birgit and Penny walked there, they couldn't hear any sounds but the whistling of a light breeze through the trees. Penny imagined herself back in the days of King Arthur and the Knights of the Round Table. She felt transported to a much earlier time, since she could neither see nor hear the traffic on London Road.

Later, Birgit and Penny walked to the village church at the opposite end of High Street. The gravestones in the churchyard mesmerized the American girl. Some of them went back to the 1300s, before Columbus discovered America. More than anything, this small country churchyard brought home to Penny the interconnection of humankind and history, and why people called Europe the *Old Country*.

The girls returned to London the following day. From there they crossed the Channel to Paris and boarded the train for their first major destination, Vienna.

20

During the four days Birgit and Penny spent in Vienna, the city of Johann Strauss and Gemütlichkeit, Freud and Mahler, Karoly and Hitler, they experienced a history lesson come to life. Some cities shout their greatness: New York, London, Paris and Rome proclaim their status as world capitals. Vienna had been a world capital for two millennia, but unlike those other cities, Vienna languished as a *doyenne*, a Grand Dame, a once beautiful woman whose day was long past, but whose charm is eternal.

Birgit and Penny stayed in a small, narrow two-bedded room in a student hostel in the First *Bezirk,* the Inner City. They traipsed their District and immersed themselves in its culture. Penny could have covered Vienna's *Kunsthistorisches Museum* in a couple of hours, but she kept returning for the next two days. The *Kunst* enthralled her with its incredibly rich collection of European art, including a few rare paintings by Franz Hals and Hieronymus Bosch, who foreshadowed modern art by five hundred years.

Vienna oozed charm. Horse-drawn carriages, *fiacres*, carried wealthy businessmen, and, in the evening, lovers, along the *Ringstrasse*.

On their second afternoon in Vienna, Birgit and Penny decided to splurge. They went up to the *Cobenzl*, a fancy restaurant high above the city, in the Vienna Woods. From there, they planned to take the bus down the hill into Grinzing with its legendary *weinstube*, restaurants where they served new local wine and old-time entertainment.

Penny had always loved high places from which she could see the surrounding countryside. Sitting at an outdoor table, Birgit and Penny watched the sun descend. The lights of Vienna came on one by one and truly transformed Vienna into a city of dreams. They'd been sitting at the table nursing their cups of coffee for twenty minutes when a pleasant-looking man in his mid-twenties approached their table. He asked them, in accented English, "Would you mind a little company in exchange for my paying the check?"

Birgit and Penny looked at one another and smiled. "Are you from Vienna?" Penny inquired.

"No. From the East."

"A Communist country?" Penny did not want this European man to think she was a provincial American ignoramus with no knowledge of the larger world.

"Americans and their English cousins call it that. We prefer to call Central and Eastern Europe a place where we've chosen a socialist economy rather than capitalism. It really doesn't matter what you call it, does it? Like most people in your country, we just try to muddle through life as best we can, keeping ourselves, as I believe you Americans might say, 'under the radar.'"

Penny found herself fascinated and charmed by the man's openness. "How come you're able to travel to the West?"

"*Gnädige fräulein*," he said, reaching over and kissing Penny's hand, "Austria is not *quite* 'the West.' It was, until quite recently, a neutral country. Czechoslovakia, my most recent destination is behind the Iron Curtain. The city where I was born is less than forty American miles east of here."

As evening settled over Vienna and talk among the three of them grew more intimate, the man swept his arm from one side of the carpet of lights to the other, pointing out St. Stephen's, the city center, and finally a large, brightly lit area with a huge ferris wheel in the distance. "The *Riesenrad*," he said reverently. "Built sixty-three years ago to celebrate Franz Joseph's fiftieth year as Kaiser. The only ferris wheel from its time still in use today."

As they gazed toward the horizon, a blond-haired man a couple of years older than Birgit and Penny approached them. "Excuse me, but did I hear Danish being spoken?"

"You did," Birgit remarked, switching effortlessly to Danish.

"Arendt Christofferson, Aarhus."

"Birgit Petersen, København. Østerbro."

The two started yammering rapidly, so wrapped up in their own conversation they hardly seemed to notice that Penny and the other man were still there.

"Looks like your companion has found a new friend. I feel I have found a new friend as well." Penny felt a chill, even though there was hardly a breeze stirring in the woods above Vienna. "Our two Danes introduced themselves immediately. I've been talking with you for," he glanced at his watch, "forty-five minutes. Please excuse my discourtesy in not asking you your name or telling you mine. I'm Lev Arkady."

"Russian?"

He laughed. "If I were a dog, you'd call me a mongrel. I'm a wandering Jew, a rarity after the last War. Born in Bratislava, but I've been traveling all through Central and Eastern Europe for the last fifteen years."

"Eight out of every ten people at my high school in Los Angeles were Jewish."

"And you're not?"

"I'm not really any religion."

He paused for a moment. "I imagine you've had lots of suitors by now, a beautiful young woman like you." Penny's heart lurched. The man's flattery seemed absolutely sincere. As Penny looked more closely at him, he did not seem handsome in the classical sense, but he was by no means unattractive.

"Well, uh, not that many."

"I'm surprised."

"I had a serious love once. His parents were posted to Nairobi. He left with them."

"I'm sorry," he said simply. He seemed to realize that silence was more sensitive than meaningless words. At that moment, a waiter came by. Lev ordered two demitasses of Turkish coffee. "You were shivering a moment ago. I thought a hot beverage might warm you." Looking around, Penny found that Birgit and her new-found fellow were nowhere to be seen.

Recovering her equilibrium, she said, "I'm Penny Fullerton." The man rose to his feet, took her hand, and bowed formally, a grin on his face. "Welcome to Vienna, Penny Fullerton. One of the most romantic cities in the world is honored with one of the loveliest young women visiting the country."

Penny felt herself blush. "You don't live in Vienna?"

"Or anywhere else for very long."

"What do you do?"

"Nothing very important. I travel from place to place."

At that moment, Birgit and Arendt reappeared. She had high color in her cheeks. "Penny, could I speak to you for a moment in private?"

"Of course." Penny excused herself. They walked toward the ladies' room.

"Would you think me terribly rude if I asked you to let me

spend the evening with Arendt alone? I noticed you and that other fellow seemed to be hitting it off quite well together."

Penny raised her eyebrows. "Something I should know?"

"Ask me no questions and I'll tell you no lies."

"He *is* awfully cute."

"Yours or mine?"

"Well … both of them, really," Penny said.

"The American discovers Europe and its 'loose morals.' Just in case, do you know how to get back to the hostel?"

"Take the bus to the streetcar terminus, then take the tram back toward Stephansdom?" Penny said.

"Right. Am I to believe you also might not be returning tonight?"

"As you said …"

The girls both joined in, giggling, "Ask me no questions and I'll tell you no lies."

A few minutes later, Birgit and Arendt said their goodbyes. Penny watched as they drove off in a Volvo, which looked like a 1948 Ford. When she and Lev were alone once more, Lev said, "Penny, you must be quite hungry by now."

"I'm starved."

Lev gave her an odd look, then recovered. "Ah, an American idiom," he said. "During my childhood years that statement had a much more serious meaning."

This time, it was Penny's turn to be embarrassed. "Two different worlds," she murmured.

"Perhaps we can bring those worlds closer." Lev rose suddenly. "There's the bus. It only comes by once every forty minutes, so if we don't catch it now, it'll be a long walk or a long wait."

"Where to, My Prince?" Penny asked, surprising herself with her boldness.

"How lovely that sounds," Lev remarked seriously. "Might I suggest we take the bus to Grinzing, walk along the main street, and pick out whatever looks good?"

The bus descended from Cobenzl through a wide street canopied with leafy green trees, with walled residences abutting both sides. They exited at the second stop and found themselves in a charming village that bore no resemblance to the pretentious buildings of the inner city. As they wandered up and down the street, Lev pointed to an attractive vine-covered building and said, "Look, they've got a special sign out. The first pressing of their new green wine. That would probably be as good a place as any."

When Lev and Penny entered the building, she found it entirely different from the way it had looked from outside. They went through an arched entrance and immediately into a large open space exposed to the sky. Picnic tables and long benches spread throughout the space. A quartet wandered from table to table singing songs. Everyone in the *heuriger*, that's what they called the place, seemed to know every song, because the audience sang right along with the musicians.

A buxom young woman in a very low-cut white blouse with red and green piping brought them a carafe of white wine and two huge wineglasses almost as soon as they'd sat down. "*Taffelspitze?*" she asked.

"What's that?" Penny asked her companion.

"Boiled beef flanken."

"That sounds so boring. I thought Vienna was known for its wonderful cooking."

"Like *sachertorte* and *apfelstrudel*?" Lev teased.

"Well, you have to admit that *taffel*-whatever-she-said and the way you translated it doesn't make it sound like the most appetizing entrée I've ever eaten."

"Trust me?"

"Why not?"

"*Jawohl, Fräulein, zwei taffelspitze mit kartoflnsalat und rotkol, bitte.*"

"Now *that* was a mouthful," Penny said.

"Wait 'til you *taste* a mouthful. Feeling adventurous?"

"Yes."

"Then let's join in the singing."

"But I don't know *any* of these songs, Lev."

"More than half these people don't know the words. Just hum along, even if it's la-la-la. Maestro!" Lev called out, when the quartet had stopped playing for a moment. "*Bitte, 'Wien, Wien nur Du Allein?'*" he asked, handing the man a couple of bills.

"*Natürlich.*"

As the combo launched into the syrupy-sweet song, the patrons hummed along with the verse. When it came to the chorus, the entire restaurant except Penny and one or two others erupted at the top of their voices.

In Penny's mind everything meshed together into one of her life's most perfect moments. The wine, the camaraderie, and a companion who brought all the magic into focus. What could be better than this? Then the *taffelspitze* and the rest of what Lev had ordered arrived, and for Penny, heaven touched the earth. Melt-in-your mouth strips of beef that looked like the corned beef she'd eaten back in Los Angeles, but that's where the similarity ended. Spices that melded together as melodiously as a baroque concert, accompanied by hot potato salad, the best she'd ever tasted, and buttery sweet-and-sour cabbage, all washed down with light, piquant, sweet white wine. And through it all, the lovely refrain.

Afterward, Lev and Penny wandered into the street. She felt warm and mellow and *very* romantic. In her eyes Lev had grown handsomer by the moment.

"Penny, look," Lev said, pointing to the sky where a full moon had made its appearance, bathing their steps in a silver light. "I know a place we can go where the magic of this evening will continue."

Thoughts entered Penny's mind, half guilty, half wanton, with fear of consequences battling with what she had missed for so long. But Lev surprised her with his suggestion, which was not what she'd thought it would be.

"The *Stadtpark*, the City Park," he said.

"Why there?"

"Trust me," he replied.

When the tram arrived at one of the many entrances to the large central park, Penny heard the refrain of violin music in the distance. Lev took her hand. She didn't resist and even more certainly she didn't *want* to resist. He led her toward the sound of the music. Soon they came to a fenced-off area where an audience of fifty sat at tables, nursing wine or coffee. Lev and Penny stayed beyond the fence, thirty meters away, where they could easily see and hear the orchestra playing Strauss waltzes. The musicians and the ballet dancers who danced to the music were young and extraordinarily attractive. The men, dressed in faux military uniforms, came out of old picture books. The women wore brightly colored ball gowns.

"Come, dance with me," Lev urged in a soft voice.

It was a dream out of the last century, something Penny had never experienced before. She felt mesmerized as Lev led her in a gentle waltz under the trees. He was a smooth, accomplished dancer, easy to follow, and masterful. Penny's thoughts wandered and refocused. *Could I be falling in love in the space of a few hours? Impossible! Idiotic! But maybe not so crazy after all.*

An hour later, they left the park. Penny didn't feel tipsy, but she felt a warm buzz in her head, and in other places as well. Lev led her to the middle of Imperial Vienna, the *Rathaus,* the City Hall. When they got there, Penny gasped as she saw a white canvas three stories high and as wide as the building, which displayed a movie of a Mozart opera. Below the screen she heard the noise and saw the flashing lights of a street fair. Lev bought each of them a sausage and a large buttered pretzel. When Penny asked Lev what time it was, he said, with an enigmatic smile, "It's still early. It won't be midnight for at least ten minutes."

Penny didn't want the evening to end. She'd never felt so *alive*, so electrified in the moment. Without a word, she suddenly reached her arms around Lev's neck, pulled him toward her, and, in the middle of the thousands of people in the public square, she kissed him hungrily, passionately, more so than she'd ever kissed any man before, even Andy. She ground her body into his and was gratified when she felt his response. Soon he was kissing back, returning Penny's passion in equal measure.

"Let's ..." she whispered. "Are you staying nearby?"

"I am, Darling," he said. "But not tonight. We mustn't spoil this night of nights by doing something we shouldn't."

"But you want to. I can feel you do. I feel wicked. I've never felt so ..."

"As much as I want you, that is exactly why we should *not* do anything more tonight, Penny Fullerton. Once your American morality kicked in and you thought calmly about what happened, you'd never forgive yourself and you'd harbor resentment against me for the rest of your life."

"But ..."

"Why, look at that cheat!" he said, pointing to a game of chance ten meters away. "They've fixed it so the house wins nine times out of every ten."

"What are you talking about, Lev?" He quietly and skillfully showed Penny exactly how the booth game worked. "Want to have some fun?"

"Even more than I've already had tonight?"

"Different kind of fun. I'll show you how to beat that charlatan at his own game. Pretend you're a naive American. Scream and shout like crazy when you win, and …"

Half an hour later, a thoroughly demoralized proprietor was dazedly trying to figure out how he had lost a thousand schillings, about forty U.S. dollars, to a silly American ingénue. Penny's disappointment at not being able to consummate one kind of conquest was assuaged by the sheer excitement of having prevailed in an entirely different contest.

On the way back to the student hostel, Lev and Penny held hands and occasionally kissed, chastely this time.

"When I was growing up, I loved going to the penny arcade near my home."

"A penny arcade?" Lev asked. When the young woman explained the American term, he brightened visibly. "That's exactly how I make my living. What you call a penny arcade has been around for more than a hundred years. Did the arcade you went to have shooting galleries? Skee-ball? Horse racing pinball games?"

"My God!" Penny exclaimed. "I never dreamed I'd meet up with … gotten … close to … someone who was as wild about arcades as I am."

"It's a living," Lev responded mildly. "I think you Americans would say, 'It keeps me off the streets,' although that statement doesn't seem right."

"You're not married?"

"Never have been."

"Anything serious?"

"There was a young girl once … a prostitute …" He told her about Agata. At the end Penny found herself weeping so copiously she couldn't catch her breath. "Other than your Andy, have you ever …?"

"No."

"Me neither. Perhaps that's the real reason I said 'no' earlier this evening. I hope you didn't feel I was rejecting you."

"Maybe a little bit, but now I understand why."

"Penny, might we be ... friends?"

The young American smiled, a quiet smile that started deep inside of her and became as gentle as his words. "Only if you tell me one thing before we part tonight."

"Anything."

"That song they played earlier tonight in the restaurant, *Wien, Wien nur Du Allein*. What do the words mean?"

"Everything and nothing, really. The song was written fifty years ago, a year before World War I changed everything. I'll translate the refrain into English:

'Vienna, Vienna, you alone will always be the city of my dreams.
There, where the cute old houses are, there, where the lovely girls walk.
Vienna, Vienna, you alone will always be the city of my dreams
The place where I am deliriously happy, Vienna, Vienna, my Vienna.'"

Penny started weeping again, this time out of sheer joy at life. Lev started singing the refrain in German. When they reached her hostel, he graciously kissed Penny's hand, then softly kissed her lips and her eyes as he bade her goodnight.

❦

Birgit did not return that night. Penny didn't care, but at the same time she wanted to tell Birgit, to tell anyone for that matter, *everything* that had happened that evening. She wanted to shout it to the world. Maybe it was infatuation, maybe it was love, but whatever it was, it felt like nothing else on earth. Penny had never felt so *alive*, so happy simply to *be* alive!

The clock on the bedstand read 1:45. Penny didn't feel like sleeping, although she was exhausted. Just before she crashed into bed, she started scribbling the silliest things on a notepad at her tiny student desk. "Mrs. Lev Arkady. Penny Arkady. Mr. & Mrs. Arkady. *Frau* Arkady. *Herr und Frau* Lev Arkady." She felt her eyes grow heavy. Tears, happy tears, lay just below the surface as Penny pulled the covers up around her neck. The tall, gangly girl she had once been had metamorphosed. Lev was right. She *was* truly a beautiful, desirable young woman.

21

"Well, if it isn't Miss 'Ask me no questions and I'll tell you no lies,'" Penny said the following morning when she awoke and stretched languorously like a cat, still under the covers.

"Oh, you're still alive?" Birgit responded gaily. "I was just about to call the undertaker, or at least the housekeeper to throw you down the laundry chute. In case you're unaware, it's eleven o'clock. I see no sign of anyone else. Should I?"

"That's for me to know and you to find out. Actually, nothing happened, not that I didn't *want* it to. What time did you get in?"

"Seven this morning. Just in time for breakfast."

"And Arendt?"

"Better than the breakfast," Birgit said, laughing. "Are you going to see Lev again?"

"God, I hope so. He knows where I'm staying, but I haven't the slightest idea if he's still in Vienna." As dreamlike as last night had seemed, and as smitten as Penny had been, it had all happened so fast that she couldn't bring herself to feel sad, whichever way the incipient romance ultimately went. "What's on our menu today? More Arendt?"

"No. He hopped into his Volvo and said he was driving to Salzburg, then over the Grossglockner Pass to Italy. He suggested we go with him. I thanked him, but declined. I've got his address in Denmark. How about we do the Schönbrunn today?"

"Sounds good to me." And it was. Up to that time, Penny had never seen a real palace where kings and queens had actually lived. Franz Joseph was born there in 1830 and he died there eighty-six years later in 1916, during the raging days of World War I. Queen Elisabeth of Austria, Sisi, had walked there. Paintings of her appeared throughout the palace. In her day, people said no more beautiful woman had ever worn a crown. From the pictures on display, Penny thought she was certainly one of the most beautiful women who'd ever lived.

As she wandered through the rooms, Penny was overwhelmed by the sheer *majesty* of the place: solid mahogany tables that rose from below the marble floors; place settings etched with gold, *real* gold, not gold leaf, in elegant, graceful patterns; crystal chandeliers of the highest quality; and matching gold cutlery. She looked out the back and beheld a man-made forest and a huge manicured lawn going all the way out to the horizon.

Later that afternoon, the two roommates returned to the "Fürichgasse Hilton," both exhausted from their activities of the night before. As young and vigorous as they were, they realized that if they were going to absorb whatever Vienna had to offer in the evening to come, they wouldn't be able to enjoy it fully without a long afternoon nap.

The only disappointment came when Penny entered the hostel and the attendant gave her an envelope with a note inside. Opening it, she read the plain letterhead, "Lev Arkady, Entertainments" with no address. The body of the note said,

"*Dearest Penny,*

"*Last night was one of the most amazing and wonderful in my life. I hope it was for you as well. What a shame we had to meet on my last night here. I have an engagement with a small circus in Poland. I'll be traveling with them for the next few months. If fate wills it, we'll meet again. Have a wonderful journey through Europe. You deserve only the very best life has to offer, and I wish it for you. Please try not to forget me. I'll not soon forget you. Fondly, Lev.*"

◦◦❧◦◦

In the three days Birgit and Penny spent there, it became apparent that Venice held a unique place on the planet. They walked from one end of the town to the other or they rode through the Grand Canal in a vaporetto, a large motorboat which served as the Venetian community bus. There were no cars and no roads, but hundreds of walkways enabled the girls to easily navigate the entire city. And there was so much to see.

On their third and last day in La Serenissima, Penny noticed her skin was itchy. She thought nothing of it. *Probably just a skin allergy. If it keeps up, I'll have it checked when I got back home.*

Penny and Birgit traveled from one end of Italy to the other, from Lake Como, where charming, raffish men didn't hesitate to stare frankly and appreciatively at Birgit and Penny when they donned their skimpy two-piece bathing suits, to the Vatican City, where the handsome Swiss guards made them purchase long pants which covered their calves, despite the fact that it was ninety degrees outside. Hill towns and Capri's Blue Grotto and the unmatchable Amalfi Drive. Dancing on the beach adjacent to the Adriatic Sea at Pineto and flirting with American Navy guys at Livorno and Naples. The entire country presented a comic opera come to life. Penny felt so welcome here, so much at home, perhaps because she'd become so used to transplanted Italians, or the sons and daughters of transplanted Italians, whose pop music ruled the airwaves.

Penny's only concern was that the itching didn't stop and she noticed a slight fever which came on at night. But the itching and fever abated the day after the girls crossed the French frontier. "Do you think I could have been allergic to a country I loved?" Penny asked Birgit, jokingly.

"Could be," Birgit replied nonchalantly. "I'm just glad you're back to being your old self. You seemed a little worn out during the last few days."

"Probably all that travel catching up with me. There's a street fair in Menton tonight and I'm sure up for that!"

Even though Menton was just over the border from Italy, Birgit and Penny could tell in the first half hour they were there that France differed from its neighbor to the southeast. People of both sexes seemed somehow *sexier*. The street fair emphasized the *joie de vivre*. A guy who couldn't have been more than sixteen came up to Penny, boldly stuffed confetti down the front of her blouse, then giggled and trotted jauntily away as she turned to grab him. Birgit tripped the fellow and she and Penny descended on him, grabbing nearby confetti, stuffing it down his shorts, then tickling him 'til he was out of breath with laughter.

Penny felt herself being tickled from behind. Turning, she saw it was a girl her own age. The gamin jabbered away in French. Penny was delighted that she actually understood every third or fourth word. She tried her own college French, haltingly at first, then, as a group of kids who'd gathered around them nodded encouragement, more fluently. Later, they all sat down at a nearby picnic table that had been set up on the periphery of the small park and, using bits of French, bits of English, some German, some Danish, and mostly gestures, they managed to talk about what young people everywhere seemed to talk about most, clothes, records, and, as always, the opposite sex.

Three weeks later, after meandering through the south of France, into Switzerland, and back into France again, Penny and Birgit made it to Paris, the City of Light. During the past few days, Penny had noticed the return of the itching and she felt lethargic, but she felt it was just her body preparing to conquer Paris, to live twenty-four hours a day and to burn the candle at both ends, for who knew when she'd return?

The moment Penny arrived at the Gare du Lyon and exited the train, she felt magic in the atmosphere, more oxygen in the Parisian air than anywhere else in the world. No itching, no tiredness, just absolute excitement. For the week they spent in Paris before they took the train to LeBourget Airport, Birgit and Penny painted that town every color of the rainbow.

Penny had drunk alcoholic beverages before. Back in the States there'd been something of a forbidden fruit thrill when you drank before you were twenty-one, but here everyone had a glass of wine with dinner and sometimes lunch. Penny noticed she felt a slight pain under her arms an hour or so after she'd sipped wine. The easy cure for that was she simply stopped drinking wine.

At LeBourget, Birgit and Penny cried a little because their wondrous summer was coming to an end, but they had a huge scrapbook of memories in their minds, and they'd have so much to share when they got back to what now seemed like such a small, provincial little college town, especially since they were now citizens of the larger world.

22

Shortly after school started, Penny's symptoms returned with a vengeance: a light, almost imperceptible fever that came and went. Night sweats, which she'd never experienced before. A sluggishness that made it hard for Penny to keep up with her classes or take part in the bustle of campus activities. Conversely, Penny struggled to fall asleep at night, no matter how exhausted she'd felt during the day. Most curious of all, she noticed a swelling under both her armpits. These bulges felt hard, like small rubber balls, but when she looked under her arms, they didn't seem to show. Penny seemed to be losing weight. Stepping on the scale each morning, she noticed she was effortlessly shedding pounds. At last she'd look like the slender-waisted girls who wore tight-fitting jeans.

At first, Penny didn't tell anyone how she felt. Surely the swelling would go away and the fever would subside.

Birgit was the first to notice something amiss. "Aren't you losing a little too much weight?" she asked. She looked at Penny's legs, which had a bit of a rash, then noticed her ankles seemed swollen. "Maybe you should see a doctor, just to make sure everything's O.K. How long have you had the swelling?"

Penny shrugged. "A couple of weeks, maybe a couple of months."

The following week, Penny and Birgit had planned to go on a hike with a few other girls from the dorm. Since Penny was the tallest and had always been athletic, it should have been an easy trek for her. Nevertheless, she had difficulty walking. Birgit looked at her oddly, then took Penny's arm and walked along with her. Penny didn't want to worry her best friend by telling her that almost every step she took hurt. By the time they returned from the walk, less than two hours later, Penny felt spent.

"Your friend is very sick," the surgeon said bluntly. "We need to admit her immediately and run some tests."

When the test results came back, Dr. Stuntz faced her directly. "Penny, we're sending you by ambulance down to U.C.L.A. Medical Center."

"What is it, Doctor?" Penny asked uncertainly.

"It's called Hodgkin's disease."

"*Hodgkin's* disease?" she asked, thoroughly confused. Penny had never heard of it, and no one breathed the word *cancer*. Though, of course, that is exactly what it was.

A nurse took Penny upstairs for her appointment. When the receptionist called out her name, she went into a small examining room and sat in a chair. The attendant told her she could remain in her hospital gown.

After a few minutes, the door opened, and the tallest Asiatic man Penny had ever seen walked in, wearing dark gray trousers and a blue cotton shirt with the sleeves rolled up. He wasn't wearing a white coat, he didn't carry a stethoscope, and his eyes were large, round, and consummately gentle. Penny had expected a much older man. He looked to be in his early forties. When he reached out to shake Penny's hand, he introduced himself as Jacob Lo.

Dr. Lo didn't say much, which added to Penny's confusion. At first, he seemed mildly forbidding. There were none of the pleasantries in which her previous doctors had engaged, not even the obligatory smile, but that was fine, since Penny didn't feel much like smiling either. Dr. Lo eyed her carefully, taking in her hair and face, even studying her hospital gown. Penny was sure she looked a sorry sight in the baggy brown bathrobe that had become her daily uniform. Who needed to dress up for a doctor, anyway?

If Dr. Lo held back on some of the niceties, he also spared Penny the endless questions she had been asked in recent weeks. He seemed able to tell at a glance the answer to all of those questions.

Instead, as he examined Penny rapidly, with a sure, firm, confident hand, he asked questions no other doctors had asked: What did Penny like most about school? Did she have any hobbies? Was she planning to go to graduate school? What were her favorite books and authors?

Penny had only one question for him: "Do I have Hodgkin's?"

"You might," he replied, as lightly and noncommittally as if she'd asked him whether she had a cold. "You might."

A few days later, Dr. Lo came to see Penny in the examining room. Without fanfare, he described the tests he was ordering. During the next several days, they took countless x-rays. She would be in and out of different gowns, hustled into dark, cold rooms with monstrous metal machines she had never seen before. She took tests that lasted minutes and tests that took hours to perform and made her ill.

The staff treated her kindly. Even by the billing clerks constantly reassured her, "Worry about getting well, not about the bills."

Penny went home to Jack's apartment. Several times a week, she traveled to U.C.L.A. Hospital where she met privately with Dr. Lo. He would examine her, chart her progress, and see how she was faring.

Penny determined she would survive. She forced herself to dress up when she saw Dr. Lo. She acted poised and upbeat, even though she wasn't feeling either. She refused to cry, no matter how sad she felt, no matter what news he delivered. When Penny and Dr. Lo talked, it rarely concerned medical matters. Mostly they chatted about books, his favorites and hers, and hobbies. She learned of his many pet peeves, from the defeated presidential candidate, Richard Nixon, to the blatant sex that seemed to be creeping into even mainstream novels.

"How could you possibly know how I'm doing without conducting a thorough exam?" Penny asked him one day.

"By looking into your eyes," he replied.

The test results came back. Penny's illness had spread far beyond the site she'd originally noticed. She had secretly glanced at her chart, which said that out of four possible stages of Hodgkin's, the fourth being the worst and hardest to treat, she was in stage three.

Dr. Lo never discussed Penny's prognosis; he never even used the word. He didn't cite odds of survival or years to live. He simply spoke of the need to begin treatment, which he minimized by saying it would consist of several weeks of radiation. He made it sound as simple and innocuous a taking a course of antibiotics. He warned of only one major consequence, it was unlikely she would ever be able to have children.

When the radiation treatment became so intense she could no longer eat, Mi-Ra Paik thought of an ingenious solution: ginger and olives. She began to bring Penny cans of black olives with no pits, the enormous ones labeled "Colossal." Penny couldn't bear to look at food. The mere thought of eating made her ill, but she was somehow able to nibble at the olives and the ginger root. Slowly, she would eat an olive followed by a small bite of the sweet, hot ginger. While all around her, the patients in radiation became weak from the treatments, collapsed, or dropped out, never to be seen again, Penny continued to eat ginger and olives.

Despite Jack's efforts to bring in foods that had been her favorites from an early age, she was hardly able to eat as much as a spoonful of anything else. Penny became convinced the olive and ginger regimen, not the radiation treatments, were healing her.

Birgit called from San Luis Obispo every day. It must have cost her a fortune, but she told Penny that she was far more important than a milkshake. "How are you doing, Penny? Are the radiation treatments working? Are you cured yet?"

There were no answers that fall or during the mild winter that followed. *Cured* was a vague term, used only on TV and in women's magazines. There was only the chance that the relentless treatments, if Penny could survive them, would interrupt the disease's pernicious advance.

There were times when Penny felt so weak that all she wanted to do was sleep. Mi-Ra came to Jack's apartment every couple of hours to feed her ginger and olives. Penny took them grudgingly. Mi-Ra fed her and tended to her as patiently as if she were a small child.

In early April, Birgit came down to Los Angeles. Penny appeared thinner than ever and frail. She stared at Birgit, beaming and gorgeous in a bright green sweater that set off her long, white-blonde hair, as if she were a visitor from another planet.

The girls visited for hours. Birgit asked why Penny hadn't bothered to comb her hair. Penny was afraid to tell Birgit the truth: if she brushed it too much, some would fall out. Until now, it had been Penny's secret. Her hair had grown longer since Europe, and it was only falling out in the back, where she'd been heavily radiated. Penny figured that if she arranged it artfully, no one would notice. Birgit took out a hairbrush from her handbag and began to lightly brush Penny's hair with it. They both pretended not to notice the thin strands that landed on Penny's shoulder.

One morning, Birgit announced she was taking Penny out to lunch. Nothing Penny said could stop her. She drove to West Hollywood, to a restaurant called Micelli's on LaCienega. Although Penny ate almost nothing, she felt chatty.

All around them were young businessmen, wearing suits. Penny stared at them. Elegant men, wild-looking men, young actors, agents, lawyers, bankers. Penny pointed them out to Birgit, remarking how wonderful they looked. They seemed rich and important. Penny told Birgit that someday she'd marry a man who wore expensive clothes.

At that moment at Micelli's, as Penny nibbled at a breadstick, for the first time since she'd been diagnosed, "some day" seemed like a possibility. After lunch, the two friends wandered up LaCienega to a boutique. Birgit encouraged Penny to go in. She went to a rack and pulled out a knit sweater in a rich shade of blue, clingy with a plunging neckline. "Don't you think it's too low cut?" Penny asked Birgit, fearful she would say yes.

"It's perfect. Why don't you try it on?"

Penny walked out in her new sweater, feeling resplendent and, for the first time in months, pretty and sexy.

As spring wore on, Penny dared to ask Dr. Lo if she might be able to go back to Cal Poly in the fall.

"You *will* go back to Cal Poly," he declared. His confident tone brooked no resistance. Because his voice sounded so brisk and refreshing, Penny began to feel hopeful. Perhaps she might one day be well again.

Within months, it seemed as if it had never happened.

There were no obvious traces of Penny's illness except she was pale and still tired easily. She concentrated on eating and trying to regain some of the weight she had lost.

One day, shortly after the treatment had ended, Penny developed a high fever. She returned to U.C.L.A., but Dr. Lo was nowhere to be found. The emergency room doctor on call prescribed horse pills she could barely swallow. When Dr. Lo returned, Penny showed him the pills and he ordered her to stop taking them. The fever disappeared as mysteriously as it had come.

In September, Penny returned to San Luis Obispo. With the exception of Birgit, she kept to herself. She no longer had many friends and no boyfriends. Illness had made her wary. She decided to take life's gifts sparingly, like olives, one at a time. Penny lived for her checkups with Dr. Lo, once a month at first, then every couple of months. She felt safe there, as if she were out of danger inside that little examining room, with him at her side. He did nothing much except talk. He no longer prescribed medicines, injections, or tests. As long as Penny looked well, and he insisted he knew the moment she walked in, that proved that the disease had weakened, and they could move on to more important subjects.

They chatted for hours, as if his other patients, duties, and responsibilities were put on hold while he and Penny huddled in the small room that hadn't changed from the day she'd first climbed onto the gurney, a desperately frightened young woman with no hope at all.

One day, a couple of years after the treatment, Penny asked if she were cured. She had read about five-year marks and ten-year marks, or even remission.

Dr. Lo frowned at the word *cured*. Hodgkin's, he declared, wasn't curable. "It will return," he warned. "It will come back."

Penny went home so panic-stricken she couldn't sleep or eat. Of course, she couldn't confide her fears to anyone. Cancer was not the stuff of cocktail party conversation.

The following day, without bothering to make an appointment, Penny returned to U.C.L.A. and demanded to see Dr. Lo. She wanted to know when "it" would be coming back. He looked at Penny, somewhat startled. She could tell he was in a pensive mood. She had learned over the months that there was no kinder or more caring human being on earth than this tall, gangly Asiatic man.

He gently took Penny's arm. "Some of us have this much to live," he told her, indicating the space from her fingertips to her wrist, "and some of us have this much to live," he said, showing her the much longer space from her wrist to her shoulder, "and you don't know, and I don't know which it will be, so forget about it."

And that was the closest Dr. Lo and ever came to discussing Penny's "prognosis."

23

"It's been almost a year since the Hodgkins went into remission. You haven't spent any money that I can tell, you haven't dated, and you've had a pretty boring year. Why don't you spend a month with me in Scandinavia? You've seen the south, but my homeland and its neighbors are pretty spectacular too."

"I don't know," Penny replied. "The thought of another five-day car trip to New York and ten or twelve hours in the air might be a little hard to take."

"Oh, come on, girl," Birgit snapped. "Like your friend Dr. Lo said, you don't know how long you have or you don't have. If you pack yourself into an icebox full of self-doubt and 'I can't do it, it's too hard,' you'll die before you've *lived*. Besides, there've been a lot of changes in two years. They're flying from New York to Copenhagen in five hours. All the big international airlines have started flying jets. SAS has an over-the-pole flight from L.A. to Copenhagen."

The more she reflected on Birgit's words, the more Penny came to realize her best friend was absolutely right. She *had* closeted herself in the year-and-a-half since she'd been diagnosed, *Acting like I'm made of glass.* She had been asked out on dates, but she'd always made excuses. She'd missed out on a year-and-a-half of life and the only thing she had to show for it were grades that got her on the Dean's list. Big deal. After her bout with Hodgkins' she was not looking for a thrill ride on life's roller coaster. Still ...

By May, Birgit had coaxed another Cal Poly friend of theirs, Dana Wagner, to make it a threesome. Dana asked if they'd mind if her older brother, Dave, who was graduating U.C.L.A. with a bachelor's in electronic engineering, came with them. "It never hurts to have a man along. Might be some protection." The three girls laughed because they knew Birgit would be on her home turf.

"It's O.K. with me," Penny replied. The thought of an older guy, an *American* older guy, and an engineer, sounded good to her.

During the month they spent in Scandinavia, the four young people immersed themselves in the city of Hans Christian Andersen and Birgit Petersen for a week before renting a Volvo and driving up to Stockholm. Penny, who'd regained the spirit she'd lost during her illness, exuded the confidence of an old European hand, even though it was only her second journey to the Continent and her first time in Scandinavia.

During the trip, Dave Wagner proved to be a most congenial companion: easygoing, pleasant to be with, good looking in a chiseled-face kind of way, and six-foot two-inches tall, a man Penny could "look up to."

As the summer and the Scandinavian journey approached their end, Penny realized that rather than a lightning rod of lust and excitement, she craved steadiness, a life's companion who would not make inordinate demands on her, a friend and partner more than a flash of chemistry. Dave Wagner seemed to feel the same way. As summer gave way to fall, their courtship progressed naturally, with no hassles and no great drama. Neither was surprised when Dave proposed to Penny during his first semester in the Master's program at U.C.L.A.

Shortly after her twenty-second birthday, the newly married Penny Wagner went to work as an assistant manager at a small engineering firm in North Hollywood. Six months later, she was more shocked and delighted than Dave to discover she'd beaten the odds set by almost every doctor except Jacob Lo, and was pregnant. Jim emerged healthy and lusty on July 4, 1964, followed a year later by Kassy.

When Dave secured a well-paying position as an electronics engineer at Teledyne, the family moved to Encino, where they purchased a larger home than Penny had ever lived in. Dave's parents lived in Studio City, at the conjunction of Los Angeles and the San Fernando Valley, close enough to be convenient baby sitters, far enough away that the two generations didn't have to spend dinner together every night.

By the beginning of 1968, Penny had settled into the American dream: two kids, both of whom were enrolled in a nearby pre-school; a Volvo station wagon, tennis with girlfriends twice a week, an exercise class three days a week at the local club; and annual physical exams which, thank God, had shown no re-emergence of Hodgkins.

Life was a good place to be, aside from the pesky, nasty little war in Vietnam which came into her home via Chet Huntley and David Brinkley at six o'clock each evening. Since none of her relatives or friends had anyone *over there*, the perpetual reference to body counts, this offensive, or that battle, created only a mild background buzz on the TV. Teledyne was a major defense contractor and Dave received regular bonuses. While he occasionally came home from work as late as eight at night, after she'd put Jimmy and Kassy down, for the most part he was home in time for dinner and they took turns bathing the kids.

Their lives had settled down to an every-day's-more-or-less-the-same existence. On Monday, January 22, that changed when *Rowan and Martin's Laugh In* premiered on NBC. The world may not have been all that funny, but *Laugh In* sure was. Whatever else they did, Penny and Dave were sure to be home every Monday night at eight to catch it. Little could the Wagners have expected that the next twelve months would be the most turbulent period the United States had known since the American Civil War.

※

Penny wiped the sweat off her brow as she and her sister-in-law Dana walked off the court and into the nearby lounge. Dana ordered an iced tea for herself and told the waiter to bring a tall glass of water for Penny. They'd just started nursing their beverages when the noon news issued from a TV set suspended from a wall near the bar.

A grainy black and white close-up photograph of the back of a middle-aged man with his pistol raised filled the screen. A small, slender, much younger man with thick bushy hair, who couldn't have been more than eighteen, stood with his hands behind his back, no doubt shackled, his eyes closed, seemingly weeping. The barrel of the pistol was less than a foot from his head.

"In Saigon, combat photojournalist Eddie Adams brought the Vietnamese war home to a level that underscores the human element of the conflict much more graphically than nightly body bag counts," the announcer said. "In this photo released by the *New York Times*, South Vietnamese Police Chief General Nguyen Ngoc Loan is shown executing a Viet Cong prisoner, Nguyen Van Lem, in a street in downtown Saigon. The worldwide reaction to this picture has polarized both sides of the issue …"

Penny stopped drinking her water in mid-sip and gaped at the photo. The simplicity of the shot was terrifying. On one side of the police chief, a soldier in combat fatigues looked on menacingly. On the other side of the prisoner, someone who looked like a postman was running up a street abutted by square three-story buildings. The terror in the prisoner's face was riveting.

The newscaster went on, "Those who support our South Vietnamese allies pointed out that the day before yesterday Viet Cong forces launched a series of surprise attacks across South Vietnam on *Tet*

Nguyen Dan, the first day of the year in the traditional lunar calendar and the most important Vietnamese holiday. Their goal in what is now being called the *Tet* Offensive was to strike military and civilian command centers throughout South Vietnam and to spark a general uprising among the population. Meanwhile, a growing number of antiwar protesters, many of them about the same age as the prisoner who was executed, condemned the United States for supporting what they called a corrupt puppet government which routinely committed war atrocities …"

"Wow!" Dana Wagner remarked. "Pretty sickening."

"What, the picture or the war?" Penny asked.

"The whole thing. Does anybody even know why we're there in the first place?"

"I've never given it much thought."

"Neither have I, but maybe we should. We seem to have gotten so used to hearing more than we need to hear about it every night that it's no more real to us than those old World War II newsreels. You ever notice most Americans over there seem to be Black?"

Penny scratched the side of her nose uncomfortably, but said nothing.

<hr />

At the end of that month, Walter Cronkite, the single most trusted voice in America, who'd just returned from a trip to Vietnam to cover the aftermath of the *Tet* Offensive, closed his nationally televised editorial report, "Vietnam – Who, What, When, Where, Why?" with the statement, "We have been too often disappointed by the optimism of American leaders, both in Vietnam and Washington, to have faith any longer in the silver linings they find in the darkest clouds. They may be right that Hanoi's offensive has been forced by the Communist realization that they could not win the longer war of attrition, and that the Communists hope that any success in the offensive will improve their position for eventual negotiations. But it now seems more certain than ever that the bloody experience of Vietnam will end in a stalemate. This summer's almost certain standoff will either end in real give-and-take negotiations or terrible escalation; and for every means we have to escalate, the enemy can match us. That applies to the invasion of the North, the use of nuclear weapons, or committing one hundred, or two hundred, or three hundred thousand more American troops to the battle. And with each escalation, the world comes closer to the brink of cosmic disaster.

"To say that we are closer to victory today is to believe, in the face of the evidence, the optimists who have been wrong in the past. To suggest we are on the edge of defeat is to yield to unreasonable pessimism. To say that we are mired in stalemate seems the only realistic, yet unsatisfactory, conclusion. It is increasingly clear to this reporter that the only rational way out will be to negotiate, not as victors, but as an honorable people who lived up to their pledge to do the best they could."

Following Cronkite's editorial report, President Lyndon Johnson reportedly said, "If I've lost Cronkite, I've lost Middle America."

On March 31, President Johnson announced that he would not seek reelection.

Four days later, the Reverend Martin Luther King was shot dead at the Lorraine Motel in Memphis, Tennessee. Riots erupted in every major American city and lasted for several days afterwards.

The bond that had held the United States together for more than a hundred years was starting to fray.

❦

During the same month, a phonograph record was released in the United States. The song had originally been offered to Tony Bennett, who'd turned it down. Thereafter, it was offered to a sixty-seven year old Black man. The song initially sold fewer than 1,000 copies because the head of ABC Records did not like the song and did not promote it, but it was a major success in the United Kingdom, where it reached number one the same month President Johnson announced he would not run for President. The song made Louis Armstrong the oldest male ever to top the charts, and the words became both an anthem and an antidote to what was going on in the world that March.

> I see trees of green, red roses too
> I see them bloom, for me and you
> And I think to myself
> What a wonderful world …
>
> The colors of the rainbow, so pretty in the sky
> Are also on the faces, of people going by
> I see friends shaking hands, sayin', "How do you do?"
> They're really sayin', "I love you"
>
> I hear babies cryin', I watch them grow
> They'll learn much more, than I'll ever know
> And I think to myself
> What a wonderful world.

BOOK III
THE TIMES THEY ARE A'CHANGIN'

24

Lev awoke at six in the morning. He'd been in Kiev for the last two weeks. During his fortnight in the Ukrainian capital, Alexander Dubček had replaced Antonín Novotný as First Secretary of the Slovak Communist Party, becoming the *de facto* leader of Czechoslovakia. The change of regime merited a small article at the bottom of page six in *Segodnya*. It had caught Lev's eye, first because no matter how long he'd been gone, he still considered Bratislava his home town, and second because it was his *job* to know everything there was to know about everything that mattered in his life.

As he rubbed the sleep from his eyes, he reflected briefly on the dream from which he'd just awakened. A tall, attractive girl he'd met in Vienna more than seven years ago, what was her name? He searched his memory, but all he could recall was that she'd been American, so wide-eyed and innocent. The Americans he'd met were so different from Eastern Europeans. They walked with their heads held high, shoulders back, a spring in their step, as if they owned the world. Which, for the most part, they did. Of course there was that mess in Vietnam … but that was their problem not his.

Penny. *That* was her name. Odd. She still invaded his dreams every now and again. Not frequently, but often enough. Probably married with a couple of kids by now. Shame, really.

His own life had developed into a routine which, if not unpleasant, was predictable. At thirty-four, Lev managed to maintain a profile low enough so as to go unnoticed by the authorities. He always remembered what brand of cigarettes or brandy or nylon stockings the border guards preferred. His midway shows and games played to larger audiences each season. Never married, Lev traveled widely. Last year, he'd ranged from Tallinn to Istanbul, from the Black Sea to Prague, and, thanks to his assortment of passports, into the West as well.

Along the way, he'd amassed an ever-growing series of acquaintances from whom he regularly managed to borrow apartments, and often feminine companions, for brief periods of time. These lodgings were considerably roomier than sleeping in his lorry and far cheaper than even the most run-down transient hotel rooms. Despite the drab grayness and economic strangulation in the Socialist Workers' Paradise, Lev had put by a significant cache of funds in a series of numbered accounts in Switzerland. In addition to the passbooks he kept with a friend in Vienna, he had duplicate passbooks in bank safe deposit boxes throughout Eastern Europe.

Two weeks ago, he'd cadged the use of a friend's apartment as well as the favors of that man's former girlfriend. Despite the cold Kievan winter, his bed had been quite warm at night.

He ducked with practiced deftness between the hanging clothes and crumbling bathroom fittings and showered. Praise God the apartment had never run out of hot water and there was enough to allow him the luxury of actually shaving in the shower while raising his body temperature sufficiently to face the frigid morning. When he'd finished, he turned the taps as hard as they would go, then finished them off with a wallop of the wooden mallet at hand.

The last recollection of his dream disappeared with the water slowly seeping down the antiquated drain.

The bedroom was the smallest of the three rooms that made up the tiny apartment: an alcove with a cupboard and a bed. But Lev was accustomed to confined spaces. While he dressed and packed his small cardboard valise, the apartment block began to wake up.

First, through the adjoining wall, came the Vitalys' alarm clock sounding six-thirty, followed by their crazy mongrel dog howling to be let out. *The poor Vitalys, I must take them a small gift before I leave.* Last week Yekaterina had lost her father and on Friday Igor's brother had been rushed to the hospital with severe appendicitis. *I'll give them some honey.* In the same instant he found himself smiling at the thought of the young widow in Tambulosin who'd given him several jars of the sweet stuff, and several other sweet memories besides.

After the Vitalys came the petulant cries of the Nekratievs' baby son cutting his first teeth and a moment later, through the floorboards, the boom of their new Japanese stereo thumping out the latest British rock. *How on earth could they afford such things? Elizabeth was always pregnant and Sasha earned a hundred fifty rubles a month.* After the Nekratievs came the dour Karpovs. Nothing but Radio Kiev for them. A week ago, a large segment of the Karpovs' balcony had fallen down, killing a policeman and a dog. Some cynical college students in the block had wanted to take up a collection for the dog.

Lev had quickly acclimatized himself to his surroundings. During the past three winters, he'd become a block legend as a "go to" man. On Mondays there was a chance of fresh chickens and root vegetables, which he'd purchased privately from several small villages east of L'viv over the weekend. His friend Tanya's uncle functioned as a dealer for smallholders. Lev must phone Tanya later this morning.

The theatre tickets. As soon as he picked up his lorry, he'd go over to the offices of *Segodnya* and collect the two front-row seats which the editor, Barzinye, had promised him after Lev had given him a lead, which had led to the newspaper uncovering a minor scandal in the city's waterworks administration.

After brunch and shopping at the local flea market for low-end prizes to give away at his entresorts, Lev would trade his theatre tickets with the porter, Moritz, who had pledged him thirty bars of imported French soap wrapped in decorative paper. He'd give three of those fancy soaps as a gift to the young woman who'd been such a joyous nighttime companion. With the remainder, Lev would buy the bolt of pure wool green cloth that the manager of a small textile mill was keeping locked in his storeroom for the traveling showman.

This afternoon, just before he embarked for L'viv, he'd hand the cloth and an ancient Singer sewing machine he'd carried for years, to Handelsmann the broker in exchange for a newer East German sewing machine and two "cowboy" shirts in his size.

As he stepped out of his apartment into the wide boulevard, he bundled his greatcoat tighter, appreciating the warmth of the black lamb's wool karakul on his head. Standing on the cold pavement, he loosened his wrists and shoulders and rolled his head round his collar to relax himself for the day ahead. He turned his mind outward and let the city's conflicting smells and sights and sounds envelop him. The stink of Russian petrol, tobacco, cheap scent, and icy water running in the gutters. The sporadic charges of commuter cars, the belching brown lorries thundering through the potholes in pursuit. The eerie emptiness in between. The Russian limousines with their blackened windows, the unmarked buildings splitting before their time. Were they office blocks, barracks, or schools? The dough-faced boys smoking in the doorways, waiting. The chauffeurs and taxi drivers reading newspapers in their parked cars, waiting. The unspeaking group of solemn men in greatcoats and hats, staring at a closed door, waiting.

From the metro, a group of teenaged girls in woolen skirts and sweaters and boys in denim jackets, seemingly oblivious to the cold, walked purposefully to work or to school, their expressions uniformly glum. The early food lines had a restless, unsettled look. Grim-faced labor heroes and war veterans, their breastplates of medals jingling as they waded through the crowds, had an air of being late for wherever they were marching. Doing nothing was itself an act of opposition. *Because by doing nothing, we change nothing,* Lev thought. *And by changing nothing, we hang on to what we understand, even if it is the bars of our own jail.*

Hearing a voice close beside him, Lev swung around and discovered an old couple in their best clothes asking him the way to somewhere. He was vaguely aware of the area for which they were searching, and politely pointed his finger in the general location. They nodded their thanks silently.

Lev retraced his steps, pausing at windows spotted with an accumulation of dust and caked snow, examining what they offered. Painted wooden dolls. For whom? Dusty tins of fruit or perhaps fish. Battered packets hanging from red string, contents a complete mystery. Jars of pickled herring. He approached the parking garage. A drunk-eyed peasant woman pushed a bunch of dying tulips wrapped in newspaper toward him. Rummaging through his pockets, he found a crumpled ruble note and pressed it into her withered, wrinkled hand.

A green Lada was parked outside the garage, its radiator smashed. The driver was leaning over the hood, detaching the wiper blades as a precaution against theft. The hubcaps had already been removed and were resting in the opened trunk where, presumably, the wipers would join them in a few moments.

The only differences between Kiev, Moscow, Warszawa and Berlin were street names and languages. The people, the cars, the trucks, the drab, gray cheerlessness of one place could be transplanted to another with no great effort of the imagination. *How unlike Vienna*, Lev thought. He wondered what London, Paris, and Rome would look like.

Ducking into a nondescript basement restaurant a block away from his borrowed apartment Lev, feeling hungrier than usual, ordered the standard Ukrainian breakfast fare, hot tea, boiled *kasha,* the ever present buckwheat groats, fried potatoes, bread and butter. The waitress, a large-boned middle-aged woman who'd known him for the past three years, nodded at him and gave her best excuse for a grin, displaying a mouth filled with steel fillings and teeth brown from years of harsh cigarettes.

"Leaving today, eh?"

He grunted.

"West?"

Another noncommittal grunt.

"Be nice to travel all the time."

"The grass always seems greener in the next pasture."

"Isn't it?"

"Gets lonely."

"Come now, Lev. They say you've got a woman in every town between here and L'viv. Probably a parcel of kids, too. Buncha' little half-kikes," she joked. "No offense."

"None taken m'dear. You know the old saying about how Jews are such optimists. On the eighth day out they cut a quarter of it off before they have any idea how long it's going to be."

Lev made no attempt to hide his Jewishness. Indeed, he played on it to his advantage wherever he could. Better to be everybody's "good Jew." Screw 'em with a smile.

That afternoon, his errands accomplished and having collected his van, Lev had gotten ten kilometers out of Kiev when two police vehicles, blue lights flashing, signaled him to pull over to the side of the road. An officious-looking, bemedaled man of fifty emerged from the lead vehicle, walked over to the lorry and presented a card case. The man told Lev in Russian that he was to be taken to police headquarters and detained for questioning.

"Are you KGB?" he asked the officer.

"Perhaps, perhaps not."

"And I, Sir, demand to see my Consul-general," Lev said, his tone distinctly bolder than he felt.

"Which one, Pan Arkady?" the officer asked lightly. "Your citizenship is rather ambiguous, wouldn't you say? Which of your many passports are you using today?"

"So you know who I am. Is that supposed to frighten me? You are obviously aware that I travel freely within the Socialist world, that I have no criminal record."

"*Da*," the man replied equably. "But you have not always paid the duties on goods you've transported across national frontiers. And, might I add, the goods you bring across borders are not always entirely legal."

"That's absurd!" Lev said hotly.

The man said nothing, merely smiled enigmatically.

"I have nothing to say to you until I speak with an avukat."

"As you wish, Pan Arkady. Of course, if you are detained that could be a long time, a very long time indeed. "

"What do you mean 'if'?"

"Would you like a cigarette?" the officer inquired solicitously.

"No, thank you."

"I'll have one," he said, coughing. "Dreadful habit, but I'm afraid it's one of my vices. Now, Pan Arkady, would you join me for a brief walk?"

"Do I have a choice, Major?"

"Ah, you are an astute man indeed," the officer answered, impressed that Lev recognized his rank. "Of course you do," the man chortled. "You might take a brief walk, have a little chat with me, and proceed on your way, or then, again, you might enjoy the free accommodations of a glorious Soviet hostel for some time."

"A prison, you mean?"

"Please, Pan Arkady, a re-education center."

"You make a very persuasive case, Major."

The officer turned on his heel, walked over to the lead police car, and spoke briefly with the driver. Throwing his half-smoked cigarette to the ground and stomping the ash out, he traipsed back to the second car and peremptorily dismissed it. The driver of the first car shut down the engine. "You're sure you'll be all right?" he asked.

The major removed a handgun from a half-hidden holster under his coat and pointed it toward the sky. "Have you ever known me to be otherwise, Lieutenant?" he asked. "This man and I would like to take a short stroll so I can ask some pertinent questions. Stand by and guard his van if you will."

"Of course."

As they started down a nearby trail, the Major asked solicitously, "Your health is good, Pan Arkady?"

"As far as I know," he remarked carefully. He had learned early on that law enforcement officers were not always his friends. "Is there any reason you made this invitation I could not refuse?"

The man paused, lit up another cigarette, and said, "My name is Karel Svoboda."

"Not a typical KGB name," Lev remarked.

"Does Boris Orlov sound more genuine?"

"If that's the name you go by. You're Czech? Slovak?"

"The latter."

"Am I to guess there's a reason I was 'detained' by a KGB officer, Major Orlov?"

"*Da*. I have been charged with instituting a crackdown on smuggling operations within the great Soviet Republic of the Ukraine."

"And I'm one of the bigger fish in the River Dnieper?"

That brought a belly laugh from the officer. "Hardly."

"May I ask the real reason, Major?"

"You may. But first let us move off a little ways down the path."

"Why?"

In response, Svoboda walked over to the nearest tree, plucked something that looked like an acorn, opened it, and showed Lev the battery.

"How do I know there aren't more devices planted along the trail?"

"You don't, Pan Arkady. There may well be more. You'll have to trust me."

"Trust you?" he responded, his eyebrows lifting in surprise. "You're *their* agent, their public face, the one who detained me, or don't you remember?"

"I remember quite well, Pan Arkady. You will also note I did not promise that you would or would not be arrested. I merely requested we have a small, private chat."

"I'm listening," Lev said.

"Pan Arkady, I have been a public servant for nearly thirty years."

"Yes?"

"One does not survive in the current regime without being a pragmatist. Don't get me wrong, I am in all ways loyal to my country and I would never do anything to betray my country's best interests."

"Czechoslovakia's, the Ukraine's, or Russia's?"

"For someone so diplomatic you are very direct," the officer said, smiling. "Our Soviet government, the beloved organ of the people, may continue in power for the next hundred years. Or it may not." Lev looked at him wordlessly. "How much international news have you heard?"

"About Dubček?"

"Precisely."

"Not much. Most likely a pragmatic bureaucrat like his predecessor," Lev said.

"He may be much different than you think," Svoboda replied.

"I can't see how that would be. He's certainly Brezhnev's man."

"Maybe. Maybe not."

"What do you mean?"

"You think the Russian bear is all powerful, a monolith?" The Major paused, bent over and picked up an aluminum can, stamped the aluminum can flat with his boot, and tossed it into a cloth bag he was carrying. "This for the rag picker. A few *hryvnya* apiece to add to my retirement." He chuckled. "You think our Muscovite rulers are all powerful?"

"Don't you?"

"In Moscow, yes. In Leningrad, certainly. Even in Kiev, because the Ukraine is a Russian dumping ground. But the farther you go afield … Ceausescu, Broz, Hoxha…"

"Are you saying Dubček will turn into one of them?"

"I think you may be surprised as months go by. You are aware that the only voices allowed to speak are those which tow the government line?"

"Isn't that the same everywhere, Major … uh … Major …"

"Karel will be fine while there are just the two of us," the officer said. "Of course, no one *needs* to complain about our glorious rulers while all things are good. But a few of us, those who *think*, are not all that enamored of the glorious socialist workers' paradise. While we are capable of putting a rocket into space or producing the largest man-made missile in the world, there are massive shortages of just about everything we *really* need – sugar, butter, gasoline, meat. It could be that the forces of discontent are beginning to outnumber those of the duly constituted legal authority."

"What does that have to do with me?"

Svoboda lit another cigarette with the ash of the one he'd not yet finished. "As I said earlier, I am a loyal public servant. I emphasize the word *public*. While I am loyal to our noble Soviet cause, I have a wife and three nearly grown children. My first loyalty is to them. You may see much more liberal policies as Mr. Dubček solidifies his position in Czechoslovakia. Socialism with a human face, if you will. It never hurts to maintain friendships on both sides of the fence. Do you understand what I am saying?"

"Of course."

"Pan Arkady, you travel to many places. You are not an important public figure. You slide effortlessly under nets set for bigger fish. If I were to be seen transmitting a message of support for Mr. Dubček, it would mean my job, perhaps even my life. On the other hand, those of us who secretly wish Mr. Dubček well, who pray that his policies might actually free us a little from Soviet, shall we say 'oppression,' … well, if you were somehow to pass a message to a series of half a dozen friends in various towns …"

"I see. You'd trust me to do that? How could you be so naïve? You've known me for less than an hour."

"More."

"How could you?"

"Your father was an English teacher at the *gymnasium* in Jewish Bratislava."

"How could you possibly have known that?" Lev asked, shocked.

"He was one of my first teachers," Svoboda replied quietly. "When your family left Bratislava, my father paid him a fair price for the furniture he left behind.

"Are you Jewish?"

"No. More what your people would call a 'Righteous Gentile.' Your father taught me to raise my voice against injustice wherever I found it."

"Yet you are KGB?"

"There are many of us in KGB. Not all of us are bound to obey our 'master.'"

"How can I turn you down?" Lev asked. Then, answering his own question in a soft murmur, he responded, "I can't. Not after what you've told me." Louder, he continued, "Your driver?"

"One of us as well."

Over the next several minutes, Svoboda gave Lev a list of men and women with whom he should communicate and pass a message of solidarity. As they returned to where the police car and Lev's van were parked, Svoboda unobtrusively handed Lev a folded piece of paper.

After Svoboda and his deputy had departed, Lev unfolded the note, which had the names and addresses of the Major's confreres. At the bottom of the note he read, "In the past we have done everything badly for the sake of the future. Now we must do everything right for the sake of the present. When we fail, God gives us what we deserve: another Stalin, another Brezhnev, another purge, another age of terrified monotony. Please try to remember, Pan Arkady, that there are truly good people in every society, and as naïve as we may seem, we believe that in the end right will triumph."

25

In early March, Lev arrived in Berlin. He found the address he'd been given in Friedrichshain, a flat area of industrial grounds and warehouses between the Östbahnhof and the River Spree, 27 Karl-Marx-Allee, to be a gargantuan warehouse, indistinguishable from any of a hundred industrial buildings in the vicinity. Lev parked his van in the dirt parking lot. Three dozen cars and vans, mostly Trabant 601s, Ladas, and Škodas, but even a few Volkswagens, crowded the area adjacent to Building 27. He emerged from the van and walked forty meters to a glass door marked "B." Underneath, he read the name "Willi Straus, *Surplus Waren*" in small discreet letters.

It took the better part of a minute before the door was answered by a barrel-chested, mustachioed man his own age, who wore a checked shirt, American-style blue jeans, and a pair of overalls.

"Herr Strauss?"

"You must be Lev Arkady. Major Svoboda wrote that you might be coming. You have not been followed?"

"Not that I know of."

"Wouldn't matter if you had been." He laughed. "Karel, being a loyal KGB man is used to seeing spiders where there are no webs. You know his uncle Ludvik just became president of Czechoslovakia."

"Should we be talking like this? Here?" Lev raised his eyebrows.

"Why not?" the other responded good-naturedly. "If *these* walls have ears, they'd be deaf by now from all the noise I tolerate each day. Besides, did Karel Svoboda ever tell you what it is we *do*?"

"No. You're the third person on his list, and so far I've learned nothing."

"It's about noon. You hungry?"

"Starved. I had only a sweet roll for breakfast this morning."

"There's a cheap cafeteria nearby, but I bring my lunch every day and it's more private in my office. I have plenty to share if you'd like."

"Thank you. I'd appreciate that."

Lev followed Strauss up a small flight of stairs. When he walked into the broker's office, he looked out a one-way glass window from which Strauss could see everything going on below. "Security, such as it is," the owner said. His office was pedestrian and functional: a wooden desk, three chairs, an equal number of file cabinets, a small refrigerator, and miscellaneous office equipment. Strauss reached into the refrigerator, took out a large chunk of salami, some black bread, and two bottles of *ersatz* Coca Cola, then took a knife from a side drawer, two plastic plates, some mustard and two apples, and laid the spread out in front of Lev. "Help yourself."

"Thank you. So far, Karel Svoboda's friends did not impress me as revolutionaries or cloak-and-dagger types. A fat, sixtyish butcher, a down-at-the-mouth haberdasher; and, of course there's you. Not meaning to insult you, but you don't look particularly vicious or dangerous."

"Nor do you," Strauss rejoined jovially. "A carnival huckster?"

"An entertainer."

"Same thing. You ply your trade by making people happy, by helping them think they'll get rich. You bring happiness wherever you go, and not simply by your many tales. At each stop along the way, your arrival is a major event. Villagers invariably find space for you."

"That's true."

"Perhaps even, umm, companionship for your bed."

"I'll not deny that," he grinned.

"As much as your games of chance and your stories, you bring news from the world outside their villages, a letter or message from a loved one in a distant place, a source of fresh life. Whether they're Jews like you and me or gentiles, villagers wanted to hear gossip, not the political messages spread by our beloved socialist leaders in Moscow, Warsaw, even this model of the best the Socialist Worker's Paradise has to offer." Strauss chuckled.

"How is what I do going to change our world, make our glorious society better?"

"Come with me," Strauss said. "I want to show you something I think you'll like."

Lev followed the merchant down another flight of stairs into a huge warehouse filled with rows and rows of merchandise. Lev heard numerous forklifts displacing huge crates and, at a loading dock, massive trucks onloading and offloading more unopened crates onto pallets. Strauss had to shout above the din to be heard. "We'll take one of these *Apis*," he said. "It's made by Piaggio. The *Vespa's* big brother. The consignment I want to show you is half a kilometer down the third row to the left."

"An Italian mini-truck?" Lev asked. "But Italy's a capitalist country."

"And the DDR Mark or the Swiss franc speaks an international language. They'll sell to anyone as long as the letter of credit's good."

As they drove down the rows of the warehouse, Lev remarked he had never seen so many trade items in one place. He'd heard that the East could not compare with Western Europe or the United States when it came to plenitude, but Willi Strauss's warehouse, packed from floor to ceiling with all manner of goods, matched anything Lev could imagine: everything from tractors to oil derricks, books to pleasure boats, fertilizer to stone marten coats. All of the goods seemed to be in pristine condition.

When Strauss brought the truck to a stop, Lev stared in awe. He'd heard of these machines, of course, but he'd never seen so much as one on his annual peregrinations. Like a starved cat in a fish market, he could feel himself salivating. Ten of them sat on stands, their gleaming chrome finish, glassine screens, and single arms singing a siren song, urging the showman to come closer.

"My God!" Lev exhaled involuntarily.

"Thought you'd like 'em. The American army's transferring Warner Kaserne outside Munich to the Bundeswehr later this year. I found out last October that they were selling off surplus and I was able to buy these ten beauties through an intermediary in the Bundesrepublik. Bally started making electromechanical push-button machines five years ago, so there was no reason to ship 'em back to the States, and Munich's got so many American bases with casinos they couldn't give them away."

"Mechanical?"

"Entirely. These are the genuine article – last of the one-armed bandits." Lev placed his right hand reverently on one of the machines, gently caressing its firm solidity, admiring the three rows of reels. "Try your luck, Herr Arkady?"

"With what kind of coin?"

"It can adjust to all kinds, but it's best if you use tokens. Here," he said, digging into a leather cup by the side of one of the machines and coming up with a handful of bronze-colored slugs. "Try your luck."

Lev a token, placed it in the coin slot, and pulled down the handle. The spring-loaded appendage retracted with surprising strength. The three wheels made a whirring mechanical sound until, left to right, each reel slowed. The first reel stopped, three cherries in the center. The second reel showed three cherries as well. Lev felt a sudden adrenalin rush as the third reel slowed ever so slowly and finally came to a stop. "*Yes!!!*" Lev shouted as the third reel displayed a third set of three cherries. Instantly, ten tokens clinked into the chrome tray below.

"Care to try again?"

Lev didn't even hear Strauss's remarks. He was already busily putting in a coin and pumping the handle. As fast as the reels came to a stop, he poured another token into the coin slot. Fifteen minutes condensed into what felt like five. By the time Strauss firmly grasped his arm, Lev still had five tokens left, four more than he'd started with.

"Hypnotic, isn't it?"

"If it was adjusted right, I could abandon all the rest of my games and make a fortune from these alone. How long will they last?"

"These are fifteen years old. The Mills Company, the American manufacturer, guarantees 'em for twenty-five years, but since they're mechanical and the gears are built using only steel parts, I'd say they'll last closer to fifty. Easy to work on, easy to repair, and built like military tanks."

At that moment, Lev was like a man besotted by the most desirable woman he could ever imagine. He had to have all ten of the machines, no matter what the cost. He'd beg, steal if he had to, exhaust his entire fortune, the equivalent of ten thousand United States dollars, to have these machines. They'd require only a small segment of the attention he had to bestow on his other games of chance.

"They're automatically pre-set to pay back eighty-two percent of all tokens played. Of course you can adjust them up or down, but the American casino operators found that a machine that pays back more than four out of every five coins is bound to make them rich."

"And," Lev said, licking his fingers, "they don't even notice that the owner makes eighteen percent on every penny invested. How much would they cost me, Herr Strauss?"

"They'd be a bargain at fifteen hundred dollars U.S. per unit."

Lev's face dropped. Even with an eighteen percent return, where would he get the money, more than one-and-a-half times his total capital? He hadn't even thought of the cost of transporting the slot machines or how he'd store them.

As if reading his mind, Strauss abruptly changed the subject. "You came here to discuss freedom fighters, not merchandise, did you not?"

"That's true. Why, then, did you whet my appetite only to dash my hopes?"

"Precisely because our confederates believe in fair treatment."

"You're talking in riddles."

"You don't want to play the slots any longer?"

"And become even more upset?"

"I have another office twenty-five meters down this row," Strauss said. "It's quieter and we can talk in private."

Within two minutes they were ensconced in Strauss's auxiliary office, this one furnished even more sparsely than the other digs. A mid-sized conference table, five cheap chairs, a hanging cage with two canaries, and nothing more.

"All right, you wanted to talk," Lev said.

"What did Major Svoboda tell you about our clandestine operation?"

"Nothing."

"Cigarette?"

"No, thank you."

"There are revolutionaries and then there are revolutionaries."

"More doubletalk?"

"Have you ever heard the phrase, 'From each according to his ability, to each according to his needs'?"

"Karl Marx, 1875."

"Correct. According to Herr Marx, in the ideal communist society, every person should contribute to society to the best of his or her ability and consume from society in proportion to his or her needs. Do you fancy yourself a foot soldier, Herr Arkady?"

"At thirty-four, I'd hardly think so."

"Yet you 'came to the colors' when Karel Svoboda called."

"Because of a statement he made which might or might not be true."

"What is it you do best?"

"In your front office you called me a 'carnival huckster.'"

"Not as an insult." Strauss held his hands up, palms out. "Simply an acknowledgment that you are a master at entertainment – and at relieving folks of their excess money, such as it is."

"Mmmm," Lev grunted noncommittally.

"Foot soldiers, revolutionaries have the highest ideals, but they can't survive by eating air. Some of them even occasionally beat back a dram or two of liquor. They need uniforms, they need … things. No matter what anyone tells you, Lev Arkady, no revolution ever succeeded without filthy lucre."

"Money," Lev provided.

"You've heard the phrase 'Money doesn't grow on trees?'"

"If money doesn't grow on trees, why do banks have branches?"

Willi Strauss laughed so hard his palms slapped his thighs. "Eloquently put." Becoming more serious after several moments, he continued, "One, you are not cut out to be a violent gunman. Two, you are excellent at getting money to stick to your fingers. From each according to his abilities ..."

"You'd want me to be a fundraiser for your revolution?"

"Chaim Salomon, a Jew like us, did it and funded the American Revolution."

"Exactly what do you have in mind?"

"Herr Arkady, I told you that ten slot machines would cost fifteen thousand American dollars. I saw the look on your face. It was as if the most beautiful woman in the world had thrown water in your face or kicked you in the gutter."

"No secret I was, er, surprised."

"Did you even think about how you were going to transport ten slot machines which weigh fifty-three kilos apiece not counting the stands, all over Europe? Or how to ensure you'd be able to keep those machines secure and provide space for people who want to try their luck?"

"Vaguely. But when I heard the price ..."

"So I gathered." Strauss reached into a drawer in his side of the conference table and withdrew two glasses and a green bottle. "Schnapps?"

"Are you trying to temper my disappointment, Herr Strauss?"

"No, Herr Arkady. To make you an offer."

"I'm listening."

"What if I told you I could let you have the ten slot machines on their stands, plus a cargo van that could easily hold the machines and fold down so that twenty people could gather comfortably in the space around the machines for virtually nothing? I'd add ten thousand slugs, a token machine so you could press any slugs into coins to fit the machines, and enough raw material to produce a hundred thousand additional tokens if you need them. Finally, the machines would be secured to the van so completely that it would take a direct hit by a missile to dislodge them."

Lev's mind raced at the thought. "Thirty thousand dollars?"

"Between thirty and thirty-five with extra parts and insurance coverage."

"I thought as much."

"What if I could let you have the whole package for two?"

At that moment Lev noticed the two canaries tweeting in the large cage hanging in one corner of the room. "Who would I have to bribe or kill, Herr Strauss?"

"The second part of your remarks, no one. The first part, the freedom fighters."

"Meaning?"

"You'll gross eighteen percent from the machines. If you were to pay three percent of that gross to help make life better for the millions …"

"Leaving me fifteen percent. How long would I have to pay this? Don't get me wrong, I'd happily pay forever …"

"That's pretty much what they have in mind."

"How would my benefactors know I wasn't cheating them?"

"They wouldn't. It's entirely on the honor system."

"And if I didn't pay? Would my life be in jeopardy?"

"Of course not. The day you stopped paying, everything would simply be repossessed by the registered owners."

"So I wouldn't really own the machines?"

"The Chinese entered into a ninety-nine year lease with the British for Hong Kong. The Americans entered into a similar lease for the Panama Canal. Happens all the time. You think you'll be around another ninety-nine years Herr Arkady?"

"Where do I sign?"

Willi Strauss smiled broadly. He opened another drawer and took out five copies of a very simple one page contract. The owner of the machines and paraphernalia was Höfer, G.m.b.H., Vaduz, Liechtenstein. "Whether or not the current political climate in Czechoslovakia changes is of no consequence. You enter into an honest business deal and your remittance is due to the Union Bank of Switzerland in Bern on the first day of each month. Nothing to tie you to anything except a Liechtenstein corporation. I can assure you our Soviet friends do exactly the same thing."

"One last thing, if I may, Herr Strauss?" Lev said, unable to mask his delight. "Since you seem to know so much, do you have any idea what these machines might bring in on an average day?"

"I'd wager in a ten hour day each machine would bring in the equivalent of $200 U.S. So figure two thousand dollars a day. Your fifteen percent would be three hundred a day, the owner of the machines would get sixty dollars a day. Assuming you work two hundred-fifty days a year, that would come out to fifteen thousand dollars a year for the 'company,' and five times that much for you. Of course, you'd be the one bearing the expenses of transporting and setting up the machines …"

26

Within two weeks, Lev's slot machines became the most popular games of chance on any circus midway or country fair where he chanced to light. Willi Strauss's prediction was accurate. Lev promptly paid every ruble, złoty, or crown he owed to Höfer, G.m.b.H. through banks throughout Eastern Europe, who were only too happy to spread their branches wherever Lev chose to deposit the money that had figuratively dropped from trees.

Shortly after he realized he had found the geese that laid golden eggs, Lev's fertile mind gave birth to three new ideas. Two of them would enhance his fortune almost immediately. Although the third did not bear fruit that quickly, it would have the most profound effect on his life in the long run.

His winter stay in Kiev had given rise to the first of his stratagems. He'd traded something or other for two western "cowboy" shirts, aware that for most of the century, ever since Karl May's *Winnetou* books, audiences in Europe, particularly in Germany and Poland, went wild over anything that projected the image of the American cowboy. Lev now had ten symbols which, like nothing else ever seen in the small towns of Eastern Europe, proclaimed the American Western dream: the same type of slot machines that graced Las Vegas, Nevada. He played that image for all it was worth.

In Warsaw, he had a tailor fashion three complete cowboy outfits. He already had two shirts. Working with the tailor, he embellished these with chaps, a belt with a huge silver-colored buckle, and a neckerchief. The tailor had access to what looked passably like Western boots and an outsized cowboy hat. Although no true cowboy in the 1960s wore anything resembling Lev Arkady's garish outfit, the showman now sported a perfect imitation of what Europeans saw when American Western movies played to sellout crowds in Warsaw, Budapest, Vilnius, or Berlin. He painted the sides of the van in a western theme, cactus, dry sage hills, a crescent moon, a chuck wagon, and some cowpokes riding the range. He gave the slot machines whimsical names, "Billy the Kid," "Butch Cassidy," "Wyatt Earp," and similar titles that evoked images of the wild west.

Although he profited mightily from bringing America to Minsk, Łodz, Krakow, and Budapest, Lev found he was still limited to 18%, minus the three percent for Höfer. Eighty-two parts went back into the hands of the gamblers. If only he could find a way to enhance the profits by enticing the rubes to accept something other than money in return for their handfuls of tokens.

The answer came when he saw that every crowd contained not only men, but women and children as well. Children had absolutely no interest in money. They preferred *things* like goldfish in small bowls, stuffed bears, cap pistols, and sheriff's "gold" badges. Women were always happiest when their children were pleased. Lev had learned long ago that when a woman is happy, she would make her man *very* happy.

Of course, Lev realized he could purchase bright gewgaws in bulk for mere pennies and that the *actual* value of these prizes had absolutely no connection to what the gawkers *perceived* as their value. Within a fortnight, Lev set up a special corner of the van that featured prizes instead of money in return for tokens. Why settle for exchanging the tokens for mere coins when, for one hundred tokens, you could take home a unique and special gift for your beloved child? The audiences never connected the dots to realize that what Lev gave away for "only a hundred tokens" had cost him a tenth of that sum.

Finally, Lev gave himself a genuine American name when he was on the midway. Gone was the Eastern European Lev Arkady, replaced by the "genuine"

American showman "Luke Carter." Initially, this presented a bit of a problem. Although Lev spoke at least six languages, one of them English, fluently, his accent was central European. Lev spent every evening during the next two months listening to shortwave broadcasts from the United States and disk jockeys on America's Armed Forces Radio and Television Service, slowly but steadily picking up the American dialect with a decided southern drawl. By the third month of his studies, Luke Carter could, if no one listened too closely, easily pass for a native American speaker.

※

In April 1968, Prime Minister Dubček launched a liberalization campaign which increased freedom of the press, freedom of speech, and freedom of movement. For the first time in a Communist-dominated society, the government encouraged economic emphasis on consumer goods. Even more staggering, Dubček proposed the possibility of a multiparty government. At a huge public rally in Wenceslas Square, he said, "Socialism must make more provision for a fuller life of the personality than any bourgeois democracy." Dubček vowed to limit the power of the secret police and provide for the federalization of the ČSSR into two equal nations, the Czech

Republic and Slovakia. His foreign policy included both maintaining good relations with Western countries and cooperating with the Soviet Union and other Communist nations. He spoke of a ten year transition in which democratic elections would occur and democratic socialism would replace the status quo. By June 1968, censorship was abolished. Czechoslovakia stood poised to enter the family of Western European nations as an equal.

For the first time in his life, Lev began to wonder what it might be like to settle down in one place, or at least one country, marry, father children, and run his small but burgeoning entertainment empire from a home base. Karel Svoboda had been right: there were changes – changes he could, perhaps, believe in.

⁂

"Mister President?"

"Come in, come in, Lev Arkady. Such a young man to be so successful in the socialist world. My nephew told me you might be calling on me." The man looked like a kindly grandfather, but Lev knew that Ludvik Svoboda had proved himself to be a canny survivor.

After the outbreak of the German offensive against the USSR during World War II, Svoboda became head of the Czechoslovak military units on Eastern front. A hero at the Battle of the Dukla Pass in fall 1944, a year later he had attained the rank of general. Svoboda lived in obscurity until Nikita Khrushchev succeeded to power. Then he returned to public life and headed the Klement Gottwald Military Academy. A few months ago, on 's recommendation, Svoboda had been elected President of Czechoslovakia.

"Tea, Mister Arkady?"

"If you please, Mister President."

The president rang a small bronze bell and within moments a well-tailored middle-aged woman brought a silver tray bearing a ceramic teapot, milk, sugar, a pair of bone china cups, and a plate of cookies.

"I must say Mister President, your government appears to be serious about 'Socialism with a human face.' How is it working out? Really?"

"For the present it is promising," Svoboda said carefully. Lev noticed that the president's eyes shifted uncomfortably, glancing around the room as if there might be listening devices hidden anywhere. When he was certain no one was in sight, he put his right forefinger to his lips. "How long has it been since you've been to Prague, Mr. Arkady?"

"Three years."

"It's a lovely day. Why don't we take a stroll alongside the Vltava so you can get a better idea of our socialist progress?"

Lev caught the warning look and immediately replied, "It would be my pleasure."

Soon the two were walking like old friends over the Charles Bridge, Prague's most famous route over the stately Vltava River. "Can you talk frankly now, Mister President?"

"What do you hear from my nephew?"

Lev knew that regardless of the anonymity of the crowd, he should keep his answers as brief as possible. "Brezhnev is not pleased."

"So I gather."

"Do you think his days are numbered?" Both men knew Lev did not mean Leonid Brezhnev.

Svoboda shrugged. A little farther along the bridge, he remarked, "I've heard you're considering settling in Prague."

"Perhaps?"

"You might better consider Leipzig or Warszawa."

"Vienna?"

"Better still. *Dobré odpoledne, jak se máte pane* Gustav? Good afternoon, Gustav, how are you?" Svoboda asked brightly, turning to a street artist, looking every bit the happy leader of a happy land. At the end of the bridge, they turned right and headed toward the Old Town.

"Odd of you to say."

"I've survived," Svoboda said simply. "As have you until now. It'll be harder for you to 'stay under the radar,' now that you've become conspicuously more successful. *Höfer* appreciates your efforts, Mister Arkady. It would be unfortunate if its property were to fall into the wrong hands."

"Meaning?"

"Vienna."

"How long do I have, to enjoy the beauties of the summer in Prague?"

"Sooner rather than later. And Mister Arkady?"

"Yes?"

"It would not hurt to go even further west. I'm told you speak English with a pronounced American accent. A genuine Czechoslovak passport could be arranged in short order. It might serve you better than the seven *ersatz* books you've been carrying for the past twenty years, particularly if you were to become a political refugee. Don't smile, I'm sure you're not surprised I know such things. At least you wouldn't be a 'stateless' person, even if the state might be questionable."

※

On August 14, 1968, Lev Arkady left the Czech capital, one of the world's most beautiful cities, heading south and east toward the old imperial Habsburg capital by way of his hometown. By the seventeenth, he reached Bratislava where he revisited friends he'd made over the past fifteen years.

As he crossed the Danube and approached the Austrian frontier, where he was waved through with not even a brief inspection stop, he was curious as he looked east toward Hungary and saw an unusually large number of troops and tanks moving west and massing on the Czechoslovak border.

27

Two weeks after his arrival in Vienna, Lev was ensconced in his luxurious room at the Hotel Sacher, watching the late afternoon newscast over the Österreichischer Rundfunk, when the telephone light blinked on and off unobtrusively. He had no idea who'd be calling him here, at this moment, but, given he'd survived by being extremely cautious, he answered carefully, assuming a common Viennese surname. "Schmidt."

"Mister Carter?"

Now his suspicions were aroused. "*Wer ist das?* Who's speaking, please?"

"You don't know me. I'm calling from Feldkirch"

"Your name?" Lev continued suspiciously.

"My name is not important, Mister Carter. Do the names Svoboda, Willi Strauss, and Höfer mean anything to you?"

"They might or they might not."

"Listen carefully, Mister Carter. Karel Svoboda has been liquidated. Willi Strauss took the Kaliningrad-Visby ferry and made to it Gotland less than twenty-four hours before a series of unexplained explosions leveled his warehouse. The operation's been blown. The KGB and their fellow-traveling lackeys are rounding up everyone they can find. Take your Czech passport, at least five thousand *schillings* and …"

There was a click on the other line. Lev kept calm as the voice continued. "According to my watch it's been fifty seconds. I'm sure the Sacher is bugged. It takes them three minutes to trace a call… "

Within ten minutes Lev hailed a cab and directed its driver to take him to a storage facility near Schwechat airport, eighteen kilometers southeast of central Vienna, where he'd stored his garishly decorated truck and his slot machines the day he'd left Czechoslovakia. No sooner did the driver arrive at the warehouse than Lev saw a cordon of armed guards surrounding the place. There should be no need for such security at a shabby warehouse in an even shabbier neighborhood unless …"You're sure this is the address you said?" the cabbie muttered.

"Yes, but I've changed my mind," Lev replied, as one of the guards broke ranks and approached the taxi. "Take me back to the hotel." He peeled off a wad of *schilling* notes. "Sorry for the inconvenience."

"Don't have to be sorry. More money in it for me."

"Take a circuitous route."

As the cab wound its way back into the City, Lev glanced back from time to time. He'd noticed a gunmetal gray Volga GAZ-21 behind the taxi when the cab had left Schwechat. He glanced back every so often, noticing that the Russian car remained eight or nine car lengths behind. Occasionally a car would come between the GAZ and the taxicab, but the Volga remained within sight.

Lev hoped the area around the Sacher would be congested so there might be an opportunity for him to disappear into the anonymity of the large hotel. His hopes flared when the taxi pulled into the main parking circle and a beige Škoda suddenly cut in front of the approaching GAZ-21. The Volga's driver pounded on his horn and barely avoided crashing into the rear of the Czech sedan. The two drivers jumped out of their cars and started shouting at one another. Lev had no time to listen. He quickly peeled off several more *schilling* notes, shoved them at the driver and jumped out of the cab.

As he started toward the front entryway of the hotel, he found his path suddenly blocked as a Fiat convertible swerved around the two shouting drivers and skidded to a halt where the cab had been moments before. The driver of the Fiat, a striking blonde, snapped sharply at him. "Mister Carter, get in *now*! Take your chances with the Russians, who are waiting just inside the hotel or take a chance on me."

Without breaking his stride, Lev turned and jumped into the small Italian sports car. The Fiat took off as the woman expertly negotiated onto the nearest street.

"I suppose I should say, 'Thank you for saving my life,' even before we make introductions," Lev said.

"You might," she replied coolly, but we won't know each other that long."

"Why not?"

"You're getting off at Südbahnof," she said, handing him a ticket. "Your train leaves at 7:29 this evening. You'll have twenty minutes after we get to the station to make your train."

Lev glanced down at the ticket. Klagenfurt in the Carinthian Lake District, the southeasternmost part of Austria. "What then?" he asked.

"You'll be met by one of ours."

"'Ours?'"

"Yes," she said, pushing the Fiat through an intersection as the signal turned red.

"I got a call from Feldkirch less than an hour ago, male. He told me …"

"Svoboda and Strauss are gone and they're looking for you."

"So I learned when I went out to Schwechat to retrieve Höfer's property."

"We got it out just before the Russians surrounded the place."

"Where are the machines now?"

"In hiding."

"You won't tell me where?"

"Correct. For your own good. Don't worry, they're safe."

"Yes," Lev sighed. "But how am I supposed to make a living with them gone?"

"Excuse me? How much do you have stashed away in Switzerland?"

"Uh …"

"A million-and-a-half Swiss francs as of the end of last month. Enough to see you comfortably through the rest of your life. As for our people, you've provided enough during your time that we're not hurting. And you can stop looking at my breasts now, Mister Carter," she continued, neither offended nor with any hint of false modesty.

"Do you mind if I ask …?"

"It won't do you a bit of good. My name is Irena, I'm twenty-six, Czech, my lover's two years older than you, and here we are at the Südbahnhof. Goodbye, Mister Carter. Have a nice life."

The train pulled into Klagenfurt's Hauptbahnhof at quarter to midnight. Lev, who'd left Vienna with nothing more than the clothes on his back, his Czech passport, and five thousand Austrian *schillings*, was famished. He'd had nothing to eat since lunch. Aside from a vending machine which dispensed half-stale sandwiches, there appeared to be no place to get any food at this hour. As he approached the machine, he cursed his bad fortune when he found he did not have enough change to buy a sandwich.

"Tough luck, eh pardner?" The voice had an American accent. The speaker, a tall, whip-thin man of sixty, wearing a cowboy hat, seemed remarkably out-of-place in the southern Austrian train station.

"You wouldn't be looking for Luke Carter, would you?" Lev asked, affecting his own ersatz southern American drawl.

"Matter a'fact, pardner, I'm looking for Uncle Buck. That'll be your new name for awhile, Son." The man stuck out his hand. "Tom Lodge."

This is surreal, Lev thought, as he shook the extended paw. Five hours ago, the world he'd known had fallen apart. Now hungry, exhausted, and most likely smelly, he faced what might have been anything from a KGB goon to exactly what the man purported to be, an old-time American cowboy.

"You're a … a Texas cowboy?"

"Hardly. My accent's as phony as yours. I'm supposed to drive you from here to Ljubljana, where you'll meet your new employer."

"My … new … employer …?" Lev said slowly.

"Mister O'Rahilly."

"Mister O'Rahilly?"

"An Irishman. I'll explain on the way to the apartment. I trust you're hungry?"

"Just a bit."

"And tired?"

"An understatement."

"Mister O'Rahilly rented an apartment five minutes from here. Some grub, a hot shower, and a good night's sleep, then you can reconnect with your western gear, even down to the LC belt buckle."

"How …?"

"As the lady in Vienna told you, your people have learned to survive in the jungle called Eastern Europe."

◆◆◆

"My people?" Lev asked Lodge at breakfast the next morning.

"The Höfer group," Lodge said. He had shed thirty years by shampooing out the gray hair and washing the makeup off his face. He wore denim jeans and a plaid open-necked shirt. "They're the ones who got in touch with Mister O'Rahilly."

"Who's Mister O'Rahilly?"

"Does the name Radio Caroline mean anything to you?"

"No. Should it?"

Lodge smiled enigmatically, then deftly changed the subject. "You've been in the entertainment business most of your life?"

"Mmm-hmm," Lev said, spearing another pair of sausages and spooning more scrambled eggs onto his plate.

"Let's just say that you'll be staying in the game, but expanding your horizons."

"Okay," Lev said. "I've pretty much run my own life for awhile. Do I get a say in any of this? First off, why are other people assuming control of me?"

"Because they feel responsible for getting you into this mess."

"I'm not following you, Mister Lodge."

"Tom."

"Tom, then. I went into this with my eyes wide open. Like everyone else in the world, there was a little greed involved."

"More than a little," the other man grinned. "If it hadn't have been you, there'd have been someone else. Fortuitous choice for both sides."

"I could have made it to the West on my own."

"Might have," Lodge said. "Maybe. The Bear's an octopus, tentacles everywhere. The Höfer folks thought it'd be best if you had some help. He who fights and runs away, and all that."

"I'm not a fighter."

"Your people think you'll be back to resume your way of life another day. The leopard doesn't change his spots. You wouldn't want to miss the fun of what you've been doing. Give it a year or so and the Russkies'll go on to the next urgent problem. There's always a new bunch of malcontents waiting around the next corner."

By noon, Lev was nervously pacing the floor of the apartment. "I thought we were going to leave this morning."

"Not safe yet."

"In Klagenfurt?"

"Not a good idea to take chances in broad daylight."

"It's only thirty kilometers to the border."

"A lot can happen in thirty clicks. You'd be surprised how little it takes. An unfortunate accident at an intersection, a sniper ... Speaking of which, it wouldn't hurt for you to look the part."

He tossed Lev an authentic-looking American passport. As Lev looked through the passport, he read Richard Buchanan "Buck" Shaw, 1017 Oak Road, Bakersfield, California 93304." The passport photo showed a man of early middle age with crinkly lines in his face and a gray-black moustache.

"A little makeup, a false wig and moustache, and you'll pass just fine. You can wear my hat from last night to complete the picture."

Lev and Tom Lodge left the apartment at seven that evening, just as twilight shut down the day. They packed into a dark gray Volkswagen bug. Lodge took a secondary route into the eastern Alpine foothills. It took an hour to negotiate the twenty twisting miles to the Yugoslav frontier. Lodge honked the horn several times before a disgruntled old man waddled out of a nearby cottage, still wearing a stained bib-napkin stuffed into his shirt, and grumpily lifted the single-arm gate by hand. He didn't bother to look at the car's registration or the inhabitants, but desultorily waved them on.

After another hour on the tortuous mountain trail, Lev and Tom came to the main road into the capital of the semi-autonomous Slovenian province of Yugoslavia. Halfway between Ljubljana and Brnik Airport, they arrived at the Hotel Silvester, shortly after nine-thirty. Lodge asked the concierge to advise Mister O'Rahilly of their arrival and to tell him they'd be having a late dinner in the dining room.

They were just starting in on their soup course when another tall man, a few years younger than Lev, sporting the long-hair Beatle style, approached their table.

"Evenin' Mister Lodge," he said, his eyes twinkling.

"Well, if it ain't the poor man's Brian Epstein," Tom rejoined.

"Thankfully still living and no need to get high on drugs," O'Rahilly responded equably. "This must be whatever-his-name is, Arkady, Carter, Uncle Buck? Hey, Uncle Buck *baby*! Welcome to the world of the pirates!" He smiled ingratiatingly. "How's it feel to be on the other side of the Curtain, Mister Arkady?"

"Been West several times already, Mister O'Rahilly."

"If you want to call Vienna the West," O'Rahilly continued smoothly. "Even West Berlin is hardly the FRG," he said. "I mean *really* West."

"Haven't been there yet. Ljubljana's not exactly the cowboy capital of the world."

"Neither is Texas anymore," Lodge interjected. "Nowadays it's Hoyo de Manzanares, near Madrid, at least to the Italians."

"Spaghetti westerns, they're calling 'em," O'Rahilly added. "Take a second tier American TV cowboy actor, bring him to Europe, and who knows? The guy might have a career ahead of him. Funnier things have happened. Sergio Leone went through nine guys who turned him down flat before Clint Eastwood agreed to take the job."

"What time's our flight to London?" Lodge asked, shifting the subject.

"London?"

"Your new home when you aren't in international waters, Mister Arkady," O'Rahilly said. "The JAT Caravelle leaves at noon tomorrow. I suggest we pack it in, get some sleep, and be ready to rock and roll tomorrow morning."

28[1]

"Okay," Lev said, once the jetliner had attained its cruising altitude. "How'd you get involved in this whatever-you-call-it that you want to get me involved in?"

"Radio Caroline," Tom said. "Pirate radio." He was in the center seat of three on the right side of the aircraft.

"Last night Tom called me the 'Poor Man's Brian Epstein.' He wasn't far off the mark," O'Rahilly said. "I grew up in Greenore, County Louth. Left to make my fortune in Jolly Olde. For awhile I ran the Scene Club in Soho, then I branched out into managing a number of pop music artists. One of 'em was Georgie Fame."

"I've never heard of him."

---

[1] The events described in this section actually took place from 1965 to 1967. For continuity of the story the author has "adjusted" the calendar to 1968. To be historically accurate, by that time, the English government had passed the Marine Broadcasting Offences Act, which made it a crime for a British subject to supply pirate radio stations with water, food, records, fuel, or labor. Eight of the ten radio station that were all around the coast of England closed down. Radio Caroline survived for another year.

"Hardly anyone outside of England ever has. I recorded Georgie on my own independent label, which nobody'd heard of either. Took the record to the BBC and tried to get it played. That's when I learned that if you weren't EMI or Decca, you might as well save your breath. I went over to Radio Luxembourg and got pretty much the same response. Their shows were 'owned' by EMI, Decca, Pye and Philips. They played only music from the paying label.

"That pissed me off," O'Rahilly continued. "I decided if you can't get the establishment to give the little guy an even break, the little guy's got to make his own break."

"So you started your own illegal radio station?"

"It wasn't illegal at the time," Lodge said. "When Ronan started Radio Caroline it was transmitting from international waters. It was only after we started getting ten million listeners a week that the BBC bitched to Her Majesty's Government and they started talking about the Marine Broadcasting Offences Act. It'll probably pass by next year."

"But you're still operating?" Lev said.

"For the time being," O'Rahilly said. "Everyone hates us except the people, and if enough of 'em love us, what are they going to do, shoot us out of the water?"

❧

"Why me?"

"'Cause you know Europe, 'cause you sound American enough, and 'cause Höfer's a little guy fighting the government, like me. They said you were one of their most valuable assets, but they had to put you on ice for awhile and asked if I could help."

"So sight unseen, or should I say voice unheard, you said yes?"

"Something like that. They told me a bit about you and, to be frank, you sounded perfect. Pretty ballsy putting together that American cowboy act behind the Curtain."

"But 'Uncle Buck'?"

"If we're going to do it right, we've got to plug into every American idiom we can. Our cousin across the pond talks about the British Invasion, the Beatles, the Stones, the Who, and a dozen or more acts. Nowadays all you need to do to make it big in the States is to have long hair and a Liverpool accent. Free trade's a two-way street."

"Meaning?"

"Mister Arkady, one of the reasons you were so successful behind the Curtain was that you gave your audiences something they couldn't get at home. The BBC's got enough Limey music to boot us off the airwaves in a minute. They're just starting to catch on that there are three kinds of American music. They're light on Black music and twenty years behind the times when it comes to Country and Western."

"Country and Western?"

"What Americans call C and W started out when emigrants from the Scottish highlands settled in the Appalachian Mountains and brought their music with them," Lodge said. "That music became popular in the twenties, spread down to the Deep South and across the Bible Belt to Texas, then farther west. Look at your American passport."

"Bakersfield, California," Lev said. Never heard of the place."

"Radio Caroline's got to keep up with the times or, better yet, anticipate what's coming next. The latest incarnation is the 'Bakersfield Sound.' Bakersfield's a town of a hundred-fifty-thousand, two hundred clicks north of Los Angeles. Used to be Nashville was the only legitimate place to record Country and Western and New York was the center of Rhythm and Blues. No more. Los Angeles is the new powerhouse and Bakersfield's close enough to L.A., just over the Grapevine, to make it a serious feeder."

"That's how you decided you needed an 'Uncle Buck?'"

"Name associations are important. The Bakersfield sound is guys like Merle Haggard, Dallas Frazier, and Tommy Collins, but one name stands out above all the others: Buck Owens."

"Sounds like a name you'd call a donkey," Lev said sardonically.

"Owens' father was a farmer in Texas. 'Buck' was a donkey on the Owens farm. When little Alvis was four years old, he walked into the house and announced his name was going to be 'Buck' from then on. The name stuck."

"But name association?"

"Two of the biggest names England has sent around the world are Tom Jones, whose real name is Thomas Woodward, and Arnold George Dorsey, better known as Engelbert Humperdinck. *Tom Jones* comes from a racy English novel out of the 1700s. Humperdinck wrote the opera *Hänsel and Gretel* in the 1890s. Instant name recognition."

"So Buck Owens is a country and western singer in Bakersfield, California. How's that going to get me name recognition in England?"

"The most popular TV show in the United States these days is *Rowan and Martin's Laugh-In*," O'Rahilly said. "Our man in the States advised us they're working on a country and western version of *Laugh-In* which they'll call *Hee-Haw*. Buck Owens is going to be one of the two hosts on that show. If it takes off ..." O'Rahilly said.

"One step ahead of the game, one step ahead of the BBC," Lodge joined in.

⁂

"O.K., Buck *baby*, you're about to set foot on your new home," O'Rahilly said jauntily. "But first we're going to survey our domain."

They'd landed at Gatwick the day before. From there, they'd motored down to Harwich, Essex. After spending the night at the less-than-luxurious Kingscliff Hotel, they'd boarded the tender that would take Lev out to sea and his first taste of life aboard Radio Caroline.

When O'Rahilly, Tom Lodge, and their newest recruit set out into the early morning fog, Lev, who'd lived his life inland, had no idea what he'd find anchored out there. He has seen advertisements for sea voyages in the windows of travel agencies in Vienna, Warsaw, and Budapest. In his mind he pictured a gleaming white cruise ship.

Lev Arkady / Luke Carter / Uncle Buck came in for a rude awakening. The tender plied a daily route, carrying mail and passengers to pirate radio stations anchored off the East Coast of England, stopping at Radio England/Britain Radio, Radio London, and finally at Radio Caroline. Their first stop was at Swingin' Radio England which shared quarters with her sister station, Britain Radio, aboard the MV *Laissez Faire*.

"Interesting history," O'Rahilly said. "A few years back it transported American GI corpses, casualties of the Vietnam War, back to America."

The *Laissez Faire* looked to be a gloomy vessel indeed. The disk jockeys' quarters were on the lower decks, where they camped out in sleeping bags.

"Swingin' Radio England and Britain Radio are owned by an American consortium. They use a slick Top-40 radio format, complete with American deejays. Frankly, I don't know how long they'll be around," O'Rahilly ventured. "I don't think English listeners are ready for that kind of high energy radio. The Brits prefer more laid-back and chatty communication."

Their next stop, Radio London, housed aboard the MV *Galaxy*, had once been a Navy minesweeper. It still bore the utilitarian gray color of a military vessel, with streaks of rust accenting the hull. Against the gray sky and gloomy green seas, she looked grim and foreboding, by no means a visual representation of the "Wonderful Radio London" image portrayed in the jingles and deejay patter that interspersed the music. Living conditions on the *Galaxy* seemed a lot better than those aboard the *Laissez Faire*.

Finally, a mile farther out to sea, the tender reached its ultimate destination, the *Caroline*, a one-time Danish passenger ferry. She may have been old, but she wore her age with elegance, and was clearly head and shoulders above the other ships. As the tender drew near, the water churned beneath them and Lev's stomach rose up and down as he prepared to set foot on deck for his first taste of life as a pirate on the high seas.

A deckhand caught the lines thrown from the tender and secured the two vessels together. Lev waited until the ocean swell lifted the tender level with the *Caroline's* deck. Without looking down at the heaving sea between the two ships, he leapt aboard. Once safely on deck Lev looked up and saw a group of long-haired, unshaven, half-dressed, disheveled-looking figures approaching him. They looked like escaped prisoners. For the slightest moment, the East European man with the wide-brimmed cowboy hat wondered if he'd been dropped off on a convict ship by mistake.

The men were, in fact, nine disk jockeys, newsreaders, and technicians who were working their fourteen-day shift aboard Radio Caroline. Some were departing for a week-long shore-leave as their replacements arrived.

A huge bear of a man stepped forward and gripped Lev's right hand with an oversized paw. "You're the new kid in town, eh?" he said in a strong English accent which seemed country-rough. "Dave Lee Travis, Lancashire," he said, grinning. "I'm the lunchtime guy on this ship of fools. I hear tell you'll be our country guy."

"So they tell me."

"Polish?"

"With a name like Luke Carter?" Lev asked, raising his eyebrows.

"Slovak then."

"How would you know that?"

"When you're in radio, you learn to distinguish all kinds of accents. Your American accent, by the way, is superb. We've got Limeys, Canucks, Yanks, Aussies, Danes, New Zealanders, you name it. You're the first from behind the Curtain."

"But you said my American accent was …"

"Could'a fooled me, Mate. I'm Emperor Rosko," a dark-haired man, several years younger than Lev, said. "You lookin' at Alfie for a reason?" he asked.

"Well, uh … that is … You'll forgive me, but it is a bit unusual seeing a grown man walking around with a bird on his shoulder."

"Alfie's a Mynah. Assists me on the morning gig, so I figure he's entitled to ride along when he's not working. A wandering Jew, eh?"

"Seems like you've been clued in about me."

"That, plus I'm a Member of the Tribe. Good ol' dad's got a history like yours."

"Emperor Rosko?" Lev said, arching his eyebrows.

"Mike Pasternak," the younger man said, reaching out his right hand and gripping Lev's with a firm friendliness.

"The only Pasternak I ever heard of was Joe Pasternak, the American film producer."

"That's m'dear ol' pa," the other replied. "Sixty-nine and still going strong. Just as Jewish as you and me and just as much of a mongrel. He started out on the Hungarian-Romanian border. It feels so great to have a new face, a new nationality, and a Jew to boot, around here."

"Jay-zus," O'Rahilly, who'd been standing quietly off to one side, said. "A regular United Nations I've got here. Well, guys, call the new kid on the block anything you want, but take care of him 'til he gets accustomed to this tub. I'm back to the big city." With that, Ronan O'Rahilly stepped gingerly back into the tender and it shoved off.

❧

"What's he really like?"

"O'Rahilly? One of the nicest guys in the business, He'll bend over backwards for us, die or kill for us. He'd probably pay us a lot better if he could turn a profit from this venture, but none of us are really in it for the money. So you really scarpered out of the East when things got a little warm?"

"*Got* scarpered out," Lev rejoined. "Not really my choice, but events made it look like my life might be shortened somewhat. What about you, Mike?"

"I got my start on the water. Of course, the U.S. Navy's idea of a boat, an aircraft carrier, was quite a bit roomier and pricier than this old tramp. Grew up in L.A. listening to Lord Tim Hudson and Wolfman Jack."

"Ooh – ooh – owoooooh!"

"Bugger off, old man," Pasternak said genially to a tall, sandy-haired fellow who'd mouthed the wolf howl as he brushed by while Mike and Lev were talking. "Or sit down and join us, your choice."

"Old man?" Lev raised his eyebrows. "He can't be older than me."

"Simon Dee, thirty-three, here's to Thee and here's to We!" the newcomer said, raising a bottle of beer. "This is as strong an alcohol belt as we get on this boat."

"Simon was the very first voice anyone heard when Radio Caroline busted the cherry on Easter Sunday '64," Pasternak said. "Been here ever since."

One by one, half a dozen other men came up to their table. Lev, who'd always been more or less a loner, felt a rush of warmth for the sudden outpouring of bonhomie.

"Is it like this every day?" he asked Mike Pasternak.

"When we get a new guy. Gives us something to do and someone new to talk to during the down-hours. And let me tell you, there's a helluva lot of down time. It's great for the first two days, but then it gets boring as hell. Two weeks on, one week off. Most of us can't wait for the week off."

"Good enough lodgings, food's okay, but boss's rules are no ladies overnight and nothing stronger than beer or ale. Take a dozen horny guys in their twenties and early thirties and after a week of showers every four days, boredom, and no sex … well, you get the picture," Dee said.

"So you're Simon Dee," Lev said. "And I'm Uncle Buck and Mike's Emperor Rosko. You're not going to tell me Simon Dee's your real name?"

"Nope. I am a mite fancier than your other guys. I've a got a real uptown English moniker I do. Cyril Nicholas Henty-Dodd."

"You're bullshitting me."

"I shit you not. How far d'you think I'd get using that name on pirate radio? And I need the job. Since I got out of the RAF in fifty-eight I've been a bouncer, an actor, a waiter in a coffee bar, a photographic assistant 'til I loaded the wrong film into the camera for a fashion shoot, a laborer, a leaf-sweeper in Hyde Park, a vacuum cleaner salesman …"

Dee was interrupted by five beer-swigging, shaggy-haired, odoriferous men doing a raucous rendition of the bridge from Frank Sinatra's newly arrived hit, *That's Life*.

"He's been a puppet, a pauper, a pirate, a poet, a pawn and a king.
He's been up and down and over and out, but he knows one thing:
Each time he finds himself ... flat on his face,
He picks himself up and gets back in the race. ..."

"Loverly," Emperor Rosko drawled sardonically. "Hey, Arkady, I'm sure Mister Dee'd love to sit and jaw for awhile, but it's time he got off his fat arse and did his talk show."

And that was how Lev Arkady became an air personality on Radio Caroline.

29

While Lev's new digs were infinitesimal compared to his previous "home," the mindset of its inhabitants exuded a sense of freedom he'd never experienced before. The *Caroline*, 188-feet from stem to stern and displacing 763 tons of water, was distinguished by a 168-foot-high mast, the transmitting tower. The main deck ran around the outside of the ship. Midway between the fore and aft sections, Lev went through a mahogany door that led from a short passageway to two different destinations. To the right, the place he'd found so convivial last night, the lounge, a large room surrounded by windows. A long table bolted to the floor comfortably sat twelve people.

Opposite the lounge, Lev climbed half a dozen steps and entered the record library: over a thousand LPs and 45 RPM records. Beyond the library, he stepped into the broadcast studio, the reason for the ship's existence.

The bridge, which included the captain's cabin, occupied the next floor up from the main deck. The stern deck became Lev's favorite place to get away from the crowd when he wanted solitude. In days to come, he'd sunbathe, sit, or simply lean over the rail watching the ocean. The ship's bow, by contrast, contained winches, chains, ropes, and the base of the tall mast.

Last night, an exhausted Lev had dropped off to sleep moments after he'd been shown to his cabin, a wood-paneled room which contained a bed, a place for clothes, and a porthole. The porthole had large bolts which, Mike had told him, he'd better close and bolt tight during a storm, lest he be drenched by a wave. The showers and toilets were at the end of the passage which led to the cabins.

Below it all, the engine room ran the entire length of the underpart of the ship: a huge engine connected by a thick shaft to the propeller, an electrical generator, and transmitters with dials, switches, knobs, and controls. A thick cable ran from the transmitters through a large insulator to the outside and the mast.

In his next few days on board, Lev discovered two distinct cultures confined to the limited spaces of the *Caroline,* which had previously been the MV *Fredericia*: Dutch-speaking, methodical, down-to-earth, efficient sailors, and English-speaking, pie-in-the-sky disk jockeys. Sometimes they complemented one another. Other times they may have lived on different planets. The law of the sea is that the captain is king, but this was different. The *Caroline* was not going anywhere: its only purpose was to broadcast. Everything had to be subservient to that end. Life on Radio Caroline clashed with the tradition of the ocean.

Lev commenced his latest profession in the least-desired time slot, 2:00 to 6:00 a.m. O'Rahilly's business-savvy decision to link two 10-kilowatt transmitters together gave the pirate station ample power to blanket southeastern England and a good slice of Western Europe day and night.

Within thirty days, "Uncle Buck's Corral" was garnering enough interest from England's somnambulists and the sleepless creatures of the night that Tom Lodge, who lived his life between Caroline House in Mayfair with his wife Jeannine and their three kids, and the *Caroline,* decided to experiment.

"Lev, I'm going to try you in a couple of different time slots. You'll be doing two hours, from seven to nine a.m. with Emperor Rosko and Alfie. Then you'll share the mike with Dave Lee Travis in drive time, four to five-thirty in the afternoon."

"How do they feel about that, Tom?"

"Quite happy, both of them," Lodge said. "They'll take anything that'll jack up our ratings and keep us ahead of Radio Atlanta."

"The new Aussie station?"

"Yeah. We've owned the radio waves for six months. Now, they're camped out only three miles away. Ronan told me it's already confused our advertisers. There's a hold on all potential advertising until they determine which of us has the largest audience."

"He thinks I can help save the ratings?"

"O'Rahilly's given me free rein to run the station any way I want. I believe putting you on split shifts will work. How do *you* feel about it?"

"I'm invading *their* territory, even though they're my two closest friends on the ship, other than you."

❦

Less than three months later, an exuberant Ronan O'Rahilly bounded onto the deck of the *Caroline*. "Okay, guys, I've made a deal with Alan Crawford, the owner of Radio Atlanta. Radio Atlanta is about to become Radio Caroline *South*."

Lev was the first to break the silence. "Have you bought the *Mi Amigo?*"

"Goodness, no!" O'Rahilly replied. "Crawford still owns the ship, but we've entered into a joint venture to sell advertising. This ship will sail up north and become Radio Caroline *North*. That way we'll cover the whole U.K."

"Where will Caroline North be anchored?" asked Mike Pasternak.

"That's top secret, Rosko," O'Rahilly said with a grin. "You'll know when you're almost there. If the government were to find out, they'd create problems. The real question is who's staying on this ship to go up north and who's going over to the *Mi Amigo* for Caroline South?"

"I'll go wherever you want me to go," Lev said agreeably. "After all, you've engineered one helluva change in my life. I owe you."

"Since you're such a loyal company man," Ronan said, "I suggest that you and Tommy ride this tub to the new location and then we can talk some more."

✧

Saturday, November 15, promised to be a surprisingly warm, sunny late fall day. Many thousands were likely to be all along the English coast. Lev and "Emperor Rosko" alternated Saturday morning shifts, so whoever didn't work that weekend could sleep in late. Lev, whose turn it was to run the morning show, awoke and looked out the porthole. A bright gibbous moon shined down on the Kentish coast, then the White Cliffs of Dover. The *MV Caroline* was on the move. 6:00 a.m. Time for Lev to go on the air. He had no idea where the vessel was sailing. The only person who knew was the ship's Dutch captain, who'd been given sealed orders. That just added to the excitement.

Lev Arkady settled into the studio, hit the button on the cartridge tape player, and out came Buck Owens' "Act Naturally," his theme song. "Howdy, Buckaroos!" Lev began. "Good morning from old Uncle Buck on a beautiful Caroline morning. Here's some good ol' Country and Western music for sashaying around the breakfast table while *we* sail around the coast of England …"

Two hours later, Tom Lodge came down to spell Lev, while Uncle Buck took a well-needed toilet break. On his way back to the studio, he went out to the deck to stretch. The ship was approaching Beachy Head and he wanted a closer look. He scanned the shoreline with a pair of binoculars.

"Oh my God!" Lev shouted. The sight of Beachy Head, completely covered with people, astonished him. Then it hit him. People had come to see the *Caroline* pass by! Lev rushed down to the studio.

"Tom!" Lev shouted. "There are thousands of people watching!" Lev scrambled up the ladder to the bridge, grabbed a mirror, and began reflecting the sun onto the shore.

When it was his turn to go back on the air, it took all of Lev's control to try, unsuccessfully it turned out, to keep the excitement out of his voice. "Well, buckaroos, it's Uncle Buck back at the switch and we're passing Beachy Head. Hey, y'all, the Big Buck has an idea that might by fun. Those of you girls on the beach listening to Radio Caroline, take your mirrors out of your purses and reflect the sun at us. Reflect it onto Radio Caroline so we can see you. You can't miss us, we're the ship with the big, big mast."

An instant later the coastline lit up with flashing lights. Everything was sparkling. This went on all day, all along the coast. The Deejays kept reminding Caroline's listeners "We're the ship with the big, big mast." As the sun set in the west, people began flashing car headlights. The *Caroline* flashed its lights back as the twilight turned to night.

That evening, the *Caroline's* Dutch captain came into the studio. Tom Lodge put him on the air. With his strong Dutch accent, he resolved the mystery of the *Caroline's* destination. He announced that the vessel was heading for the Isle of Man in the Irish Sea, and they were going to drop anchor in Ramsey Bay.

Next morning, the ship sailed off the north coast of Cornwall into a gentle, welcoming sea. On the air, Uncle Buck crowed, "It's Sunday morning and I sure miss breakfast in bed and reading the Sunday paper. But in the meantime, here's an oldie-but-goodie, just perfect for the way we're travelin', the Hollywood Argyles and *Alley Oop*."

Within twenty minutes a speedboat rushed out from the coast, came alongside the *Caroline*, and threw a bundle of newspapers onto the deck. As the ship sailed out from the coast of Wales, Lev noticed that this coastline was sparsely populated, no lights, no boats, no mirrors. The seas were calm that night. The night and the music blended into one. Lev slept deeply and contentedly.

Next day, *Caroline* arrived at the Isle of Man. "Hello, Isle of Man!" Lev said on the air. "This is Uncle Buck. If you're listening to Radio Caroline, we'd like you to use your mirrors to reflect the sun onto our ship so we can see you. If you don't have a mirror handy, flash your headlights."

Nothing happened. During the next two hours, the air personalities tried everything. No response. Lev asked Tom Lodge, "What's going on?"

Tom seemed just as mystified.

"Something must be wrong," Lev said. "Maybe we're not welcome here."

This baffled the entire staff. The Radio Caroline personalities were loved by thousands of people in England. All along the coast they had been welcomed with cheers, mirrors, and headlights, but now that they had arrived at their destination, there was no response. To not be welcomed by the Isle of Man would be most awkward. The self-governing British Crown Dependency of fifty thousand souls, located in the Irish Sea between the islands of Great Britain and Ireland, was to be Radio Caroline North's new home. The staff needed the support of the Isle of Man's populace in order for its battle against the British establishment to work.

That afternoon, Tom and Lev, who'd bundled up in parkas to keep out the chill wind that blew in from the Irish Sea, walked on the sun deck, quietly discussing the strange lack of enthusiasm that had greeted their arrival at the Isle of Man. Suddenly, Lev saw a small boat moving out from the coast, which looked like no other boat Lev had ever seen. He pointed it out to Tom Lodge.

"It's a canoe," Tom said. "I saw a lot of them when I worked in the Northwest Territories."

"Northwest Territories?"

"Canada."

"Oh." Lev took his hands out of his pockets and blew on them to get the circulation going. "Anywhere near Toronto?"

"Couldn't be farther away. Yellowknife is way up north."

"How did you end up here?"

Tom pulled out a pipe, tamped in some tobacco, and lit up. "I ran a fishing business on the Great Slave Lake. We cut holes through the ice and caught fish with nets. In winter, the temperature often got down to *minus* 51 degrees Celsius, sixty degrees below zero Fahrenheit."

Lev whistled and pulled his parka tighter.

"One day when I was eighteen, the ice broke apart, sending me, my companion, and our three sled dogs drifting across one hundred miles of open water. My companion died, but a native trapper rescued me. Three years later, I partnered with a guy named Joe Boschman. One night he took off with all our fishing equipment and left me broke. Eventually, I hooked up with the CBC as a broadcaster up in Yellowknife. After I learned to imitate the American DJs of the day, I was looking for a bigger world than Horse's Arse, Canada, so I begged for an assignment overseas and got London. The rest …whoa! Look at that, Lev! Those men in the canoe look like they could go on paddling forever."

As the two men on the *Caroline* watched, the canoe came alongside. One of the men held up an envelope in his right hand. "My wife wouldn't let me come home until I brought you this," he said.

Tom reached over the railing and took the envelope. Without another word, the two men canoed back to shore. Opening the envelope, Tom broke out into a big grin.

"Puzzle solved?" Lev asked.

Tom handed him the letter. From the fold in the page, Lev took out a sprig of heather. He read the note out loud. "Welcome to the Isle of Man."

Suddenly Tom laughed. "Now we've really been welcomed by the people of the Isle of Man. This is it! These people have said yes!"

The two Deejays on board *Caroline* waved to the receding men in their canoe and shouted, "Thanks a lot, guys!" The two men waved back and returned to paddling. And in this low-key, heartfelt way, the gentle Celts of the Isle of Man welcomed pirate radio to their coast.

⁂

The Isle of Man may have welcomed *Caroline* but the British government was not pleased. Anthony Wedgwood-Benn, Postmaster General in charge of the ministry that controlled radio in Britain, denounced pirate radio on TV. "The pirates are a menace," he said. "I believe the public would support action to enforce the law. I'm quite convinced that the pirate ships have no future at all."

The Government recognized the pirates as being outside of their jurisdiction. Their response was to treat *Caroline's* personnel as foreigners. When they came ashore, they had to go through customs with their passports.

After the next election cycle, Edward Short took over the Postmaster General position from Wedgwood-Benn. No better than his predecessor, he promised legislation to put all pirate stations off the air.

No one liked pirate radio except the people. By year's end, more than ten million people professed to tuning in, often secretly, to the pirates in general, and to Radio Caroline North and South in particular.

Lev could not hide the shadow of anger that loomed within him. Since he felt closest to Mike Pasternak, Emperor Rosko, a fellow Jew and, at least through his father, a fellow East European, he unloaded one day after his shift, when the two of them were playing Blackjack in the lounge, oblivious to a howling wind that raged outside.

"Mike, I believed that by leaving the Iron Curtain behind I'd breathe the air of real freedom."

"You can't say we don't have that, Lev. We say and do whatever we want on board this glorified rust bucket."

"Yes, provided we stay *on* this glorified rust bucket. Step onto English soil and we're not treated any differently than an enemy alien."

Pasternak stood up, went to the electric tea kettle, poured hot water into two battered ceramic cups, reached into a red, white, and green cardboard box and extracted a pair of PG Tips tagless teabags. "Black or white?" he asked Lev.

"Black, thanks. Never could get used to the English way of spoiling a perfectly good cup of tea by putting milk into it."

"The British are a strange lot," Pasternak said, returning with the cups and shoving one toward his friend. "Even to their habitual cuppa'. By the way, d'you know how the English came to use black tea?"

"Nope, but I trust you're going to educate me soon enough."

"About three hundred years ago the British were trading regularly with China. The tea they brought back was the green stuff. One day, so the story goes, they pulled into port and there was no green tea available on the wharf. The Limeys raised such a ruckus that one of the Chinese merchants said, 'We've got some old tea that got soaked and turned black. Just give it to 'em and say it's the latest rage in Kowloon.' That's what they did. Lo and behold, the English loved it. From then on they insisted on black tea when they came a'calling."

"Bullshit."

"Maybe, but it's a good story. I see from your face you've got more serious stuff to talk about. That's why I brought over some tea. Makes it easier to listen," he said, loudly slurping as his lips touched the hot liquid. "So you think there's no difference between the East and the West?"

"Not really," Lev said. "On the surface they all parrot their own ideologies like it's the Second Coming. Depending on where you are, Communism is the great evil and Capitalism is the great salvation; Communism means dictatorship and Capitalism, they call it democracy, means freedom for everyone."

"Meaning they mix up an economic system with a political system and try to draw sharp lines in the sand."

"Exactly."

"Welcome to the real world, pardner," Emperor Rosko said, affecting his own version of a Texas drawl. "Doesn't matter whether you're over here, over there, or in Timbuktu, Africa. *I* want power and once I have it, I'll do everything I can to hold onto it and to keep you from getting it, no matter if it means I put you in jail after a proper show trial, or I hire someone to shoot your kneecaps off."

"Great," Lev responded. "You really think it's like that all over the world?"

"Always has been, always will be," Pasternak said. "You think things were any different in ancient Egypt?"

"Don't know, I wasn't there."

"Doesn't matter whether you were or not. This two-legged little species of ours has always been competitive and combative. No one's satisfied to be the low man on the totem pole, but since the guy who *is* the low man has no chance at all of winning against the big, rich, powerful guy, he ends up fighting with the *next-to-lowest* guy. Trust me, I've seen it in the good old U.S. of A. The Mexicans and the Blacks account for five percent of the American economy. They're so intent on battering one another to get a bigger slice of that five percent of the pie that they don't realize that they'll never come near getting anything more than five percent. Probably the same where you come from."

Lev thought back to his time in Eastern Europe. "I guess you're right. The Poles and the Ukrainians have always fought over the worst pieces of land. Doesn't really matter who owns it, the Jews always get hind tit, even on *that* piece-of-shit real estate. You're not optimistic then, no matter where the land or who's in power?"

"I'm not optimistic and I'm not pessimistic. I'm just a realist who likes to play rock music, and I'll be along for the ride as long as the *Caroline* continues to be the ship that rocks the world."

30

"You can stay here or you can move on to a bigger playing field, Lev. Your choice."

"So the rumors I heard are true?"

"Might be. Ronan wants to see you and me at Caroline House as soon as possible. This afternoon wouldn't too soon for the boss man."

"I can understand why he'd want to talk to you, Tom. You've been management since he started, but why me?"

"Ratings."

"Ratings?"

"Yeah, in case you hadn't noticed the public loves the idea of the crossover cowboy who plays both C&W and who's on top of rock as well. You've pulled in consistent number one ratings in your time slot in Liverpool, Manchester, and Dublin. Mine is not to question why … the big guy said to bring your ass along."

Contrary to the image of David versus Goliath which Radio Caroline wanted to portray to its listeners, Caroline House was a palatial four-story structure at 6 Chesterfield Gardens, ideally located in a cul-de-sac off Curzon Street in the heart of London's Mayfair District. Radio Caroline's headquarters occupied a strategic West End position at the confluence of the entertainment world and the music business. Oxford Street, Piccadilly Circus, and Carnaby Street came together nearby. The place teemed with smiling, enthusiastic young people, fans wanting a piece of the energy, music people wanting their records played, and tourists from Europe and the States.

The entrance had four pillars with a large door opening into a tiled vestibule. As Lev entered, he saw a wide, curving, blue-carpeted staircase. "Nice," he murmured.

"That it is," Lodge said. "Today we'll avoid the crowds and take the elevator.

The elevator was large enough for Lev, Tom, and two other people. Tom recognized one of them. "Hi, Eric, I'm Tom Lodge. I'd like you to meet one of my sidekicks from Radio Caroline, Uncle Buck. Buck, this guy's Eric Burdon of The Animals."

Burdon smiled and shook hands with Lev. Then, to Lev's surprise, he pulled a six-gun out of his satchel, a revolver. It was shiny, strangely real, and strictly illegal in England. He looked at Lev with a gleam in his eye. "I just got this. Isn't it beautiful?"

"Yes, it is," Lev said, not knowing what else to say. "But what for?"

"I just love guns, Mr. Buck. And this is a real cowboy gun. You've probably seen hundreds of them, I'm sure, but it's one-of-a-kind to me."

The elevator door opened. Tom pointed to the right and Lev walked down the wide, teak-floored hallway toward the front of the building. As they entered Ronan O'Rahilly's office, which ran the full front length of the building, Lev saw that one wall was wallpapered with a huge photograph of Radio Caroline North, Lev's home for the past several months. Opposite that wall, two floor-to-ceiling windows opened onto Chesterfield Gardens. Ronan signaled Lev and Tom to sit while he continued his phone conversation.

"Of course you can't, Mister Short. I understand you perfectly, but I assure you we are not doing anything illegal. All of our broadcasting will stay in international waters. We are like birds, flying freely across the ocean. By the way, can I interest you in a free ocean holiday in the North Sea? No? Pity. Oh, well, that's too bad then. Goodbye, Mr. Short."

Ronan hung up and addressed the two men who'd just come in. "I love speaking with these government officials. They're so locked into their circumscribed British sense of self-importance they have no fun in life."

Tom and Lev laughed. Then Tom turned more serious. "Why'd you have us flown down, Ronan?"

"Well, it's like this," O'Rahilly said. "While you've been up north, another broadcast ship arrived from Texas, Radio London."

"I know," Tom replied. "Singing American radio jingles and the Drake Format, the typical American Top Forty radio sound. Powerful stuff."

"The most recent survey showed that Radio London has ten listeners to Caroline South's one. Alan Crawford's programming was too conservative. No punch. So all of Caroline South's advertisers switched to Radio London, Crawford went broke, and I ended up buying Caroline South."

"Fantastic! I love it!" Tom said.

"That's where you come in," Ronan continued. "You've created a sound and programming on the North ship that really says what we are all about. I want you to take over Caroline South and get our audience back from Radio London. You're a huge fish in a mud puddle where you are. We need the London market in order to survive. To do that, we've not only got to stick a hot poker up the BBC's nose, we've got to kick the living shit out of the competition."

"I can do that," Tom said confidently. "But I'll need three things: an assistant program manager, I think that's why you had me bring Lev down with me; a whole new radio staff; and free control of the music."

"Why do you need new deejays?"

"I need to start from scratch. I need young guys who love the current music scene, adventurers. A different kind of programming to beat Drake. A fun, high-spirited ship."

"Bucky?" Ronan turned to Lev.

"I haven't had time to get old. As you Brits say, 'In for a penny, in for a pound.'

※

"O.K., Tom, how do you propose to change Caroline South?" Lev and the newly-appointed station manager had purchased their fish and chips, fried plaice and soggy French fries wrapped in newspaper and doused with vinegar, at a nearby stand and were munching their early evening meal as they walked through Hyde Park.

"Each show has to have its own unique character. You and Rosko are perfect examples. Completely different ends of the spectrum. You and that farkin' mynah bird of his make the perfect trio. Dave Lee Travis is another good guy."

"You think Ronan will allow you to empty out Caroline North?"

"Most likely not. But he wants to get that same electricity powering up South."

"What's so different about them now?" Lev asked.

"South plays middle of the road stuff."

"Doesn't Radio London do that?"

"Yeah, but I see a great difference between the new Caroline South and Radio London. Drake Format's successful in the States, but it's still an automated system. Deejays are locked into a routine, not as tightly controlled as the BBC, but still restricted to what's on the play list. I want the deejays to choose their own records. It'll always outshine an automatic system."

❦

As Lev climbed off the tender and onto the *Mi Amigo*, Caroline South, he found it was, to put it bluntly, "different" from the *Fredericia*. Where *Caroline North* had been a legitimate ship and arguably luxurious, the *Mi Amigo* made no pretense of being anything but a dumpy, dingy, cramped little cargo vessel which sat low in the water. She was half as long as the *Caroline*, weighed one-sixth of what the larger ship displaced, and sported a 141-foot-high broadcasting tower. The *Mi Amigo* reacted to every wave.

The first meeting with Tom's new squadron was crisp and to the point. "Here's the situation, guys. We've got to get the audience back from Radio London. That's the main thing, and the *only* thing."

"They have a great sound," Dave said. "Are we going to use the Drake Format?"

"No, we'll never beat them that way. We're going to use a new formula. It's never been tried before. Here it is. First, the deejay is not allowed to prepare his show in advance. You get all the records and albums you might want to play on your show and you place them around you in the studio on the console. There'll be a box for the Top 40, a box for the new releases, a box for our favorites, one for oldies-but-goodies."

"Then what?" asked Rosko.

"You only decide what to play next when the one before is playing. No prep."

"That could be a bit dicey," Lev ventured.

"Maybe, Buck, but you've got to *feel* your show, not think about it. You've gotta' be right in it, enjoying it, too. Then you'll always know what to play next."

"Kinda' like being spontaneous." This from Robbie Dale.

"Yes, and here's the trick," Tom continued. "You have to really *listen* to your own show. None of this turning down the monitor and relaxing 'til the record ends. You've got to be your own show's number one fan. And when you go ashore and do gigs, get involved with the local music scene and bring back those experiences to Caroline South and to your audience."

Everyone soon acknowledged that Uncle Buck was the *de facto* assistant station manager. When Tom took leave, Lev stayed behind to ensure that Caroline South worked like a well-oiled machine. The reverse took place when Lev went ashore.

Lev had always been a consummate charmer, whether on land or sea. Within a month after coming aboard Caroline South, he rented a small flat near Caroline House, well within his budget. The times were changing since he'd first come West. The girls in their miniskirts advertised unabashed sexuality and the young men seemed to have discovered new confidence with their colorful clothes.

When the 'birds' learned that Lev was single, thus clearly available, and even more when they discovered that he was the famous "Uncle Buck" of Radio Caroline fame, there was scarcely a night onshore when he slept alone. One of his 'friends,' who'd stayed with Lev during an entire week of shore leave, told him, after they'd engaged in a particularly passionate spate of lovemaking, "You know, Buck, you're a sexy guy and a great lay, but you might try wearing something more exciting than those cowboy duds."

"Holly, that's for young bucks. I'm almost thirty-five. I'd just look silly."

"You're certainly not at the end of your road," she said. "Not if your little friend is an example. You didn't know what I'd be like 'til you tried me out, Luv. Turned out to be quite fun." Although

Lev was too experienced to blush, he felt uncomfortable with her bold forwardness. Whether he wanted to admit it or not, there was something far more seductive in the old ways. "Besides, I'd like you to meet my employer," the girl continued. "She's a great fan of Radio Caroline."

As Lev and Holly walked into Carnaby Street, Lev immersed himself in the brightly etched, sensual atmosphere. The girls wore miniskirts, the guys bell-bottoms. He heard music everywhere, and not the music of the staid old BBC. Romance suffused the air, no doubt fueled by the fact that the pill was no longer restricted to married women. Carnaby Street was abuzz, and King's Road was hip.

Dressed as he was, Lev felt out of place. He was magnetically attracted by the vibrant clothes in a new boutique, which were unique in both design and color.

"This is where I work," his friend announced. "Uh-oh, here comes the boss lady." She glanced quickly at her watch. "Thank God I'm on time."

A striking young woman with stylishly-cut hair came forward. "Hey!" she said. "With that cowboy outfit you've got to be Uncle Buck! Am I right?"

"You sure are, ma'am," Lev drawled.

"Great to meet you in person! I'm Mary Quant."

They shook hands and Lev looked around the woman's shop. "It's beautiful," Lev stammered. "You're a real knock-out."

"Thanks. We've got new styles to match the music you play on Radio Caroline."

"I never thought I'd say this, but I love this gear," Lev said. "I could speak about them on my show or in my personal appearances if you wouldn't mind."

"That'd be great," the woman replied. "Help yourself to whatever you fancy."

"I ... uh ... that is ... I wouldn't even know where to begin," he said haltingly.

"Perhaps I might help you then," Quant said mischievously. She directed Lev's friend-of-the-night to fetch several items of clothing. "I want to make sure our cowboy friend has appropriate attire to wear when he returns to his boat."

"Ship," Lev interjected.

"Whatever."

Twenty minutes later, a bemused and befuddled Uncle Buck emerged from Mary Quant's boutique carrying an oversized bag with the name of the proprietress emblazoned on it. If one were to peek into the bag, the observer would see a complete cowboy outfit, including boots and belt buckle. Such an onlooker would also see a completely metamorphosed man attired in a satin turquoise shirt with full, puffy sleeves, lace on the cuffs, and a flounce along the bottom. The collar had a white braid sewn in a wavy pattern. The aquamarine-and-blue satin pants were tight on the thighs and came with wide bell-bottoms. Where once there had been cowboy boots, Uncle Buck wore bright blue shoes with large gold buckles. Atop his head sat a red beret. The former "cowpoke" looked like a character out of HMS Pinafore come to life ninety years after Ralph Rackstraw had strutted his stuff on the stage of the Opera Comique.

As Lev wandered into Caroline House, he was greeted with admiring, flabbergasted, stares. Ronan took one look at his protégé and barked, "Perfect! One of our Caroline North boys had to cancel out and we need someone to emcee a Kinks concert this afternoon. What'd'ya say, Bucky Baby, wanna' do a fun gig? You look ... uh ... perfect for the part."

"As Uncle Buck?"

"Why not? It'd add to the excitement of the 'new' Caroline South. By the way, your pocketbook will be happy to know that this week we passed Radio London. Twenty-three million listeners can't be wrong."

※

Lev donned a coat and dark glasses and slipped in via the backstage door. The band was setting up and the audience was arriving. Lev peeked through an opening in the curtain. The place swam with high-energy teenagers chatting, running here and there, and calling out to their friends. *This is going to be a good concert,* he thought.

The moment came. Lev ran out on stage in his new threads, grabbed the microphone, and the audience went wild. "This is Radio Caroline bringing you the best rock and roll in the universe!" he shouted. The audience cheered again.

A girl in the front row grabbed Lev's ankle and pulled. Uncle Buck fell forward onto a group of girls clustered in the first few rows. They screamed as he collapsed into the middle of them. Many hands pulled on his shirt, grabbing in all directions. Lev could hear it rip. As it tore, they pulled harder and harder. Suddenly it came right off his back in a few jagged pieces. Lev scrambled, topless, back on stage and watched with amazement as the group of girls tore his shirt into many pieces. Each one wanted a Radio Caroline souvenir, whether it was from Uncle Buck or any other deejay.

Undeterred, bare-chested, Lev shouted into the mic' "Do you want more?"

"Yes!" they roared as one.

"Are you ready to go all the way?"

"Yes!!"

"Alright, then. Here are the Kinks! Now go total!"

The band crashed in with their first chord and Lev ran off stage. "Wow!" he exclaimed to the nearest stagehand. "I never knew love could be so violent."

31

January 9 was cold and stormy. Snow was falling along the coast. That morning Uncle Buck had been playing some lively music, but nothing warmed up the day. The wind kept getting stronger and the *Mi Amigo* started to roll and heave. With each wave, the whole ship creaked and groaned. Soon all hands had to secure the portholes and doors. By evening, the little ship was rolling around in the turbulent North Sea. One of the deejays succumbed to seasickness, so Lev took over his shift. He opened with the Beatles' *Day Tripper* and closed with *Eve of Destruction* by Barry McGuire. By the end of the show, Lev was so tired he immediately went to bed.

A few minutes before dark on Thursday, January 25, 1945, Papa, Mama, and the two children, Lev, who'd be eleven next month, and three-year-old Eva, Lev's baby sister, gathered around the old, serviceable radio receiver the partisans had left when they'd visited last September.

For the past year-and-a-half, since they'd left Bratislava, the Arkady family had been dodging both the Germans and the Russians. If the stories told by the partisans were true, the Nazis had systematically eliminated millions of Jews. While the Soviets had been steadily, inexorably advancing, squeezing what blood remained out of the collapsing Third Reich, Papa knew there had never been love lost between the Cossacks and the zhids.

A dozen years ago, Papa had become the new English teacher at the gymnasium, the high school in Bratislava's Jewish section. Shortly afterward, his parents had arranged through a shadchan, a marriage broker, that Papa and Mama meet. By the time Lev's father had broken the glass under the chuppah, the wedding canopy, it was clear that the parents had engineered a fine match. A year later, in 1935, when Papa was twenty-five and Mama two years younger, Lev entered the world. Before the Nazis came. When life was normal.

By the time Lev was four, he spoke his native Slovak, as well as German, fluently. A year later, he could read books in those languages, as well as Magyar and English. While it was not unusual for adults in that corner of East-Central Europe to speak many languages, Lev's early mastery of four gave him a leg-up on his peers.

Mama and Papa had taken him to art museums and to concerts in the nearby park. Their home was filled with books, a Victrola, and an assortment of classical phonograph records. Most precious of all, a cabinet even higher than Lev was tall, housed a radio. Ah, the things that came from that magical instrument! Strauss waltzes and Verdi operas, programs from Budapest, Prague, Warsaw, and even farther away! As he listened to the radio, sometimes for as long as two hours a day, Lev became amazed at how differently each station reported the news. If signals coming out of Berlin, Leipzig, Vienna, and Venice were to be believed, the poor Germans in Bohemia and Poland were being decimated by the natives. The Austrians had welcomed their German protectors with garlands of flowers.

On the other hand, in the twilight hours between sunset and darkness, when Lev and his father listened to the B.B.C. from London, or to signals coming from France, Holland, or the Soviet Union, they'd get a very different picture. Granted, a five-year-old boy, even one as intelligent as Lev, might not understand the deeper meaning of these conflicting messages. But as he became six and then seven, Lev's comprehension grew as quickly as he did. The boy became aware of meetings carried on in hushed and increasingly desperate tones by members of Bratislava's Jewish community who'd gather in his parents' home.

One evening, toward the end of 1943, when Lev was eight and baby Eva was a year old, Mama and Papa gathered the family together just after dinner. "We must leave Bratislava tomorrow morning."

"Why, Papa?" Lev had asked.

"Because it is not safe for Jews to remain here. You've seen how many of your friends have moved in the last year?"

"Yes."

"Some of them made it out in time. Others ..." the words hung in the air.

"But our radio? Our phonograph records?"

"A friend has agreed to sell them for us," his father replied. "We'll need that money to live on. We can't take much with us. Some books, a Kiddush cup, my talles," he added, holding up his ritual prayer shawl. "Lev, you must start packing now, tonight. Take only those things that are most special to you."

Not entirely shocked by this turn of events, since almost every Jew over the age of five had developed an inner sense of foreboding, Lev spent the last night in the only home he had known, gathering and packing things he thought he would need: a heavy coat, a pocket-sized English-German dictionary, a stuffed toy dog, a bag of marbles, a small pocket knife his parents had given him on his last birthday, last year's school class photograph, and a small Bible.

During their first months on the run, the family had moved first to Komárno on the Hungarian border, then to Bad'an, east of Nitra, where they'd rented the use of a farmer's barn for a month; then to a fisherman's shack on the Hron River; from there to Dúbrava, and thence into the Tatras, a northern slice of the great Carpathian Mountain chain, which straddled the frontier between Slovakia and Poland.

In July 1944, the family stumbled onto an abandoned cabin in a tiny valley high in the eastern Tatras. They'd purchased cheap peasant garb so they'd be indistinguishable from others in the area, then started farming a patch of ground in front of the cabin, raising enough to sustain themselves and a little extra. Once a week Mama walked to the nearest village, ten kilometers away, where she traded the excess beets, potatoes, and cabbage they'd grown for wheat and rye seeds, a rooster, and two laying hens. Soon enough, eggs had hatched and now they not only had eight chickens and more trade goods to take to market, but they'd been able to enjoy the unheard-of luxury of chicken dinner once every two weeks.

On the days Mama went to market, often taking Eva in a cloth hamper tied around her neck, Papa taught Lev the history of their people and rudimentary algebra, as well as card games, such as gin rummy, follow suit, highest one wins, and sixty-six.

After three partisans had visited in September and left the radio, a handgun, and fifty rounds of ammunition, Papa taught his son how to use the firearm, which he'd hidden in the shallow cellar, and which, he said, might save their lives someday. Of course, Papa had never used any of the ammunition the Partisans had left, but if the time came....Once established in the cabin which had become their home, Mama and Papa had told Lev that while it was safe enough in the daytime, they must be extremely cautious not to light too large a fire after the sun went down, lest they be discovered.

In addition to the treasures Lev had brought with him from Bratislava, the family had a few special possessions: a battered Tanach, the Five Books of Moses; the silver Kiddush cup; Papa's talles, and Mama's *shabbos* candles, as well as coats, blankets, and cooking utensils. The partisan visitors had taught Papa how to sharpen and maintain the magneto which, in the absence of electricity, would enable the radio to receive local stations and, at twilight and dawn, signals from as far away as London.

When winter descended on the valley, the Arkadys learned how propitiously the cabin had been located. The mountain which rose immediately to the north protected their valley from the worst of the winds. By the time the first frost came, Papa had honed his skills in hand-cranking the magneto so that a single charge of the receiver would last almost five minutes before he had to re-crank the handle. The transmissions from London came through best just after sundown. Since no Partisans had come their way since September, the radio and Mama's weekly market trips provided the family with their only news from the outside.

Now, in the chill twilight of late January, 1945, Papa cranked up the radio. Lev bundled himself in one of the family's blankets while Eva and Mama huddled in another. Moments later, as Papa was turning slowly from signal to signal, a sharp male voice speaking in English cut through the maze of whistling and static.

"This is the United States Armed Forces Radio. Today a spokesman for General Patton's Third Army announced that it had liberated Bastogne, effectively ending the Battle of the Bulge...." Papa tuned to the frequency he'd listened to each evening for the past four months. The incredible message was repeated and amplified, accompanied by the familiar tolling of a large bell. "This is the B.B.C. calling from London. Earlier today, the American 501st Airborne Division met up with the 101st Infantry. The Yanks reported that the German Ardennes Offensive, Unternehmen Wacht am Rhein, the Battle of the Bulge, is over. According to sources close to General Patton's Command, the American forces suffered more than 89,000 casualties including 19,000 killed, more than 47,000 wounded, and 23,000 missing."

Although Lev and his parents wanted to whoop for joy, they knew better. Their thrill at this news, which surely marked the beginning of the end of the international chess game in which Germany had reigned as Grand Master for a decade, was greeted not by victorious shouts, but by smiles and eyes bright with hope.

"The last of the German reserves are now gone," Papa said quietly. "The Luftwaffe's been shattered. The German forces are being pushed back everywhere. It's time for a celebration, eh, Mama?" he said, squeezing her arm.

Lev's mother nodded.

"Lev, go down into the cellar. In the wooden chest at the far end of the room you'll find a very special bottle of wine your mother and I saved from the day we got married, long before the war. We promised each other we'd save it for a time like this."

"Is it more special than Pesach, Papa?"

"The best combination of Pesach and Purim, Lev. It looks like the most murderous villain since Haman will finally be defeated and we Jews may soon be free to live our lives in peace. Now, go quickly, my son. I may even let you have a sip of wine."

Lev had scarcely shut the basement door when he heard a loud crash above him, followed by screams and the sound of gunfire. He didn't know how long he remained quiet, fearful, as the crunch of loud boots and the voices of a number of men grew louder, then softer, as they searched throughout the house. Finally there was silence. When Lev finally emerged from the cellar, it was totally dark. He remained still for several moments, listening for any sign of life. There was none. Still cautious, he crept silently toward the front door of the cabin. "Mama? Papa? Eva?" No sound. "Papa?" he called more forcefully. Nothing.

Suddenly his foot pushed against something heavy and soft. Some third sense told him this was not as it should be. He knew by heart where the emergency store of candles was kept. He tiptoed to the back of the tiny cottage, reached into the pantry, and extracted a candle and a box of wooden matches. Striking the match against the box, he inhaled the sulfur smell as it burst into flame. He advanced toward the front of the cabin, holding the candle in his hand.

"Papa?" He stopped in his tracks and retched uncontrollably. Everywhere he looked there were bloody remains of what had been the bodies of his family scattered throughout the room. Mama and Eva were recognizable. Papa's head had been blown off.

⸎

Lev awoke in a cold sweat. He didn't know whether he'd truly screamed out loud or if it had been part of the dream. It didn't matter. The dream always came back to haunt him, sometimes once a year, other times four or five years went by before it returned. He could never escape it. But he was pulled into wakefulness as terror replaced terror.

32

He felt the *Mi Amigo* rolling rapidly, tilting at crazy angles, and threatening to upend his small cabin. This was followed by a strange double shudder, and a vibration through the hull, as if something were smacking the vessel's structure. Lev, filled with foreboding, tried to work out in his half-awake mind what this strange motion could be.

Something's definitely wrong. As he debated getting up, two rolls to port seemed to stop before they should, as if something prevented the ship from riding the swell properly. Seconds later, the world fell apart around him.

Riding the crest of an enormous wave, the *Mi Amigo* rolled heavily to port and slammed hard into something solid underwater, with all the force of a hundred tons of metal hitting a solid brick wall. The ship bounced up in the air, catapulting Lev out of bed. He went flying through the air, landing on the opposite side of the room as the ship went the other way, hard to starboard. Every fixture and fitting leapt from the benches, snapping the metal restraints, and rained down on the nearly horizontal wall around him.

As the ship went down, almost flat on its side, tons of machinery and equipment all over the vessel broke free and crashed into the walls. Then another roar erupted as thousands of tons of seawater came over the now-submerged starboard deck and hammered its way into the ship, breaking open portholes, forcing open doors, squeezing through every nook and cranny, every fissure in the normally above-deck accommodations.

The ship hung there, almost on its side, for a few seconds, then slowly she rose again, turning the wall on which Lev had landed back into a wall and not a floor. Another rumble of machinery and furniture followed, crashing back down onto the floors again.

The vessel resumed its normal rolling and crashed heavily again onto an unseen object, with a tearing, grinding noise, as the hull slid across something obviously very hard – and huge. Lev lay on the cabin floor, bruised, battered, and covered with loose objects. His mind racing, he knew he'd have to get out of the now wrecked cabin, and into the company of the others. He might at least find safety in numbers and perhaps find out what was happening.

Lev reached the bridge at the same time Mike Pasternak, Dave Lee Travis, and Ronnie Dale came pounding up the stairs.

"Shit," said Mike.

"Yeah," Dave Lee said. "

I think we are in deep shit indeed."

The coastline, which for most of the night had been invisible, was clearer now. They could see rows of yellow street lights stretching off into the distance, across the sea. From the port side it looked much closer than usual, but the size and the direction were all wrong.

Lev concluded that the *Mi Amigo* had broken its anchor chain sometime during the night and drifted away, but the question was, *where*? With no instruments to guide them, they were helpless. There was nothing to do but call the Coast Guard, despite all that that entailed for the crew of a pirate ship. With tension mounting, Lev took the handset of the ship-to-shore radio.

"Dover Coast Guard, this is *Mi Amigo*. Do you read us?"

There was no reply. Mike adjusted the power setting on the radio.

"Dover Coast Guard, this is *Mi Amigo*. Do you read us?"

This time the reply came back crystal clear. "*Mi Amigo*, this is Dover Coast Guard. Go ahead."

"Dover, *Mi Amigo*. Could you give us a position check, please? We should be about one mile southeast of the Falls Head buoy, but we've had it pretty rough for the last few hours, and we can't find our bearings."

"*Mi Amigo* go to Channel 80 please and we will DF."

Lev tuned to the new channel. "Dover Coast Guard, *Mi Amigo*. I'll give you more time to track. Testing 1-2-3-4-5, testing 1-2-3-4-5. This is *Mi Amigo*, over."

The reply came back from the Coast Guard instantly, in a very different and deadly serious tone of voice. "*Mi Amigo*, Dover Coast Guard. How many on board?"

"Oh, shit," muttered Mike Pasternak. "We must be in serious trouble. The only reason they'd ask how many of us there are is if they need to know how many people they have to rescue."

"Nine including crew." Lev replied.

"*Mi Amigo*, do you have any idea of the situation you're in?"

"Er … we had a bit of a bang a few minutes ago and thought something might be wrong. We couldn't find our bearings. That's why we called you."

"*Mi Amigo*, you are aground on the Goodwin Sands. We've scrambled a helicopter. Do you wish to come off?"

We couldn't be, Lev thought. The Goodwin Sands were eighteen miles away from Falls Head – *and the deadliest spot for shipwrecks off the entire south coast of England!*

"We have located you, *Mi Amigo*. You are aground on the Goodwin Sands. Do you wish to abandon ship?"

"Hang on, please, Dover. I'm alerting the crew."

No one on the *Mi Amigo* needed to be told about the Goodwin Sands and its reputation as the "great ship swallower." Hundreds of ships and thousands of men had ended their lives there after running aground in storms. Any other captain or crew would have abandoned ship immediately. But this was the *Caroline* crew. If they lost the ship, they lost everything. The unanimous vote was to do everything they could to save the ship.

Soon all of them were back on the bridge, wearing life jackets. An RAF helicopter arrived above them, its blades almost inaudible in the storm, and caught the ship in a powerful spotlight. Dover came on the radio again. "*Mi Amigo*, strongly advise all hands to abandon ship."

"Many thanks, Dover," Mike replied. "Do you know who we are?"

"Yeah," a much younger-sounding voice replied. "You're those crazies on Radio Caroline. We're not supposed to say anything, but we really love you and the moment the higher-ups aren't around we tune in. I recognized Uncle Buck. You must be the guy with the parrot, Emperor something-or-other."

"Almost correct, Dover. He's a mynah."

"The cowboy?"

"Nawww, man, the bird. The guys have decided we're going to stay and try to save the ship if we can."

"Kinda' foolhardy, but we'll call the chopper back and send out the Ramsgate lifeboat to drop anchor nearby and rescue you all at the first sign of trouble. Good luck."

After the helicopter flew off, the ship continued battering itself to pieces underneath the deejays and the crew. As the men on board thought of every conceivable way of saving the vessel, the radio sprang to life as Dover Coast Guard called back. "*Mi Amigo*, do you want us to send out a tug from Dover to assist you?"

"What do you think?" the captain asked Lev.

The deejays formed a tight circle and engaged in vigorous conversation. "A tug from Dover means a tow to Dover if we get the ship free from the Goodwins," Robbie Dale, the youngest of them said.

"Yeah, and the arrival of a pirate ship in a British port means a massive salvage fee to get it back, probable detention by the British government, and a big victory for the bad guys," Mike added.

Dave Lee Travis chimed in, "But without the tug, the *Mi Amigo* would dig a hole for itself within hours, break its back, and sink within a few days ... if it doesn't capsize and kill us all first. A sunken ship is worth even less to Caroline than a captured one."

Accepting a British tug would be a terrible gamble, but the men concurred unanimously that it was their only hope. Lev resumed broadcasting, "Dover, *Mi Amigo*. Could you please send the tug?"

"*Mi Amigo*, the tug will be with you within the hour. Ramsgate lifeboat will be with you shortly. Keep in contact. Dover out."

The deejays took stock. They had hit the sandbank and nearly rolled over at 3:50 a.m. It was now 4:15. It would not be dawn for a long time. The storm raging outside was savage. Swells from the northeasterlies were still lifting the *Mi Amigo* up, hammering it down again on the hard sand, driving the ship further onto the sandbanks, with much tearing and scraping along the hull each time it did so. The men organized themselves into pairs. Robbie and Dave Travis went down into the depths of the engine room to check the level of water in the bilges. If there was a hole, the water would be rising and they'd be in deep trouble.

Down in the very bottom of the ship, they were right above the grounded section of the hull. Everyone could hear the scraping and grinding. Each time the boat slammed down on the bottom, it seemed as if the floor beneath them was about to give way. If the ship rolled over, they wouldn't have a hope in hell of getting free.

Luckily, the water in the bilges was at the normal level. The men quickly made their way upstairs to give this news to the Dutch captain. The main levels were a different story, several inches of water still in the main corridor, the galley totally flooded, the mess room carpet sodden from waves which had sprayed through the edges of the still-sealed portholes. Back upstairs, they found the captain talking to the Dover Harbor Board, whose representative was asking whether whoever was in charge was willing to sign the standard Lloyds salvage agreement.

Miraculously, the ship's little generator was still running at full tilt, providing the vessel with light and power despite the fact that it was situated directly underneath a leaky hatch on the front deck, and water must have been literally cascading down on top of it. Lev went into the newsroom and switched on as many exterior spotlights as he dared, so that their rescuers would have light to work with. The generator struggled with the unexpected load. The lights dimmed for a moment before coming back up again.

Visibility started to improve. They could see the Goodwin lightship about two miles away, and, further off in the same direction, the lights of France. Huge waves still came toward the ship from the northeast, lifting the boat up, then breaking into smaller waves near the stern. The bow rose and fell, twisting from side to side, but the stern was now firmly embedded in the underwater sandbank, increasing the strains on the hull.

At 6:00 a.m., they heard a news report on Invicta Radio about their grounding. Still no sign of the tug. Dover Coast Guard told them the tug was on its way, but was not due for another hour.

As time went by and there was no sign of the tug, the men on board *Mi Amigo* felt more and more isolated and vulnerable. The small ship, after a period of relative stability, started twisting and banging on the bottom again, with such ear-piercing metallic scrapes that they felt it would spring a plate at any moment. Robbie, Mike, and Dave went downstairs, checked the bilges, and examined the main level. As the ship rolled and thumped around and the waves hit them, the amount of water making its way in had begun to increase. The corridors and floors were under an inch of water again. Water was forcing its way up through the drains as the boat smacked against the bottom. Only the mess room seemed safe and relatively dry.

When the three men returned to the bridge, worse news awaited. "I just got another call from the Coast Guard," Lev said wearily. "The tug's been delayed again. It won't get here until well after 7 a.m., and …"

Suddenly the ship was lifted up in a massive wave and came crashing down onto the sandbank with a bumping, grinding noise. It made an alarming lurch to one side, then settled again. But it was now listing fifteen degrees to starboard and did not right itself. Following in the tail of the first wave, another huge breaker smashed into the desperately wounded vessel, throwing both the deejays and the crew off their feet. When they got up, the ship was listing farther down to starboard than before. Wave after wave came toward the stricken ship. Each one left the vessel a little closer to being on one side. Horrifyingly, the ship was not even trying to right itself again.

"That's it," said the captain. "We're coming off." No one disagreed.

Lev rushed to the radio. "Ramsgate lifeboat, *Mi Amigo*. We wish to abandon ship."

"*Mi Amigo*, Ramsgate lifeboat. We will be with you shortly."

"*Mi Amigo*, this is Dover Coast Guard. The helicopter has been scrambled."

Another wave, another lifting of the ship, and they banged ferociously onto the bottom again, ending up still farther over on one side. It was now difficult to stand upright. The churning sea, visible from the bridge, was getting closer and closer.

Suddenly, there was a noise like thunder from the top of the bridge. The windows of the two doors leading out onto the back deck turned white in the most concentrated hail of spray the men had ever seen. Those on board looked at each other, their fear mounting. Whichever way they got off the ship, they would have to go outside, which meant braving the spray, which was coming in increasingly vicious bursts every time the stern slammed down into the shallow water.

Another comber tilted the boat farther over, another resounding bang on the bottom took everyone off their feet. A monsoon of spray swept across the ship and hammered on the roof. The boat's inhabitants struggled to their feet again, clinging to whatever they could to keep their balance.

"Come on, come on, where is that damned lifeboat?" cursed Robbie.

"*Mi Amigo*, this is Ramsgate lifeboat. Have you a lee side?"

Lev peered out into the first light of dawn and could see only massive breakers and churning water all around him. "Ramsgate lifeboat, come to our starboard side. We'll have less distance to jump from there."

"Agreed, *Mi Amigo*, we're just moments away."

The ship was taking an incredible pounding now, juddering up and down on the bottom, the sound of tortured metal from underneath competing with the blasts of spray thundering over the metal decks. Jumping into a lifeboat in these conditions would be almost suicidal but what choice did they have?

The lifeboat rounded the *Mi Amigo's* stern and attempted to come toward the stricken vessel. It was still a hundred yards away when it was caught up by a big wave and hurled sideways in the water.

"It's gone over!" shouted Dave Lee Travis. "The lifeboat is on its side."

Lev climbed back up the floor to the ship-to-shore radio, bracing himself against an instrument console. "Ramsgate lifeboat, this is *Mi Amigo*. Are you all right?"

Silence.

"Ramsgate lifeboat, this is *Mi Amigo*. Are you all right?"

There was silence for a long moment, then a reply. "*Mi Amigo*, this is Ramsgate lifeboat. We have run aground."

Fear clutched tightly at the throats of the men as the boat took another huge wave and was battered down again. The ship now tilted at a thirty-five degree angle. They were stuck fast on the Goodwin Sands, the tug nowhere in sight, as the vessel smashed itself to pieces, moments away from rolling over. Now their rescuers were stuck too.

Mike grabbed the radio. "Dover, how long before the helicopter reaches us?"

"Ten minutes."

At that moment, the boat went over even farther. Too fast. Soon it would be on its side, its inhabitants hurled out into the icy water. Ironically, although there was not enough depth for the *Mi Amigo's* considerable draft, there was more than enough water to fill her up if they went sideways, and more than enough seawater to drown in.

"Everybody over to the port side," the captain called. "If we go over it may still be above water." Another huge wave headed toward the ship.

"Stand by, this may be it," Lev said quietly. The ship tilted over more than forty degrees. He managed to make it to the radio set. "Dover Coast Guard, *Mi Amigo*. Communications might fail at any moment."

"*Mi Amigo*, can you launch your life raft?"

"No way of getting a life raft into the water and then jumping into it. We'd be washed away."

"Helicopter will be with you soon." The tone changed, "Dover Coast Guard to tug *Dexterous* and any other vessel in the area, you may have to search for bodies in the water."

The men on board looked at one another in horror. Dawn was breaking fully now. They could see the churning, bubbling mass of sea around them. Strange currents were created by the shifting sands. The massive breakers combined to make the water look mad with rage. They wouldn't last a minute in that maelstrom.

"God bless you and protect you, *Mi Amigo*. You were the good guys," said an unknown voice on the radio, a crew member of a ship somewhere out there, listening in to the drama and wishing them well.

Another huge wave was coming.

"*Mi Amigo*, Rescue Helicopter 166. We will be with you in two minutes," came the reassuring voice of an RAF pilot. Even as he spoke, Lev could hear the massive rotor blades as the chopper passed overhead. He could see it settle into position a hundred feet above their stern. Maybe they'd get out of this alive after all.

"Right, we are abandoning ship now, out this way," Mike called, opening the bridge door onto the little balcony leading to the back deck. The men formed a human chain and struggled out into the wilderness.

Once outside, the wind and chopper noise deafened them. Within seconds, they were soaked to the skin and almost blinded by the spray. They edged their way down the stairs onto the back deck, gaping at the seething seawater just a few feet below them, waves breaking over what had been the starboard deck, and pounding the side of the ship. The back deck tilted and jumped beneath them, as if wanting to throw them into the sea. They reached the base of the back tower and grabbed it, huddling around it for support. The stern kept smashing down into the water. Within moments, each of them had swallowed so much spray they felt sick. They were frozen stiff, drenched, and disoriented, but they managed somehow to cling to the tower.

The helicopter approached, lowering a winch man. One by one, each of the ship's inhabitants were strapped into safety harnesses. Lev felt the beginning of another earthquake-like smack onto the seabed beneath him, and then he was in the air, just as the spray attacked the ship again. His body like ice, his lungs filled with seawater, he had a brief glimpse of the back tower and some stays slicing through the air right in front of him.

Lev banged his head against something solid in the air above him. The next thing he knew, strong hands were pulling him into the helicopter and ripping the harness from him to send it below again for the next man. As soon as the last two men and the winch man were on the end of the rope, the helicopter turned and headed back toward Kent, even as the three were being hauled up through the air. As they turned toward shore, Lev had one last glimpse of the *Mi Amigo* at sea, trapped in the middle of a boiling mass of water, huge waves breaking over her, tilting at a fifty degree angle, and lit up by lights and spotlights.

As the helicopter flew away, she was still semi-upright in the water, somehow managing to look sad, abandoned, and beautiful all at the same time.

※

It took more than forty-eight hours, two huge salvage tugs, and four Harbor Board crews to pull the battered radio ship, which refused to sink, off the Goodwin Sands. As Lev, accompanied by

Ronan O'Rahilly and Tom Lodge, pulled up to the quayside, it was heartrending to see the *Mi Amigo* looking so small and cold and frail, tied up at a dock that was normally used for giant superferries. The three Radio Caroline executives knew, without saying it, what was ahead of them: the official detention order on the ship, the massive salvage bill, and the endless inspections aimed at preventing her from ever escaping from British jurisdiction.

After all the years of freedom in international waters, countless thousands of hours of voices spoken and songs spun through the air by the ship and her crew, the day of reckoning had arrived. Lev looked at the others and smiled weakly. "It's time to face the music," he said.

BOOK IV
CHANGES

33

In May 1973, Birgit Petersen, now Birgit Mouton, married and living in Dijon in the heart of France's burgundy district with her husband Jean-Claude, paid a visit to Encino. It was the first time she'd seen Penny in five years. She was surprised to see that Penny, who'd been living the good life of America in the early seventies, seemed much sadder than Birgit remembered, and a bit dowdy.

On the drive to the Valley from LAX Penny said, "I suppose I don't look too great, huh?"

Never one to shy from directness, Birgit said, "Maybe not as bad as you did when the Hodgkins was in full swing, but you're getting close. What the hell happened?"

"Life happened. After Bobby Kennedy's assassination and what followed, my faith in the 'system' collapsed. The freedom and goodness, the promise that had been America when I grew up turned out to be a lie. Don't get me wrong, materially we're doing just fine, kids in private school, Dave away more that he should be, but, what the heck, he needs to work the long hours so we can live the way we do.

When they got to the house, Birgit went into the kitchen as effortlessly as if she'd lived in the place for the past five years. Everything was still where she'd remembered it. Within two minutes she was brewing a pot of black tea. "None of the designer teas and other crap they drink in your country," she said. "Thank God you still held it together enough to keep the cupboard stocked with Five Roses."

"Dave, not me," Penny said. "He found a place on the corner of Olympic and Doheny where he could pick it up. There's shortbread in the service porch cupboard."

As the two women sat on the light wooden chairs at the tiny kitchen table, Birgit sipped her tea contentedly. "Mmm, good stuff," she said. "Helluva lot better than that Lipton they sell here. The closest we come to this is PG Tips from England." She faced her friend and looked directly into her eyes.

"So everything's good but nothing's good. Is Dave having an affair?"

"Same old Birgit. You sure cut to the chase." She took a shortbread cookie from the plate in front of her, dipped it into the hot tea, and nibbled.

"Well?"

"I don't know. I wouldn't blame him if he was. It's been three months since …"

"My God, girl, are you saying …? Don't tell me he hasn't been interested?"

"I'm sure he has. I was too into my own self to care about sex. The kids run me ragged, I'm into two book groups and on God-knows-how many committees for this, that, and the other."

Birgit picked a shortbread cookie from the plate, crunched it decisively, and immediately grabbed another.

"Penny Jo Wagner, how long have we been friends?"

"Fourteen years this coming September.

"And we've always leveled with each other?"

"Uh-huh. Sometimes I've thought too much so."

"O.K. I'll level with you now. Making love once every three months is going to send Dave into the arms of another woman and may well send you guys to the divorce court sooner that you think. Don't bullshit me with that 'shocked' intake of breath. Whether you want to admit it or not, you know as well as I that when sex is good, that gets you through eighty percent of any problems in the marriage. Heck, even when it's not that good, it's way ahead of most everything else. But if there's no sex for more than a week, you've got a lot of explaining to do, mostly to yourself. Yes, I will have more of that delicious tea," she said sweetly, pouring herself another full cup.

"You don't understand. He works 'til all hours of the night, I'm exhausted when he comes home, and … I guess that sounds pretty lame-ass, doesn't it?"

Birgit said nothing, but simply sip-slurped her tea.

"He's a good man, Penny. And you're a good woman. Something made you turn in a direction that's made things go into a tailspin, an unnecessary tailspin."

"What do you suggest, Doctor Freud or Dr. Ruth or whoever?"

"Just remember, Penny, you are the same girl that willed yourself, yes, *willed* yourself, to beat Hodgkins disease. You didn't give up on yourself then, and you damn well better not give up on yourself now. Remember what your friend Doctor Lo said when you asked him how long you were going to survive?" She paused for a moment.

"What ever happened to Dr. Lo?" Birgit asked.

"I don't know. That was twelve years ago. I never kept up with him."

"You think he might have said you're cutting off part of the distance between your wrist and however long you've got?"

Penny thought back to her first year at Cal Poly. This was exactly the type of conversation they'd always had. This was why they were closer than had they been blood sisters. She stood up, put the teacups and saucers in the sink, and ran water while she rinsed them off. "Did you come here to help me find some kind of epiphany?"

"Sorry, Penny Jo," Birgit responded. "Despite what you might read in everything from the Bible to *Cosmopolitan*, there's no such thing as a sudden great flash of light and a choir of heavenly Hosannahs. Life's its own epiphany. The best you can do is to take one small step at a time and hope you don't fall into a mud puddle and break your leg. Want to know what I think?"

"I fear another lecture is coming." But Penny smiled.

"I think you're bored to death and you're hiding from that boredom."

"You mean I should take on a lover?"

"That might cure you for a month before you'd get bored again. No, I think what you might consider is something more positive, more meaningful. Apropos nothing at all, I listened to a radio program in Dijon a couple of months ago. They had a dog psychiatrist on. Silliest damned thing I ever heard. Someone called in and asked the guy, 'Why would a dog need a psychiatrist? We give them everything. Love, attention, food, they don't want for a thing.'

"The psychiatrist said, 'Maybe that's the point. When a dog herds sheep on a farm, or goes hunting with his master, or even when he guards a junkyard, he's got a job to do. He feels *needed*. He's too busy *doing* something to be bored. He feels, as much as a dog can, that he's got a *reason* for being here. But now we don't need a dog to herd sheep anymore, so the dog's become someone's spoiled, pampered toy, and his sense of worth is nonexistent. We really don't know what a dog feels, but it's a fairly common belief that everyone has to have *some* purpose, and if it doesn't have a purpose and feels useless, that dog or cat or man or woman tends to find ways to try to beat the boredom'"

"Makes sense," Penny said.

"Made sense to me, too. A bored animal chews furniture or digs holes in the backyard, or poops on the carpet."

"You're saying I reacted like an animal?"

"Bingo, my friend! Gold star for the lady. You don't chew furniture, you simply bury yourself in stuff that's so far beneath what you're capable of doing you might as well be in suspended animation. I think you're bored because you're thirty-two, you think you're wasting your life being nothing but a mommy, as you'd probably call it, and because your husband is climbing the ladder of success in a profession where you have as much training as he does, and probably a lot more creativity."

"You think I should go back to work?"

"Drop the word 'back.' You never worked a day in your life at what you were trained to do. Did you ever think you might fail at engineering? That it was somehow a man's profession?"

"Well … uh …"

"And that, my friend, answers the question of why you are where you are. That'll be $5,000 in shrink fees."

As they walked into the Wagners' capacious living room, Penny found herself genuinely laughing. "You really think I could?"

"Maybe, maybe not. Did you ever ask the question, 'Can I beat cancer?' or 'Can I stand up to those toughs at Venice Beach?' Or … let's get down and dirty, Girl, 'Can I turn Andy Burgess on if I strip all the way to nothing?' Life is challenge, Penny."

She paused, picked up a small statuette of two lovers embracing, and looked at the writing on its base. *Count the stars in the sky. Measure my love for you.*

"You walk through life step by step. Regardless of what happens, you keep walking ahead until your time comes. Muddling through life the best you can, is its own epiphany. Remember what we did a hundred years or so ago, when you'd realized you just might survive Hodgkins?"

"Mmm-hmm," Penny murmured. "You made me take my dad's old Pontiac to Micelli's on LaCienega. For the first time in a year, I felt I might still be alive and I might still be around some day to marry a rich guy. I felt withered and skinny and useless …"

"A little bit like now?"

"Maybe. After lunch you forced me to go to a boutique and look at clothes, which was the very last thing I felt like doing. But you pushed me in the door, Miss Denmark with her long blonde hair and superboobs. So just to humor you, I went to a rack and pulled out a clingy, low cut blue sweater. I thought it was way too revealing, but you said, 'It's perfect. Why don't you try it on?' and when I walked out with my new sweater, I actually felt sexy, even though I was nothing but a bag of bones."

"You think it might be time to go back to LaCienega?"

Penny glanced at her watch. Dave was at work. It would be four hours before Jim and Kassy came home from school.

"Why not?"

And they did.

That might not have been the start of Penny's journey back to the real world, but you'd never convince her of that.

❦

"Kind of thin on experience," Penny half-joked to the employment counselor, a striking blonde woman fifteen years older, who seemed genuinely interested in her.

"Maybe," the woman said. "But you impressed some important people when you worked on the Bobby Kennedy campaign in sixty-eight. You have two children. I surmise you dropped out to help them along when they needed you most."

"Something like that. Do I notice a European accent?"

"Hungarian," the woman, whose name was Eva, said. "I escaped some years ago, at a time when I could barely speak English. For the first couple of years, I worked as a hostess at a restaurant in Washington, D.C. My vocabulary was limited to 'Good evening,' and 'This way, please.'" She laughed. "If I was able to get where I wanted to be, why not you?"

After an insightful half-hour interview, the woman said, "I won't kid you by saying it's not a challenge. But this is 1973. Women are becoming a force to reckon with in the workplace. You've got an engineering degree from Cal Poly San Luis Obispo, and some real-world experience that made you a few friends in high places. I can't promise you anything, but we at Ability Search have a reputation for getting things done."

❦

"Penny? Eva June at Ability Search. I might have something interesting for you to consider. Do you know the term 'logistics?'"

"Arranging to get things from Point 'A' to Point 'B.'"

"Exactly. I've got a small startup company that just moved to Memphis, Tennessee … They've got twenty-two small aircraft."

"How small a company can it be if they've got that kind of inventory? Even if they had only one Cessna 172, I can happily use a job, any job, Eva, but you pegged it right when you said family comes first. Dave's been with Teledyne for years and he's not moving. Besides, it's not as if we need the money…"

"I didn't say you did. Actually, it's just as well you don't 'cause this company is a real shoestring operation. They need someone to go back to Memphis and train there for six weeks, then become their part-time logistics manager at Burbank. When they heard that you had a great PR run with Kennedy *and* an engineering degree, they said they'd like to talk to you. While they can't afford to pay you much more than minimum wage, they'd sweeten the pie by giving you a few hundred shares of stock in the company, not that that means a damn thing, 'cause their stock is probably worth less than five cents a share. But what have you got to lose?"

"Do you mean my virginity or my husband?"

Warm laughter erupted at the other end of the phone. "A sense of humor like that can't hurt either. What say you talk it over with your husband and call me back in a couple days?"

❦

"Forty-two days?" Dave said equably. "Nothing much to lose. The stock might be worth a little money some day, and it gets you in the professional door, so why not go for it? What'd you say the name of the company was?"

"It sounds a lot more pretentious than it probably is. They call it Federal Express."

❦

Since Penny had started with FedEx four-and-a-half years ago, the few hundred shares she'd been given as a bonus when they promoted her to full time were now worth in the six figures, making her both financially independent and self-sufficient. Dave had continued his steady ascent at Teledyne. Each of them had reached a plateau in their professional lives. Jimmy and Kassy were a reflection of Richie and Joanie Cunningham on the *Happy Days* TV show.

Every day had a certain sameness. Dinner out twice a week, a play at the Ahmanson once a month, six visits to the Philharmonic each year, a once a week visit to the nearest of the Paiks' eight martial arts centers, three hundred days of sunshine a year, more money than they could use, a marriage that, while not electric with passion, had settled into a mutually satisfying friendship. No real highs, no real lows. Life was easy, privileged, unchallenging.

Ten months ago, Dave had suggested they take flying lessons for no particular reason other than that it might come in handy some day. "Besides, it would be fun flying all over the place in no time, showing off for the kids … "

"I don't know," Penny replied. "It sounds scary."

"This from a lady who's a black belt in tae kwon do, who beat back a pretty frightening disease some years ago," he said, patting her on the arm, "not to mention jumping into an executive position with FedEx?"

"O.K., expensive, then."

"Yeah, right," he said. "If you're so all-fired worried about *that* aspect, I'm sure we could find ways to write it off without even pretending to be dishonest. Tell you what, honey, Van Nuys Flying School is offering a 20-minute introductory flight over L.A. for seventy-five bucks to see if we'd be interested in learning to fly. I'll make you a deal. I know I'd like to learn, but why don't you go up alone with the flight instructor and see how you feel about it? "

❦

By the time Penny had put sixty hours into flying lessons, her exhilaration showed. She'd soloed as far as Bakersfield, then over to Santa Maria before flying back to Whiteman. One afternoon, two weeks before she was to test for her license, she and Hank, her instructor, were flying south toward Oxnard when he suddenly cut the power to minimum. Penny stifled her panic and her need to scream when Hank quietly told her, "When you're up in the air, always expect the unexpected. This is not like a car, you can't just pull over to the nearest gas station or expect the Triple-A to come."

"What do I do?" She noticed that her voice was tremulous. "I can't expect you'll be with me either."

"First and most important, stay calm. Second, stay calm. Remember what you learned at ground school?"

"Y-yes." At that moment she didn't remember a thing, but Hank's voice continued smoothly, comfortingly.

"Look to see if there's any flat place that might be long enough to set the plane down."

"Like an airport?"

"That'd be best, but you can't always depend on it. Again, keep your cool."

"But what if there's no time?"

"You're at ten thousand feet. A light plane's more like a glider than a rock. Remember what I told you about descending? Flaps up ten degrees."

She did, and the plane slowed noticeably. More panic as the airspeed needle dropped from one hundred-twenty to one hundred.

"Good. Check your rate of descent."

She did. "Five hundred feet per minute,"

"No engine running and your airspeed's steady," Hank said. "You're at ninety-five hundred and let's say the altitude on the ground is five hundred. Gives you nine thousand feet of drop 'til you land."

Penny's heart stopped racing. She started to concentrate on looking for a flat area where she might land. She started doing calculations in her head.

"Eighteen minutes," Hank said, his voice maintaining the same calm monotone. "Heck of a long time to find a place to land, and you can go twenty-five miles in any direction before you do. Just thought I'd do the figuring so you can concentrate on landing."

Penny's eyes lit on a large, flat patch of ground about three miles away. Farm land. She pointed toward it.

"O.K., you've got one landing site. As you get closer, you can look out for trees, telephone poles, wires, and such. Good idea to scout other possibilities. Start circling slowly. Plenty of room to do that."

As she started to circle, all the while keeping a steady descent, Hank took the microphone and called, "L.A. Center, Cessna four-five-five-four zulu."

"Five four zulu." A disembodied male voice came over the speaker.

"Five-four-zulu, Skyhawk one-zero miles east of Oxnard at seven thousand, student on board. Practicing emergency landing."

"Five-four-zulu, turn transponder to one-two-five-five." He did.

"Five-four-zulu, confirm we have you at six-six-hundred. No targets nearby. Descent approved."

During the next five minutes Penny's sense of fear diminished to almost nothing. This was simply a job like any other and she concentrated. When the aircraft reached five thousand feet, Penny pointed to another field, this one somewhat longer than the first and away from any inhabited area.

"Good. Keep circling 'till you get down to two thousand."

She did, dutifully, keeping her eyes constantly moving from left to right and back, as she'd been taught. When they'd descended to two thousand feet, Penny repeated the landing procedure she's learned rote, "Flaps up to twenty degrees, airspeed ninety." The aircraft nosed up.

Just as suddenly as the engine had cut back several minutes ago, it suddenly came back to life with a roar as Hank pushed in the gas. She didn't even have time to be nervous as the noise level increased and the plane started climbing.

"Excellent job, Penny!" her instructor said, patting her on the arm. "You've passed your last big hurdle with flying colors. Let's take this bird over to Oxnard and have a well-deserved cup of coffee and a pee-stop."

During the next two years, Dave and Penny spent several weekends exploring California and Arizona aboard their Cessna 182, a muscular four-seat single-engine plane they'd purchased. By the time 1980 came to an end, both Jim and Kassy had learned to solo, although they couldn't get their pilots' licenses before they were seventeen.

Often, when she was thinking of nothing else, Penny found herself humming the refrain of Peggy Lee's *Is That All There Is?*, or mouthing the words to a song she'd heard a few months before, *I've Never Been to Me*.

In her teens, Penny had been tall, attractive, but never the knockout bombshell some of the girls at Hamilton had been. More and more nowadays, particularly as she looked at what, to her, was a beautiful body and a striking face, she thought back, not without longing, to the awakening of her sexual desires with Andy Burgess, a hundred or so years ago. *What ever happened to Andy? If we had stayed together and become serious? What then?*

Even more often, she found herself daydreaming about that European man she had met for one unbelievably magic evening in Vienna when she was nineteen. Before the Hodgkins. Lev something-or-other – *Arkady*, that was it. In her imagination, more than just once, she had magnified their few hours together into the *real* grand passion of her life, the one that had stopped short and never materialized.

34

"Wujek, looks like you really became 'Holier than Thou,' even though in your present garb I'd hardly have mistaken you for God's Anointed," Lev said irreverently. The two men had arranged to meet in utmost secrecy in a nondescript cabin in the Žabia Valley, a no man's land between Poland and Slovakia, two kilometers from Mengusovské Lake.

The older man, dressed in ski pants, boots, a heavy woolen sweater, a scruffy leather coat, and a ski mask, which he'd removed on entering the cabin, was accompanied by a younger priest, Stanisław Dziwisz, who'd been his personal secretary for the past thirteen years. Dziwisz sat in a far corner of the cabin, brewing a pot of tea.

"Reminds me of a joke," Lev continued. " An old Jewish grandfather and an old Catholic grandfather were in Krakow one day, elaborating on how high each of their children had risen in life … 'My son made it to be the Pope Himself!' said the Catholic, gloating. 'Nu, and *then?*' the old Jew asked.

"'What do you mean and then …?" his Catholic friend said, aghast. What did you expect him to be, Jesus Christ?'"

"'One of *our* boys did it,'" the man who was still "Wujek" to only a few of his closest associates finished the old joke, winking at Lev.

"So what do you expect me to call you?" Lev asked.

"How many names have you known me by over the years, 'Mister Carter?'"

"Let's see …" Lev began, counting the fingers of his left hand by gently striking them with his right forefinger. "Karol, of course. That was thirty-four years ago …"

"Ah, yes," Wujek smiled and winked. "You were ten years old, buck naked, and tied to a tree near Old Amos as I recall."

"Then there was Andrzej Jawień the poet and Stanisław Andrzej Gruda, the playwright and actor," Lev continued, ticking off the next two fingers. There was talk about a Jewish girlfriend, Ginka Beer. Of course that was before you got ordained."

Father Dziwisz looked up sharply, but said nothing. Wujek's expression betrayed no emotion, but his eyes seemed to cloud over, as if thinking about a different path his life might have taken.

"Ah, yes," he murmured under his breath, "Slender, incredible eyes, a superb actress… " He looked steadily at Lev.

"Then there was Wujek – 'Uncle' – so you could remain a *human* friend when you became the Archbishop. And now, of course, Your Holiness, John Paul II," Lev concluded. "Is it true what they say about the Pope's hat being so heavy?"

"The Tiara, the Mitre, the Zucchetto, or the Camauro?"

"Any of them, take your choice."

"The 'Pope's hat' can be as light or as heavy as the wearer lets it be."

"Still the poet," Lev remarked. "Aside from the fact that I'm probably the only one in the August Presence who can still call a spade a 'shit shovel,' and not be damned to hell, is there any reason I was summoned to a very private meeting with the Holy Father himself?"

"There is," John Paul replied. "And might *I* add, you seem to have acquired all of Old Amos' brass balls and charm. You've also done an amazing amount of good over the years without being caught in the net. Höfer and all that."

Father Dziwisz brought two plain ceramic mugs of tea over and handed one each to the Pontiff and to Lev Arkady.

"I'd have to attend Confession every moment of my life if I didn't say I made a hefty fortune for myself from my so-called 'good works.'"

"Doesn't make them any worse for the fact that you made a profit, Lev. I don't recall hearing that anyone was deliberately hurt by anything you've done. A decade ago I was one of 'Uncle Buck's' regular listeners. But to answer your question, I asked you here for a reason. Shall we go outside for a little fresh air?"

Lev, whose years had attuned him to every inflection, not only in the words a man spoke, but in the way he spoke them, nodded. The air was brisk but not cold. The Pope, after ensuring there were no others within the clearing, addressed his friend.

"Unlike the media which tells me what I want to hear or what I don't want to hear, depending on their point of view, I trust you to tell me the real fallout from my June visit, what the little people are thinking. I know our Communist leaders intended to use my visit to show the people that even though the Pope was Polish it didn't affect their capacity to govern."

"Frankly, Karol, you handled the situation in the best way possible. Amos would have been proud of you. You used the power of the Papacy to duck politics altogether. You started out with an enormous advantage, and then you exploited it to the fullest."

"Meaning?"

"You head the one institution that stands for the exact opposite of Communism. You're a Pole, but because of who you are and what your represent, the regime can't touch you. By identifying with you, the Poles disdain the compromises they have to make to live under the regime. So they came and they listened. You told them to be good, not to compromise themselves, to stick by one another, to be fearless, and that God is the only source of goodness.

"When you said 'Be not afraid,' I was in the audience when millions shouted in response, 'We want God!' How could the regime fight that? They couldn't. Had you chosen to turn your soft power into hard words, the regime might have been drowned in blood. Instead, you simply led the Polish people to desert their rulers by affirming solidarity with one another."

"Interesting turn of phrase. Almost as if you're anticipating what I want to say."

"*Solidarność?* Solidarity? Lech Wałęsa's movement?"

"Exactly. What do you know about him?"

"Mostly hearsay."

"But you *hear* what the people *say.*"

"Just about the time the *Mi Amigo* went into drydock and I found my rear end back on this side of the Curtain, he organized the strikes at the Gdańsk Shipyard. Since then, he's been on the government's shit list, under constant surveillance by the Polish secret police."

"So you *do* keep your ear to the ground?"

"Höfer's been involved from time to time."

"I've never said you're not a perceptive man," the Pope said, grinning. "But standing out here while our mouths are the only parts of our bodies moving does nothing to keep us in shape. Let's walk awhile.

As they did, John Paul II expounded on his half-formed plan. "You've heard of the *Istituto per le Opere di Religione?*"

"The Vatican Bank?"

"Yes. The Bank is a major shareholder in the Italian *Banco Ambrosiano*."

"Roberto Calvi's operation. 'God's banker.'"

"Correct. It would not be expedient for the world to know that the Church is getting its hands dirtied in earthly politics."

"May I cut through this, Holiness?"

"So now it's 'Holiness'?"

"Whatever you want to call it, Karol. The Church wants to show solidarity with *Solidarity* but no one's supposed to know that?"

"Mmmm," John Paul murmured noncommittally.

"And *someone* might want to arrange for an unknown and unsuspected person, someone visibly *not* connected with the Church, to transfer a substantial sum of cash money that never appears anywhere on anyone's books to an equally trusted nonentity, who in turn will …?"

An hour later, the two men returned to the cabin from their hike. During that time, Lev had outlined his plan to implement what John Paul wanted to achieve.

When His Holiness, the Spiritual head of the largest church in Christendom, entered the cabin, he was laughing so hard his face was almost purple, tears streamed from his eyes, and he found it hard to catch his breath.

Father Dziwisz, startled by the Pope's appearance, rushed over with a wooden chair and bade his superior sit immediately. He rushed to a nearby sink, wet a dish towel with cold water, and brought it over to John Paul, prepared to bathe the Pontiff's face.

"Your Holiness …?"

John Paul took a few deep breaths and his color returned to normal. "There's no need for that, Stan," he said to his worshipful junior. "It's ... it's ..." He broke into uncontrolled spasms of laughter again. "You remember what you and I were talking about on the way up here? In private, of course?"

"I do," Dziwisz said cautiously, recalling the Pope's admonition that in Poland anyone could be listening to anything, and even this remote cabin could be bugged.

"Our Jewish friend has come up with a plan that is so ... so ..." John Paul coughed to keep from laughing, "absurd," he continued, "that only a man named Amos, whom he and I knew in another lifetime, could have come up with such a scheme and, what's more, made it work."

Although Lev had told John Paul that when his stint on Radio Caroline came to an end, he'd found his rear end back on the eastern side of the Iron Curtain, that was only half true. He resumed exactly where he'd left off, successfully and profitably plying his huckstering trade in the Socialist Workers' Paradise.

Still, while his personal fortune multiplied geometrically in his Swiss bank accounts, Lev had never forgotten his humble roots, nor the moral debt he owed Karol Wojtyla, not a personal debt, but a much larger debt to Lev's people, which the Pope undoubtedly had long ago forgotten. There were still enough Jews in Poland who had confirmed to him time and again that it was true.

What was widely known was that Wojtyła had helped protect many Polish Jews from the Nazis during the Holocaust. What was not generally known, during the Nazi occupation of Poland, a Jewish family had sent its son, Stanley Berger, to be hidden by a Gentile Polish family. Berger's biological Jewish parents died during the Holocaust, and after the war Berger's new Christian parents asked a young Polish priest named Karol Wojtyla to baptize the boy. Wojtyla refused to do so, stating that the child should be raised in the Jewish faith of his birth parents, not as a Catholic. It is said in the Talmud that he who saves a single soul has saved the Universe. By that simple act, Karol Wojtyla had done his part to save one small part of the remnant Jews that survived the ovens.

Could Lev do anything less than repay the debt? And as long as the Pontiff's request was so minimal as to require no great effort on Lev's part, there was no reason why he couldn't have a great deal of fun in the process.

While Luke Carter continued to travel from Estonia to Bulgaria and from the Turkish frontier to the Croatian coast, and to ubiquitously appear in all these locales with his irreverent patter, his slot machines, and four associates who now assisted him in his greatly expanded show of shows, Lev refused to let Uncle Buck die, which necessitated his living another life on the Western side of the divide.

Hof, situated in the northeastern corner of Bavaria, five miles from the tiny town of Luby in Communist Czechoslovakia, had a population of only fifty thousand, but Lev had been enchanted, both by Hof's location, and by the lively cultural mecca it had become when he'd put down roots in 1970. Hof boasted an annual film festival, a small but growing orchestra, a choir, a youth symphony, and a ballet. The annual Hofer Volksfest was the largest of its kind in eastern Bavaria and western Bohemia. Within two years of his arrival, Lev had become a member of the festival board. The mayor was not averse to the dramatic increase in the size and success of the folk fair after Lev Arkady / Luke Carter had come to town.

Lev built a small studio at the back of his home. During his three days a month in Hof, he recorded a series of broadcasts as "Uncle Buck," which were then sent to a number of stations throughout Western Germany, and to the Voice of America.

While northern Germany is predominantly Lutheran Protestant, Bavaria has always been a Roman Catholic stronghold, so it was no surprise that when Lev revealed his plan to the Mayor, Dr. Heun enthusiastically agreed to it. The plan was further facilitated when Dr. Heun told Lev that almost all of the participants he intended to enlist were fluent in Polish and many had relatives where the plan was to be executed.

35

On July 2, 1980, Lev received a message with no name or address. "Gift from Uncle arrives 5 July, M.V. White Sea, Stocznia Szczecińska."

Three days later, a middle-aged Catholic priest arrived at the Port of Szczecin, the morthwesternmost city in Poland. When he asked where he might find the White Sea, he was directed to a small cargo vessel of indeterminate age. Within ten minutes, he was joined by a similarly clad Black priest, who addressed him respectfully, handed him a small leather briefcase, and bowed slightly. The Caucasian nodded in reply, returned to his car, and drove to Old Town. He parked in front of St. James the Apostle's Basilica.

When he entered the squat building, Archbishop Majdański greeted him. The "priest," Lev Arkady, handed the briefcase, which he had not bothered to open, to the archbishop, then took his leave.

The following day at three in the afternoon, Lev met a younger man with a bushy moustache, whom he had only seen in newspaper photos and on the television, in a small bar in Sopot, halfway between Gdynia and Gdańsk.

"Archbishop Majdański has a small gift for you from Wujek," Lev said. No names were used.

"I'm sure one of their lackeys is in this room, watching and listening as we speak," Wałęsa replied

"Are you going to the concert at the entrance to Long Street on the twelfth?"

"I have no idea what you're talking about. I've never heard of it."

"One of choir singers will be wearing a gray rucksack on her back. The rucksack will have a large red patch with the number 5 on it."

"How will I …?"

"Eleven in the morning. Good day, Pan Zelisky. I have an appointment in Olsztyn this evening."

He made an abrupt exit. When the Solidarity leader stood and started to leave the booth, he saw that the man with whom he had been talking had left a gray rucksack bearing a large red patch and the number 5. When he lifted it, he found it was empty.

❧

The Hofer Volksfest was to start on the last Friday of July, which meant that Lev's enlistees would have time to work the plan to and return in time for the Fair.

Early in the morning of July 7, 1980, a Blaguss bus carried thirty-eight passengers, half of whom carried musical instrument cases, twenty-two miles, from Hof to Luby, where they were met by a bus owned by the Polish State Transportation Authority. Nine hours later, the passengers reached their destination.

❧

July 8, was a typically warm day in Gdańsk. By ten that morning, it was 21° Celsius, 70° Fahrenheit. Hardly a breeze stirred off the Baltic. Saturday, an abbreviated day for most of the dock workers, had started at six that morning. By ten-thirty, most of them had packed what there was to carry in their rucksacks and headed south along the canal toward their homes, which lay inland, beyond Gdańsk's tourist magnet, the newly rebuilt Old Town. The foreigners who'd spent the preceding night in hotels east of the quay, had either finished breakfast early or decided to eat in Old Town. By shortly after nine, most of them had crossed the bridge over the canal. An hour later, tour buses bearing the next wave of the day's visitors arrived. The day's catch of tourists was meager by international standards, but by quarter to eleven, three hundred people were strolling through the pedestrian-only streets.

As the clocks from several nearby towers and churches bonged or chimed eleven times, there was a momentary silence in Old Town. When the visitors saw what was happening, a sudden murmur soon turned into an excited buzz.

From out of nowhere, thirty-eight people materialized, half of them carrying musical instruments. They ranged from twenty to seventy. Some wore skimpy shorts and halter tops. Others wore formal evening wear. Still others wore blue jeans and bright print shirts and dock workers' industrial clothing. All of them seemed to be headed toward the Long Street entrance to Old Town. The crowd gravitated toward this spectacle.

Moments later, without so much as tuning their instruments or adjusting their voices, the musicians started playing and the choir started singing the Ode to Joy from Beethoven's Ninth Symphony. Although by no means of the heroic size required to perform this great masterpiece, the group was remarkably melodious. Soon the choir was joined by fifty people in the immediate vicinity, most of whom had no idea of the words to the *Ode*, all of whom were willing to belt out la-la-la's to accompany the familiar theme with which they'd grown up.

A small woman accidentally bumped against a taller female choir member, causing the rucksack the chorister wore to slip from her shoulders. The smaller woman colored in apparent embarrassment and bent down to pick up the rucksack. As she did so, the rucksack worn by the smaller woman slipped from her back as well. As the small woman mumbled her apologies to the larger one, the two rucksacks, which looked very much alike, got confused. No one within range of either woman could tell that the two rucksacks had been switched. The smaller woman scurried away, her new, and substantially heavier, rucksack on her back.

The symphony continued for another three minutes, after which the thirty-eight members who'd originally appeared walked away in thirty-eight different directions, without even waiting for the storm of applause to die down.

On August 14, 1980, after another food price hike led to a strike at the Lenin Shipyard in Gdańsk, a strike of which he was one of the instigators, Wałęsa scaled the shipyard fence. Once inside, he became one of the strike leaders. That strike inspired similar strikes, first at Gdańsk, then across Poland. The Strike Coordinating Committee legalized itself as the National Coordinating Committee of the Solidarity Free Trade Union. Wałęsa became its chairman. Solidarity grew quickly, soon claiming over ten million members, more than a quarter of Poland's population. Wałęsa held his position until December 12, 1981, when General Jaruzelski declared martial law. On October 8, 1982, the general outlawed Solidarity. In 1983 Wałęsa returned to the Gdańsk Shipyard as a simple electrician. That same year, he was awarded the Nobel Peace Prize.

According to an influential historian of the Cold War, Pope John Paul's trip to Poland in 1979 led to the formation of Solidarity and began the process of Communism's demise in Eastern Europe. When the Pope kissed the ground at Warsaw airport, he began the process by which communism in Poland, and ultimately elsewhere in Europe, came to an end.

36

"My God," Penny said. "It's been a year since your dad passed." The "kids" – Jim was now in his third year at U.C.L.A. and Kassy had gone north to U.C. Davis, near Sacramento – had gathered at the family home for the winter break. "He was forty-nine, way too young to go," she continued. "And he was in good shape. A heart attack of all things."

"What's to say?" Jim responded. "You and he couldn't have been better parents. Kids grown and gone. …This year's been a really empty nest for you, Mom."

"Not that empty," Penny said, hugging them both. "You'll always be my little boy and my baby girl, no matter how long we live."

"Where do you go from here, Mom? I've got another year before I start vet school. I'd be happy to take time off, come down and be with you for awhile."

"No, Kassy. You need to get on with your own life. Besides, what would Roger think if his girlfriend went running home to mom at every turn?"

"He'd better damn well get used to it or the girlfriend would be gone in a heartbeat," she said. "Oh, my God, what a horrid thing of me to say, Mom. I'm so sorry."

"That's just a turn of the phrase, Kass. I took it that way."

"What *are* you going to do, Penny? Why don't you come over and stay with me for awhile? Lord knows you can afford it and then some. You can help in the vineyards."

"And keep track of your little ankle biters, Birgit? You need a Nanny?"

"Jean-Claude wouldn't mind if you and I went on vacation for a few weeks. Tina and Chris are old enough to make it on their own, with a little help from the neighbors."

"Why not, Mom?" Jim joined in. "You and dad were so busy working, you never got to travel. A change of scenery might do you good."

"What do you think, Kassy?"

"Sound goods to me. You're not that old, Mom. Forty-five's not grandma territory yet. And face it, you're pretty hot for an older gal."

"Kassandra Wagner, how dare you! Your father's been gone only a year and you're packing me off to a house of ill repute already!"

"You're sure as heck not ready to burn yourself on the funeral pyre," Jim added. "Kassy's a little more direct than me, but sooner or later you're going to have to get back to the business of living. Dad would have wanted that. I'm not saying you have to go to France tomorrow, but why don't you give it some thought?"

Penny and Dave had always lived below their means. The Trust they'd set up would easily see her through the rest of her life, but Penny was not one to let the grass grow under her feet. Although she was now head of Fed Ex's Los Angeles operations, as the memory of Dave started to fade gently, then more rapidly, she often thought about what Birgit and her children had said. It was not that dating wasn't an option. She did not try to fool herself that her life as a woman should come to a premature end. It was just that Penny still wasn't ready.

❦

Penny arrived in Paris in the late spring of 1988, shortly after her forty-seventh birthday.

"About time," Birgit remarked. "You still wearing widow's weeds?"

"If you mean have I dated yet, the answer is no. Not that I've closed that chapter of my life, it's just that no one interesting has come knocking at my door."

"Are you doing anything to market yourself?"

"Not really."

"Maybe it's time," Birgit said. "Like your daughter said last year, you are still one hot mama."

"This is not the way I normally dress," Penny said lightly. "It's been twenty-five years since I was last in Europe and I thought, 'What the hell have I got to lose?'"

"As you Americans say when you think no one else is listening, you're still a 'piece of ass,' although it's probably become a bit rusty from not being used for awhile."

"You are so-o-o diplomatic, my dear."

"And *you* are such a bullshitter."

"How long are we staying in Paris?"

"Two nights will give you a chance to reacquaint yourself with *La Reine du Monde* before we drive back to *Bourgogne*. Not enough time, but you can never spend too much time in the City of Light. Since you're here for the better part of the month, I figured we'd give you time to begin end your journey where you ended it in 1960."

❦

Jean-Claude Mouton was the stereotypical sophisticated country Frenchman, handsome, urbane, and possessed of an overflow of Gallic charm and slightly graying hair. Tina, nineteen, and Christopher, seventeen, were strikingly attractive young people. Tina had recently started living with her boyfriend, Michel, in an adjacent town. She, Michel, and Christopher greeted Penny with a huge spring bouquet and two bottles Mouton estate-grown burgundy when she arrived.

"Alas, everything but a gentleman friend for you," Birgit chided her friend. "Still, one can never tell what might happen on our journey."

Over a delicious dinner of chicken stewed in burgundy wine, potatoes *Lyonnaise*, and *haricots verts*, green beans, discussion turned to the ladies' upcoming journey. "I propose we go into the heart of Europe, where you've never been Penny. Switzerland, Austria, and Czechoslovakia."

"We've already been to Vienna."

"I was thinking more along the lines of Hallstatt, which is simply the most beautiful place in the world, Prague, which could rival Paris in the next forty years …"

"Would you mind picking me up on the way back?" Jean-Claude asked. "By that time you may have had your surfeit of the Continent."

"By all means, my love," Birgit said. "*Helas*, the travails of the poor working man."

Mouton lifted his eyebrows. "My Dear, as you are too well aware, someone has to work to support our extravagant lifestyle."

"*Oui, mon peuvre petit*," Birgit said. "My poor hardworking husband." To Penny, she added, "Our money is derived from our twenty-one hectares of Burgundy's best wine, plus an estate which Jean-Claude inherited. His true work is on the Board of a do-gooder organization in Vaduz, Liechtenstein, where he spends two days each month."

"It is a valuable service we provide."

"It's a secretive organization called Höfer G.m.b.H., which almost no one has ever heard of, that provides funding for socially worthwhile activities," Birgit added.

⁂

"You're right, Birgit. I predict this city will be the next Paris. I don't know which I enjoyed more, Hallstatt, Budapest, or Prague."

"And, of course, Vienna?"

"That, too," Penny said, a bit sadly. "It wasn't quite the same, though."

"We were nineteen back then. The start of our lives. So much water has gone under the bridge since then."

"Two old ladies with grown kids. Who'd have thought it would go by so fast?"

"Oh, Penny, we're not in the grave yet. Forty-seven is far from the end."

"It wasn't for Dave."

"It could have been you or me, but it wasn't, and if you want to get maudlin, it really *could* have been *you* way back when."

"Why do I feel that life's like a roll of toilet paper – the closer you get to the end the faster it goes?"

"Little Ms. Optimist, you can think that way all you want, but you really never know what's around the next corner."

"I do. The Jewish ghetto and *Stare Mesto*, the old town."

"Uh-huh. Six million people who never knew what tomorrow might bring. But they still held to their faith in God and to their faith in *life* until the very last moment. And so, my friend, should you."

⁂

West of Innsbruck the fore-Alps towered over them. Penny gasped, "Is this tunnel never going to end?"

"Probably," Birgit responded. "It's about fifteen kilometers in all."

"I'd get claustrophobic except for those openings on the sides. How far is Vaduz?"

"About an hour. Not much to see there. Some hills and a not particularly charming village that prints a lot of postage stamps and stock certificates. Five thousand people. Not much of a capital, but then again the Grand Duchy is tiny."

"Where do we pick up Jean-Claude?"

"Malbun, a ski resort nine miles beyond Vaduz. Their meetings always take place at the Familienhotel Gorfion, which looks like just about every other Alpine pension. It's far enough away from anyplace anyone has ever heard of, so it protects their privacy."

"How many people will be at the meeting?"

Birgit laughed brightly. "According to Jean-Claude, maybe five."

The Peugeot wound through the hills until it reached Malbun. The concierge, Henri, whom Birgit knew from several times before, met them at the front door. "Bonjour 'dames, they're in the meeting room waiting for you. Quite a crowd this time."

Birgit's eyebrows arched. "Forty? Fifty?"

"Seven." He led them to the conference room. "*Messieurs, Herren*, the ladies have arrived,"

As they entered the room, Penny heard a sudden sharp intake of breath.

"My God! It couldn't be! Penny? Penny Fullerton?"

As she gazed across the room in the direction of the voice, she felt her knees trembling and her face must have gone white.

"Lev?"
"Yes."

⋘⋙

Words didn't stop tumbling out of their mouths during the two hours they walked through the village and the surrounding mountain paths.

"I never knew … No one said … Jean-Claude only told me that his wife was bringing a girlfriend …"

"You never married? I can't believe it."

"And you? You look even more beautiful than you did all those years ago."

"And you are a consummate flatterer. I know I don't look the same. I *can't* look the same. Twenty-seven years and two grown children … I'm a widow …"

"I'm sorry."

"Dave was a good man. We were married twenty-two years. He was forty-nine when he died. You're …?"

"Fifty-four, no children. Life's been good."

"Mine as well."

"Boy? Girl?"

"One of each. Twenty-four and twenty-three. Older than I was when we met."

Little words. A lifetime of missed memories. A return to life.

⋘⋙

Later, when they lay resting side by side, the room suffused with the musky scent of their lovemaking, she looked over at him, her eyes aglow. "Thank you, Lev," she said quietly. "I may be far from the way I once was, but you certainly made me feel like the most desirable woman in the world."

"You are, Penny," he said gently. "It's certainly been more than worth the wait."

"Did you ever think of me during those years?"

"Truthfully? No less than a thousand times."

"I'm glad," she said, squeezing his hand affectionately. "Me, too."

"While you were married?"

"Many times. Many, many times. Surely there've been women in your life?"

"I won't lie to you. But this has truly been … Not since …"

"Agata?"

"You remembered?"

She reached over and ruffled the whitening hairs on his chest. "We compressed a lifetime's worth of memories into one evening. An evening which, I might add, did not finish quite as I had hoped it would. A thousand times? Maybe a hundred times that. And now we've completed what we started all those years ago… They say that life begins at whatever age you find love. Our lives have just begun, Mister Lev Arkady."

⚜

Dear Jim & Kassy,

… So now you're about to get the shock of your lives and I hope you don't cast your dear old mother out of your lives. His name is Lev Arkady. I first met him when I was nineteen, on my first trip to Europe with Aunt Birgit … ,. Aunt Birgit swears she had no idea he'd be at the meeting. And … …! I love you both so much! Your Mom

P.S. His life story reads like a cross between James Michener and Indiana Jones! I swear it!

⚜

Mom,

 When do we meet the guy?" Kassy

❦

 You're no dumbass. You've always been the smartest woman I know, but I won't call you a smartass! Go for it! I love you. Jim

❦

 J. & K.
 He said, "Pick a place you'd like to go. A place you've never been." Without thinking, I said, "Last year I saw a picture about Mount Ararat, where Noah's Ark supposedly put down." I said it as a joke. Lev said, "Turkey's a big country. You'll need at least three weeks to see it. Can you afford the time?" Should I go? Help!

❦

Yep! Jim.

❦

 What have you got to lose? Your virginity? Again? - K

37

Penny and Lev met their pilot, Hüsseyin Ovacık, at a small airstrip south of Doğubayazit. He was busily checking out their aircraft, a DeHavilland Beaver, when they arrived shortly after 8:00 a.m. Penny approached the high-winged single-engine craft, a "taildragger" with fixed landing gear and struts bracing each side of the wing. "This plane looks pretty small to be attacking such a huge mountain."

"Not to worry," the pilot said. "This is the strongest aircraft for its size ever built. I've flown it for almost twenty years. It has never given me one minute's trouble. I fly around Büyük Ağrı at least thirty times a year. As you Americans say, 'no problem.' Big, strong airplane, big, strong pilot."

"How high will we be flying, Hüsseyin Bey?" Lev asked.

"Twenty thousand feet, three thousand feet higher than the summit. But we won't fly over the mountain. It is safest to stay at least ten miles away from the peak and fly around it. We have permission to fly over Iranian airspace, but I try to stay on the Turkish side of the mountain. As soon as we get to twelve thousand, five hundred feet, it's required by international law that we have oxygen for everyone. We'll start early, before winds pick up and clouds cover the top of the mountain."

They found the aircraft roomier than they'd expected. The pilot sat in the front left-hand seat. Lev sat next to him. Penny sat in the next row of seats.

"It's a good idea to wear earplugs," the pilot said, handing them plastic packets. "This is a noisy plane."

Moments later, the plane took off. The Beaver required only a third of the three thousand foot long airstrip before it leapt into the air. Lev marveled at how slowly the plane seemed to be flying. He pressed the intercom button on his headset and asked the pilot, "Are you sure we're going fast enough to stay up?"

"Oh, yes," the pilot said, laughing. "One hundred ten miles an hour."

"It seems like we're sitting still."

"That's because we're flying much higher than the surrounding land. Everything looks much smaller and it feels like we're going slower, too." When he reached twenty thousand feet, he leveled the plane and headed toward Ararat.

As he neared the mountain, Lev looked anxious. "I thought you said we'd stay at least ten miles away from Ağrı Dağ."

"We're a good twenty miles away." He pressed the radio communications switch and continued in English. "Kars Tower, Beaver three-two-eight-one-seven, seventeen west of Ağrı Dağ, request permission to overfly Iğdir, then southeast."

"Eight-one-seven. Surface winds three-zero-zero at two-zero knots. TAF Hercules reports strong updrafts and downdrafts southeast of Iğdir, advise caution."

The two passengers concentrated on the stunning vista below. The aircraft seemed to hang in the air. Although Lev saw that the airspeed indicator showed one hundred twenty-five miles per hour, the mountain and the ground hardly seemed to move. What seemed like an hour later, but was only twenty minutes according to Lev's watch, the sturdy craft passed over a featureless town and turned gently to the right. Another quarter hour and they seemed much closer to Mount Ararat.

Without warning, the aircraft descended rapidly and seemed much nearer to the ground than Lev felt was safe. He poked the pilot to gain his attention.

"Downdraft," the pilot said. "There should be an updraft within a minute and we'll be climbing even faster than we're going down."

"I don't know …" Lev began, then stopped in mid-sentence as the plane suddenly climbed steeply. He was just starting to relax when the aircraft went into a steep descent again, followed by a spate of turbulence that shook the craft like a giant hand.

He looked over at the pilot, who'd suddenly gone white. "*Kalp!*" he gasped. "My heart! *Allahhhh!*" The pilot let go of the wheel and doubled up in pain. Moments later, he'd ceased his breathing and turned blue.

Lev had no time to look back at Penny. He had the dual control wheel in his hand, but with no flying experience he was terrified.

Penny took control of the moment. She touched his shoulder, pointed to the radio, and said calmly, "Dial 121.5, press the communications button, and call '*Mayday!*' three times. We're not going anywhere that fast that we won't get help."

It took less than ten seconds for him to receive a response, thank God in English. "Aircraft calling Mayday, Erzurum Center, please identify yourself and your location."

Penny signaled to Lev to hand her the microphone. She replied, "DeHavilland Beaver … we're very near Mount Ararat … I can't tell the altitude, it keeps going up and down rapidly."

"Beaver, are you a pilot?"

"Affirmative," Penny responded. "But I'm in the rear seat and no way to get up front. My companion is flying from the right seat."

"Put your captain on the radio, please."

The plane gave a sudden lurch upward and Lev's hands tightened on the wheel. "The captain had a heart attack. I don't know if he's alive," Penny said, her voice calm.

"Beaver, do you have a transponder?"

"Yes, Sir. Small yellow bulb in the center of the instrument panel?"

"Affirmative. Is it blinking?"

"Negative. Time you spoke with the man flying the plane. I'll try to help as best I can from the rear seat."

"All right. Beaver, listen to me. Please follow my instructions to the letter. First thing, flip the small switch up." Lev did, and was encouraged as the small yellow light started blinking. "I have you on my radar, Beaver. You are eight miles north-northeast of Büyük Ağrı. Look up at your compass, it's at the very top of the instrument panel, in the center of your windshield. What do the numbers read?"

"They're whirling around, but they seem to center on one hundred fifty."

"Beaver, make an *immediate* left turn. *Gently* push in the left side foot pedal and turn the wheel *gently* to the left. Keep doing that until I say Stop."

"Y ... yes, sir," Lev said, concentrating on the controller's words, silently blessing the disembodied voice. "The plane's still going up and down and rocking hard."

"That's all right, Beaver. You're not in danger. Just concentrate on turning slowly to the left. My radar shows you turning north, away from Büyük Ağrı. What does the compass show?"

"Thirty."

"Good. Keep turning left until you hit three hundred. How's the turbulence?"

"A bit better."

"The pilot?"

"Not good."

"Any other souls on board?"

"Just the lady, the pilot, and me. Where are we now?"

"Thirty miles south of Yerevan, Armenian Socialist Republic. We'd like to keep you in Turkish airspace and get you as close to Kars as possible."

The ride had just smoothed out and Lev was starting to breathe regularly when the engine coughed and started to sputter. The engine caught, then faltered, caught, faltered again, and quit. Instinctively, he called out *"Mayday!"* again.

"Beaver, Erzurum Center still with you. You're heading is fine."

"Th … that's not the problem, Sir. We've lost power. We're going down."

"All right, Beaver, listen carefully. What is your altitude?"

"Twelve thousand and falling rapidly."

"All right. Push the wheel forward very slightly, to keep your airspeed up. Do not, repeat, *do not* turn the plane in any way. Look down and around the countryside for the most level piece of land you can see."

Penny looked as well. There appeared to be a long, flat valley between the rolling, mountainous land. Penny tapped Lev's shoulder and pointed to the valley.

"Erzurum Center, I see a valley slightly to my right."

"Good. Aim for that valley. What is your airspeed?"

"One hundred thirty."

"Perfect. Keep that speed up and point the nose of your aircraft down a little more. What's you altitude?"

"Ten thousand."

"Good. Do you have any power?"

"No."

"All right. Avoid any turns because my radar shows high mountains on either side of you. The elevation of the land is fifty-two hundred feet. Do you have flaps?"

"I don't know."

"Look to your left, about the center of the plane. You should see something that looks like an emergency brake on a car."

"I see it."

"Lift up on the lever."

He did. The airspeed quickly dropped to ninety miles per hour. "Uh-oh. My airspeed has gone way down."

"That's all right, Beaver. Point the nose farther down." Lev did. "When your airspeed shows one hundred, leave the plane in exactly that position and push the *right* foot pedal gently."

Lev noticed that his hands, which had been squeezing hard on the wheel, had started to tremble. The controller's voice jarred him. "Beaver, my radar will lose you at six thousand. When you get to that altitude, start to flare for landing."

"Flare?"

"Pull the nose back up as high as you can."

"But we'll crash!"

"You'll probably have a hard landing, but you'll survive. The plane won't stall until you're going about sixty miles an hour. If you're within seventy-five feet of the ground you'll be just fine."

"Stay with me as long as you can, Erzurum. Just in case."

"Will do, Beaver, but you're off my radar now."

The plane settled down gently. The actual landing wasn't that jarring, but, as with all taildraggers, the Beaver's nose was high, and Lev couldn't see the huge boulder directly ahead of the plane. The aircraft crashed into the boulder at forty miles per hour. And everything went black.

38

"I think my right leg's broken and my wrist doesn't function normally. How about you, Penny?"

"Bruised, shaken up, but still in one piece. Is the pilot …?"

"Yes. The front end of the aircraft's a mess."

"Try the Electronic Locator Transmitter." She pointed to where it would be.

"Not working."

Within an hour of their landing, Penny and Lev fashioned a splint for Lev's leg and managed to move him out of the plane.

"No emergency rations or supplies on board," she said. "Nothing but barren wasteland as far as I can see. We may as well be on Mars."

"No telephone lines or signs of habitation?" Lev asked.

"Nothing. Not even a stream. Fortunately, we've got a three-liter bottle of water in the hold. Otherwise, we'd really be in trouble."

They sat in a patch of shade created by the plane's shadow. Penny had given Lev four ibuprofen tablets while they were splinting his leg. It was the best she could do.

"Erzurum Center caught our Mayday signal and had us on radar until ten minutes before we landed," Lev ventured. "The emergency transmitter is not functioning, which would arouse them. I wouldn't be surprised if someone's looking for us right now. Every survival handbook I've ever read says we should stay put right where we are, so we're a stationary target. We'll need less water that way. If necessary, we can survive a couple of days without food."

"What if we're attacked?" Penny asked.

"What's for them to steal? A smashed-up plane ... A lovely American woman," he said. "On the other hand, you're *my* woman. In this part of the world a man's honor would be questioned if he so much as looked at another man's woman. Hospitality to the guest and aid for someone in distress are the first rules of behavior in the Middle East."

⁂

They removed the red shirt the pilot had been wearing from the corpse. After they'd carried his remains to a piece of scrub and covered the body as best they could, they fashioned a makeshift flag, which they strapped to the top of the aircraft. By sunset, they'd neither seen nor heard any sign of anyone.

When darkness came upon the land and wolves started howling in the distance, they climbed back into the aircraft for the night. They'd carefully marshaled their supply of water, so that half of it was left. Penny had given Lev four more ibuprofen. Just before returning to the plane, each took a turn privately relieving themselves, so they need not leave the craft until daylight.

During the moonless night, the wolves' baying became louder. Each of the survivors slept restlessly, a couple of hours at a time. Just before dawn, the wolves' howling ceased. It was then that Penny said, "I can't hold it in any longer. I'm going outside to squat."

"It's only half an hour until daylight. Can you hold on 'til then?"

"No."

"Let me come with you, then. You can never tell what might be around."

"Okay, but let me go first. You'll have trouble getting down."

She had just descended to the ground when she heard a low growl. Turning, she saw a single gray wolf, its teeth bared. Penny gasped and quickly started back up the stairs, her bodily needs forgotten. The wolf snarled and leapt, barely nicking the skin above her boot with his teeth. Acting from pure instinct, Penny kicked at the beast. Her boot caught the animal squarely on its muzzle. With a scream and a whine of agony, the maddened beast turned in continuous circles, its mouth gushing blood mingled with foaming saliva, then slunk away into the rocks.

Back in the plane, Penny started shaking. She looked at her leg, which itched a little bit near the tiny break in her skin. There was a tiny droplet of saliva around the cut. "Oh, God, no!" she said. "Please, God, don't let it be what I think it is."

39

"How's your leg feel?" It was sundown. They'd not seen any sign of human habitation all day.

"It started itching like mad a couple of hours ago. I don't want to even think about what that might mean."

"You haven't touched any water all day. You're sure you're not thirsty?"

"Not at all. I guess I'm trying to conserve what water there is. Funny, I haven't been hungry all day either."

"The wound seems to be closing all right."

"How's *your* leg?"

"Painful but I can hobble out to search the area."

A few moments later, Lev returned, his look serious and concerned. "No sign of life, but I found the remains of last night's wolf."

"The remains?" Penny asked.

"From its looks, the animal was ill even before it bit you."

"Oh, my God!" Penny gasped.

"Now we really have no time to lose." Lev felt queasy, but pulled himself together, realizing Penny's life was at stake. "We've got an hour before it gets dark. We've got to gather every stick of wood we can find. I'll toss anything we can possibly burn out of the plane. If we're not found tonight ... Our only hope is to build as big a fire as we can and pray that someone sees it."

Unknown to the terrified survivors, their plane had come down northeast of Oktemberian in Soviet Armenia, less than twelve miles from Yerevan. By sheer happenstance, a small group of amateur astronomers had chosen that particular night to drive a borrowed van southwest, beyond the city lights and were now setting up a portable twelve-inch telescope and two smaller four-inch units.

Efrem Harunian, eleven, had come home with an excellent school report card earlier that week. His father had decided to treat the lad to an outing in the wild countryside outside the capital. Once the excitement of being outdoors well after his normal bedtime had worn off, Efrem, who knew basic astronomy but was not an aficionado, became more interested in the sounds of night and the sights of the seemingly endless horizon. He had very good eyesight. As Efrem scanned the distant horizon, he thought he saw a very dim, flickering light on the horizon to the south.

"Papa," he called "I think I see a fire over there." He pointed to the far distance.

"It's probably just a reflection off a rock. Come over here. I think you'll love this view of Saturn. You can see the rings and even one of its moons."

"But, Papa ...?"

"Efrem, it's nothing," his father said in a tone that brooked no argument. "Besides, we need you over here to help steady the large telescope.

The fire started to flicker and die down.

"Can you make the fire any larger?"

"I don't think so, Penny. We've got one more piece of dry wood and a canvas bag. I could siphon a few cups of fuel from the wing tank, but trying to throw that on the fire could cause the whole plane to explode."

"We've got to do something. I refuse sit here helplessly and die. Wait a minute. Did you say the plane could explode? Is there some way we can move far enough away from the plane so that if it did explode …?"

"We couldn't move that far away before it got really dangerous."

"Could we hook something resembling a fuse up to the aircraft's wings?" Penny asked. "Do we have any rope or rags in the plane?"

"Maybe," Lev replied, ignoring the pain in his leg. "I'll look."

◆

"What did you think of Saturn's rings, Efrem?" his father asked. "Fabulous, yes?"

"Very interesting, Papa," the boy said dutifully. He looked out toward where he'd seen what he thought was a fire. It had died down. Perhaps Papa had been right after all.

◆

"I found half a dozen rags and a thirty foot coil of rope."

"Can you siphon enough fuel so that if we set the rope on fire it can burn all the way to the fuel tanks?"

"We've got no choice," Lev replied decisively. "If we aren't rescued tonight, there may not even *be* a tomorrow."

Fifteen minutes later, they had thoroughly soaked the rope and the rags with aircraft fuel. The smell of the gasoline sickened Penny, even from the small hill, fifty yards away. Lev managed to limp to her side. He touched the rope to the fire. Within a few moments, it started to burn.

∞

The Armenians had taken notes for the past ten minutes. Efrem had started to doze near the van. His father came over and put his arm around the boy. "We'll be done in another quarter hour, son. Do you need a wrap?"

"Please. Do you mind if I nap for a while?"

"Not at all. I'll get you a blanket in the van."

∞

The flame made it halfway from the end of the rope to the fuselage when the fire went out. "Damn!" Lev swore softly. He hobbled as swiftly as he could toward the plane, ignoring the heat from the wood and the pain radiating up his broken leg. When he got to within ten feet of the aircraft, he held the burning piece of wood against the rags and the rope until both had ignited once again. He screamed with pain as a shot of flame singed his hair and his broken leg buckled out from under him.

The fuel-soaked rope seemed to fight the fire for an instant. It appeared as though it would go out once again. But then a stray spark caught the next rag, and then the next. The fire picked up speed as it neared the wing. If only it kept up this momentum, it would be ten seconds at most before …

Using his arms and his one useful leg, Lev dragged himself toward a nearby rise thirty feet from the plane, his only hope. The fire inched closer to the aircraft…

∞

"Father!" Efrem shouted suddenly. "There it is again! Over there! Look!!"

"Efrem, you've fallen asleep. You're dreaming. Quiet down."

"No Father!" he yelled. "I swear by the Holy Jesus there's something over there!"

Another of the amateur astronomers confirmed Efrem's sighting. "It is something!" he said. He lifted a pair of binoculars to his eyes. "It's a fire all right. Maybe an explosion," he said. "Can anyone train the telescope in that direction?"

Shortly afterward, Efrem's father sucked in his breath. "If I didn't know better, I'd say it's an aircraft, it's on fire and … My God! It just exploded!"

"Start the van. I don't know how far away it is, but there could be people there!"

※

The explosion ripped the plane to pieces. Superheated shards shot out in every direction. A small piece of the fuselage skinned the top of Lev's forehead. As he reached up and felt a pool of warm liquid, a second, larger piece sliced through his left arm. Then everything dissolved.

※

Penny mumbled incoherently. The interior of the van, crammed to capacity, stank of unwashed bodies, human fear, and the sickly odor emanating from Penny. It was close to two in the morning when the van reached the highway. Forty-five minutes later, they arrived at Yerevan State University Medical Center.

The duty physician, Arov Nikssarian, lost no time weighing the patient and injecting Penny with human rabies immune globulin into and around the site of the bite. Within an hour of the first injection, he administered rabies vaccine. He told his assistant the woman would be given five such injections over the next twenty-eight days.

"I've read about these injections," the assistant said. "Huge needles and …"

"It used to be that way when Louis Pasteur invented the treatment, but we've progressed since then. We'll deliver the vaccine into her shoulder muscle, so it will be fully absorbed. We'll give her another shot two days from now, a third one in a week, a fourth one in two weeks, and the last one four weeks from tonight."

40

Lev Arkady, barely alive, lapsed into and out of consciousness. The blood on his forehead had congealed quickly, cauterized by a shard that had fallen from the dying aircraft. His left arm, between the shoulder and the elbow, sliced all the way down to the bone, hung to his torso by a thin thread of ligament and muscle tissue. His leg was now broken in three places. Lev's unconsciousness afforded blessed relief.

He'd had neither food nor water for twenty-four hours. The blazing midday sun gave way to a wind that fanned sand and dust into his wounds and into his lungs. Images of Istanbul and Penny wafted through his mind, periodically washed in a red halo. He could not move, could not even raise his head. As it became colder, he shivered involuntarily. It would only be a matter of time, an hour or two at most…

Urdu Kamlican, fifteen, and his younger brother Ulgan, Kurdish villagers from Mahmutbey in the border country between Iğdir and

Oktemberian, had heard about a downed aircraft when they listened to the afternoon news on Radio Yerevan. Believing there might be some salvageable material left in the plane, they'd ridden their ponies to the area where they thought the craft might be. As Urdu climbed a nearby rise to try and spot the destroyed airplane, he came upon the still, nearly lifeless form of Lev Arkady.

"Is he dead?" Ulgan asked, gazing at the charred, fragmented body.

"I think so," Urdu replied. He stepped gingerly toward the body and shoved gently at it with the toe of his shoe. A soft sigh escaped Lev's lips. Both boys jumped back as if they'd been stung by a wasp.

"He's alive!" the younger boy exclaimed. "What should we do, older brother?"

"Leave him be. He's as good as dead anyway. Let's see if there's anything we can scavenge in the wreckage."

"Wait. Please help me," Lev managed to stammer in his delirium. "In my pocket ... some money ..." He could not move and faded out of consciousness.

The boys, who were not inherently avaricious but simply very poor, reached into Lev's charred pants pockets and brought out several large denomination Turkish notes. Their discovery bound them morally to help the man, even though he was dying.

"We must give him a little water," the older bother said. He went to his pony, grabbed a water pouch, took off his shirt, poured a few drops of water onto the shirt, and gently rubbed the wet cloth over Lev's mouth and face. Lev moaned. Urdu poured more water onto the shirt, and squeezed his shirt until the liquid found its way into Lev's mouth. He continued until he'd exhausted half the water in the pouch, then poured more into the shirt and covered Lev's face with it.

"We can't load him on one of the ponies," Urdu said. "There's more that's broken than not. It's three kilometers back to the village.

He'd be dead by the time we got back. If only we could fashion some kind of sledge."

"The plane?" his younger brother asked.

The boys found nothing of value they could take back to the village but, to Lev's better fortune, the resourceful brothers found a small, flat, segment of wing, two feet wide and six feet long, thin enough for them to drag toward their ponies and sturdy enough to bear Lev's weight. They fashioned a primitive travois, which they connected by rope to the saddle on one of the ponies. Moving the nearly lifeless Lev onto the makeshift sledge was more difficult, but they did it slowly and gently, taking half an hour to do so. They secured Lev's body by a cross-tie system. While they couldn't stop all of the bouncing and jarring on the ride back to the village, in Lev's semi-conscious state, he had no idea that the boys had saved his life.

※

The Erzurum duty officer's reverie was interrupted by a buzz on the intercom in his office. "Yes?" he snapped, not even knowing who was signaling him.

"Sir, there's a telephone call from a man who says he's the *muhtar* of a small Kurdish village, Mahmutbey on the Armenian frontier. ..."

Within three hours after the call, Turkish Air Force sent a helicopter from Kars to pick Lev up and fly him to the nearest medical center, where he was treated by a general surgeon. Two days later, he was evacuated to Numune Burn Center in Ankara.

At the beginning of the second week, Doctor Sunay advised his patient, "You're very lucky to be alive. During the next month there'll be times you'll wish you weren't."

"I don't feel any pain right now," Lev said.

"That's because you've got so much morphine pumped into you," Sunay replied. "Your leg seems to be healing just fine. Your left arm is something else again. The cut was so deep I fear it will be useless for a long time. Whether or not you ever get the feeling back will be up to the therapists and to God."

"I hadn't planned on being a concert pianist. Any word about my friend…?"

"No word of her yet."

"But it's been two weeks."

"Turkish authorities overflew the area where the plane went down. It's in Soviet Armenia. They found nothing."

41

"Mrs. Wagner, it appears you're out of danger. All the vital signs are excellent."

"Any word about my companion?"

"An agent of a company called Höfer managed to smuggle a note that your friend survived the fire. He's in Numune Burn Center in Ankara."

"Did they say anything about his condition?"

"Unfortunately, no," Nikssarian responded.

"How soon can I get out of here and back to Turkey?"

"Ah, that may be a bit of a problem, Mrs. Wagner."

"How so?"

"Politics too often interfere with human lives. You're an American citizen. The best way to deal with your situation is through the Israelis. Armenia and Israel have cordial relations, but neither maintains an embassy in the other country. The Israeli Chargé d'Affaires is based in Tbilisi in the Georgian SSR. He visits Yerevan twice a month. He's not due back for another ten days. The American consulate is here at sufferance, since the Soviet Union and the United States have cool relations."

"Couldn't I can simply go to the American consulate and leave this country?"

"It's not that easy, Mrs. Arkady. The Turks, who are great friends with the Americans, have picked up the story of the crash. They're saying the plane landed in Turkish territory and Armenians kidnapped you. Soviet Armenia is rejecting the story and claims a group of amateur astronomers rescued you and saved your life, even though you're in Armenia illegally."

"That should make it even easier for me to get back to Turkey," Penny said.

"I'm afraid not. Yerevan and Ankara have no diplomatic relations. The Armenian authorities feel the longer they can keep you here, the better."

Penny pondered what the Armenian doctor was saying. "Why are you telling me these things, Doctor Nikssarian? Couldn't you get you into trouble?"

"I'm outside the political stream. While this hospital is not immune from scrutiny, I've simply told you the way things are. I've said nothing to betray any state secrets."

"So you're under orders to keep me here?" she asked.

"No. The normal rabies treatment is twenty-eight days. The authorities haven't bothered us yet."

"Yet?"

"I received a call from KGB last week and dutifully reported that you were in hospital here. They put two and two together and found out this could be a cause célèbre. That large bouquet of flowers on the nightstand beside you came from them."

Penny, who'd not noticed the flowers before, turned and admired them, then asked, "Have their agents visited my room?"

"Undoubtedly," Nikssarian said. "They have plants in every major facility in the capital, most likely an orderly. It could be a doctor or part of the housekeeping staff."

"So there's no way I can escape their 'protective' custody?"

"I'm afraid not," the Armenian doctor said. However, when he said it, Penny noticed he had unobtrusively winked.

✸

Doctor Nikssarian returned close to midnight, accompanied by a short, burly orderly who wore a surgical mask and pushed a small gurney. Penny came awake instantly. Doctor Nikssarian closed the door behind him. "I'm sorry we disturbed you, but it's necessary to perform surgery," he said. "It's just a small procedure but it should be done immediately. We should not wait until morning."

Penny started to protest when the doctor put his fingers to his lips. The orderly pressed a piece of paper into Penny's hand. "No surgery. Room bugged. Must talk."

Once in the dimly-lit operating theater, the doctor spoke. "The smaller operating rooms are not subject to surveillance. I'm sorry if we startled you, but we had no other way to do this. I have a small favor to ask." Penny nodded for the physician to continue.

"My niece Nadya is a graduate student at the State University. The authorities claim she's, um, been involved in the recent anti-Soviet rallies. Our Soviet brothers are very sensitive to this sort of thing. They want to make examples."

"And Nadya is an example?" Penny asked.

"Three of her closest friends were detained last night. They haven't been heard from since then. The KGB always comes by at about three in the morning, when they're least expected. They catch their quarry at their weakest and most vulnerable."

"Couldn't Nadya simply disappear? Armenia's as large as Maryland."

"One of America's smallest states," Nikssarian said sardonically. "I'm afraid it's too late for that. The KGB has been keeping a careful watch on her. They know Nadya's one of the local leaders of the Armenian Nationalist Patriotic Front."

"You said you had a small favor to ask?" Penny said.

"You know the problem we discussed earlier this afternoon about getting you out of Armenia? I can probably hide Nadya here for twenty-four hours at most. Sometimes we are very thankful for Soviet bureaucracy. Even though you have been under KGB surveillance, the authorities require that we report the presence of all foreigners in our hospital. We must make sure they're registered with their consulates. The American consulate is a twenty minute ride from here. Do you have an American passport?"

Penny looked down at the floor. "No, Doctor Nikssarian. I left my passport with the hotel's registry in Istanbul. We assumed we'd be gone less than a week."

"A problem, but not insurmountable. I have some friends at the American consulate. Remember what I told you about KGB having its eyes and ears everywhere?"

"Yes."

"Occasionally we advise our Western friends when we think it important that they turn their attention toward certain events or people with whom we come into contact."

"So the Americans know I'm here?"

"Correct. Even as we speak, one or two American agents shadow their KGB counterparts in this hospital, although even I don't know who they are."

"You said you had a favor to ask?"

"Yes. We've reported you're under treatment for rabies and will have to remain in Yerevan for a month. Truthfully, you need not remain in hospital. I've arranged that tomorrow morning an ambulance will deliver you to the American Consulate. You'll be accompanied by the ambulance driver and a hospital orderly …"

"Nadya?"

"Correct. Once inside the Consulate, she'll ask for asylum as a political refugee, and I thought …"

"That I'd sponsor her application?"

"Would that be too great an imposition on you, Mrs. Wagner?"

"Of course not. I don't see any risk for me, but what risk will there be for you and your family?"

"I can, and will, publicly disavow my niece's defection. Her mother will express shock and outrage. Her father's managing a mine in Gyumri on an extended assignment, so he won't know about this."

"But you said the KGB's watching her," Penny said. "They must know she's disguised herself and come to the hospital."

"As far as they know, she had dinner with her mother earlier in the evening, then went to bed at ten o'clock. This orderly," he said, pointing toward the burly person accompanying him, "has been on duty since five this afternoon. But I've forgotten my manners. I'd like you to meet my niece, Nadya Vartunian."

The 'orderly' peeled off several lawyers of towels and gowns to reveal a tiny, dark-haired young woman who could not have been more than twenty-three, nor weigh more than a hundred pounds, and who, Penny noticed, was quite attractive.

"Good evening, Mrs. Wagner," she said in English. "It might seem unpatriotic of me to say, but I've been a fan of America ever since I could remember."

"Have you ever been outside Armenia, Nadya?" she asked.

"No, but my family lived in southeastern Turkey for hundreds of years. After the slaughter of our people, what was left of the family fled to Yerevan."

"Would you consider sponsoring her?" Dr. Nikssarian asked.

"Happily," Penny said. "But if the KGB truly is watching every vehicle that leaves the hospital, aren't we likely to be stopped?"

"Once they find Nadya's not at her home, they'll search the entire hospital."

"Could you call the American consulate, even at this hour, and find out how we might contact the American agents at this hospital?"

The doctor shrugged. "I'm certain the KGB would be watching any of Nadya's relatives. I wouldn't be surprised if they monitored all my telephone calls."

"Is there some way *I* could call the duty officer?"

Doctor Nikssarian smiled. "I just happen to have the private number of the consul-general in my possession, but you must wait at least half an hour after you get back to your room before you call out. That will give me time to return to my quarters."

Forty-five minutes later, Penny rang the night operator at University Hospital. She was peremptory, and, although pleasant enough, her tone brooked no room for argument. "This is Penelope Wagner in Room 317. I have just received word that my associate, who was with me when our airplane crashed, has survived and is in Ankara. Please connect me to 572727 immediately."

"But Madame, it is one o'clock in the morning," the operator said.

"I know. That number will connect me via international telephone with my office in New York, where it is three in the afternoon. Do I need to speak with your superior or will you please put my call through?"

The operator did not need to think twice. She and her husband barely made ends meet on their two salaries. She did not need this bossy foreigner raising a ruckus. Who knew what kind of influence she might have? The only two people in the world who needed to know she even worked at the hospital were her husband and the clerk in the payroll department who cut her a check each month. "Very well, Madame. It's a local number. Are you sure it will connect to the international telephone line?"

"I am."

Four rings later a sleepy consul-general answered the phone.

"Good evening, Mister Ambassador," she said, elevating him several ranks. "I apologize for waking you at this ungodly hour. This is Penelope Wagner. My associate, Lev Arkady, is with Höfer GmbH. I have an urgent problem. I'd really appreciate it if you could give me some information."

Unknown to Penny, the telephone operator had, in accordance with specific instructions from the political commissar's representative at the hospital, patched Penny's call through to local KGB headquarters. The KGB unobtrusively recorded the call.

At ten minutes to four that morning, a gray Bulgar Renault pulled up to the hospital's Emergency Room door. A distraught man of thirty emerged from the driver's side. When the orderly came to meet him, he reported that his wife's water had broken, she was having contractions every two minutes, and he could not wait until morning to bring her in. The masked orderly who met them at the door, spoke calmly to the man, then helped the obviously very pregnant woman into the Emergency Room.

Fifteen minutes elapsed, before the man and his wife emerged from the hospital, accompanied by the duty physician. "Is this your first?" the doctor asked.

"Yes, Sir," the man replied.

"I thought as much," the doctor said. "This happens frequently. You'll have plenty of time to bring her in later this morning. Now, if you don't mind, I'd like to go back to sleep." As he returned to the Emergency Room, he grumbled to his orderly, "They really don't pay us enough to deal with these expectant fathers at four a.m."

The orderly mumbled something indecipherable and left the Emergency Room. Dr. Nikssarian momentarily thought something was a bit odd. He distinctly remembered Penny mentioning that the man in the Bulgar Renault would be there at four *thirty*. No matter. The exchange had gone off without a hitch.

Shortly before nine that morning, Penny entered the ambulance that was to take her to the American consulate. "Are you sure this is necessary?" she asked a rather sleepy Doctor Nikssarian. "I feel healthy enough to catch a public tram or a bus."

"It's part of the bureaucratic requirements I told you about yesterday," the doctor replied. "It's also protocol that you be accompanied by an orderly."

"Very well, then," she said. "But I still think it's unnecessary."

The ambulance had been on the road less than ten minutes when a cordon of police vehicles, red lights flashing and sirens blaring, signaled the ambulance to pull over to the side of the road. An officious-looking, bemedaled man of fifty emerged from the lead vehicle, walked over to the ambulance, directed the driver to roll down the window, and presented a card case. He spoke in Armenian and Russian. The driver said nothing. The man told Penny in English that the ambulance and its inhabitants were to be taken to police headquarters and detained for questioning.

"Are you KGB?" she asked the officer.

"*Nyet.* Ministry of the Interior."

"And I, Sir, am an American citizen. I demand to see my Consul-general," Penny said, her tone distinctly bolder than she felt.

"You can, and will see him after we're finished questioning you, Mrs. Wagner," the officer said in heavily accented English. "As for you being an American citizen, that is not the highest status to have in the Armenian S.S.R."

"If you know who I am, you know I'm on my way to the American Consulate, that this trip has been arranged by the hospital, and that everything's in order."

"That is not quite so, Mrs. Wagner. KGB advised us you are illegally transporting a citizen of the Armenian SSR to the consulate to seek asylum."

"That's absurd!" Penny said hotly.

"You admit you have met Nadya Vartunian?"

"I have nothing to say to you until I speak to the American Consul-general."

"As you wish, Mrs. Wagner. That could be a long time, a very long time indeed."

"I'm sure Doctor Nikssarian will call the Consulate to check on my arrival."

"I very much doubt that. Doctor Nikssarian has been picked up for questioning. We expect he may join you sooner rather than later."

By that time, four more police officers had surrounded the ambulance. They were polite but firm in propelling Penny into the back seat of one of the squad cars. The senior officer, who identified himself as Captain Artakian, sat in the right front seat as the Polish-built Warszawa police cruiser took off. No one said a word during the twenty minute trip to police headquarters. When they arrived, the captain directed his detainee to a bare ten-by-fifteen-foot room.

"Mrs. Wagner," he said to Penny pleasantly. "It would appear you have much to answer for."

"I will say absolutely nothing until I have seen the United States representative."

"That is fine with me, Mrs. Arkady. But I fear that may take some time."

"What do you mean?"

"Would you like a cigarette?" the officer inquired solicitously.

"No, thank you."

"I'll have one," he said, coughing. "Dreadful habit, but I'm afraid it's one of my vices. Now, Mrs. Wagner," he said, lighting up. "I would like to play you something on this tape recorder."

Penny listened in shock, then in mounting horror as she heard her own voice. "Good evening, Mister Ambassador. I apologize for waking you at this ungodly hour. This is Penelope Wagner. My associate, Lev Arkady, is with Höfer GmbH…"

She did not speak as she heard herself relating Nadya Vartunian's dilemma. After some moments of silence at the other end of the line, the Consul-general asked Penny to describe Nadya. She did. "Listen carefully, Mrs. Arkady. We have a Marine Sergeant on detached assignment to our Consulate. He's Ms. Vartunian's height, but stockier." The consul-general went on in specific detail about how a man with a very pregnant wife would drive a Bulgar Renault to the State Hospital Emergency Room at precisely 4:30 a.m., and how this man would drive a very different, but still very pregnant, "wife" – Nadya Vartunian – out of the hospital fifteen minutes later.

Penny remained silent as the Captain turned off the tape. "The telephone operator at the hospital had strict instructions to patch any outgoing call into the KGB. So, it seems we have an American citizen coming across the border into Armenia, aiding and abetting an Armenian dissident attempting to commit treason, and conspiring to commit a treasonous escape to an unfriendly foreign state. As I said, Mrs. Wagner, it seems you've got a lot to answer for."

42

Nadya and Doctor Nikssarian were summarily tried and sentenced to three years' imprisonment. Before Doctor Nikssarian was whisked away to Yevtushenko, he smuggled out news of Penny's capture, through an easily bribable guard, to one of his trusted colleagues who, in turn, advised the United States consulate, who passed word to Turkish authorities in Ankara. In this manner, Lev learned that Penny had survived.

The Turkish press reveled in disclosing that Penny was being held *incommunicado,* without bail, in an Armenian prison awaiting trial on a plethora of trumped-up charges. Of course Penny was a citizen of Turkey's great ally. That made the case sensational enough on a local level. More important on the international level, Turkey had, for more than seventy years, borne the brunt of Armenian fury and a strongly dedicated public relations campaign against the "genocide" that had allegedly taken place in Turkey in 1915. Now the Turks were able to demonstrate the beastliness of the Armenian state. The media did not miss an opportunity to capitalize on Penny's bad fortune and the Turks' good fortune.

For the next month, each side waged a war of words. The United States and Turkey publicly demanded the immediate release of Penelope Wagner, American citizen. Soviet Armenia chided the Americans for deliberately interfering in the internal affairs of a sovereign state, giving the lie to the United States' proclamations of independence.

In Ankara, Lev's condition improved slowly. Since he was not allowed to leave the hospital, he watched news accounts of Penny's incarceration and the verbal battles surrounding her pending, but never announced, trial, with growing frustration.

Congress passed a joint resolution condemning Penelope Wagner's treatment and demanding her immediate release. The Soviet Armenian government ignored the plea and told the American Congress to mind its own business.

Meanwhile, Penny dwelt in relative comfort. Given the furor her arrest had engendered, the Armenian authorities were careful to ensure she was treated with utmost courtesy. She was afforded ample food, a two room apartment with private bath, access to a radio and books, continuing medical care, and any items she requested for her needs. However, her communication with the outside world was effectively blocked.

It was now September, 1988, two months after Penny's arrest. There had still been no court proceedings, not even a preliminary arraignment. Her demands to see the American consul-general were denied. The world's media turned to other, more immediate headlines. Penny was relegated to the status of a non-person. The only people she saw on a daily basis were the cleaning woman and the orderlies who brought her food. Once a week, Captain Artakian visited her for half an hour.

On his sixth such visit, Penny intuited, not from his words but from his manner, that Captain Artakian was far more cordial than he had been in the past. "Your health is good, Madame Wagner?"

"As well as can be expected," she remarked carefully. She had learned early on that her entire suite had been bugged. She had discovered eight such hidden recording devices in the time she'd been incarcerated. "When may I expect court proceedings to start?"

"I have heard nothing."

"And my requests to see anyone, the Consul-general, a lawyer, my associate?"

"Pan Arkady is still in hospital in Ankara," Artakian responded.

"What about my friends?"

"Miss Vartunian is in the Women's Prison. Doctor Nikssarian is at Yevtushenko."

"They've already been tried and sentenced while I haven't even being charged."

"It's somewhat different with you, Madame Wagner."

"The Armenian radio mentioned me in passing," she said. "Others are interested."

"A mild way of putting it. The International Red Cross has requested, and our patriotic Soviet government has acceded to that request, that you be given a letter from your companion."

Penny brightened visibly. "Please, may I see it now?"

"Of course," he said, extracting not one but two sealed envelopes. At her sudden start, Captain Artakian made a quick hand movement to silence anything she was about to say. "Why don't you read your friend's letter?" he said. "Would you mind terribly if I used your toilet facilities?" He put his finger to his lips.

"Do what you must. I have no choice, do I?"

In response, he made as if to go to the bathroom, then closed the door but remained outside. As she watched, he carefully removed all eight of the hidden microphones she knew about, then took out four more she didn't know existed. Going into the bathroom, he returned a few moments later with two additional devices, then signaled her to hand him her prison-issue shoes. He removed one more device from the space between the sole and the top of her left shoe.

"I was told your 'babysitters' were acting up. My superior suggested I replace them. I was told to show you where they were, so you'd know to behave yourself. I will replace them momentarily, but I thought we'd use this time to speak frankly," he said.

"How do I know there aren't more devices planted around the room?"

"You don't, Madame Wagner. For all you or I know, there might well be more. I'll have to ask you to trust me."

"Trust you?" she responded, her eyebrows lifting in surprise. "You're *their* agent, their public face, the one who arrested me, or don't you remember."

"I remember quite well, Madame Wagner. You will also notice you have not been mistreated or abused in any way since your, umm, tenure as the guest of the Soviet Armenian government began."

"You said you wanted to speak frankly. I'm listening," Penny said.

"Thank you. As you are aware, I am a senior public servant. I have been such for nearly thirty years. One does not survive in the current regime without being a pragmatist." She noticed that, although accented, his English was perfect and he did not stumble over any sophisticated English words. "Don't get me wrong, I am in all ways loyal to my country and would never do anything to betray my country's best interests."

"But?" she urged him on.

"Ah, you Americans are so direct," Captain Artakian said, smiling. "I've heard that whenever someone says the word 'but' you don't listen to any words that went before, only those that follow."

"True."

"Our Soviet government, the beloved organ of the people, may continue in power for the next hundred years. Or it may not."

Penny looked at him wordlessly. "How much news have you heard? International news, I mean?"

"Not much. Aside from the occasional mention of my name on the Armenian radio and the few seconds of broadcast I can get from Kars and Artvin before the Turkish airwaves are jammed, I hear lots of Armenian popular music."

"Then you really don't know," Captain Artakian continued. "Things are not always what they seem amongst our overlords in Moscow. ..."

"So the American media's intuition is correct," she said softly.

"I beg your pardon?"

"Contrary to what your government believes, Captain Artakian, I was never sent into Armenia to spy. The plane in which I was flying crashed in Armenian territory by accident. Prior to that, I was advised while I was still in America that the Soviet regime was by no means as unified and secure as Gorbachev had led us to believe."

Artakian rose to his feet and walked around her room. He lit a cigarette. "I forgot, you don't smoke," he said, crushing it out on the heel of his shoe. "Forgive me."

Penny remained silent.

"Madame Wagner, you are well treated, but there are massive shortages of just about everything we need in Armenia, sugar, butter, gasoline. There's talk that our great friend has spent so much in Afghanistan that there are few rubles and no military forces left to send to what they view as a troublesome backwater. Miss Vartunian's associates are becoming much bolder. The forces of malcontent are beginning to outnumber those of the duly constituted legal authority."

Penny nodded.

"As I said earlier, I am a loyal Armenian public servant. I emphasize the word *Armenian*. While I am loyal to the *Armenian* cause, I have a wife and three nearly grown children. My first loyalty is to them. You are an American citizen. It never hurts to maintain friendships on both sides of the fence. Do you understand what I am saying?"

"Of course," she replied.

"It is time for me to replant your little friends," he said, indicating the second, unmarked envelope he had earlier handed her. "If you need anything, please submit any request you might have through the cleaning lady." Captain Artakian clicked his heels in a mock military style, screwed the bugging devices back in, and took his leave.

The typed letter from Lev described where he was and the nature of his treatment, but little more detail than that. He professed eternal gratitude to the God who had saved her life, and a pledge that he would not cease his efforts to obtain her immediate release. He ended the letter by saying the doctors anticipated he'd be released from the hospital within the next month. *A month!* My God, she thought, that's a lifetime. She composed the letter in her mind that she would write back to him that evening, not believing for one moment the authorities would ever let it leave the grounds of her residence.

She opened the unmarked envelope Artakian had handed her. It said simply, "Four days from now at three o'clock in the afternoon you will be picked up and taken to the Court of First Instance in downtown Yerevan, where you will be arraigned. Take everything you need with you. Please remember there are those among us who are truly *Armenian* patriots. Artakian."

❦

At the appointed time, the cleaning lady escorted her into the waiting Warszawa and entered the Interior Ministry car with her. The chauffeur said nothing as he drove into downtown traffic. The Warszawa stopped at the curb in front of the Justice Building for a few moments. When no one came to greet the car, the driver pulled into traffic once again. Ten minutes later, he turned into a side street. Two blocks up the street, she saw a large property surrounded by a ten-foot high black iron fence. The Warszawa came to a driveway beyond which there was an electric gate. The driver pushed a set of numbers in a mounted box by the side of the gate. The gate swung slowly open. Moments later, Penny was discharged at the front door of the American Consulate. The cleaning lady and the driver nodded a curt dismissal and the Warszawa drove away.

43

A nondescript middle-age man in a western cut gray suit, his hair clipped short introduced himself as Frank O'Neil, United States Secret Service. "You are not officially here, Mrs. Wagner," he said. "My instructions are to get you to Erebuni Airport."

"Not Zvartnots?"

"No. The authorities monitor every flight into and out of Zvartnots. Erebuni, Yerevan's domestic airport, is hardly used at all." He pointed to a pile of peasant clothes and heavy shoes, and handed her a small, cheap cardboard suitcase. "You're the same height, but your build is more robust than one of our housekeepers. Those are her clothes. At some distance you'll be able to pass. First thing, put on the scarf. It's the best we can do on such short notice."

Within the hour, Penny walked out the rear door of the Consulate, where a dark blue Chevrolet sedan awaited. "You think the authorities won't track an obviously American automobile?" she asked.

"I'm sure they will, Mrs. Wagner. Our friends watch our every movement into and out of the Consulate. What we are doing is anything but suspicious. One of our housekeepers leaves the Consulate every day at noon to pick up her daughter from daycare. She and her husband live near Sheram Street. We drop her off downtown at Andravar Street, where she catches the shared taxi, the cheapest way to travel. She gets off at Sheram Street, the third stop. You'll stay on the van 'til its last stop, Erebuni Airport. Once you're there, there'll be further arrangements."

"What if I'm spotted?" Penny asked.

"No problem," O'Neil said, as the Chevrolet turned into traffic. "There'll be someone on the van the whole way to make sure you get safely to where you're going."

"How will I recognize him?"

"You won't. You won't even know if it's a him or a her until the last stop. Then you'll receive further instructions."

Penny had been waiting at the stop less than three minutes when a brown-and-white van bearing a large number four on its front window pulled up. She joined ten other people crammed into the van and paid her fare with a 100 dram coin. During the trip, she sat silently in the van, gazing out the window. The day was bright and sunny. She could see snow-topped Mount Ararat in the distance. Turkey was there. So was Lev. Her heart raced as she thought about him. If only he could see her now. She smiled inwardly. Soon she would be with him.

At Erebuni Airport, the five people remaining in the van clambered out. Just as she was about to exit, an older woman who'd been sitting in front of her signaled for Penny to follow. Penny looked around. There was no one else who'd even taken notice of her. "Are you …?"

"*Da*," the woman answered. "Follow, please."

When they'd walked fifty feet from the stop, an older model brown car of indeterminate make pulled up. "Madame Wagner?" its driver, a young man, asked.

"Yes."

"Please get in. We're going to Armavir Airfield."

"Armavir?" Penny said, her suspicion rising. "But I was told Erebuni."

"Too public," the man replied equably. "No one checks Armavir. It's very small. No scheduled airlines fly there. Much easier to get you out of Armenia."

Penny realized she had no choice in the matter. Earlier this morning, she'd been a prisoner on her way to the criminal court in a hostile land. She'd been whisked secretly to American soil, but she'd been there less than an hour when she'd been given ambiguous instructions. So far, she'd not been apprehended. There had been representatives, just as Frank O'Neil had said there'd be. Yet her nervousness did not abate. She got in, and the sedan pulled away from the curb.

By the time they reached Armavir, it was late afternoon. The field looked forlorn, virtually abandoned. The terminal building was a squat, boxy one-story affair. There were three older model Cessnas and an ancient DC-3 sitting silently on the tarmac. As Penny entered the building, she saw a large map of the surrounding area, encased in glass. Turkey was twelve miles away. She could probably walk to the border in four hours. Once there, she would immediately identify herself ... But then, reality dawned on her. She had no identification papers of any kind.

"It's all right," her driver said in unaccented American English. "The plane'll be here momentarily. You'll be out of Armenia in a couple of hours. Some *chay*?"

"Yes, please," she said.

The young man went over to a kiosk. Penny watched as the woman attendant filled a half-cracked cup from a samovar. Her attention was momentarily diverted as a small, unmarked jet aircraft touched down and screeched to a stop at the far end of the runway.

She turned and saw the man nodding. "There's your plane," he said, looking at his wristwatch. "A few minutes early. It'll get you out of this country sooner. I brought you a sugar cookie as well as tea. You must be famished. The plane will fuel up and the crew will take some time before they come to get you."

Penny reached for the tea thankfully. It would be the first nourishment she'd had since early morning. She wolfed the cookie down, surprised at how delicious it was. The tea tasted unusually sweet, but it was hot and felt good going down. She glanced at the wall clock. Five past four. Her eyes felt heavy, undoubtedly from knowing her ordeal was nearly over. Tonight, she'd be with Lev in Ankara.

"How long will it be until the crew is ready?"

"Thirty minutes."

"Do you think I have time to take a small nap?" she asked.

"Oh, yes. I'll wake you up in plenty of time."

Moments later, she was deeply asleep and snoring softly.

❦

When she awoke, it was dark. She felt dizzy, as though she'd been drugged. She was in a single bed, covered by a thin blanket, in a small room. She lay quietly for several minutes, trying to dispel the heaviness in her head. As her eyes accommodated to the dark, she made out the only furniture in the room: the cot, a small table, and a lamp. She felt no sense of motion. Although she knew she'd been supposed to fly out of Armenia, she could not remember boarding or getting off an aircraft. "I must have been more exhausted than I thought," she said to herself. She waited several moments before the cobwebs began to clear from her head, then reached over and turned the light switch. The lamp glowed dimly. She saw a framed print with Arabic writing on the wall to her right.

Penny was mildly surprised to see the flowing letters. She knew Turkish had been written in Arabic for hundreds of years, but that script had been abandoned since the days of Atatürk. She wondered why there would be such a print here in Ankara, unless it was an oversight or, more likely had been placed in the room to accommodate the growing number of Arab tourists to the Turkish capital. More awake now, Penny felt her bladder would explode if she didn't go to the bathroom soon.

She swung her legs off the cot, not nearly as dizzy as she'd been when she awakened, stood up, and went toward the door. Odd. Locked from the outside. She banged softly, then more insistently. Moments later, she heard a key being inserted and tumblers moving as the key turned. The door opened. A woman twenty years her junior said, "Ah, you are awake, Mrs. Wagner. Good. If you need to use the facilities, the loo is just down the hall."

"Thank you, Miss …?"

"Rosa Dudayev, Mrs. Wagner," the woman said, smiling.

After she returned from the toilet, Penny saw the young woman still waiting by the door to her room.

"Rosa Dudayev?" Penny said. "That's an unusual name for a Turk. Have you been in Ankara long?"

The young woman had just started to answer when a door down the hall opened. An impeccably dressed man strode toward Penny. As he came closer, Penny felt the soft down on her arms start to prickle.

"Ah, good morning Madame Wagner. I trust you had a good rest?"

"I don't believe we've met, Mister …?"

"For your purposes, Signor Black will do. It seems you are destined to be my guest for awhile."

"And just how long do you think you'll be able to keep me as your 'guest,' Signor Black?" she replied calmly. "I'm sure Turkish Intelligence knows exactly where you are. I wouldn't be surprised if the Turkish police are watching this very building."

"I very much doubt that, Madame Wagner," Black responded casually, lighting up a cigarette and blowing the smoke in her face. "They have no jurisdiction here."

"You're crazy," she replied. She realized that Rosa Dudayev had absented herself from the room as soon as Signor Black had entered. "How could they not have jurisdiction in their own capital city?"

"Oh, that they do," Black said. "What makes you think you're in Turkey?"

"The American Consulate told me I was going to leave Armenia, and … and …" She realized with a sinking feeling that the American Consulate had never told her exactly where she was going to go when she left Armenia.

"Did you enjoy your tea, Madame Wagner?" Black continued smoothly. "A bit sweet, wasn't it?"

"You … you drugged me," she said, her memory now becoming quite clear.

"Ah, not I, not personally in any event. I suggest however, that henceforth you'd best be more respectful of me. We may be together longer than you think. Certainly until the appropriate authorities decide to, as they say in America, 'bail you out.'"

"Would you mind telling me, Signor Black, exactly where I am?"

"Of course. Welcome to Itum-Shale, seventy miles south of Groszny, in the Freedom-loving Islamic Republic of Chechnya."

44

Lev Arkady had finished his fourth week of physical therapy when he got the news that Penny had gone missing.

"What exactly do you mean, 'missing'?" he demanded of the young attaché who'd told him. "American citizens simply don't vanish into thin air."

"Mister Arkady, all I know is what I've just told you. Captain Artakian arranged a ruse to get her to the Consulate. Frank O'Neil arranged for her to get to Erebuni, where an American Embassy 727 aircraft was sitting on the tarmac awaiting her arrival. She never showed up. The woman who'd been detailed to watch over her mistakenly believed that a man in a brown sedan was the agent with whom she was supposed to connect. The last she saw, Penny Wagner drove away with the man."

"American security couldn't do better than that to protect her? How in heaven's name was she allowed to ride through Armenia's capital alone? How could she have slipped through your fingers?"

The attaché shrugged helplessly. "Look, Mister Arkady, I'm sorry …"

"Sorry's a damned weak word!" Quickly he quieted down. "Listen, Mister …?"

"Hudson. John A. Hudson."

"May I call you John?"

"I'd prefer 'Art.' I understand your frustration, Mister Arkady."

"I'm sure you do. Listen, Art, I didn't mean to vent on you. None of this is your doing. Please understand I don't hold you responsible."

"Kill the messenger?" Hudson smiled ruefully.

"Isn't that the truth? Do you have any possible information?"

"Not a clue." Changing the subject, the young diplomat asked, "How are you doing, physically? I understand you've been here almost three months."

"How do I look to you, Art?"

"Your face is pretty beat up. How's your leg?"

"With all the P.T. they've given me and the weight training I've been doing on my own, I feel pretty good. They tell me there's only a half inch difference between my right leg and my left. They've inserted a plastic orthotic in my shoe that makes them equal. I can even run, I can use my arm, and they say that with two or three more operations my upper body will look almost as good as new. Listen, Art, is there any way you can get me out of this hospital?"

"You're a free man, whatever kind of citizen you are. Why don't you just leave?"

"The doctors don't want to release me yet. They keep putting it off. I think they suspect that if I'd gotten out earlier I might have done something rash to get my friend back, and that might have caused international repercussions."

Hudson shrugged. "As far as I know, your lady is not in Armenia anymore."

"What if I were to go into Armenia?"

"I wouldn't advise it, Sir."

"Is there any way the Consulate could get me into Yerevan quietly, so I might talk to Frank O'Neil or somebody who might know something?"

"The Embassy's telling everybody to stay as far away as possible from any place that could be a breakaway republic. Armenia's as high up on that list as you can go."

"OK, John Arthur Hudson, future Ambassador to God-knows-where. I don't give a rat's ass about putting myself in danger. Three months ago I was given up for dead. If our government wants to keep American citizens out of harm's way, that's their problem. If our government can't find my companion, that's *my* problem. I will find some way to get out of this hospital if I have to break down every door in the place. I'm asking you, man to man, can you find any way in the world to get me into Armenia?"

"Let's go down to the cafeteria," Hudson said. "The walls have ears." When they were seated at a table, sipping coffee, Hudson said, "There is a way, but it's got to be hush-hush."

"I'm listening."

"There are no diplomatic relations between Ankara and Yerevan. Zero, *nada*, none. In the crazy way things work in this part of the world, even Uncle Sam is not allowed to fly direct from Ankara to Yerevan, but Israel, which is friendly with both Armenia and Turkey, has the largest egg production plant in the Middle East. There's an Embassy flight twice a week, an old, slow C-54 – the 'egg flight.' It carries all the chickens and eggs we need, both to Turkey and to Armenia. The plane leaves here at 10:00 p.m. and lands at Ben Gurion just after midnight. After it loads up with eggs, it flies from Tel Aviv to Yerevan, where it lands just before 4:00 a.m. The plane leaves Yerevan at 4:30 and flies back to Israel, reloads more chickens and eggs, and lands at Ankara about 9:30 in the morning. A friend of mine's an Air Force captain who flies the route. She told me they keep the doors between the cockpit and the rest of the plane shut pretty tight because it smells like a flying chicken coop. If there's an extra passenger or two on board, no one at Zvartnots Airport wants to wake up to check them out at four in the morning. Plus, all occupants of the plane have diplomatic immunity, and the pilot files a manifest with the Armenian authorities which they review maybe once a month."

"Could you get me on the egg flight?"

"Yep. Of course, there'd be absolutely no record of you being aboard. You'd be a stowaway. If you're caught, the U.S. government will deny they even know who you are. They'll be hollering to put your ass in the slammer faster than anyone else."

Three days later, Lev Arkady, who'd convinced the hospital authorities he was sufficiently healed to leave the hospital, took the airport bus eighteen miles north to Esenboğa International Airport. He arrived at seven thirty in the evening. After a leisurely dinner at the airport restaurant, he ambled out to the tarmac. Shortly before nine o'clock, a USAF truck stopped adjacent to him.

"Going out on the egg flight?" the driver shouted good-naturedly.

"Uh-huh."

"Girlfriend in Tel Aviv?"

"Something like that."

"Man, I've heard those honeys down there are hot," the driver, a young airman, said. "You can't get anything in Turkey, not even the clap. Wish I could afford to go down there for a weekend."

"Maybe you could," Lev said, casually slipping the young man a fifty dollar bill.

"Hey, thanks, bud. That was completely unnecessary, but I sure appreciate it."

"No problem, Airman," Lev replied. "Just a little something to let you know we appreciate what you guys are doing here, manning the farthest outposts of democracy."

"Enlisted housing's pretty grim. I've got eight months. Can't wait to get home."

The truck pulled up at a small, old-fashioned aluminum hangar at the far end of the field. A single pole with two sodium lights illuminated the area. A four-engine propeller plane waited quietly under the lights. As Lev alighted from the truck, he was shocked to see a petite, attractive woman wearing an Air Force flight suit.

"Hi, I'm Colleen Miller," she said. "Art Hudson told me you were gonna' hop on when I had my back turned." She chuckled. Lev liked her immediately.

"You could say that, Captain. How were you so lucky to get this assignment?"

"Connections. Listen, if you'd like, there's a third seat in the cockpit we hardly ever use. You can take your choice, fly cabin class or fly chickenshit class."

"All the way to …"

"Just about …" Captain Miller replied. "Fifteen minutes outta' Zvartnots, you gotta' hunker down with the chickens, 'cause we don't know you're on board."

During the flight, Lev spent the hours going over and over the plan he and Art Hudson had concocted. He studied exactly which shared taxi ran from the airport to downtown, the closest street to the American Consulate, exactly where Captain Artakian's precinct headquarters were located, the restaurant frequented by Frank O'Neil, and the date and time Hudson had arranged for Lev to meet him there. Lev had been provided with a Canadian passport and visa identifying him as Lawrence Biegel, businessman, one thousand Soviet Rubles, a return ticket from Yerevan to Moscow and then on to Toronto, enclosed in an Air Canada envelope, a document proving he had reservations at the Razdan Hotel, and a letter of introduction to a well-known Armenian export house. He had packed a small suitcase with toiletries, underwear, two changes of clothes, a large plastic bottle of ibuprofen tablets, and a warm, kapok-filled jacket.

By the time he landed, Yerevan's early morning chill had set in. Lev, who'd been in the controlled temperature of the hospital for more than three months, could not believe how painful his joints were as he alighted from the plane. Only one man, a civilian, met the plane. While he concentrated on loading a few crates of eggs onto his truck, Lev unobtrusively wandered away from the aircraft, limping stiffly along the perimeter road toward the barely-lit terminal a quarter mile away.

By the time the sun came up, Lev Arkady, who'd sponge-bathed and shaved in an airport lavatory, and who'd eaten a breakfast of croissants and tea, emerged from Zvartnots' main terminal and casually walked to the van station outside the arrivals lounge.

❦

Lev listened with growing frustration as Frank O'Neil told him that no one at either of Yerevan's two main airports had seen anyone remotely resembling Penny. "There's a third airport, Armavir," O'Neil said, "but it's abandoned, no tower, a short, pockmarked runway, and no one's filed a flight plan into or out of that field for years."

"Could she have gotten out of Armenia by any other means?"

"Walking over the mountains to Georgia. Maybe to Azerbaijan. Since the Azeris align themselves with the Turks, those borders aren't particularly safe, but just because borders exist doesn't mean that hundreds of people don't cross every year."

"So the trail turns cold just outside Erebuni Airport?"

"Uh-huh."

"I thought America was one of two superpowers in the world," Lev said.

"I wouldn't be surprised if within the couple of years we're the *only* superpower left," O'Neil replied. "In this part of the world, that doesn't count for diddly squat. Even with the Soviet Union fragmenting more every day, Uncle Sam isn't about to capitalize on the mess. You saw what happened in Afghanistan. There are many people more intelligent than me who say *that's* what has brought the Soviet Union crashing down. Thank God the U.S. is too smart to get involved in that rathole. Let the friggin' mullahs and the Taliban have their dry-ass mountains."

"So there's no hope?"

"I didn't say that. There's always hope. That's what I'm supposed to tell anybody who asks. Good evening Captain Artakian," O'Neil said as a middle-aged man stopped at their table."

"Good evening, gentlemen," Artakian replied. "I trust you are enjoying our fair country's hospitality, Mister Arkady? Or would you rather I call you by your new Canadian name?"

"No, that's fine, Captain," Lev said. "I heard of the kindness you showed Penelope Wagner while she was in your custody. I appreciate it."

"But you'd be more appreciative if I had any clues," he said equably. "Officially I can't help much. Armenian jurisdiction extends no further than our own borders. Armenia is weak, times are very hard. We can't even control our own nation of three million. *Unofficially* ..."

"Yes?"

"How long would it take you to pack your suitcase?"

"It's already packed. Why?"

O'Neil piped up. "Gentlemen, it's better if I don't hear this conversation."

"You're probably right, Mister O'Neil," Artakian said. "Not that it would make much difference. Are you allergic to dust, Mister Arkady?"

"No. Why?"

"Concrete and sand kick up a lot of dust when they're being transported. An Otsekian Brothers truck will stop across the street from the hotel where you're booked to pick up a load of concrete on its way to Alaverdi within the next hour."

45

Lev slept for five hours during the nightlong trip through the mountains. The sun had already risen when the driver dropped him off at a thirteenth century Monastery. "Is most famous building in Debed Valley," he said in broken English. "You give this to priest at entry door," he continued, handing Lev a small envelope. With a barely muffled roar and a clashing of gears, the truck took off in a cloud of blue-black smoke, leaving Arkady in its wake.

The priest, who wore a light cassock, was pale, with a shaved head. He nodded wordlessly as Lev handed him the envelope. After glancing at the contents, he motioned Lev to follow him down a hall to a large cell. When the priest opened the door, Lev saw two young women, one slight, pretty, and dark-haired, the other equally attractive, but taller and more robust looking.

"Good morning, Mister Arkady," the priest said in English. "Please pardon my prison pallor. My name is Arov Nikssarian. I'm not a priest. Until my recent incarceration at Yevtushenko penitentiary, I was a doctor at Yerevan State University Hospital, where I had the privilege of treating your brave, lovely friend, Mrs. Wagner. She risked her life to try to get my niece, Nadya Vartunian, out of Armenia during the recent troubles," he said, nodding at the smaller of the two women, "Alas, it didn't work. Nadya and I were each sentenced to three years' imprisonment. But there have been changes in Armenia. As a result, we find ourselves free for the time being."

"Penny wrote me about you, Doctor Nikssarian," Lev replied. "To say my thanks are profound would be an understatement. You're aware that Penny's gone missing?"

"Yes, she seems to have dropped off the face of the earth."

Lev rubbed his eyes, which were puffy from lack of sleep.

"Would you like some coffee or tea, Mister Arkady?" Nadya asked.

"Either one is fine, please." He ground his hands into his thighs, trying to massage feeling back into them. Turning to Doctor Nikssarian, he said, "Captain Artakian arranged for me to come here. I didn't know why at the time. He said it was best not to ask."

"Strange things happen in this part of the world," Nikssarian said. "Cross-border friendships are precious. My Nadya was in her first year at the university when she met a girl from the Georgian SSR. They stayed in touch, even when Nadya was sent to prison. When Nadya was released, Rosa crossed two borders to celebrate Nadya's freedom."

"Two borders?" Lev said.

"As far as the Soviet Union is concerned, it's all one country, but Nadya's friend had been working at a temporary job just over the Georgian border in Chechnya when she saw something I think will interest you, Mister Arkady." Lev looked at the taller woman. "Mister Arkady, I'd like you to meet Nadya's friend, Rosa Dudayev."

◆◆◆

"It's been several days since I saw her, Mister Arkady. I can't promise she's still there."

"How did you – ?"

"My cousin Mikhail and his wife, Anya, have worked at the compound for the past year. They have no love for the rebels, but nowadays jobs are very hard to come by in the northern Caucasus and they need to eat. Anya's mother became ill in September. They told Mikhail they could not spare Anya, even for a week. I had ten days' vacation time from my job in Tbilisi. I'd never been to Chechnya, so I agreed to replace Anya. The third day I was there, Signor Black appeared. Two days later, Mrs. Wagner came."

"Signor Black?"

"I didn't like him from the moment I saw him. He believes every woman is his next conquest. He apparently had … has … designs on your lady?"

"That bastard!" Lev swore. "Is she still there?"

"Anya sent word that as of two nights ago she was still there. It is your lady friend's great good fortune that Signor Black was called away to Aleppo the day after she arrived. She's under constant guard, but at least he hasn't been there. Anya told me he's due back in Chechnya day after tomorrow."

Lev paced the floor of the room. "How far is the compound from here?"

"Seventy kilometers to Tbilisi. Another eighty to Itum-Shale."

"So," Nadya chimed in, "it's a matter of getting Mrs. Wagner out of Chechnya and getting her back to Georgia, which has excellent relations with Turkey."

By that time, Lev no longer noticed the pain in his legs. He was anxious to get going immediately, now that he knew Penny was within ninety miles.

A short, stocky man in his late thirties, with ruddy complexion and curly dark hair, entered. Doctor Nikssarian brightened. "Mister Arkady, as I said earlier, this part of the world is a strange cauldron of nationalities where friendships cross many borders, often shifting allegiances. Simcha La'or is officially a third secretary with the Israeli embassy in Tbilisi. It's best we not know what he really does. He'll be the key to you and Mrs. Wagner returning to Tbilisi. The route will be somewhat circuitous."

❦

"This is absolutely obscene," Doctor Nikssarian said. "And you're a Rabbi, an ordained man of God."

"Almost. I've still got a year of study ahead of me before I'm ordained."

"As serious and urgent as this whole thing is, you fellows are comic relief," Lev said, unable to suppress his laughter. "You look like Latin American guerilla wannabes."

"Wannabes?" Nikssarian asked, raising his thin eyebrows.

"An American phrase I learned in another life," Lev responded. "Never mind. You look like the real thing."

Ariel Levine, who could not have dreamed that in less than five years he'd be the Chief Rabbi of Tbilisi, and the mild-mannered Doctor Arov Nikssarian were identically dressed in rough buckskin outfits with bandoliers crisscrossing their chests. Each held a large, old-fashioned rifle.

"Let's go over the plan again," Simcha continued. "You fellows will make a show of trying to kidnap Signor Black. You feign frustration when you find he's not there and you then try to kidnap Penelope Wagner. When you get to Penny's room, she'll be gone."

"And then?" This from Lev.

"You'll take whoever shows you to Penny's room at gunpoint, tie him up, and put him in the back of the car," Simcha continued. "The car is a beat-up old Moskva with Azeri license plates. You'll let whoever's in charge know you're taking this man as hostage to your confederates across the Azeri border, and that any attempt to follow you will result in your prisoner's death. They're sure to follow you as soon as they believe you can't see them anymore. That'll give you a five minute head start on them. You don't need more than two or three of those minutes. There'll be a Russian State Police cruiser with flashing lights off to the side of the road. You'll pull over behind the cruiser. A uniformed policeman will order you to get out of the Moskva, leave the prisoner behind, and get into the police car. When your prisoner's associates come to get him, he'll only be able to tell them truthfully that you abandoned the car and drove off with the police."

"How will we take the lady to safety?"

"You won't," Simcha said.

"What?" Lev looked bemused.

"Everything these people do will be a ruse to distract attention from you and Mrs. Wagner. I'll give you more detailed instructions when we get closer."

"Simcha, I don't know what to say. I can't thank you enough for your help. The Israeli consulate has really gone above and beyond the call of duty on this one."

"No thanks are necessary, Mister Arkady. We owe the Chechnyans a few sharp raps on the knuckles. As Doctor Nikssarian said, we have friends in strange places. What do you know about Mrs. Wagner's physical and mental condition?"

"She's an expert in martial arts. She'll handle herself well in an emergency."

"Excellent."

"If that's the case, why can't we simply all leave the compound together?"

"Because we'll be in Chechen country all the way to the 'real' Soviet Union. Signor Black and his people will have every road covered. Black will undoubtedly consider an escaped prisoner, and a mere woman at that, an insult to his authority, not to mention his manhood. So when they check us out …"

"An empty bucket."

"Precisely."

"Will there be other players?"

"Friends."

"Of which we won't speak?"

"True."

"I trust there'll be something more than friendship in it for them?"

"Of course."

"How will we recognize them?"

"They'll find you in a shit wagon."

"No, really?"

"You'll travel in a farm wagon covered with manure for the first few miles." Turning to the others, Simcha said, "We'll divide up within the hour. Simcha, the ladies, and I will drive up to the farmhouse. Doctor Nikssarian, Rabbi Levine, you're on your own."

"And the police cruiser?" Nikssarian asked.

"God, working through the Israeli consulate, will provide," Simcha responded. "It's always convenient to have friends inside the Georgian State Police Department."

46

"Darling Rosa, I thought you'd been taken from my life forever."

"Today's your lucky day, Gyorgi," she responded. She'd developed a real liking for the twenty-two-year-old guard, Raskov, who was not Chechnyan, but, like her, a hired Georgian laborer. She knew he was smitten with her. "Anya's mother's ill again."

"I'm so sorry to hear that. How long will you be here?"

"Two or three days."

"Then we'll have time to talk?"

"Thank you for standing up to Signor Black when he tried to get fresh with me."

"He is not a gentleman," Gyorgi remarked acidly.

"Aren't you worried that if he sees the two of us together …?"

"He'll be in Syria for at least another two days."

She winked at him flirtatiously. "What about Mrs. Wagner?"

"She's still here, and none too happy either."

"Is she in the same guest room?"

"Unfortunately no," Raskov replied. "Signor Black's keeping her in his own suite of rooms, under the heaviest guard in the camp, until he returns."

"Have they become … lovers?" she asked casually.

"Hardly. He flew off to Aleppo the day after she got here. Signor Black is necessary for the financial survival of the revolution, but no one would be sorry to see him gone, permanently."

Damn! Rosa thought. *Not only will that make it harder to get to her, but it'll be next to impossible to get word to the others in time.* "Gyorgi," she said warmly. "I'm one of the few people here she trusts. Could I see her for a few minutes, just to say hello?"

"Well …" he said uncertainly. "Signor Black left word no one was to see her."

"What harm could there be in my spending a few moments with her? I'd be happy to have you search me …" she saw his eyes light up with interest, "provided there's a woman close by to protect me."

"Rosa!" he said, abashed. "Surely you wouldn't think – ?"

"Of course not, Gyorgi. You're too much of a gentleman, and a Georgian, which means you know how to treat a woman."

"*Are* you armed?" he asked.

"Of course not. Truly, you can search me if you want," she said, taking his right hand and pressing it to her pants pockets, her stomach, and her shoulders.

"No, no, I trust you."

"You can stay in the room with us the whole time. I just want to say hello to her."

⁂

Penny flushed with pleasure when she saw Rosa. They hugged and spoke inanities. Penny, who knew she'd have to be cautious, asked if Rosa had heard anything from the outside. Rosa responded there were rumors about how poorly things were going in the Soviet Union, but otherwise no really exciting news.

"Have you heard anything about Lev?" Penny asked.

"Not a word," Rosa replied, but Penny was quick to catch the other woman's sharply raised eyebrows while Rosa was sure her back was to Gyorgi. Suddenly, Rosa grasped at her stomach. In response to Penny's questioning look, Rosa said, "It's nothing really. Just some indigestion from the journey. Is there a loo I could use?"

"There's a private bathroom in this suite."

"I'll only be a moment."

While she was in the bathroom, Rosa spotted a clothes hamper in a corner of the room. She opened it. Seeing there were only women's underclothes in the basket, she taped the message to the bottom of the lid. Then, she flushed the toilet, washed her hands, and emerged from the room, her hands wet.

"Mrs. Wagner, I hate to be a pest, but there was no towel in the restroom and I wasn't about to dry my hands on the soiled underwear in the hamper …"

"I'm sorry, Rosa," Penny said. "Would you mind using a kitchen towel?"

"Of course not."

⁂

Penny found the note less than two minutes after Rosa Dudayev had left. The instructions were explicit. While she felt this might be a genuine opportunity, her experience in Armenia made her suspicious. After all, the American Consul had also given her detailed instructions. "You fool me once, shame on you. You fool me twice, shame on me," she said softly. On the other hand, she'd recognized Lev's handwriting.

She tore the note into tiny strips and shoved them under the living room rug. Just before sunset, she asked the guard outside her door if she might take a short walk along the camp perimeter. "You can have someone accompany me if you wish."

The guard summoned young Gyorgi Raskov and directed him to keep watch on "our important guest."

"Would you mind if I brought her friend Rosa along, Sergeant?"

"I can't see what harm it would do. She seemed much happier when she saw the Dudayev woman earlier today, and if she's in a better mood, you-know-who will be easier to live with when he returns."

North of the Georgian frontier, the great, wild mountains of the Caucasus gradually descend into foothills. The land flattens out between the Chechen steppe and the Great Russian forests. It is a place of small farmholdings and endless skies. In early fall, the land is golden with sheaves of wheat and bales of drying hay. It is a land of few private automobiles. *Kamyons,* huge trucks plying the international highways, rule the larger roads. One sees more horse-drawn wagons than motor vehicles on the byways.

Just after Penny, Rosa, and Gyorgi had started their walk, a Soviet police cruiser pulled up to the camp's entrance. A loudspeaker blared from the headquarters building, "All duty guard personnel report to the front gate! We have a report of a potential armed incursion. I repeat, all guard personnel on duty, report to the front gate immediately!"

Raskov looked at the women. "Don't worry, Gyorgi," Rosa said. "I'll watch Mrs. Wagner. Even if she wanted to, how would she escape? By hitching a ride on that farm wagon yonder? And where would she go if she could escape?"

"You're right," Raskov said. "I should be back in thirty minutes at the most."

⁂

Ten minutes after he'd left, Rosa spoke softly to Penny. "There's a small cornfield nearby. The tall stalks haven't been cut yet, so there's room to hide."

"So the instructions were real?"

"The wagon should be here within the hour. Hide yourself as best you can until you hear a girl calling out for some animal, then make a run for it."

The two women switched clothing. Penny, although taller than Rosa, was slender enough so that the bulky peasant clothing fit her well. Once garbed in a headscarf, she was indistinguishable from other females in the area.

⁘

Within the hour, Penny and Lev, whose reunion had been joyous but subdued, lay in the farm wagon, under a blanket atop which lay a thin veneer of hay. The hay was covered by a large pile of manure. The short, grizzled farmer driving the wagon shouted out the imagined name of some animal every minute or two. His daughter, wrapped in a shawl and loose clothing, punctuated the farmer's entreaties by occasionally yelling out the same name. A mile up the road, discouraged by their inability to find the lost animal, they turned into a rutted path leading to their cottage.

⁘

The Soviet State Police officer told the guards, "We have reports of an Armenian insurgent group in this area. They've taken up arms against the Soviet government. We don't believe Itum-Shale is a target, but this camp has a cache of weapons that could prove useful to them." As he was speaking, a nondescript Moskva pulled up to the gate. Through its badly scratched side window, its driver, a uniformed man of late middle age, Simcha's present disguise, nodded to the Soviet officer, who continued, "With your permission, Lieutenant Markov from our Groszny regional office will examine your headquarters building for anything unusual. If you experience any problems, let him know and we'll respond immediately. I suggest you remain here until I return."

The police cruiser pulled into the camp, followed by the Moskva. No sooner were they out of hearing range, the senior guard snarled, "Fucking Soviet bullies. They think they still own the world! Can you imagine they think we're on *their* side?"

"It's all right, Captain," his lieutenant replied. "Let them play their power games as long as they leave us alone. Have you heard anything about insurgents?"

"Nawww. Just an excuse to rub our nose in the dirt by showing us they can still come in here without an invitation any time they want. I suppose we'll have to stay here until that cruiser comes back. No sense messing with them."

The Moskva followed the Police Cruiser to the headquarters building. The patrol cruiser then returned to the main gate. When he was sure no one was looking, "Lieutenant Markov" popped the trunk and two "insurgents," Doctor Nikssarian and Rabbi Levine, jumped out.

"It's fortunate we only had to share each other's company for ten minutes," Levine said. "It was already getting pretty stuffy."

"Are you sure you know what to do if anyone asks anything?"

"I just hope they don't look closely enough to see – "

"You don't look that bad," Levine said. "Unless someone really examines you at close range. Besides, it's the best we could do on such short notice," he continued. "Fortunately, one of our congregants retired from *Gosfilm* after thirty years in the makeup department. What's the plan now?"

"We were given three miniature devices and shown how to conceal them in the main security office. The operation should take less than an hour. Camp security probably won't detect them in that time. They've only got a three mile range, but that's all we need, since I'll be on a side road less than two miles from here."

When he returned to the gate, the Soviet Security Officer said, "Nothing looks suspicious, but you should keep your eyes and ears open tonight." He touched the second and third fingers of his right hand to the visor of his service cap and pulled away.

A few minutes later, the Moskva followed in the cruiser's wake. "Captain," Lieutenant Markov said to the head of camp security, "I'm sorry to have troubled you. I've just received a radio call from Groszny. The insurgents have been surrounded twenty miles north of here, and the danger is past. I regret any disturbance we've caused."

✦

"Good evening, Captain." The senior camp security guard was startled as he faced two evil-looking, rifle-bearing men who stood waiting as he entered his office.

"Who are you?" he barked, "And just what the hell do you think you're doing?"

"Now, now, Captain, there's no need to get defensive, *offensive*, actually," one of the armed men said. "*We* know who we are, and that's sufficient for our needs. We also know why we're here. It does not concern you."

"Smoke?" the other man said pleasantly. "Ah, I see you're not interested in niceties. Very well then, we'll get to the point. We're not interested in you and we're not interested in the little soldier games you're playing at this camp. We want Black."

"Who – ?"

The first man came closer to the guard and shoved the barrel of the rifle into his belly. "We told you that was none of your business. Where's Black?"

"He's not here," the senior guard answered truthfully.

"We're told he's holding an American woman hostage. Where is she?"

"None of your goddam business," the captain growled.

In response, the second man smacked him across the face, not hard, just enough to sting. "Wrong answer, Captain. Want to try again?"

"You think you're frightening me?" the guard snarled. "There are over a hundred men in this compound. You may kill me. You may even kill a few of my forces, but your chances of getting out of this camp alive are nonexistent."

"Look," the first man said calmly. "We told you we're not interested in you or in what goes on here. Be reasonable, man. We've been told your people don't hold Black in high esteem."

The guard's look softened somewhat. "I'm listening."

"Black may be here, or he may not, but if he's the mouse, the woman's the cheese. She comes with us. Bait for the trap. How important is she to your mission?"

"She means nothing to us, but if he comes back and she's not here – "

"He'll what? Shoot you? You just said there are over a hundred men here. There are two of us. There's one of him. His chances of getting out alive would be half of ours."

"You don't understand. The Chechen Independence Movement needs arms and money. Black's the source of that money and most of our weapons."

The second man said, "How would he know Mrs. Wagner was kidnapped? Don't look so surprised, Captain, we know her name."

"How could he not know?"

"Detail an expendable man to take us to her room. We'll knock him out. Don't worry, we won't hurt him, and we'll take the lady."

"Do I have a choice?"

The first man, Rabbi Levine, said, "All life is a choice, Captain."

The security man hesitated for an instant, picked up an old-fashioned, heavy black phone on his desk and dialed three numbers.

"Lieutenant Grechko, find Gyorgi Raskov and send him up here. No, it's nothing I can't handle."

❧

Less than a quarter hour later, the two armed men and the young guard who'd been detailed to go with them returned to the captain's office.

"You lied to us," Nikssarian said. "She's not there."

"What do you mean she's not there?" the captain asked incredulously.

"She's gone, Captain," the sentry answered. "Nothing's missing except Mrs. Wagner. Her clothes are all in place."

"What do we do now?" asked the captain.

"We wait for Black to return."

"That could take days," the captain said.

"We've got time," Nikssarian said.

"I think not," the captain said. In a split second he'd reached under his desk, grabbed a service revolver, brought it up and fired into Nikssarian's stomach. A red flower spread through Nikssarian's midsection. Within moments, the doctor was dead.

What happened thereafter was a blur. Rabbi Levine instinctively fired point blank into the captain's face, pulping it in an instant. As the young guard raised his firearm, Levine barked, "I can make it two as easy as one. Someone's going to pay for this. Do you want to be next?"

"N...n...no, Sir," the young sentry stammered. "P...p... please, Sir, I have a mama and daddy in a s...small town near Tbilisi. I d...didn't mean any harm, Sir. I was just, just o... obeying orders," he blubbered. Then he looked down at the floor. "It doesn't matter anyway." He started sobbing. "If you don't kill me, they will."

The two men stood facing each other, each uncertain what to

do next. As the enormity of what had happened started to sink in, the two men, each holding a firearm aimed at the other, were visibly shaking. Levine spoke first.

"Tbilisi? You're not a Chechen?"

"No, sir, but jobs are scarce in Georgia and one needs to eat."

"What did you mean, 'If I don't kill you, they will?'"

"I was the last one to see Mrs. Wagner."

"Explain."

"She's been housed in Black's quarters for days. She wanted to take a walk outside, just to get a bit of fresh air. A young woman named Rosa Dudayev, who'd worked here in the past, had just come back to work again. Miss Dudayev suggested she accompany Mrs. Wagner. The captain detailed me to walk with them to make sure nothing happened. Then I was called back to the main gate. It's not my fault …"

"What's not your fault?"

"That Mrs. Wagner wasn't there when you went looking for her."

At that moment, the door to the office burst open. Simcha La'or stood there, his sidearm raised, pointing it at the young sentry. He looked around the room, saw the grisly sight, and flinched for a moment. "I heard what happened, Rabbi," he said. "I got here as quickly as I can. Who's this young man?"

"Gyorgi Raskov, Sir," the sentry replied. Somewhat incongruously he added, "Are you going to kill me, Mister … Mister …?"

"La'or, Guard Raskov, and the answer is no. You're not really one of them. It's not your time to meet the Angel of Death. But I think it is time for us to go for a ride."

47

By the time the sun set, Penny and Lev were seated in rough wooden chairs in a hut made of pine planks. A man who called himself "Sergei" had introduced himself as "the friend of your friend," and now sat facing them. His English was fluent, although he spoke with a heavy accent. "It was kind of Mister La'or to make provision and to advise us where we might pick up the merchandise. My associates will ensure you have a safe trip to Georgia, just east of the Military Highway."

Lev, who'd participated in the "goods" game for most of his life, knew not to ask what kind of merchandise Sergei was to pick up. Their host, a tall, man of indeterminate middle age, with full black beard flecked with gray, continued. "Have you been to this part of the Soviet Union before?"

"No."

Penny, dressed in long, loose-fitting clothing and modest headscarf, sat silently.

"The Military Road, started by the Russians in 1799 and completed sixty tears later, has been protected by military outposts since the nineteenth century. It's two hundred-twenty kilometers long and crosses the Greater Caucasus Mountains, from Vladikavkaz to Tbilisi."

"I trust we won't travel on that Highway?"

"We'll stay on mountain trails, far away from any roads."

"Because of war? Bandits?"

"Both. My friends will try to make certain, at least as certain as one can be in the Caucasus, that you'll most likely make it safely to Georgia. Ah, time for dinner." Three women garbed much like Penny and silent as ghosts, entered the room unobtrusively. They placed a large pot of rice and another filled with stew at a nearby table. The fare was simple, delicious and filling, accompanied by tankards of ice-cold spring water.

"Are you Muslim?" Lev asked casually.

"Whatever you wish to believe, that's your choice. The 'civilized' world views my people as a pugnacious bunch of savages. But we're not as bad as Cossacks, not as bad as Georgians, and not as bad as Russians, that's for sure."

"You seem rather urbane for a simple mountain man," Penny interjected.

"Thank you," Sergei replied proudly. "I graduated Tbilisi State University, which doesn't mean a damned thing in the West, but it's the oldest university in the Caucasus. I trained as an engineer. Our Soviet overlords employed me for twenty years."

"So you may be Muslim or you may not?" Lev persisted.

Sergei smiled shrewdly. "My people have a selective approach to religion. We're religious, but not so religious that we aren't secular. If some crazy Russian policeman ever tried to enforce the criminal code in this part of the world, half of us would be in jail and the other half would be standing in the street with Kalashnikovs, getting the other half out. We love God, drink too much, fight, boast, steal, forge a little money, deal in drugs, and wage blood feuds. We'll fight any enemy to the death, but we can't be organized into groups of more than one."

Lev broke out a bottle of wine from the rucksack Simcha had given him before he'd dropped them off, handed it to Sergei, and sat quietly, waiting for the man to continue. Sergei opened the bottle and poured a draught for Lev and one for himself.

"Alliances and politics? Not in this part of the world," the mountaineer continued. "You can make any promise you like, break it, and we'll believe you again tomorrow. We've suffered indignities you wouldn't believe, yet you'll never see them on the evening television news because we're only a small piece of worthless land so remote no one anyone's ever heard of us or even gives a damn. We've got nothing, we'll never have anything, but what little we do have, we share with anyone who's a guest, even if he's murdered a dozen of our people and is certain to murder a hundred more tomorrow."

The radio on an adjacent table gave a shrill squeal, followed by a message neither Lev nor Penny could understand. Sergei barked a monosyllabic response, turned abruptly to his guests and said, "Time for you to go to sleep. My associates will be here at four tomorrow morning."

❧❦❧

An army bus with small steel windows and kit bags on the roof picked them up a few minutes before four. Dawn was not yet breaking over the Caucasus. The sun would not rise for another three hours. The bus showed placards in front and back bearing the number 518. A fat man in sloppy army uniform drove them through the black night. Three dark young men wearing flak jackets sat behind him, holding Kalashnikovs on their laps. Five other men sat in the back seats. Sergei, Penny, and Lev sat in three vacant seats in the middle of the bus. Their conveyance was lit by faint blue lights.

As the bus rolled along, Sergei spoke to Lev and Penny in a low voice. "When I came home to my village, my friends and relatives still liked me. I had worked for the Russians, but they understood that everyone needed to work for someone in order to eat. My brothers and sisters were proud of me, since I was the only college graduate in the family. The Russians coddled the North Ossetians while they stuck it to the South Ossetians and the Ingush."

"What is your nationality?"

"I am a mongrel, a hybrid, able to speak enough local dialects to get by almost anywhere in the mountains, able to shift my identity to whatever I need it to be."

"Kind of like me," Lev mused.

"I listen to their radio, read their papers, and keep my ear to the earth, as they say in the Caucasus. Your friend Simcha reads the tea leaves well. In two years the Soviet Empire will lie dead in its grave and the Russian Empire will be climbing out. Ten, fifteen years from now there'll be a new strong man. That's the way the Russians are. Ukraine gone! The Baltics gone! Georgia going! The whole Caucasus going! And the Russians will try to grab us back. You can bet money on that!"

The bus slowed down. "Pretend you're asleep. Put your head forward, close your eyes," he murmured.

The bus stopped. A draft of icy air ripped through the interior as the driver's door opened. Sergei pushed past the passengers. From beneath his lowered lids, Lev saw a figure in a long gray overcoat step aboard and grasp Sergei in a swift embrace. He heard confidential murmurs and saw a fat envelope change hands. The man in the overcoat departed, the door slammed shut, and the bus eased forward. Sergei remained standing in the aisle. They passed a barracks and an empty, floodlit field. They passed a canteen and saw Soviet solders eating under fluorescent lighting. The bus advanced slowly. Sergei remained standing, one hand in his pocket. They approached a checkpoint. A red-and-white boom blocked their path. The three dark men laid their Kalashnikovs on the floor. The boom rose and the bus passed through.

The bus rolled toward the dark side of an airfield, following black tire tracks in the snow. A battered twin-engined transport plane appeared in the headlights, its doors open, its gangway in place. The bus slowed, then stopped in front of the gangway. At Sergei's signal, everyone except the driver jumped out of the bus, into the freezing dawn.

The plane's propellers were turning and its landing lights were switched on. In the cockpit, three white faces shouted at everyone to get a move on. Lev and Penny scurried up the rickety steps. The belly of the aircraft was bare. There were no seats in the plane, just a dozen or so web enclosures. Sergei signaled Penny and Lev to strap themselves in.

Penny glanced momentarily at Lev, who shrugged but otherwise said nothing.

The door shut. The sound of the propellers grew louder as the plane taxied for what seemed an inordinately long time, making further conversation impossible. As the engines screamed to full power and the wind whistled against the fuselage, the ungainly bird slowly, protestingly left the ground and clawed its way into the air. Through a sliver of moonlight, Lev saw three onion domes of a church rising from a hillside, the largest one gilded, the other two wrapped in scaffolding. The plane banked so steeply that for a moment he wondered whether they were upside down.

Strapped into his web-seat, Sergei started talking again, his voice tinged with bitterness. "We thought the Russians wouldn't shoot. This wasn't happening to us. Gorbachev was not Stalin. Of course he wasn't. He was Gorbachev. The Ossetians had tanks and helicopters but the Russians came along all the same to make sure no Ossetians got hurt. Their propaganda machine was great. The

Ingush were bloodthirsty savages, the Chechnyans were bloodthirsty savages, the South Ossetians were bloodthirsty savages. The Soviets and the North Ossetians were good guys. The North Ossetians shot the shit out of us and the Russians stood around and laughed while fifty thousand innocent people ran for their lives. The Russians sealed off the region with tanks and declared military rule in the 'breakaway republics.' Not in North Ossetia because the Ossetians were civilized guys, Christians."

Sergei took out a flask from somewhere in his rucksack, drank, and handed it to Lev, who waved it away. "Our people appealed to the world, but the world was too damn busy. 'Who the hell are the Ingush, the Chechnyans, the South Ossetians? That's the Soviets' backyard, isn't it? While we're pulling down the economic borders, those ethnic crazies are putting up *national* borders. They're dissidents, Muslims, criminals. Forget the Soviet criminals. Best let Gorby handle it.'"

The plane's engines faltered, then resumed on a lower note. It was losing altitude.

Penny gripped the sides of her webbing, her knuckles white. "Are we landing or crashing?" she asked, her voice much calmer than she felt.

The transport hurtled between light towers towards a black hillside, which opened to reveal a single strip of concrete. With a hard bump, the aircraft hit the tarmac, slowed, and taxied beyond the red and green lights to a concrete parking area. It stopped next to six vintage fighter planes, a single fire engine, and a few fuel trucks. The transport's propellers kept turning, beating the air listlessly, forcing the freezing air back toward the plane's door.

As it opened, the passengers scrambled out. Less than ninety seconds later, the old bird turned and headed back toward the runway from whence it had come.

The compound consisted of three houses inside a white-walled courtyard. There were two gateways, one to the road, one to open pasture. Beyond the pasture, foothills patched with shadows by the sun, folded in on one another. Above the hills rose mountains and more, higher mountains.

Lev and Penny sat at a plastic-topped table in the center of the room. Two women in headscarves scurried about, setting out food. Their host, a stocky man with a bushy moustache, spoke gravely while he grasped Lev's hand.

"He says you are welcome," said Sergei. "He says he's greatly honored by your presence here and you should sit beside him. He says we can fight our wars for ourselves, that we don't need outside help. But when anyone lends support, we are grateful and we thank God. He means every word. He's a Sufi, so we don't question his authority."

Lev did as he was bid. The older men took their places at the table, while the younger men remained standing. The women served pita loaves, fried beef in garlic, and tea. A photograph of a bearded man hung on the wall. In answer to Lev's unspoken question, Sergei said, "One of the martyrs. There are so many of them their names are buried in the shadows of time."

The Sufi host spoke rapidly in a language neither Lev nor Penny understood.

"They attacked the village at night," Sergei translated. "It had been deserted for years, ever since the Soviets knocked down the houses and drove the inhabitants into the valley. In the old days we could always be safe in our mountains, but today they have rockets and helicopters, the Russians and Ossetians."

Sergei stopped, reflecting his own thoughts to Lev. "Ossetians are bastards, but they're our bastards. We'll deal with them in our own way."

Their host continued his rapid fire barrage of talk and again Sergei translated. "The Sufis are the only ones capable of taking up the Russian challenge. A woman attended her mother's funeral ten kilometers away. When she returned, she found everyone dead, so she turned around and walked back to the village where she'd buried her mother, Next day a group of men set out. They washed the remains of the bodies, said words over them, and buried them. One of our leaders had been tortured with knives, but they recognized him."

"*My predali!*" their host said sharply, banging his hand on the table. Lev understood the Russian. "We were betrayed!"

"*Kem?*" he asked. "By whom?"

"'*N verraaier! 'N Ossetië spioen!* A traitor! An Ossetian spy!"

One of the younger men spoke softly, solemnly, in a different dialect. Sergei translated. "We shall kill every one of them. We shall find out the names of the helicopter pilots and the men who planned the operation, the name of the man who commanded it, and the names of the men who took part in it. With God's help, we shall kill them all. We shall go on killing the Soviets until they take their tanks and their guns, their helicopters and their rockets, their soldiers and officials and spies to the other side of the Terek River and leave us to settle our differences and govern ourselves in peace. That is God's will."

❦

Lev slept with the men, Penny with the women, in almost identical guest rooms, beds pushed against the walls, mattresses on the floor, and a bucket to pee in. One by one the men dropped off to sleep.

Hours passed. Lev heard roosters and the bleating of sheep. A faltering muezzin called the faithful over a loudspeaker. Lev stood, urinated in the bucket, and walked over to the nearest window. The view was eerie, hypnotic, and rivetingly beautiful: cattle shuffling in the nearby yard, mountains again, and more mountains above the mountains. He watched women driving buffaloes through the courtyard in the darkness which presaged dawn. Sergei pulled at his loose shirtsleeves.

"Time to go. Have you any money?"

"Money? I thought ...?"

"Not for us. For the young children. So they might have hope. Nothing much, a few coins, some small bills for the older ones. Only if you can, of course."

Moved by the simplicity, the smallness of what Sergei asked, Lev gathered all his pocket change, Turkish lira, Russian kopecks, some unidentifiable Armenian coins, and a few small bills, and pushed the lot toward Sergei.

"No, Mister Arkady," Sergei said, politely declining the proffered money. "It is for you to distribute."

"I have no idea how much ..."

"Any amount, no matter how small, will greatly increase the wealth of each child, and they will be thankful. Boys, girls, it doesn't matter.

When he'd distributed the piddlingly small amount, a group of eight children gathered around Lev as well as Penny, who'd awakened by this time, and sang a song to the foreigners. Neither understood the words, but both understood the emotion and the sweetness with which the melody was sung. Tears came to both their eyes.

"We should get started," Sergei said.

It was still dark. They drove first on the main road, then up a widening valley until the road became a field strewn with boulders. A jeep in front stopped and they stopped beside it. By their headlights, Lev saw a footbridge over a river and a steeply rising grass track abutting the water. On the riverbank, eight horses were already saddled. They whuffled softly. An old man in a high fur hat, boots, and breeches, and a slender mountain boy sat astride two of them.

The boy set out first, accompanied by two of the men who'd carried Kalashnikovs the day before. The fur-hatted guide went next, then Sergei, then Penny and Lev. Two other young men from the night before brought up the rear.

Sergei had given a pistol each to Penny and Lev. Now he added holsters and ammunition belts with metal loops on them for grenades. Lev started to refuse the grenades, but Sergei sharply commanded him: "Take the damn things and wear them. We're close to the Ossetian frontier, close to the Military Highway, and close to the Soviet camps. This isn't Paris."

The old guide spoke up, his dialect Ukranian, which Lev understood. "Speak quietly. Don't talk unless you have to. Don't shoot unless you have to. Don't stop unless you have to, don't light a flame, don't swear. How long since you've ridden a horse?"

"Years."

"Don't mind the mud or the steep places. The horses know the way. The horses will do the work. Don't lean. If you're scared, don't look down. If we're attacked, nobody surrenders. That's the tradition, so please observe it."

"What did he say?" Penny asked.

"I don't think you want to hear it," her companion replied.

"I can take it."

"Have it your way." He translated from the Ukrainian.

"You're right," she shuddered. "Too much information."

"I don't think we're given much choice. You've already survived a plane crash, rabies, imprisonment …"

"True, but even a cat runs out of lives eventually."

"Oh, and one other thing," the old man added sardonically. "If you want to piss, save it 'til we've killed some Russians." This was met by grim laughter from the rest.

They rode for four hours. If they hadn't been so fearful of what might await them, they might have been more fearful of the journey.

Within minutes they were looking down on the lights of villages thousands of feet below them, while the black mountain wall brushed past their faces. The sky lightened, black peaks appeared among the clouds, snowcaps rose above them, and Penny's heart lifted from the mystery of it all.

Rounding a bend, they came on herds of black, thick-coated sheep perched precariously on the slopes below them. Two shepherds huddled under a crude shelter, warming themselves before a fire fueled by dried sheep dung. Their eyes took the measure of the group's guns and horses.

Silently, Lev's group entered a forest of veiled trees. The forest rose on one side. On the other, beyond a steep dropoff which seemed like only inches away, lay the chasm of a valley full of swirling dawn mist, the sigh of wind, and the scream of birds below. Lev and Penny willed their bodies to remain quiet with each new sight of a precipice between their horses' slithering feet and the tiny, winding valley floor, and of the crumbling stone ridge, their only hold on the mountain face. Around more turns, their ears were assaulted by the sound of numerous waterfalls.

The weather changed as wildly as the landscape. Giant insects hummed around their faces, then danced away. One moment friendly white clouds drifted gently across the blue alpine sky. The next, they were cringing in the lee of enormous trees in a vain effort to escape torrential rain.

They entered a clearing. The old guide ordered the train to halt and bunch together under an overhanging cliff. One of the Kalashnikov-bearing men dismounted and busied himself with his saddlebag while he kept watch up the track. A second man sat with his back to the first, his gun held across his chest as he covered the route they had climbed. The mountain boy rode out of the trees ahead of them. He murmured something to the old guide.

"We can ride on," the guide said in Ukrainian.

"What was holding us up?" Lev asked.

"Russians."

❦

At first Penny and Lev did not realize they'd entered the village. Lev saw a wide plateau, like a sawed-off mountain, covered with smashed stones, four crumbling towers with a blue cloud rolling over them, and dark figures dotted across the landscape, which he dismissed as shepherds with their flocks. As the train drew closer he saw figures stooping, rising, and stooping again.

As gusts of frigid wind blew fiercely in their faces they heard the sound of wailing, which undulated with each movement up and down of the shadowy figures. Penny recognized the keening wail of women mourning the dead, each for herself, and each in strident discord with the others. She shivered.

They smelled wood smoke and saw fires burning halfway up the slope. Women tended the fires and small children played around them. A dead sheep hung head down from a tree. In addition to the wood smoke, Lev smelled death, the sweet, sticky smell of blood, and scorched earth open to the sky. The wind blew stronger. With each step they took, the keening became louder. The mounted group rode into the village in single file. From somewhere within, a dozen men materialized and assembled, nodding in silent respect at the old guide and bowing reverentially to Sergei.

❦

The wind died down on the plateau, leaving behind it a frigid alpine cold. Someone had provided a warm coat for Penny and one for Lev. They stood next to Sergei on the hillside above the village. A bonfire burned in the courtyard below them as men of all ages sat around it and conferred.

"What are they talking about?" Lev asked.

"Roughly translated, 'the more things change the more they remain the same. The killings go on, vengeance breeds vengeance. A new generation begins the war anew.'"

"Must it always be like this?" Penny asked.

"We say 'God knows,'" Sergei responded, "but in truth He doesn't. Not in this part of the world anyway." He changed his tone. "Tomorrow morning, three hours after sunrise, we'll cross into Georgia where we'll rendezvous with La'or's people. We will part company there, you to return to your lives, we to ours. I only hope the crossing of our paths may, in some small way, have been meaningful to all of us."

Thus it was that as the sun approached its zenith the next day, East and West bid a heartfelt farewell to one another. But the story didn't end there.

Three days later, Lev and Penny reunited with Simcha, Nadya, Rosa Dudayev, and Ariel Levine in a comfortable home on the outskirts of Tbilisi. Although they were overjoyed to come together at last, Simcha bore sad tidings.

"Sergei and his group were ambushed on the way back up into their mountains. No survivors."

Penny, who'd been a rock of strength since the Beaver had crashed in Armenia, broke down in wracking sobs. "Doctor Nikssarian dead and now Sergei gone. Despite the rough exterior of Sergei and his people, they were kind and generous and …"

"Simple and trusting to a fault," Lev filled in.

"And that, alas, is the tragedy of the Caucasus, or, for that matter, Israel and the Palestinians, the Turks and the Armenians and the Kurds ... and the world," Simcha concluded quietly.

"Will it never end?" Nadya asked.

"The torch is being passed to your generation sooner than you think, my dear. We won't live long enough to know."

❦

Within a year, conditions in Armenia deteriorated rapidly. A paralyzing strike in neighboring Azerbaijan cut fuel and other supplies, ninety percent of which were shipped to Yerevan via Baku. Deputy Chairman Kodzhamirian claimed the Armenian Soviet Republic was suffering an economic blockade, and things were at a flash point.

As summer of 1989 gave way to fall, cataclysmic changes occurred in Eastern Europe. Pro-Soviet governments in Poland and Hungary started to crumble. After weeks of civil unrest, the East German government announced on November 9, 1989 that all DDR citizens could visit West Germany and West Berlin. Crowds of East Germans crossed and climbed onto the wall, joined by West Germans on the other side in a celebratory atmosphere. A euphoric public and souvenir hunters chipped away parts of the wall. The government later removed most of the rest.

On November 26, Premier Gorbachev affirmed that the Soviet Union must retain a one party system. He added that the economic crisis facing Russia was equal to that which the Soviet Union faced in the war against the Nazis. His policy statement occupied almost three pages in *Pravda*.

Three days later, the Supreme Soviet of the U.S.S.R. ratified the Law on the Economic Sovereignty of the Baltic States. Under pressure from Azerbaijan, the Soviet Parliament relinquished its control over Nagorno-Karabakh. The new provisional council was to report directly to Baku. Two hundred thousand fled during the violence in that troubled area. Meanwhile, Premier Gorbachev arrived in Rome for three days of talks with his Italian counterpart and said, "I have arrived here in a very good state of mind."

On December 2, 1989, during a meeting aboard the Soviet yacht *Maxim Gorky* off the island of Malta, Premier Gorbachev and United States President Bush declared that the Cold War had ended. Less than two weeks later, the European Community and the U.S.S.R. signed a trade and cooperation agreement.

As the year came to an end, the news from Moscow grew steadily more desperate. The Baltics were aflame. It had become increasingly obvious to nations the world over that the only superpower in the world other than the United States of America was about to collapse. Twenty-one years after they began, the changes which had started with violence of 1968 had come full circle. It was time for a new cycle to begin.

BOOK V

CODA

48

In February 1990, Penelope Wagner changed her name to Mrs. Lev Arkady in a small, private ceremony atop a crumbling rubble pile remnant of what had been the Berlin wall. Lev had arranged to fly the newly ordained Rabbi Ariel Levine from Tbilisi, to Munich and thence to Tegel Airport, to officiate. Kassy and Birgit, the maid and matron of honor respectively, accompanied Penny, while Lev enjoyed the services of two "best men," Jimmy Wagner, who'd eagerly welcome his new stepfather into the fold, and a second man who stood five-feet-ten inches tall, the same height as the groom. His face wrapped in a thick shawl to shield him from the late-winter cold of the city, his bright eyes twinkled merrily. Lev referred to him as "my beloved Polish friend, Wujek." After the wedding, the couple held an intimate party at the Kempinski Four Seasons Hotel. Wujek, his face uncovered, toasted the couple and announced with regret that he must leave early because he had to be back at work by next morning.

Kassy's eyes nearly bulged out of her head when the man entered the room. "My God, isn't that …?" she whispered to her brother.

"Well, I don't know if you'd call him *your* God," Jim responded, a mischievous gleam in his own eye. "But yes, that's him all right."

"You don't seem surprised."

"Lev told me about the Gdansk affair a few months ago, so I knew they were friends. Still, the combination of Rabbi Levine and the Pope lends a nice ecumenical touch, wouldn't you say?"

In May, Kassy announced she was taking a year off from Vet school to become a free spirit and see the world. Happily unattached, at twenty-five, tall, strikingly attractive and athletic-looking, she portrayed the image of her mother at the same age. Kassy stopped in Israel for three weeks, where she worked on a kibbutz, before setting out for India. In October, Jimmy announced that the following June, through a fortuitous circumstance called love, Nadya Vartunian would succeed Penny as the latest "Mrs. Wagner" in the family.

The following month, Lev and Penny summoned Jim and Kassy to join them for a three week holiday in Europe. The "kids" each received an open-ended tourist class ticket ("We have not increased our fortune by spending money unnecessarily," Penny wrote) from wherever in the world they would be on December 3, to Vienna. The Arkadys met them at Schwechat Airport, eleven miles east of central Vienna, on December 5, 1991.

The rented Audi, roomy enough for the four of them, turned east on the A4 toward Budapest and thence onto the A6 to Bratislava. Jim looked questioningly at their mom. Penny said, "Your stepdad's going to take us on a little trip to where it all began for him." She squeezed his arm possessively. "Your sister and I are going to hit the hotel's Spa while you fellows do whatever it is guys do in the Old Town.

Their hotel, the Devin, a charming and elegant central European venue, could not have been more strategically placed. Its southern edge was directly across the road from the swift-running Danube and the *Novy Most* tower, the Soviet-built equivalent of Seattle's space needle. Bratislava Castle, just west of the hotel, was surrounded by Old Town.

As Lev and Jimmy walked in Old Town in the gray afternoon, they came upon a not particularly impressive stone building with seven pillars and a flat roof. "The Heydukova Street Synagogue," Lev said, sighing. "There were three Jewish house of worship in this city when I was born. This is the only one left."

"How old were you when you left Bratislava?"

"Ten. My family sold everything they could. We ended up with almost no money and whatever clothing we could carry. We were only able to get that because some kind Gentiles took pity on us."

They kept walking until they reached a block of Soviet-style apartment houses. Lev looked about sadly. "The neighborhood where I was born. I don't even remember the name of the street. It doesn't really matter, since the Nazis obliterated the whole area and the Soviets changed so many of the street names anyway. Can you speak any foreign languages, Jim?"

"A little high school Spanish," the younger man said.

"Your country is so large. Except for your neighbors to the north and south, it's separated from the rest of the world by two great oceans. Here, we were so tiny you couldn't survive if you didn't speak at least three languages. I spoke six when we were chased out of Bratislava. I don't say that to impress you."

Jimmy looked around the street. "How many Jews lived in Bratislava?"

"One-hundred thirty thousand. When we left in 1944, less than twenty thousand."

"Was there no way …?"

"None. Hungary's less than ten minutes away, but by that time, the Hungarians had caved in to the Nazis. Romania had closed its frontiers. The closest border beyond Hungary led to Nazi-controlled Croatia."

"So Poland was the only answer?" the young man asked.

"Not much of an answer," Lev replied. "Most of the Jews who perished in the War were killed in the Polish camps. What small pockets of resistance there were took root in the forests and in the High Tatras along the border." Lev glanced at his watch. "Almost four o'clock. The women should be done by now." As they headed back toward the Devin, he asked Jim, "How's the law practice going?"

"As good as can be expected, I guess."

"Which means you're getting bored? Given my life, I can hardly blame you for that. Want an ice cream?"

"What time's dinner?"

"Closer to eight than to six."

"If you'll let me pay."

"And just how many *koruna* do you have in your pocket?"

◆

They'd spent the day wandering through the rebuilt, but still haunting, center of Warsaw: the synagogue where Lev had become a Bar Mitzvah, the Memorial to the Jewish uprising, and the Ghetto itself, outlined by gold-colored bricks in the street. In the late afternoon, Lev led them to Prozna Street, without saying a word. Prozna Street, one of the few remaining blocks of the Jewish Ghetto that had survived World War II intact.

Penny, Jim, and Kassy experienced the block-long tenement building in different ways. When he saw the building at 7-9, Jim froze in his tracks. He looked up the single block and back down to the larger street abutting Prozna. His eyes riveted on the building. He stood in stunned silence. Penny turned ashen, covered her eyes, knelt down and kissed the cobblestones of the street, then gazed upward, her eyes slowly moving from window to window. Kassy took but a single look, then broke into sobs.

After a time, Lev spoke softly. "This is as it was." Posted to the inside of every window was a large, grainy black-and-white photograph of former Jewish inhabitants of the ghetto: old men with white beards wearing skullcaps and prayer shawls, grandmothers sitting and knitting in ancient rocking chairs, or serving steaming hot meals to their families; a young bride and groom gazing shyly at one another, the optimism of a long, happy life evident in their eyes. Tailors busily at work on tiny black sewing machines. Children playing in the street, boys and girls separated of course. A five-year-old girl holding her precious rag doll to her chest. A boy of sixteen wearing the badge of *Jude,* Jew, a Star of David pinned to his shirt, being dragged along the street by four Nazi toughs while his neighbors looked on helplessly. A young mother, perhaps the bride two years later, cradling a baby to her breast. A young couple with two young children, a boy and a girl, standing stiffly for a family photograph, just as people used to do so long ago.

"Warsaw … just before …" Lev's voice trailed off.

Nearly sixty years later a fifty-six year-old man, his middle-aged wife, and two attractive adults in their twenties stood transfixed in Prozna Street, their feet unable to move, their eyes shifting uncomfortably to the ground, then back to each picture, back to individual lives filled with joy, hope, longing, with the simple worries and pleasures of a single day, a single moment, without any inkling that within a very few years they, and six million of their coreligionists, would be wiped off the face of the earth, obliterated without a trace by forces which, themselves, would be destroyed only a few millimoments later.

That evening, Lev himself experienced his own memories of how desperately precious, tragic, precarious, and brief life might be, when he took his family into Warsaw's Old Town, to Castle Square, and to a place that had stood for four hundred years before it had been demolished in the War and then rebuilt, but whose walls contained memories as singularly moving to Lev Arkady as though they'd taken place the evening before.

"The *Przy Zamku*," Penny whispered. "Where you and Esther first met Agata."

"Yes."

"And you brought me here …"

"If I am to share the rest of my life with you, Penny, I felt I had to share my *whole* life," he said.

"Does it look the same?"

"Does anything ever look the same when you're older? Somehow things always seem smaller than they were when I was young, because back then I was smaller and because it was the largest, most impressive restaurant in the largest, most impressive city I'd ever seen at that time. But yes, it looks very much the same as I remember it. Hunting trophies, old paintings of the hunt and of Polish royalty… Although I never saw Warsaw until after the War, I believe this is what Warsaw looked like in the days before."

"I'm so glad you and mom asked us to come on this trip," Kassy said. "Without it, we'd never truly have been able to understand why you are what you are."

"Or the time in which you lived," Jim joined in. "It's one thing to read about history in a book. I remember when we studied U.S. History in Junior High. A bunch of stodgy old men in black-and-white pictures. But somehow, I never really thought of them as living, breathing, suffering human beings. They never drank too much or went to the toilet in the morning or made love at night …"

Penny said nothing.

"Sort of like the pictures on Prozna Street?" Lev said. "I didn't mean that in a bad way. But those pictures brought it home, wouldn't you say?"

"More than anything," Kassy responded.

"And yet, everything has a reason. I didn't just bring you here to show you things that were important to me, but to show you some things that might help you find your own definitions of what's important in life."

※

"This is the most beautiful city I've ever seen!" Kassy exulted as they strolled the right bank of the Vltava. "Every building is different."

"Goethe called Prague a symphony in stone," her mother remarked. "Or so Professor Pasinetti told me."

To their left, across the river and high atop a hill overlooking the city, the magnificent Castle and its attendant St. Vitus Cathedral dominated the skyline. Everywhere they looked, there were signs of a city undergoing a vast rebuilding project, scaffolding, power washers attacking grimy gray high-rises, graffiti-filled walls, and construction workers in hard yellow hats, carrying their tool bags with them.

"When were you last here, Lev?" Jim asked.

"Twenty-three years ago during the Prague Spring. I left in a hurry, a couple of days before they arrested Dubček, transported him to the Soviet Union, and expelled him from the Czech Communist Party."

"What ever happened to him?" the younger man asked.

"Believe it or not, the story has a happy ending. "He moved to Bratislava and they allowed him to work in the Forestry Service until last year. Odd how things change. Today he's Chairman of the Federal Assembly. There's more to this city than a gorgeous face," he continued. "Did you ever see the TV show *Roots*?"

"Yeah," Kassy said. "When I was twelve, we had to watch it as an assignment in my junior high American history class. Mom was very much into that kind of thing."

"You saw a good part of European Jewish history when we were in Warsaw a few days ago. Czechoslovakia's equally important. Josefov's only a few blocks from here…"

He led them through huge Wenceslas Square, from where word of the fall of Communism in Czechoslovakia had gone out to the world, to *Stare Mesto's* Old Town Square with its fabled clock tower and St. Tyn Church, down one of the abutting pedestrian-only streets to Josefov, Prague's Jewish Quarter. Like the rest of the area, it was undergoing immense urban renewal.

"Jews have lived here since the thirteenth century, when they were ordered to vacate their homes throughout the city and settle in this one area, the Ghetto."

"I don't see any bombed-out ruins like we saw in Warsaw," Jim remarked.

"True, and for a bizarre reason," Lev said. "The Nazis destroyed just about everything they could in Poland, Ukraine, and other parts of Jewish Eastern Europe, but early on Hitler decreed that he wasn't going to touch a single building in Prague. He set the entire city aside as a 'Museum to an exotic, extinct race.' The Allies didn't bomb it and the Soviets considered it within their sphere of influence after the War. They didn't destroy much, but they didn't spruce it up either. That's why they're doing so much today. There are six synagogues still standing within a few square blocks. All of them except one are being restored to their prewar glory. That's the one I want you to see."

Some minutes later they arrived at the Pinkas Synagogue. Lev spoke to an attendant in Czech. The woman nodded and they entered. The building had no furniture, no accoutrements, nothing except for some painted writing that occupied a small corner where two walls joined.

Lev closed his eyes and bowed. The others saw his lips moving, but they heard nothing. Afterward, he looked directly at them and they saw tears in his eyes. "They've started," he said simply. Once outside the ancient house of prayer, Penny looked at him questioningly. "They really intend to do it," Lev said reverently.

"Do what?" Kassy asked.

"They're making this their own Memorial to the Holocaust," Lev said. "The writing you saw … Eighty thousand Czechoslovakian Jews perished in the camps. Each one of those eighty thousand names will be individually inscribed on the walls of this synagogue. It will remain empty except for the names. Those names will speak louder than any Nazi bombs, louder than any outside forces, more meaningful, even, than prayers to the Most High."

"What were the words you were mouthing in there?" Penny asked.

"The *Kaddish*, the Memorial prayer over the dead," he said. "Lest any of them be forgotten."

"How long do they think it will take to finish the project?"

"Seven years. We can go back to our pension now."

"Not downtown?" Penny asked.

"No. Out in the sixth district. I think we can use the peace and quiet tonight."

Even using a very good map, it took Lev more than an hour to navigate the few miles to their lodging. The Pension Vetrnik occupied a small offshoot of a main street. There were no visible signs except for graffiti seemingly everywhere. A few helpful residents of the area pointed him in the direction of U Vetrniku. He drove the car around a long block to an entryway. It was an eighth of a mile from the entry gate to the main buildings, but he kept the symbol of the place, an old mill tower that had been erected in the thirteenth century, in sight. A small forested area surrounded the driveway. A middle-aged man, his plump wife, and a St. Bernard puppy, awaited them in the parking area.

"Welcome!" the man said. "I'm Milos Opatrny, this is my wife, Blanka, and this is our youngest child, Arnošt. He's the one most our guests remember. Your rooms are ready. Are you just in from Bratislava?"

"We arrived several hours ago. I took my family on a walk along the Vltava and through *Stare Mesto* to Josefof."

"Your Czech is excellent. You are not American?"

"Originally Slovak."

"Will you be dining with us tonight? We have typical Bohemian fare. I trust you're familiar with that?"

"The answer to both your questions is yes," Lev replied.

"My husband is very proud of his cooking," Blanka said. "He was a chef in the foreign service for twenty years. You won't be disappointed. Goose or lamb?"

"Two of each, unless you have duck?"

"Of course. We'll serve two platters of duck, one of goose, and one of lamb."

❦

Dinner was not only a culinary delight, but an aural and visual feast as well. The dining room was small, lit by a roaring fire in a corner fireplace, and their hosts served a bottle of light Moravian Grüner Veltliner. Dessert consisted of *švestkové knedlíky*, plum dumplings, and *meruňkové knedlíky*, apricot dumplings. Throughout the meal, a soft recording of Smetana's *Vltava*, more universally known as *Die Moldau*, arguably the most beautiful tone poem ever written, played softly in the background, the perfect accompaniment to their conversation.

When, after dinner concluded, Milos came to their table, the four of them stood simultaneously and applauded their host and chef.

"Pan Opatrny, you have made this one of the finest evenings I can remember," Penny said.

"Ah, but there one more thing you must see, if you would be so kind," he said. "It is very meaningful to me." He went to a nearby drawer from which he took out five flashlights. He handed one to each of his guests and kept one for himself.

Lev glanced at his wristwatch. "At ten o'clock at night?"

"If you don't mind. It's a bit chilly to walk, even though it's not too far. We can take my Škoda."

Opatrny drove them to the far end of the property. When they alighted, he told them to turn on their flashlights, then led them through a small patch of forest until they came to a place next to the fence abutting the street. He shone his flashlight on a single tombstone.

"Come closer," he said. They did. "Can you see anything you recognize?"

Lev looked at the stone, then looked closer. "There must be a story," he said.

"There is," Opatrny said quietly. "The Nazis tried to destroy the Jewish nation. They did not succeed. After the Soviets came to power in Czechoslovakia, they announced they were going to demolish all Jewish graveyards outside Josefov. One of them was near here. My brother and I felt it was a sacrilege to destroy any place where one met his God. One evening, a week before the scheduled demolition, we went to the cemetery shortly before midnight. We dug up the gravestone and brought it here. The authorities never found out. Now it doesn't matter anymore. Except to us."

Lev, Penny, Jim, and Kassy stared silently at the stone. Although many of the letters were obliterated and they could not understand what writing there was, they saw a large Star of David at the top of the stone, and the numbers 5517-5569.

"Born 1757 in the common era, died 1809," Opatrny said. "Just in case you were wondering. I think the Jewish Bible says, 'He who saves one person saves the entire universe.' Perhaps I did my part."

"You are not Jewish?" Penny asked.

"I am not. But no people deserves to be destroyed."

Later that evening, just before Jim and Kassy left for their room, the Arkady-Wagner family had a brief discussion, given what they had experienced on the journey, as to the meaning and purpose of life. They unanimously concluded that the answer to that question had two parts: to triumph over fear; and to leave the earth a better place because, for an infinitessimal amount of time, each of them had lived on it.

49

On the flight home from Frankfurt, Lev asked Penny, "What was the most meaningful experience in your life?"

Penny thought for a few moments before she responded. "There were so many," she said. "That very special night we shared in Vienna, beating Hodgkins." She blushed. "Being caught in bed with Andy Burgess the night I was babysitting… When you first see your child after he or she is born. But there is another moment almost equal to that.

"My mom died of lung cancer when I was twelve years old. A few weeks after that, my dad took me fishing at the Santa Monica Pier. Halfway down the pier, on the left, there was a huge, noisy place, a Penny Arcade. I felt funny because I'd never heard of a place named after me. Dad told me we might stop there on our way back."

At that moment, the flight attendant's voice came over the speaker. "Ladies and gentlemen, we're expecting a bit of turbulence for the next twenty minutes. Please return to your seats and fasten your seatbelts."

Although both of them were securely belted in, Lev looked down and Penny's right hand went to her stomach to make sure the belt buckle was in place.

"At first, fishing off the pier seemed exciting because it was something different and because I was spending time alone with my father. But after an hour it became boring. By two-thirty, Dad said, 'Time to call it a day.' When he cut the heads and tails off the eight little perch we'd caught and wrapped them in butcher paper, our day's catch looked pretty pathetic. Not the most fun I'd ever had.

"Dad looked at the big Benrus wristwatch he always wore on his left arm. 'Almost three o'clock. Should we stop at the arcade, Penny?' I remember I just shrugged. The day which had started out so full of promise had fizzled, but when my father took my hand in his large paw, that made everything all right.

"The Playland Arcade was warm inside. I'd never seen so many lights flashing at one time. There must have been fifty games. Ski-ball, pinball machine horse races, that kind of thing. Dad invited me to sit down and play the horse race game when the seat next to him became vacant. I didn't win, but my horse came in third, so the attendant handed me a token allowing me to play the next game for free."

Penny turned and noticed her husband was staring at her, saying nothing.

"After two more tries, when my horse didn't win anything, Dad guided me toward a different kind of pinball machine. If you got 50,000 points, you could win a small stuffed teddy bear. I got pretty close, 40,000 points. I didn't win a teddy bear, but I did win a goldfish in a small glass bowl. The fish survived for six months. To this day, I get goose bumps when I see an arcade. Of course, they're all pretty much gone today. There's cable TV and Pac-Man and Frogger, but nothing like the old-time arcade. Why are you staring at me like that?"

"You know how I started out?" he asked.

"More or less."

"When I was almost eleven, my family was annihilated. I only managed to survive because I was down in the basement when it happened. I would have died within a few days, except I was rescued by a group of partisans and taken to their camp. Less than a month later, that camp was destroyed, and they left me for dead.

"I don't know how long I'd been unconscious when I woke up bouncing around in a wagon, broken leg and all, and saw an old man named Amos. I still remember his first words all these years later. 'Hello there. Miserable day.' 'Of course, it could be worse. You could be dead …'

"Amos was the ultimate carnival huckster. In Yiddish, we called him a *luftmensch*, an 'air man,' someone who literally made his living from thin air, or, in his case, hot air. He ran a traveling arcade. He took me on as his grandson-apprentice for the next few years. My God, the memories …"

Penny noticed his eyes clouding over. He had moved on to another world, another time. He looked younger, and consummately happy.

"Do you think maybe God, or whoever we want to call Him, or It, brought us together deliberately?" she asked softly. "After all, I *am* Penny, and your last name is Arkady. I have no idea what that name means," she continued, "but it's close enough to Arcade to be something more than a coincidence."

"What do you mean?" he asked.

"Lev, how much would we need to live on comfortably for the rest of our lives?"

"At our present level?"

"Uh-huh."

He made some quick mental calculations. "My house in Hof is paid for. My savings account provides me with enough income to live on without touching the principal. Of course we want to make sure Kassy and Jim are provided for. She'll get married some day and we'll have to fork out money for that. A man is supposed to provide for his wife."

Penny laughed good-naturedly. "I'll accept all of that, but realistically, how much extra would we need to make it through our lives given our extravagant lifestyle?"

He arched his eyebrows. "Our extravagant lifestyle? Might I remind you we're flying coach. We didn't stay at the President, we stayed at the Pension Vetrnik, and we groused about that 'cause we had to pay for one extra room for both our adult kids."

"Uh-huh. I married the last of the big-time spenders."

"If we had a million dollars, make that a million and a half allowing for inflation, we wouldn't have to worry about where our next meal is coming from. Of course, we could always sell one of the houses if we had to and we might be forced to live in one place. So let's round that figure up to two million dollars, which would allow us to live higher on the hog than ninety-nine percent of the world's population."

"We've never hidden anything from one another. How much do you have?"

"Four million dollars excluding my house. Now it's your turn."

"Six, a little more, a little less."

Neither of them was particularly surprised.

"So we have ten million dollars. We could give nine to whatever charity we want immediately, and we'd never even feel it. Or …"

"I have a feeling my wife is about to say something important."

"Remember what we all agreed on back in Prague that night we saw the tombstone?" Penny asked.

"The purpose of life is to get over fear; and to leave the earth a better place because we lived on it."

"We've both done the best we can on the first part. And you, at least, have made a good start on the second part. Then it hit me when you asked what had been the most meaningful experience of my life, that we might have missed one other item about the meaning of life: to have *fun* while you're living it.'

"And you point is, my beloved?"

"No matter what happens, we can give several million dollars toward making the world a better place. Or, we can risk that 'play money' and see how much more we can give the world, and maybe have a great deal of fun doing it."

Lev said nothing for several moments, mulling over what Penny had said. Finally, he smiled and said, "Why not? I think that calls for a drink." He pressed the buzzer and a flight attendant approached them.

It was Penny who asked, "May we have two cups of water, please?"

❦

When they broached their idea to Jim and Kassy, the "kids" were ecstatic.

"Don't worry," Penny said, "if we blow it there'll still be plenty for each of you."

Jim glared at her. "As if we can't be expected to make it on our own. In most societies it's the job of the young to take care of the older generation when they age out."

Now it was Penny's turn to look sourly at her first-born. In response, he held up both hands, palms facing her. "Just to show that I have all the confidence in the world in you, I insist that I make my contribution to your new venture." With that, he reached into his pocket and placed a ten dollar bill on the kitchen counter.

"My brother the big spender," Kassy said. She extracted a twenty dollar bill from her purse and placed it on top of her brother's contribution.

"Very well," said Lev. "Since each of you is now a participant in this venture, why don't we brainstorm and see what kind of ideas we come up with to make it work."

❦

"What sells best in the world?" Jim asked one evening, during one of their sessions. "Not counting food, clothing, or shelter," he added.

Although the four of them came up with varying answers, number one on each list was entertainment.

"Even the government's in on that kind of business. Gambling's illegal but governments run lotteries everywhere. Catering to people's greed is always more palatable than calling it a tax," Lev said. "I spent my whole life making money in much the same way. Amos found a way to cadge money out of any situation. When the situation changed, he went with the flow. When your mom and I were in the plane concocting this weird idea, she told me how she still gets goose bumps when she sees an arcade. They're all pretty much gone today, victims of cable TV, and Pac-Man, but the basic idea behind the arcade hasn't died. People everywhere still want to get rich quick from as little effort as they can get away with, whether it's a horse race or the stock market. Even better if you can be entertained while you're trying to strike it rich. Whether it's 1593 or 1993, if you make something attractive enough to the younger generation, they'll flock to it like people are drawn to one another. Twenty years ago there was no PacMan. Heck, there weren't even Personal Computers."

"When I was growing up in L.A. in the late '50s, the transistor radio changed everything about beach parties," Penny added. It used to cost four hundred dollars to buy a pocket calculator if you could even get one."

"Transistor radios? Pocket calculators?" Kassy scoffed. "Get with the program, Mom. Nobody listens to transistor radios anymore. When I go running, I've always got a Walkman around my neck. Even that's on the way out. A calculator's two-and-a-half bucks and they give 'em away when you open a bank account anywhere."

"Would you guys like some coffee and apple pie? Or is that too old-fashioned?"

"Sounds good to me, Mom," Jim said enthusiastically. "And if baby sis is too into today's world to eat your pie, I'll accommodate by eating her share."

"No way, José," Kassy said. "Ice cream on top, please?"

After a brief break, they continued their conversation.

"So far, we've summed up three things. Times change and technologies change. That's a given. People's basic need to be entertained and to think they're getting more than they're paying out doesn't change. That's a given. ..." Lev paused.

"You said *three* things," Kassy said.

"Yes," Lev continued. "And what we just did proves the third thing: people who are having fun like to eat. I've got a proposal to make to all of you but I'll need a couple of days to flesh it out."

"Can you give us a hint?" Kassy said.

"I can and I will," Lev said. "I noticed an advertisement that came in one of the weekly throwaway papers a couple of days ago. If you're going to be part of this enterprise, I'll need to borrow the smallest coin you have in your pocket and I'll have to ask my wife if she has a Marks-A-Lot black pen and an 8½ by 11 sheet of paper."

When all this was delivered to Lev, he excused himself and went into the bathroom. When he returned, he showed them what he had put together. "Here's to our new venture," he said.

Penny stared at the display in amazement. "Yes!" she exclaimed. "Yes, yes, yes!"

Я-CADE™
Fun, Food & Fortune!

50

"Your mom and I could do it alone, but we thought, 'Why should you miss out on the fun?'"

"I'm footloose and fancy free," Kassy said. "Traveled out, no job yet, and another year to go in vet school. Count me in. But Jimmy's a 'law-yuh' with a fancy job. I don't know …"

"Yeah, right. As if I'm going to let my baby sister dominate this whole enterprise."

"If you don't mind my asking, how much are you making?" Lev asked.

"Sixty thousand a year, plus a ten percent bonus. Nadya hasn't got a job yet, so we've got no idea what she'll be making."

Lev wrote out two checks for one hundred thousand dollars, one each to James Wagner and Kassy Wagner. "Here's your first year's salary in advance."

"Uh, Lev …" Jimmy stammered.

"Yes?"

"I can't begin to tell you how incredibly generous this is and how much I appreciate it, but …"

"Does that mean you're not going to be part of this?" Penny asked.

"It's not that at all. It's just that …"

"Go ahead."

"My legal training could be of some assistance here. Each of you can make a ten thousand dollar tax-free gift to Kassy and the same to me. If you could cut our salaries to eighty thousand dollars and give each of us a twenty thousand dollar tax-free gift …"

❦

"Your mother and I will scout for the first location. If Penny-Я-Cade is successful, we'll have to be move quickly into at least two more venues. If that works, we'll play the double-down game, four locations then eight, and so on. Speed and daring will be essential because nothing succeeds like success and if anyone learns that we're making noise, you can bet there'll be interests waiting to clobber us using our own idea."

"I don't want to say anything to jinx us, Lev, but if this takes off …?"

"Kassy and your mom will design a food and drink menu, Jim."

"And me?"

"You and I will be in charge of picking out the games, negotiating with the game manufacturers, and leasing or buying properties. All four of us will make the final decisions together."

❦

"Gotta' be cheap, fast, and tasty," Kassy said, "and all-American."

"Kind of like the bräuhaus in Munich," Lev mused. "Very salty, to make sure they'll be drinking."

"We should serve meals from early lunch until late night. Pasta, burgers, steaks, fries, seafood, chicken, finger food, desserts. Update the menu to reflect current trends."

"Sounds good so far, Mom. What about Sunday brunch? Buffets for special events and private parties?" Jim suggested.

"Let's think about it. For sure a full-service bar."

"Unquestionably it's a high-profit item," Lev said, "but Americans are more Puritanical than Europeans, and we want to play to the family crowd."

"Table it?" Jim asked. "Back burner?"

"No, I'd like to look into it further. Sooner or later we'll have to appeal to the Yuppies, which is where the money will come from. Let's not forget, the purpose of this whole venture is to make a lot of money for a very good cause, even if we haven't yet decided what that cause will be."

⁂

"What do you know about P.T. Barnum?" Lev asked his stepson.

"Never heard of him."

"How quickly the world forgets. Phineas T. Barnum died a little over a hundred years ago, perhaps the greatest showman and huckster that ever lived."

"Greater than Amos?"

"Don't know. Never met the man. I'm not quite *that* old. Barnum's reputation was that of the ultimate gambler who would risk everything on a single roll of the dice. There were all kinds of quotes attributed to him, such as 'A sucker is born every minute.' But all that hype was self-generated. The true fact was that P.T. Barnum studied every investment he ever made so carefully he left nothing to chance. He made sure before he invested a dime that he would make a hefty return on his investment with no risk. He understood that the public's taste can change overnight. The ultimate economic surfer."

"How does that apply to us?"

"We're planning to open an arcade," Lev said. "Times have changed. Games are no longer enough. Manufacturers figured they could make more money and sell more units by going into home gaming and selling games outright to the personal computer market. The following year, arcades collapsed. Why spend a quarter to play a game once when you could buy the whole game for a few hundred dollars? Home video games will soon have better graphics than arcade games. When those arcade games are programmed for PCs people will buy those programs rather than pump coins into arcades."

"So you're saying we're dead in the water before we start?"

"Not at all, Jim. If we can anticipate the future we can move faster than the next fellow. Like when you're surfing. If you look beyond that beautiful curler to the wave beyond it, you'll be the one to catch that wave and have it to yourself."

"Meaning?"

"How much fun can it be to play a video game alone at home when the only one who knows how well you're doing it is you and when the only thing you can win is your pride? That reminds me of a tale."

"Uh … Do I hear another Amos story about to unfold?"

My God, Lev thought, *have I really become a talkative old windbag like Amos?* Out loud he said, "You do, and you'd better respect your elders and listen. Amos told me a similar tale. I've just brought it into the nineteen-nineties."

"I'm listening."

"A famous Orthodox Rabbi had a huge congregation in New York City. The Rabbi had only one weakness, his addiction to golf. He'd dreamed of hitting a hole-in-one his entire life and had never come close. One year, on *Yom Kippur*, the Holiest Day of the year, when every Jew, good or bad, is supposed to be in *shul* all day praying that his sins be forgiven, the Rabbi had the most unbelievable attack of his addiction he'd ever had. He called in sick the day before. On the Holiest Day, he drove out to Long Island and anonymously signed up to play a golf course he'd never played before. The day was mild and sunny. When the Rabbi got to the third tee, he hit his first shot. He could feel in his heart that it was the most magnificent drive ever, and he was flabbergasted and astonished when he saw where the ball went. He'd hit a hole in one!

"At that very moment, an archangel came up before the Holy One and complained. 'God Almighty,' he said, 'The Rabbi, of all people, plays hooky on the Holiest Day of the Year and instead he pleasures himself by going to the golf course after lying and calling in sick. Then he hits a hole in one? What kind of justice is that? What kind of lesson does that teach the multitudes?'

"The Almighty smiled benignly and paused a moment before He answered. *'And just who is he going to tell about it?'*"

Lev continued, "As long as folks can remember, a man has been motivated by only a very few things…"

"The birds and the bees?"

"Mostly. And the best way to get to that goal is to show the woman he wants to impress that he is stronger, smarter, richer, and more impressive than the next fellow. When I was with Amos back in Eastern Europe, they always had a game where a man tried to swing a hammer hard enough to cause a ball to hit the bell at the top of a tower. No matter what the modern world might think, things haven't really changed since those days. And to really impress that lady, the man had to have an audience. So here's what we have to do. We've got to lure the fish out of his hole so he'll come up and bite. And for that we'll need bait …"

Lev expounded further on his idea. "The Arcade as we've known it is dying. But *something* has to replace it because people will always need to be entertained. We'll fill the need by opening large amusement centers with clean, safe environments and expensive game control systems that are just a little bit ahead of what's available to home users. We'll mix the old and the new. We'll mix old reliable 'heritage' games with technology. Full service restaurants with full liquor bars and a wide variety of video games and hands-on electronic gaming options. Most important of all, we'll provide the best and most profitable bait of all, something that earned me a fortune back in Europe."

"Which is?"

"I tried to think of some way I could enhance the profits by convincing my customers to accept something other than money in return for their handfuls of tokens. The answer came when I noticed that every crowd had not only men, but women and children as well. Children had absolutely no interest in money. They preferred *things* like goldfish in small bowls, stuffed bears, cap pistols, and sheriff's "gold" badges. Women were always happiest when their children were pleased. I learned early on that when a woman is happy, she would most likely make her man *very* happy.

"I realized I could buy prizes in bulk for pennies and that the *actual* value of these prizes had absolutely no connection to what my audience *perceived* as their value. I set up a special corner of my games that featured *prizes* instead of *money* in return for tokens. Why settle for exchanging the tokens for mere coins when, for one hundred tokens, you could take home a unique and special gift for your beloved child? The audiences never connected the dots to realize that what I gave away for only a hundred tokens had cost me a tenth of that sum."

"Meaning you intend to do that in Penny-Я-Cade?" Jim said.

"Exactly."

51

And succeed they did. The initial Penny-Я-Cade opened near San Francisco International Airport. A year later, the second venue followed, breaking ground in Cleveland, Ohio. Less than eight months later, Seattle witnessed the opening of a new and exciting brand of entertainment.

By the turn of the 21st century, Lev and Penny's family dream had expanded to twenty locations across the United States. From the very beginning, the philosophy "Do Well – Do Good" motivated the enterprise. All employees were neatly groomed, uniformly cheerful and courteous, and represented the greatest diversity in the area. They were paid a legitimate living wage and treated with respect regardless of their station. At the 2001 annual meeting Lev proudly announced that since the commencement of Penny-Я-Cade, the turnover at each location was less than two percent. The Arcade-Entertainment centers became widely known as the best place in town to work.

Despite its rapid growth, Penny-Я-Cade remained wholly family-owned, but now the family played the eternal game of multiplication. Nadya Vartunian Wagner and her husband Jim had added a pair of twins, Arov and Ariel, now eight, to the family mix. Kassy, not far behind, had met and married an attorney and writer. They'd had a daughter four years ago and Kassy was "great with child," expecting her second when she waddled into the meeting. Happiest of all, Nadya announced, "We've been successful in sponsoring Gyorgi and Rosa Dudayev Raskov to California. They've been given special resident status."

Six months ago, after it appeared evident that the food operation was running so smoothly and seamlessly that it could have been run by a reasonably intelligent chimpanzee, Kassy had assumed a new position at Penny-Я-Cade, chair of a special project. She'd told Lev and her mom a couple of months ago that the project was ready to go and as the meeting transitioned to New Business, she was given the floor.

"Fellow members of the board," she began regally, a mischievous glint in her eye. "During the past several months I've been working on a secret project, although I can say that you probably have some idea of what it is. Anyway, here goes.

"Mom and Lev set the stage for this when we first started moving this fabulous idea forward. 'Make a difference,' they said. And today, I think we can. We're in twenty cities today. More are on the way. In each of these cities there are loads of public schools and facilities trying to help move the young people of the community out of the ghettoes, out of gangs, out of boredom. But we have more young people and money gets ever tighter each year.

"When I came up with my idea, Nadya and I went around to these schools and community centers and we asked what was *really* needed to make a difference. The answers surprised us. An elementary school orchestra died, not because the kids didn't want it and not because there weren't volunteer orchestra conductors, but because the schools didn't have enough instruments, or the instruments they had were in unusable condition. The string instruments didn't have any *strings* or the trumpets needed repairs. Little things, tiny things that, for the most part, would take less than a thousand dollars to remedy. But with all the school budgets going to science and math and big ticket items, there simply wasn't enough to give a lousy thousand dollars to the music program. Same thing with the art program, same with after-school activities. Teachers spend money out of their own pockets to buy things as simple as pens, pencils, notebooks, and even used books for kids to read in their spare time. Little things. Things that were 'mouse nuts' in comparison with big-ticket items. Things that simply got left behind or fell through the cracks. Sometimes they fell through the cracks because the teachers simply didn't have the time or the energy to make a request to the governing board."

Nadya took up when Kassy paused for a moment.

"We're calling the project *Agata's Heart*," she said. Lev stared, his mouth agape. "We would like the Board to set aside a certain minimum amount so we can meet every worthwhile request for funds for such things as we can find. We'll post notices and conduct meetings at every school within a radius of thirty miles of a Penny-Я-Cade. All the teachers have to do is *ask*, and we'll honestly evaluate each request. If we find it's worthwhile, we'll fund it. It doesn't matter if the request is officially sanctioned by the Board of Education or not. But it's not 'free money.' There'll be strings attached."

Kassy continued. "Part of Penny-Я-Cade is that we have an entertainment budget. We can cut that to almost nothing and, at the same time, we'll give the kids and their teachers and mentors and coaches the pride of saying, 'Agata's Heart didn't give us a gift. *We earned it.*' And here's how they'll earn it. We'll figure out how many schools or community centers or other facilities we're helping. Let's say there are fifty of those within the community we serve. We have fifty working weeks in the year. Each of those schools or centers or facilities will have their own week at Penny-Я-Cade. We'll provide the announcements, the publicity, and the venue. The kids will design and submit proposed programs to us at least a month in advance of their week. During their week, each place we'll help them put on a week of entertainment of whatever kind they want, hopefully using some of the things we've provided. It can be anything: a school orchestra with instruments that work, or with sheets of new music we've helped them purchase; a basketball extravaganza; a talent show on a grand scale. It's their week and their obligation. And their pride and their privilege."

Lev whistled appreciatively. "We cut our entertainment budget. The kids will bring their parents, their friends, their grandparents from however far away. And Penny-Я-Cade will be *the* place to go for a whole new group of consumers that week. Win-win-win-win. The Chairman hereby hands the floor over to the vice chairman, my wife. I move that we unanimously approve the creation of *Agata's Heart*, and I second my own motion. And," he said taking out a checkbook and writing with a flourish, "here is a check for one million dollars from my personal funds to start the program."

"Can't do that, Lev," Jimmy said. "Roberts Rules of Order and all that."

"Hey, whoever said this was a democracy, big brother?" Kassy asked.

That's how Agata's Heart began. In years to come, it would add substantially to the coffers of each Penny-Я-Cade, both financially and morally.

A decade later, when the patriarch turned seventy-seven, there were precisely seventy-seven Penny-Я-Cade centers in operation throughout the United States.

In February 2015, Lev Arkady celebrated his eightieth birthday. As he awoke, he went outside on his front porch to greet the day. He looked at his old watch, which had continued to serve him for as far back as he could remember. Eight o'clock.

"Why so early, my dear?" Penny, still striking a month shy of her seventy-third birthday, joined him on the porch and linked her arm through his.

From out of nowhere and from every direction, nearly two hundred people of every age and nationality and ethnic origin materialized. More than fifty carried musical instruments. Some wore skimpy shorts and halter tops, even in the San Fernando Valley's late winter chill. Others wore formal evening wear. Still others wore everything from blue jeans and bright print shirts to traditional Mexican mariachi attire. All of them seemed to be headed in the direction of Lev and Penelope Arkady's home.

Moments later, without so much as tuning their instruments or adjusting their voices, the musicians started playing and the rest of the audience started singing Happy Birthday to Lev Arkady. The orchestra followed this with the Ode to Joy from Beethoven's Ninth Symphony. Although by no means an ensemble of the heroic size, the group was remarkably melodious. Soon a choir of more than fifty people in the immediate vicinity, most of whom had no idea of the words to the *Ode*, but all of whom were willing to belt out la-la-la's in accompaniment to the familiar theme, joined in.

The symphony continued for more than three minutes, after which the musicians and the audience-participants stood waiting for the "Birthday Boy" to speak.

And speak he did.

"Many of you may know me. Others I have never met, or, if I have met you, you'll please forgive me if I don't recognize each of you by name or by sight. That happens when you get to be my age. I could tell you the story of my life and my great, good fortune, but we'd all be sleeping before the clock struck nine this morning.

"Twenty-five years ago, my wife Penny and our family committed to a pact. We were fortunate enough to have made all we needed to sustain us for the rest of our lives in comfort. But we wanted to make the world a better place than when we first arrived here. So we started with an idea, Penny-Я-Cade, and we promised one another than at the appropriate time we would give half our fortune, whatever it might be, to an organization that would help to make this world a better place.

"We never set a date when this would happen, but today's as good as any. In front of all of you, I am announcing that effective today we are starting the *Amos Foundation*. It is being funded with an initial contribution of one billion dollars, and – "

The rest of Lev's speech was drowned out. Penny squeezed his hand. They embraced and kissed in front of their thrown-together audience and in front of God. And they walked back into their home.

Epilogue

There remains little more to tell. Lev Arkady passed peacefully in his eighty-eighth year, surrounded by his family and by his beloved Penelope Fullerton Wagner Arkady, who followed him less than a year later in the fullness of her own years.

And so our story ends.

What have you done to help make the world a better place?

There's still time to do it.

The End

Acknowledgments

Although there are almost too many acknowledgments to count for those who helped me along the way, the basic inspiration for this novel came from learning and writing about the larger-than-life life of the *real* Penny Fullerton Wagner, and celebrating my son Jeff's 40th birthday at Dave & Buster's Arcade in San Diego, California.